# TEMPTATION

# TEMPTATION

## VICTORIA CHRISTOPHER MURRAY

**WARNER BOOKS**

A Time Warner Company

West Bloomfield, Michigan

The song "My Help" © 1997 by Jackie Gouche-Farris.
Unless otherwise noted Scripture quotations are from the King James Version of the Bible.

Published by Warner Books, Inc., with Walk Worthy Press

33290 West Fourteen Mile Road
West Bloomfield, MI 48322

*Real Believers, Real Life, Real Answers in the Living* God™

Warner Books, Inc., 1271 Avenue of the Americas, Now York, NY 10020

Visit our Web site at www.twbookmark.com

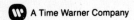 A Time Warner Company

Printed in the United States of America

ISBN: 0-446-52792-0

Page design and composition by Sans Serif Inc., Saline, Michigan 48176

Dedicated to:


My parents, Jacqueline and Edwin Christopher

. . . and parents are the pride of their children.



*Proverbs 17:6 (NIV)*

# ACKNOWLEDGMENTS

First, I give all glory and honor to Jesus Christ, my Lord and Savior. Having Him in my life is the greatest blessing of all. I thank the Lord for the lesson I learned during this process—to trust Him a little more and complain a whole lot less.

To my parents, Edwin and Jacqueline Christopher, who continue to be shining lights in my life. I have been blessed with the world's best parents.

To my sisters, Michelle, Cia, and Cecile. I love having all of you in my life. Thanks for your never-ending support and love. (And, I didn't forget you, William. It's great to have another brother-in-law!)

To my uncles Herbert Blunt and Daniel Cameron who kept me laughing and feeling loved my entire life. I'm told I have a sense of humor—if I do it's because of you. I love you both.

To my in-laws: Delores and Jim Minor, Zelda Wilson, Ercelle and Elvis Murray, Ruth and Elvis Murray, Victoria Moten, and my nieces and nephews. Thank you for giving me a wonderful extended family and for being so enthusiastic about my new career.

There is no one in the world who has been blessed with better friends. Thank you, Veronica and Joseph Austin for your immediate and complete support. (The party was terrific!) You guys are incredible. To Tracy Downs, you have always been in my corner and I love you for it. Thanks for keeping me on track with what God has planned for me. I thank God for bringing a new friend into my life. Lolita Files, I wouldn't have made it through this year without you. You are my friend, and my sister in my Christ. Thank you for your ears during all of those long phone calls.

Also, thank you to Lynette and Ulysses Brown (my brother and sister), and my "foot soldiers" who took it upon themselves to personally get the word out to everyone in L.A.

To a new friend, Dawnn Lewis, my sister in Christ: your enthusiasm and words of encouragement have been inspiring. Thank you for your friendship.

To the author-friends I met along the way. Your encouragement has been amazing and I thank you all: E. Lynn Harris, Monique Jewel Anderson, Jacquelin Thomas, Eric Jerome Dickey, Kimberla Lawson Roby, LaJoyce Brookshire, Timmothy McCann, Parry Brown, Yolanda Joe, Patrice Gaines, RM Johnson, Anfra, and all the others.

Book clubs all across the nation supported me. Thank you to all of them, but I have to give a "shout out" to: Tabahani Book Circle and my sorors, Denise Dowdy and Cheryl Henry; Minds In Motion and Dorothy Malone; Pages and Stacey Turnage; Aunt Sister Book Club and Linda Dozier; Ebony Book Club and Pat Houser; A Room Full of Sistahs and Tori Holloway; Sistas Sippin' Tea in Dallas; Circle of Friends and Shunda Blocker and Lisa Mitchell; Crystalynn Shelton (and her new club); and all the others. Thank you so much.

To all my online friends who believed from the beginning: Wilma Wilkerson, Angie Moore, Ruth Bridges, Pam Greer, Jeanette Wallington, and many others.

My thank-yous would never be complete if I didn't thank

my *St. John's* buddies. We only get together once a year, and I look forward to every November. Thank you for lining up to buy the book and then flooding the radio station with phone calls. You guys are the greatest. Thank you Theresa, Juanita (and everyone at DWP), Sandra, Rita, Mrs. Woods, Vicki, Dorothy, and Lacy.

Without the next three people, this project would have never been possible:

First, to my publisher, Denise Stinson. Wow, I don't know what to say. You have been an inspiration, my motivation, and the person who believed enough to get this project done! Thank you for your faith, thank you for your friendship, and most important, thank you for listening to God and moving this forward.

Several years ago I joined Bible Enrichment Fellowship International Church and came under the spiritual guidance of Dr. Beverly "Bam" Crawford. Though I've wanted to write my entire life, this gift was not released in me until I was placed under your teaching. Thank you is not enough. I am so blessed to be under your tutelage, and this book is a result of your teachings.

To my husband, Ray Murray. We finally got this one out, but you never stopped believing and I love you so much for it. Thank you for your never-ending support.

And to all the readers who took a chance on this "different" kind of book and then told all their friends. This book is for you! Thank you.

Please forgive me if there is anyone I left out. Believe me, it is only the result of a forty-something woman trying to get this completed in the middle of the night. Thank you all!

# One

---

"Surprise!" Kyla beamed as her startled husband jumped back. Friends shouted their greetings from the restaurant tables adorned with silver and black "Over-the-Hill" balloons.

"I don't believe this!" Jefferson grinned. He grabbed Kyla around her waist and hugged her close.

Kyla's skin tingled at his touch. After many years, he still turned her on. "We got you, didn't we?"

"That's for sure. I can't believe this."

"Happy birthday, darling!"

Cheers echoed through the restaurant again as Jefferson kissed Kyla. They lingered in the embrace and the crowd applauded.

"Hey, hey Dr. Jefferson!" A voice from the crowd interrupted their moment. "There's no room for that here, Ky. Dr. Jefferson has to be shared with everyone," Jasmine, Kyla's best friend, scolded playfully.

Laughter filled the room as Jasmine wiggled and nudged herself between Kyla and Jefferson. Standing on her toes, she said, "Here's something for your birthday I know you'll never forget." She kissed him, full on the lips.

As friends pushed Jasmine aside to offer their congratulatory wishes, Kyla frowned and remembered her husband's recent complaints about Jasmine. Now, she wondered if she should have so lightly dismissed his concerns. Taking his hand a bit too firmly, Kyla moved alongside her husband, past a smiling Jasmine as Stevie Wonder blasted birthday wishes from speakers around the elegantly decorated room. After a few body-crushing minutes, Kyla loosened her grip and allowed Jefferson to be pulled further into the crowd. He caught her eye and reluctantly let her fingers slide from his.

Kyla leaned against the restaurant's blue-suede wall and her eyes roamed through the crowd of the ninety invited guests, personal friends as well as colleagues, present to celebrate the fortieth birthday of her husband, a well-respected pulmonary specialist.

Kyla took a glass of sparkling cider from a passing tuxedoed waiter, then moved to a table, away from the swell of guests. Watching her husband over the rim of her fluted glass, she saw him stride confidently through the maze of tables on his mission to greet every guest. She was content to watch it all from the sidelines. "Thank you, Lord," she whispered as her eyes continued to follow Jefferson. "Thank you for giving me sixteen wonderful years with this man."

"Girl, things are heating up in here," Jasmine said, interrupting Kyla's prayer as she bounced down into a chair. Kyla's eyes swept over Jasmine in her red knit, hip-squeezing minidress and, although it was a little too short for her taste, she had to admit that Jasmine did look good.

Jasmine fanned her face, then took Kyla's glass and sipped her cider before Kyla could protest. Kyla got another glass from a passing waiter and crinkled her nose as the cider's bubbles rose and tickled her. She fixed her eyes on the couples on the dance floor, doing her best to ignore Jasmine and the feelings of anger she felt brewing inside.

Jasmine was tapping her fingers atop the silver tablecloth. "Well, it looks like it's going to be the party of the century, Ky." Jasmine's tone belied her words.

"At least the party of the week."

"Well, I'm not as important as you and Jefferson. I don't get invited to all those posh affairs. It's the first time I've been to a p-a-r-t-y since my separation."

Kyla's light brown eyes softened. "Are you okay? You know you can talk to me."

"Nothing to talk about. I'm fine, look at me." Jasmine made a sweeping gesture with her hand across her body. "Do I look like I'm suffering?"

Kyla smiled. "Jas, you look great."

"Yeah, The Commodores called it a brick house. And to think in a little while *I'll* be forty."

Kyla laughed.

"What's so funny?" Jasmine smirked. "Remember, two weeks after *I* hit that big number, *you'll* be joining the club."

"But, we still look good, girl."

They laughed together. "We do, don't we?" But a second later, Jasmine's smile slid away. "I just hope someone else will notice."

"Don't force it, sweetie. It might be a little too soon for you to get involved with anyone."

"Easy for you to say. You have a man."

Kyla reached over and squeezed her friend's hand. "I'm just trying to pass on some good advice."

"How can you give me advice on something you don't

know anything about? All you know is perfection and I don't feel like being perfect right now."

"I'm not perfect, Jas."

"Umph. You're as close as any human being on earth will ever be. Just ask my father, my sister, anyone we know, they'll tell you!" Her words sounded bitter.

"How can you say that? You know me better than anyone, except for Jefferson, so you know my laundry stinks just like everybody else's."

Jasmine couldn't suppress a laugh.

Kyla half smiled. "I just want you to be okay."

"I'm fine." Jasmine sighed. "I'm not going to sit here and talk all night when all of these fine men are waiting for me."

Kyla's eyes followed Jasmine as she sashayed across the room. She shook her head. But right now, she didn't have time to worry about Jasmine. Standing, Kyla edged towards the crowd, knowing it was just as important for her to meet and greet the guests as it was for Jefferson. She moved shyly along the perimeter of the room, watching as the waiters bustled around, clicking glasses, making sure none were ever empty and plates were never bare. The guests gathered in clusters and the conversation and laughter mixed with the music to form a melodic hum that floated through the air. Stepping forward, Kyla finally entered the arena and paused to chat warmly with each person, spending a little extra time with the guests she knew might later become benefactors of the Medical Center.

As she continued her stroll, Kyla was embraced and kissed at every turn as if it were her birthday. She picked hot hors d'oeuvres from the trays and, with a fixed smile, searched for Jefferson, finally spotting him at a table with a few of the other doctors. As if on cue, Jefferson turned and looked directly at her with a twinkle in his eye. Heat rushed to her face and Kyla instantly thanked God their nine-year-old daughter, Nicole, was spending the weekend in San Diego with Jefferson's mother. She turned away, afraid that others at the party would be able to discern their telepathic messages. Jefferson's gaze fortified her and she continued her stroll, pausing at the stage that had been set for the DJ.

"The music is great." She smiled at the DJ as Marvin Gaye crooned "What's Goin' On." A small circle had formed in the center of the dance floor. Jasmine was in the middle, with her arms high above her head as she cha-cha'ed with Ian Hollis, the accountant for the Medical Center, who was swaying more like an exotic dancer than a numbers cruncher. As the crowd cheered and Marvin continued to ask about picket lines and brutality, Jasmine's hips swiveled deeply.

"I had a feeling you'd like the old school theme." The DJ's words snapped Kyla back.

Turning away from the dance floor spectacle, Kyla chuckled. "I can't imagine music that I love is considered old."

He laughed. "I know how you feel!"

With an audible sigh, she shook her head. It seemed like a short time ago, but almost twenty years had passed since she had met Jefferson at Hampton Institute. Only five minutes after they had met, Jefferson had proposed to her. The memory of that night was still so clear.

She had wandered out from the Kappa Alpha Psi party, seeking refuge from the suffocating heat inside where the rooms were packed with students celebrating the completion of finals. She was squinting through the dim streetlights when a tall, mocha-skinned brother dressed in red and white fraternity paraphernalia swaggered towards her.

"Some party, huh?" the man with the huge Afro said, as he sloped against the wall.

Kyla nodded and smiled. "A little hot though."

"I like hot things," he said with a half-smile.

Ignoring his innuendo, Kyla walked across the wooden porch and perched against the rail. He followed and leaned on the fence, facing her.

"My name is Jefferson, by the way."

"Nice to meet you." She extended her hand and waited as he switched the Budweiser can from his right hand to his left.

"The pleasure is definitely all mine . . ." he answered as he took her hand. When Kyla remained silent, he continued. "So, are you a student here? I haven't noticed you before."

"I haven't noticed you either."

He laughed.

Kyla ran her hands along her corduroy jeans. The smooth voices of the Ohio Players blasted through the opened windows and Kyla snapped her fingers.

"Fire! Fire!" Jefferson sang, as his eyes danced with the music. "Fire! The way you walk and talk really sets me off to a full alarm . . ."

"It was nice meeting you, Jefferson," she said and started back towards the house."

"Wait, we haven't finished yet."

"Haven't finished what?"

"Making all of our plans. You're gonna be my wife," he said as he brought the beer can to his lips.

"You don't even know my name," she chuckled.

"Okay, wife, tell me your name."

She stepped closer so that she could see his face clearly

through the streetlights and spoke with a smile. "Kyla. Kyla Carrington."

"That's all I need to know. Everything else I'll learn over the lifetime of our long and happy marriage," he said as his hand traveled gently down the sleeve of her polyester blouse, until his fingers laced through hers.

Her eyes blinked with surprise, but she kept her hand in his. "So, Jefferson. If we're going to be married, don't you think I should know *your* last name?"

"Does that mean you *will* marry me?"

They shared their first laugh together in a scene not too different from this one.

"Hey, girl," a voice came over her shoulder. "I saw you over there talking to that Jasmine person. I was going to rescue you, but decided it would serve you right to be stuck with her all night."

"Now, Alexis. You promised you would behave," she said hugging her friend.

"I am behaving." Alexis raised her thick eyebrows, feigning innocence. She paused, lowering her voice conspiratorially. "If I wasn't I would tell Jasmine that her dress is so short, you can see what she had for breakfast!"

"Stop it," Kyla said trying to hold her laugh.

"Pastor says, 'Tell the truth and shame the devil,'" Alexis drawled as she held up one hand as if she was about to shout Hallelujah. "Anyway, sorry I'm late. Things were crazy at work. Was Jefferson surprised?"

"I think he was stunned."

"No problem getting him here?"

"That was the easy part. You know how much he loves this place."

"You worked it, Ky," Alexis said as she reached for one of the black balloons that floated above her. "Memphis restaurant has never looked better. Louise did this, right?"

"Of course."

"She's the best in L.A. She used to cater everything for my office, but recently, she's been hard to get. Hollywood has been calling her."

"I wasn't about to try to do this without Louise. But enough about this stuff," Kyla said grabbing her friend's hand and pulling her into the corner. "There are a lot of good-looking, single, successful men here."

"Kyla . . ." Alexis whined.

"Now, I'm not trying to set you up or anything."

Alexis raised her eyebrows in doubt.

"I just want you to know . . . you have *options* here."

"That's a new way of putting it."

"I just want you to be happy."

"I *am* happy. I don't need a man for that."

"But . . ."

"Kyla!" Alexis interrupted before her friend could continue. "Not everyone is going to find her Prince Charming, have the perfect child and wake up sixteen years later just as much in love as the day she married. That only happens in fairy tales and at *your* house."

"Well, you never know who you'll meet."

Alexis closed her eyes, slightly irritated, and tilted her head toward the ceiling. "Lord, please have mercy! And, please keep this chile out of my love life!"

"What are you two over here conspiring about?" Jasmine wiped her sweaty face, then tugged at her dress, trying to smooth it down over her hips. "Hello, Alexis," Jasmine said in a slow drawl, imitating Alexis' southern accent.

"Hello, Jasmine," Alexis said curtly. "Anyway, Kyla," Alexis continued, turning her back to Jasmine. "How are things going with the expansion at the clinic?"

"Great. The final proposal goes in next week."

"Does that mean they're going ahead with it?" Jasmine asked, leaning forward so that she could be heard.

"Uh-huh. Can you believe it?"

"Of course!" Alexis said. "As hard as you guys work, you deserve it."

"Yeah, just what you need—more success," Jasmine whispered and rolled her eyes.

"Hey, you," Jefferson appeared, and grabbed Kyla's arm. "We haven't danced all night."

As they stood in the center of the dance floor, Jefferson wrapped his arms around Kyla and they swayed to Lionel Richie's sexy voice. "Zoom! I'd like to fly away!" Jefferson sang softly into her ear.

"Umm," Kyla sighed and leaned in closer.

Jefferson brushed her thick bangs from her face and kissed her forehead. "Kyla, I can't believe you did this for me. Thank you." He leaned over and brushed his lips against hers, then pulled her tighter. As Jefferson sang Lionel's words into her ear, Kyla knew this would be one of the best nights of her life.

"Louise, you outdid yourself this time, lady," Kyla exclaimed as she signed her name with a flourish and handed the check to the caterer.

"I'm glad you're happy. I haven't done many private parties since I opened the Pie Shoppe. But how could I refuse this for Jefferson? By the way, I have a gift for him. I couldn't remember which was his favorite, so I baked two things—a pecan sweet potato pie and a pineapple cheesecake. They're in the kitchen."

"No, you didn't!"

Louise laughed. "I know his sweet tooth."

"He'll think he's walking around in heaven! Thank you!" As she hugged Louise, she glanced around the empty room.

"Jefferson's out front with some of the guys," Alexis said reading her friend's expression as she sat down at the table. "I just saw him. Kyla, this was a *great* party."

"I was just thanking Louise for everything. So, did you . . . meet anyone?"

Alexis rolled her eyes and ignored the question. "Anyway . . . how have things been with you, Louise?"

Louise laughed. "Great. I've been busy. In fact, I have a wedding to do tomorrow, so I've got to get going." Standing, she hugged Alexis, then Kyla. "Tell Jefferson I said enjoy the rest of his birthday."

Kyla remained silent until Louise left the room, then scooted her chair closer to Alexis, but before she could say anything, she heard Jasmine's voice.

"Still here, Alexis?"

Kyla glanced up and saw Jefferson and Jasmine walking towards them.

"Hey, you," Jefferson took Kyla's hand and pulled her to him. "Honey, everyone is raving about this party."

"It was all Louise. She left you a special surprise and said to tell you to enjoy the rest of your birthday." Kyla brushed her lips against his neck, drinking in his scent. "I want you to enjoy the rest of your birthday, too."

"Well . . . I guess that's my cue. I'm out of here." Alexis stood, readying herself to go, and glared at Jasmine when she didn't do the same.

"Hey, Alexis," said Jefferson. "Brian told me you guys had a great time together. He's a good brother."

"Brian!" Kyla said, opening her eyes wide.

"What about Brian?" Jasmine asked. She hoped they weren't talking about Brian Lewis, the doctor who had just joined the Medical Center. Jasmine had spent quite a bit of time tonight trying to get his attention, but he hadn't shown any interest in her. Now, she hoped that they weren't talking about Alexis getting together with him. That would be a dire end to this dismal evening.

"Jefferson, don't say another word!" Alexis commanded, softening her words with a smile. "You know how your wife is."

"Sorry. I was only passing along some information."

"But Alex, we can help. Jefferson has known him since they were kids, right, honey?"

"Leave me out of this. I don't want Alex killing me."

"You're a smart man, Dr. Blake."

"What are you guys talking about?" Jasmine piped in again.

"Like I said, I'm outta here." Alexis hugged Kyla and Jefferson. "Happy birthday, again. I'll call you tomorrow, Ky." Alexis looked over her shoulder. "Aren't *you* coming, Jasmine?"

"I was hoping that Jefferson and Kyla could drop me home."

"I think they want to be alone," Alexis said stating what she thought was obvious. "Where's your car?"

Jasmine grimaced at Alexis' cutting tone. "I came with some friends. Not that it's any of your business," she snapped. "Ky, would you mind giving me a ride?"

"No!" Alexis interjected before Kyla could answer. "I'll take you home."

"Alex, that would be great!" Jefferson exclaimed. "I do want some time with this beautiful lady," he said pulling Kyla closer. "I want to thank her and I have a very special way to do that." Jefferson kissed Kyla as if the two of them were already alone.

Jasmine grabbed her jacket from the table and stomped out. Alexis followed, leaving Jefferson and Kyla totally unaware of anything that was happening around them.

# *Two*

Jasmine slammed the door, kicked off her pumps and tossed her keys on the corner pedestal, piled high with unopened mail. She clicked on the lights and glanced around her pale pink and green living room. People often asked if she had decorated with her sorority colors in mind. Often she said yes, although she had never pledged a sorority. And anyway, she wouldn't have joined *that* sorority. That wasn't the sorority Kyla belonged to.

She hated coming home this late. At this hour, the house screamed its silence. As she climbed the stairs, she clamped her hands over her ears, but the quiet only grew louder. Dragging into her bedroom, her queen-sized bed swallowed her as she stretched across it. This had to be what it felt like to go crazy. First, you lose your husband, then you lose your mind.

She should have never gone to that party. It only reminded her how messed up her life was. Ever since her marriage broke up, she had put on a happy face to show everyone that she loved her new single life. They thought she was the one who had thrown Kenny out.

The small brass clock chimed softly. It was two o' clock in

the morning and it would be hours before she fell asleep. "This is all Alexis' fault!" she screamed.

Even with all of her planning, she was alone again. She should have been staying with Jefferson and Kyla tonight, just like she had many times before.

She reached for the telephone, but just as quickly pulled her hand away. Giving her body to another faceless man was something she couldn't do tonight.

Rolling over, she let her eyes roam in the dark, finally settling on the photo on the bureau. Through the open miniblinds, the streetlights illuminated the wedding picture she still kept on her dresser, and she struggled to hold back the tears.

From the moment they'd begun dating during their senior year in high school, Jasmine knew that Kenneth Larson was her key to a life she'd seen only on the society pages of *Jet* magazine. According to his coach, the high school football star had a lucrative career before him. All he had to do was choose the right college and stay healthy. Jasmine was going to be there to make sure Kenny did all that and a bit more. When he signed that big money contract, she would be at his side with a ring on her left hand.

With fortune and fame beckoning, Jasmine and Kenny entered UCLA in the fall of 1973. The first weeks were filled with freshman excitement, but it wasn't long before Jasmine realized that getting Kenny to marry her was going to be a tough task.

The freshman quarterback was not even eligible to play one game, yet women swarmed him like honeybees, leaving no question about their desires. Jasmine was beset with perfumed notes left at Kenny's room, harassing phone calls and constant interruptions when they were out on dates. By the time football season ended with the team achieving a Rose Bowl victory, Jasmine had found him in a parade of compromising positions. But her determination was stronger than her crushed pride. Keeping her head high, she continued in her mission to get the wedding ring.

For three years, Jasmine played out their situation, praying that patience would deliver the prize. But, it was her mother's death during their senior year that became the unexpected impetus toward their marriage. When Jasmine withdrew in mourning, Kenny drew closer, jumping in to rescue her from her state of agony. He took care of her—cooking, cleaning, providing whatever support she needed. The process took his mind from his flagging football career that had been fading quickly due to the presence of LaShaun Pitt—a younger, faster, more agile player who had replaced him as starting quarterback. Caring for Jasmine became his only focus.

For endless nights, he held her while she cried out her grief. Still, weeks passed before she returned to class. It wasn't until Kenny asked Jasmine to marry him two weeks before graduation that she was finally able to totally escape her despondency.

Even though the million-dollar football contract was now a bygone dream, Jasmine jumped at his proposal. She'd accomplished her mission and believed that somehow, one day they would have the life she wanted.

But it never happened. In their eighteen years, he had never made her happy. He had never been able to give her the kind of life that Kyla lived.

Kyla. Her sisterfriend for over thirty years. They'd been connected ever since that day in kindergarten when she'd been playing in the schoolyard with a group of boys and noticed the little girl with tears streaming down her face sitting against the fence.

"What's wrong with you?" Jasmine asked the girl with thick, unruly pigtails.

"Those girls over there," she said pointing. "They're picking on me."

"So? Just punch them out."

The little girl looked up, her eyes questioning.

"You know," Jasmine said sitting down on the concrete. "Punch their lights out. Kick their behind. Sock 'em in the nose."

The girl's eyes grew wide. "My mother said that Christians can't do that and God would be mad at me if I did."

Jasmine turned up her nose. "Well, your mother doesn't know anything! What's your name?"

The girl looked up and tried to smile. "Kyla."

"I'm Jasmine." Jasmine marched across the playground and demanded that the girls leave Kyla alone. And with what Jasmine had done to the neighborhood kids in the past, there was no one in the circle willing to challenge her. As the school bell signaled the end of recess, Jasmine took Kyla's hand and they stomped together past the now-silent group.

Their friendship had been sealed that day. Kyla was the friend who was always there when Jasmine needed help with schoolwork, and Jasmine was the popular one, the protector, the antithesis of the timid Kyla. Through years of birthday celebrations, pajama parties, and weeks together at sleep-away camp, their friendship continued through high school, though by their senior year, Jasmine began to notice a change in the dynamics.

One day after cheerleader practice, Kyla and Jasmine had strolled to the bus stop just as a yellow Volkswagen Beetle eased up to the curb.

"Hey, Kyla. How's it going?" the boys shouted.

Kyla smiled, hugging her books to her chest. "Fine."

"Want a ride?" the driver leaned over, yelling out the window.

"No, thank you."

"Hey, Marc," Jasmine waved.

"Hey, Jasmine. Are you sure you don't want a ride?" He said directing his question to Kyla.

"No thanks, the bus is here now. See you guys later."

As the two took their seats, Jasmine wrinkled her nose. "That Marc thinks he's so cute."

Kyla smiled. "Sounds like you're a little jealous."

"I'm not. I'm in love with Kenny."

"That's what you keep telling me, but I think you're just boy crazy."

"I'm seventeen. I'm supposed to be boy crazy. Plus, you have no idea what you're missing."

"I'm not missing anything."

"I think you're the one who's jealous because you haven't done *it* yet. You're probably the only virgin left in the senior class."

"I doubt that. But if I am, I'm proud of it."

"Well, do you plan on being a virgin your whole life?"

"Of course not. I'm just going to wait until I'm married."

"Kenny and I are getting married."

Kyla's snicker was doubtful. "When?"

"None of your business."

"I'll save my congratulations. I just think it's wrong to have sex with someone before you're married."

"That is a crazy, old-fashioned idea. Everybody's doing it. You're talking about something you know nothing about."

"I know what the Bible says," Kyla said rather weakly. "What you're doing is wrong."

"See, that's what's *wrong* with you. Not only are you judgmental, but you don't have a clue! It's all right to have sex as long as you love the person. And, not only that," she said crossing her legs, "Kenny will do anything I want because I gave it to him. You see these?" she asked pointing to her boots. "Do you know who gave them to me?"

"Kenny, so, is that why you sleep with him?"

"You haven't been listening to anything I've said. It's about love. Kenny gives me these gifts because he loves me. Anyway, why would anyone wait to have sex?"

"Maybe because God says to wait."

Jasmine sighed. "Why can't we have a normal conversation without you always bringing God into everything?"

"But, Jasmine," Kyla said sweetly as she rang the bell to get off at the next stop. "God *is* in everything." Kyla answered confidently, then jumped off the bus. She left Jasmine seething with emotions that her young mind didn't understand . . .

Jasmine bolted up in the bed, listening. A moment later, she heard it again—a banging sound, coming from downstairs. Then suddenly, it stopped. With her heart pounding, she turned on the nightstand light and tried to remember if she had locked all the doors.

She tiptoed into the darkened hallway and peeked over the railing into the foyer. The light was on and her shoes were sitting by the door just as she left them. Clicking on the hallway light, she tiptoed silently down the stairs. At the bottom, she turned on the light switch and the entire first floor became illuminated. Jasmine checked all the doors, closed the windows and blinds, safely shutting herself in. She sat down on the couch and shuddered as she wrapped her arms around her waist.

Maybe it was the furnace that she had heard. There was no one lurking in the dark shadows. She was scared beyond belief, for no reason at all. This house that she had once loved, had become a house of dread. She knew she would have to get out soon, if she were to maintain any semblance of sanity.

But, this was her final connection to Kenny. Everything reminded her of him. She had even purchased his favorite Calvin Klein cologne and sprayed it through the rooms. She needed to keep all this around her for as long as she could. This house was all that she had left.

Jasmine went to the downstairs linen closet and pulled out the down comforter. She fluffed the pillows on the couch, wrapped herself in the blanket, took one more glance around the room and lay down.

But locked doors and bolted windows could not bring her peace. And as she closed her eyes, trying to block out the glare from all the lights she was too afraid to turn off, her emotions boiled, gurgling like a volcano. Finally exploding, she no longer restrained the tears and they gushed forth freely. She cried until she slept.

# Three

Alexis hadn't turned on the answering machine and now the phone's ringing was relentless. She drew the pillow over her ears, but it continued. Without opening her eyes, she grabbed the phone.

"This had better be good," she said, her voice muffled by the pillow.

"Alexis, did I wake you?" a male voice asked.

Her eyes popped open. She sat up, catching her reflection in the mirror and smoothed her hand over her hair. "Good morning, Dr. Lewis," her voice smiled.

"Only sick folks call me doctor and sick is certainly not the word I'd use to describe you."

Alexis laughed.

"And it's no longer morning," he chuckled. "Sorry I woke you."

"It's okay. I never sleep this late," she yawned.

"Well, I promised I would call. I wanted to let you know that I enjoyed talking with you last night."

Her smile grew wider. "I enjoyed myself too."

"Good. Then, I uh . . . you mentioned that you weren't

sure if you had any plans for today and I was wondering if we could get together later."

"I'd like that."

"Is there anything in particular you like to do?"

"I enjoy all kinds of things," she flirted. "What about you?"

He cleared his throat. "Why don't I pick you up around four and then we can decide."

"Sounds great."

She gave him her address, then jumped from the bed and scurried to the mirror. Turning from side to side, she pulled her hair back. Good thing last week was touch-up time. She noticed her nails. Spreading her fingers wide, she frowned.

She punched in one of the coded numbers on her phone.

"Nancy's Nails."

"Hey Nancy, this is Alexis. I need a humongous favor."

"What, girl?"

"Squeeze me in today. Right now."

"Oh girl, it's Saturday. We're already backed up."

"Pleeease."

"Why didn't you come in yesterday?" Nancy whined.

"Because I didn't know I'd have a date tonight."

"Get out of here! A couple of decades have passed since you had a date! You told me you'd given up on men."

"Well, some things change. Please, Nancy. I'll pay you triple."

"Triple? Well, girl, just how fast can you get here?"

The day's light streaming through the bedroom window and the warm rays settling on her face awakened Kyla. With her eyes still shut, she stretched, basking in the extra hours of sleep she had gotten. Usually she greeted the dawn and got Nicole dressed, fed, and ready for her acting class. But with their daughter away, leisurely hours were laid out before them this weekend like a precious gem.

Rolling over, she allowed thoughts of last night to drift through her mind and her lips curved into a smile. She reached across the bed, patting around for Jefferson. The empty satin sheets felt smooth and cool.

She sat up, straining to listen for her husband, but knew that he could be anywhere in their capacious home. She climbed from the bed and her eyes roamed the room for her bathrobe.

"Ooh, baby. If you keep standing there like that we'll just have to start last night all over again." Jefferson came into the bedroom balancing a breakfast tray in one hand.

Kyla felt the heat rush to her face and giggled as she grabbed the top sheet off the brass-framed bed. Twisting it around her body, she turned to face her husband.

"Ah, don't hide." He tugged the sheet away from her as he laid the tray upon the bed. "I love the way you look." He traced his fingers across her bare shoulders, then kissed her softly.

"I think you're more appreciative of my body than the neighbors will be," she said, pointing to the uncovered window, then pulled the sheet around her once again. "Is this for me?" she asked, looking at the array of fruit set extravagantly on the tray.

"Yes, I did it all by myself." He wrapped his arms around her waist and kissed her forehead. "You know, Ky, I can't remember having a better birthday. Did I thank you?"

"You thanked me very well last night," she said, brushing her lips against his.

As he pulled her down onto his lap, the sheet fell and she shivered against the cool air.

"Let me warm you up." He nuzzled against her neck and planted small, soft kisses. Kyla closed her eyes and inhaled softly. "If you don't stop doing this to me, I'll never get out of here."

"Where are you going?" She wrapped her hands tighter around his neck.

"I have to go to the clinic."

She pulled back.

"I have to finish up the expansion paperwork with Brian. Remember, you're taking the proposal in for us on Monday." Jefferson took a grape off the tray and rubbed it against her pouting lips before he dropped it into her mouth. "Shannon's coming in for a few hours, so we should be finished quickly. I told her I'd be in by noon, but I was recovering. You wore me out last night."

Kyla took a grape from the tray and ran her tongue lightly against it before she fed it to him. "Maybe I could tempt you . . . to stay?"

"I'm definitely tempted," he said, his eyes narrowing. "But I've got to go."

"I thought we'd spend the entire weekend celebrating. That's why I sent Nicole to your mom's."

"Kyla, if we celebrated my birthday all weekend, I would never let you get out of this bed!"

"That was my plan." She tugged at the buttons on his shirt. "Stay." She ran her tongue along his neck.

"I won't be long." He brought her fingers to his lips. "Do

you want to go out tonight or should we stay in and finish where we left off?"

"It's your birthday. We'll do whatever you want."

"Woman, don't make no promises that you can't keep."

She tipped her head from side to side. "Oh, I can keep my promises." Her smile was seductive. "I may have been a virgin when I married you, but you've been an excellent teacher."

"And, you've been the perfect student." He leaned over and their tongues did a slow waltz. Kyla felt her heartbeat rise to the rhythm of their kiss.

It was minutes before they broke their embrace. "I'd better get out of here. I won't be able to stop in a few minutes," he said, his eyes revealing all that he felt. As he leaned forward to kiss her again, she held his head close for a moment.

"What's wrong?" he asked noticing her faint frown. "You're not upset that I have to go to the office, are you?"

"No. I understand," she said softly.

"So? What's wrong?"

"We're so happy. And it's always been like this. God has poured down infinite blessings on us."

"He has. But if you feel things are too good, just remember all those times you tell me I'm getting on your nerves."

"I'm serious, Jefferson. Will things always be this good?"

His fingers grazed the side of her face as he nodded. "We've had sixteen wonderful years and we'll have sixteen times sixteen more."

She smiled.

"And do you know why?" he continued. "Because it's not just us. It's you and me and God."

They kissed again. "Get out of here," she said, giving him a little push.

She watched his back as he strutted from the room, his gabardine slacks revealing his four-times-a-week workouts. Picking up an orange slice, she stretched on the bed, lingering in the quiet. After she finished, she put on Jefferson's terrycloth bathrobe and took the tray downstairs, laying it on the kitchen's granite countertop. She wandered into the family room, wiggling her toes through the deep cream carpet.

Thanks to Carmen's visit yesterday, the house was spotless. Kyla bounced onto the leather couch and clicked on the television. The surround-sound thundered through the room and she clicked the remote, returning the room to silence.

Now what was she going to do? She had rearranged her normal Saturday activities. Miss Imogene was overseeing the construction workers at The Compassion House and with Nicole away, she wasn't playing Shuttle Mom. The only thing she had to do was wait for Jefferson to return.

For a moment, she thought about going upstairs to her exercise room and spending some time on the bike, but she didn't have the desire to even climb the stairs. Leaning back, she picked up the Bible they kept on the end table and turned to her favorite book.

She loved the eighth chapter of Romans, Paul's letter about faith and the grace of God. From the first verse, *There is therefore now no condemnation to them which are in Christ Jesus who walk not after the flesh, but after the Spirit,* to the last verse, *Nor height, nor depth nor any other creature, shall be able to separate us from the love of God, which is in Christ Jesus our Lord,* this was one book of the Bible that left no doubt about God's love.

She reread the chapter a few times, trying to commit it to memory. But after a while, her eyelids grew heavy. Closing the

Bible, she stretched out and allowed herself to drift into a peaceful sleep.

Jasmine wasn't dreaming . . . the phone was ringing. She reached for the pink cordless phone. "Hello." Her voice was groggy.

"Jasmine, it's Serena. You sound like you were taking a nap."

"What time is it?"

"Well, it's five here, so it's two out there."

Jasmine struggled to sit up and rubbed her eyes. "I was out late last night."

"That's good. So, you're starting to get out now?"

"It was no big deal. Kyla gave a birthday party for Jefferson. Anyway, why'd you call?"

"Can't I just call my sister to say hello and see how she's doing?"

"You can, but we both know you don't. So, what's up?"

"I'm hurt. I just wanted to say hello . . ."

"And . . ."

Serena laughed. "And, Dad's here and wants to talk to you."

Jasmine sat straight up. "No! I don't want to talk to him. You didn't tell him about me and Kenny, did you?"

"No, you need to do that," Serena whispered.

"Is he standing right there?"

"Uh-huh."

"Well, I've got to go."

"What am I supposed to say?"

"I don't know. You had the big idea to call me so you figure it out. But don't tell him about Kenny."

Jasmine clicked the phone. Seconds later, when it rang again, she slumped into the couch's pillows and waited for the answering machine to pick up. She massaged her neck, trying to relieve the stiffness that settled in from a restless slumber. When she tried to stand, the ache stung her back. She always felt this way when she slept in the living room and each time she promised herself never to do it again. Sleeping on a loveseat was impossible, but that's all they had in the living room—two matching loveseats. That had been Kenny's idea—to be a little different. It seemed like a good idea at the time.

Holding her head in her hands, she sat up straight when the doorbell startled her. She sat still, silent, willing the visitor to disappear. But when the ringing continued, Jasmine remembered that her BMW was sitting outside. Her garage door had broken and she had meant to get it fixed, but she didn't even know how to begin. Kenny had always handled these things. Maybe Jefferson will do it for me, she thought.

When she realized the visitor would not be dissuaded, she crept to the door, peeked through the peephole and raised her eyebrows in surprise. She opened the door, just enough for Kyla to squeeze in, and stumbled back to her makeshift bed.

Kyla followed Jasmine to the couch, and when Kyla leaned over and hugged her, Jasmine burst into tears.

Kyla held her, trying to bring comfort as they'd done for each other so many times before. As Jasmine's sobs continued, Kyla pulled her tighter, wondering what could have gone wrong. Last night, she had thought Jasmine was taking the first steps towards recovering. For the first time in months, she had looked like she was ready to move on.

Minutes ticked by before Jasmine lifted her head. "I'm sorry," she sniffed. "I cried so much last night I didn't think I had any tears left. But when you hugged me . . . it's been so long since someone hugged me and meant it."

"I thought you were crying because you know how bad you look," Kyla said, hoping to buy a smile. It didn't work. Instead, Jasmine wept softly.

Kyla went to the bathroom and returned with a box of tissues, but when she saw Jasmine, she stopped short. "Ugh! Girl, that's nasty!"

Jasmine burst out laughing.

"At least I made you laugh," Kyla said.

"Because you're so crazy. What does it matter where I wipe my nose? I'm the only one who lives here."

"So. Your snot will still be all over that blanket and you'll never be able to use it again. Here." Kyla wrinkled her nose, stretched out her hand and handed Jasmine the tissues.

Still chuckling, Jasmine yanked a few tissues from the box. "What are you doing here anyway? I thought you'd be out celebrating."

"I wish. Jefferson had to go to the clinic. Just *had* to finish up some paperwork for the expansion."

"So the Medical Center is getting bigger and better."

"We hope so."

"They've done some incredible things over there. I know you're proud."

"I am. We've been blessed."

"That's the story of your life. Success is your middle name."

After a long silence, Kyla said, "I thought things were going a little better for you."

"I thought so too." Jasmine bit on her lip and fought back the tears that threatened to come again. "It's so hard," her voice quivered. "I never expected Kenny to walk out."

"You said you put him out," Kyla frowned.

"I didn't want to be embarrassed."

Kyla leaned over and touched her friend's hand. "You don't have anything to be embarrassed about."

"Well, I am. Especially since I'd been asking him for a divorce for years . . ."

"I never knew that."

"Yes, you did. You never paid any attention to me. You just thought I was complaining. I didn't think Kenny was listening either. Only he was. The thing is, I never really wanted a divorce."

"Then why did you say you did?"

"It's only been since he left that I realized that I never wanted him to leave. I just wanted him to be different. I wanted him to be more."

When Kyla's eyes questioned her, Jasmine continued with a sideways glance. "To be honest . . . I wanted him to be more like Jefferson."

Kyla's eyes narrowed. "Like Jefferson how?"

"I wanted him to be ambitious and successful and financially stable and give me all of the things that Jefferson gives you."

"Jasmine, I hope you never said that to him."

"Not in so many words, but he got the message. Kenny never had any drive. He would have been satisfied being a research assistant with that insurance company forever. Did you know that in the ten years he was with them, he only got two raises?"

"Maybe that's all they would give him."

"He should have found another job. Everyone knows that you have to change companies to advance. But Kenny couldn't put his energy into that. All he was interested in was hanging out. He knew every Happy Hour at every club in L.A. And on the weekends, it was worse. He would hang out and dance the hours away. It got to the point where I only saw him when he came home to sleep and change his clothes."

"I never knew that," Kyla said trying to keep the surprise from her voice.

"I wanted you to think I had the perfect life like you. And whenever we planned anything with you and Jefferson, Kenny would make sure he was there. He liked you guys. He just didn't like me."

"Now, I know that's not true. Kenny loved you. I think he kept you alive when your mother passed away. That was when I knew he was something special."

Jasmine hugged a pillow and nodded her head slightly. "It may have started out that way, but things changed. I wanted to grow, get more out of life. And Kenny wanted that too. Only he was a dreamer. The only way he was going to get anything was if he won the lottery. He let me do all the work. He was willing to go along for the ride."

Kyla looked at Jasmine as if she were seeing her for the first time. As close as she thought they were, she hadn't known that this had been going on in Jasmine's life. "So things started getting bad because Kenny didn't make the money you wanted?"

"That and the fact that I hated his job. Do you know how embarrassing it was when we went out and I had to introduce him as a research assistant?"

"What was so bad about that?"

Jasmine rolled her eyes. "Only a woman who is married to a doctor could ask that."

"Jasmine, look at all that you have."

"Oh please! I have a house that I can't afford, bills stacked to the ceiling, and a different man in my bed every week because I can't stand to sleep alone."

"Jasmine . . ."

"Remember when we said we were going to marry doctors?"

"But we were kids. Jefferson wasn't a doctor when I fell in love with him. What does it matter what your husband does if you love him?"

"It's easy for you to say that now. You and Jefferson made me and Kenny look like paupers." Jasmine tossed the pillow angrily across the room, then leaned back and folded her arms in front of her.

Kyla was surprised at Jasmine's words. "That's not true, Jasmine. But you have to stop comparing our lives. Kenny was not Jefferson and you're not me."

"Don't you think I know that! Kenny didn't have to *be* Jefferson. He just should've been a better Kenny."

"Maybe Kenny was being the best he could be."

Jasmine snickered and shook her head. There was no way Kyla would understand. "It wasn't good enough."

Kyla stared at Jasmine. "Is that why he left?" she asked softly.

Jasmine shrugged. "I don't know the real reason."

"Maybe it was because you were telling Kenny the same things that society told him every day—that he wasn't good enough. That had to kill him."

Jasmine hunched her shoulders, but said nothing.

"Did you guys ever think of counseling?" Kyla asked.

Jasmine nodded. "Kenny wanted to go, but there wasn't really a need for it. A counselor wouldn't have been able to help. All we needed was for Kenny to change even just a little bit."

Kyla paused, carefully choosing her next words. "I wish you and Kenny had been more spiritual. I wish you had God in your lives."

"Like *that* would have changed anything," Jasmine snickered.

"God does change things, Jasmine," Kyla insisted.

"How many times do I need to tell you? I'm not into God like you are. God couldn't save my marriage."

"Jasmine, nothing's too big for God. Knowing God would have changed *you* and if *you* had changed, then your marriage would have changed. But what's most important is that the Lord can get you through all of this. Let me help you get to know God again, Jasmine."

"I don't feel like getting into one of your long, boring conversations about God," Jasmine said, impatiently. "It's too late. Kenny is gone and there is no way he's coming back. When he left he said he was moving to Atlanta and hoped that he never saw me anywhere on this planet again. My marriage is over. I'm all alone."

"No, you're not. God is here. And I am too."

Jasmine shook her head like she was in a trance. "You know what's so weird about all of this? I used to fantasize about what my life would be like if I were single again. I thought it would be wonderful . . ."

"What about trying to reach Kenny? Call him and try to talk things out."

"No," Jasmine said a bit too quickly. She looked away, avoiding Kyla's gaze.

"Consider it," Kyla pushed. "Don't let eighteen years of marriage go just like that."

Tears were building in Jasmine's eyes. "He left me for another woman. Someone, he said, who loved him for who he was. He'd been seeing her for two years! I couldn't believe it, Ky. He told me once our divorce is final, he's going to marry her. I don't even know *her* name."

To hide her surprise, Kyla inhaled deeply.

"You know, Kyla, I did love Kenny. And I miss him so much. I didn't want him to leave. I just wanted him to do better and be more like . . ."

"Jefferson."

Jasmine's eyes narrowed in defiance. "What's wrong with that, Ky? You've always been so lucky. Are you the only one who's supposed to live the good life?"

"Jasmine, I'm not lucky. Yes, I've been blessed, but I've also worked hard and struggled, even when it hurt, to be obedient to God. It hasn't been easy."

Jasmine glared at Kyla. "All you know is easy. I'm sorry I told you this. You couldn't just be supportive. You have to sit back and be the self-righteous, God-quoting judge."

"That's not what I'm doing. I *want* to support you and help you through this."

"Well, if this is the kind of help you're going to give, I don't need it. Go home to your perfect life with your perfect husband and daughter and leave me alone."

Before Kyla could say anything, Jasmine stood, wrapped the blanket around her shoulders and stomped up the stairs.

Kyla heard the bedroom door slam but remained on the couch for several minutes before she moved. From the time they were young, Kyla had suspected that one day Jasmine would self-destruct and now it seemed like that day had come.

Pulling a piece of paper from her Daytimer, she scribbled a note: *Jasmine, if you need us, we're just a phone call away. Call me later. I love you. Ky.*

She rested the note against the empty vase on the table. Sighing, she picked up her backpack and went to the windows, opening the blinds and letting the afternoon sun release its rays into the house.

"That's what Jasmine needs," Kyla thought aloud. "Some light in her life." Kyla knew there was only one Light that could help Jasmine and she was determined to stand by her friend and help her find her way to the Lord. She walked to the door, paused and closed her eyes, said a silent prayer, then left, closing the door securely behind her.

Jefferson flipped through the pages and smiled. "Okay, Shannon. I think we've finally got it. It's time for us to go home."

Shannon stood and took the report from Jefferson. "Then, I'm going to leave right now. My mother is visiting and I left her alone in my apartment."

"Oh, I'm sorry," Brian said. "If we'd known we wouldn't have taken you away today."

"I needed this break," Shannon said waving her hand.

"But, I just don't want to leave her alone for too long. There's no telling how much snooping she's done already."

They all laughed.

"Enjoy the rest of the weekend," Jefferson said as Shannon walked from the office. He turned to Brian. "So, what are your plans for the rest of the weekend? Are you going to try to make it to our church? We'll be in San Diego, but I know you'll enjoy yourself anyway."

"I'll just wait to go with you next Sunday."

"I'm going to hold you to it."

"Things certainly have changed. I used to be the one trying to get you to go to church."

"Yeah, but you just wanted to have some company."

Brian chuckled. "Every breathing soul in my mother's house had to go talk to Jesus every Sunday. Rain, earthquakes, nothing stopped my mom. Remember those Saturday nights when we would stay out late?"

Jefferson nodded.

"Man, it didn't matter what time I came home, my mother was in my room before the sun was up. 'Time to get up for church, Brian,'" he mimicked in a squeaky soprano voice.

"At least you grew up knowing the Lord. No one in my house went to church at all."

"And I was so jealous. I wanted to move in with you and sleep late on Sundays."

"But the good news is that both my mother and I are born again. And, it has really changed my life."

"So you've been saying. Regina and I didn't go to church much in Boston."

"Then it's good you're back here. You're going to love our

pastor. Pastor Ford is truly anointed. This woman knows the Word of God and teaches it."

"I still can't believe you attend a church with a woman pastor. Man, I don't know if I can do that."

"Why not? The only thing that should matter is whether you're being taught the Word and Pastor Ford certainly does that. I don't know why people trip over this man/woman pastor thing. If the Bible says that we are all one in Jesus and He doesn't make a difference between men and women, in that way, then why should we?"

Brian shrugged. "I just can't imagine a skirt in the pulpit."

"All I know is that Pastor Ford has taught me what it means to be a Christian. I now have a personal relationship with the Lord. It's not about a building or a committee. It's not about rules and regulations. She teaches you to know God for yourself. It's unbelievable what that will do for your life. I've become a man because of her."

"That's a deep statement."

"That's why I want you to join us. Remember, next Sunday."

Brian smiled. "You've got it. But man, this weekend I've got big plans."

"Really? In town for just a couple of weeks and already the man is on top of the social scene."

"Yeah. I'm going out with Alexis."

Jefferson hesitated, then smiled. "Some things never change. You're still a fast worker."

"No, it's not like that. I've changed a lot."

"Good. Just don't mess up or *my* life will be hell. She's one of Kyla's best friends. They were roommates at Hampton."

Brian leaned back in the chair. "No problem. So, tell me about her. Is she involved with anyone?"

Jefferson snickered. "You should be asking her."

"I will, I just thought I could get a little inside info."

Jefferson smiled. "Not from me. It's amazing that you two haven't met over the years."

"Actually, I think we have. Wasn't she at your house-warming? Remember, when Regina and I flew here for a few days?"

Jefferson narrowed his eyes in thought. "Yeah, she was there."

"I just thought of that this morning. But, Alexis didn't mention it, so I don't think she remembers me and frankly, I don't really remember her, though I don't know how I could have missed that woman."

"Maybe you missed her because you were with your wife." Jefferson paused. "Do you miss Regina?"

"No. The divorce was the best thing for both of us."

"What about the boys? Are you sorry you moved so far away from them?"

Brian smiled. "Now those two, I miss. But, I've got it all worked out. Not only will I have them all summer, but they'll be coming out for all the long weekends, plus a week at Christmas. And I've spoken with them every day since I've moved here. Not only on the phone, but my boys have become computer whizzes and I get E-mails all day long," he laughed.

"Hey, give them my E-mail address. It would be great to hear from them."

"Will do. Anyway, it's time for me to go pick up that fine woman with those jammin' legs. Wasn't she a model?" Brian picked up his briefcase and headed for the door.

"Yeah, but if I can give you one piece of advice, my friend, it would be to get to know Alexis beyond her looks. She's an ex-model who's now a successful businesswoman. She owns an advertising agency, you know."

"Yeah. Smart, beautiful, financially together. What more is there?"

"She's a Christian."

Brian paused. "Oh, yeah?"

"Yeah, she's a member of our church. *Strong* Christian," Jefferson said, with a tone Brian had heard men use when he'd expressed interest in their younger sisters.

"Well now, I'm definitely looking forward to going to church with you. But now, I've got to go. Can't be late. I've gotta make the right first impression."

They exited the clinic together. "You have plans for tonight?" Brian asked.

Jefferson's lips spread into a wide grin. "I have a beautiful wife waiting for me and I have *big* plans for her."

"I hear you."

They laughed. As they got into their cars, Jefferson punched the button to lower his window. "Hey Brian," he yelled out. "Have a great time tonight."

"I plan to," Brian smiled.

"And another thing. It's good to have you back and working here with me."

Brian nodded and waved, then they both screeched their cars from the lot, each eager to see the woman waiting for him.

# *Four*

Brian had told Alexis to dress casual and she wondered if he realized how much stress his words generated. She had spent more time and felt more pressure wanting to make a good impression. After trying on three pairs of jeans, four shirts, and choosing between pumps, loafers or boots she'd finally emerged from her apartment. Surveying her image in the lobby mirror, she was glad she was already downstairs since she felt another outfit modification coming on.

At the sound of the beep of a car horn, she looked away from the mirror and watched Brian cruise his BMW into the circular driveway. She popped on her sunglasses and took a deep breath. When he jumped in front of the doorman to open the door for her, she smiled. A gentleman! He pecked her cheek lightly and Alexis thought she recognized his cologne.

"How you doing?"

"Great!" She smiled as he accelerated onto the street.

"You look terrific."

"Thanks," she said with a sideward glance. "You look pretty good yourself."

He released a light chuckle that she could only describe as

smooth. "Well, knowing I was going out with you, I had to do my best. I've never been out with a model before."

"I'm not a model."

"Don't try to hide. Jefferson has told me your whole history."

Alexis crinkled her nose. "I don't know if I like that."

"Why not? It's what you women do all the time. Get the four-one-one on some man. This time I got the scoop on you."

"Well, I don't know why."

"You don't know why?" Brian laughed. "Maybe it's because I want to make a good impression."

She smiled. She'd been thinking the same thing. "You've succeeded. I'm impressed—so far."

"Well, I'll just make sure that I keep on impressing you . . . all night long."

After a long pause, she asked, "So, where are we going?"

"I thought we'd hang out at the beach. I hear there's a pretty good restaurant down there and we can walk around after that."

They chatted easily as they drove to the Westside and when they pulled into the parking lot behind the Venice Beach Café, Brian once again jumped out of the car to open the door for her. He paid the attendant, took her hand and they strolled to the restaurant. When they were seated, Brian took off his glasses and stared at her.

"So, Ms. Ward . . ."

"Yes, Dr. Lewis?"

"Should we order first and then talk? Or talk a little and then order?"

Alexis pursed her lips, scrolling the rules of dating through her mind. Never appear too hungry, never eat all of your food, always order a salad. She smiled. "Actually, I'm starving. Let's order, then talk. I think I'll have the turkey burger and fries."

They gave their orders to the blond, muscular waiter/actor, then settled back as the Saturday afternoon beach crowd eagerly snatched the first warm rays of summer and strolled one of the world's most infamous strips.

Alexis looked up when she heard Brian chuckle. "What are you laughing at?"

"I was told that I was likely to see anything out here."

Alexis followed his gaze to a young woman clad only in a yellow thong bikini, Rollerblades, and a set of headphones. She whizzed down the concrete, seemingly oblivious to the legion of dogs and men trailing behind. "This must be your first time here," she said.

He returned her glance. "It is. Our beaches were a bit calmer in San Diego."

"There are some sights here."

He leaned forward. "Well, the only sight I'm interested in . . ."

She held up her hands. "Don't say it, please!" she drawled.

"I love your accent. Where're you from?"

"A question you forgot to ask Jefferson," she laughed. "I'm from Savannah."

"Ah, the Deep South."

"And, I feel right at home here. Los Angeles is just the final resting place for everyone born in Texas, Oklahoma . . . you name it!"

Brian laughed. "I've heard that before. But you've been in

L.A. for a long time. I'm surprised we haven't met before," he said, testing to see if she remembered their first encounter.

"I'm surprised too. Kyla tries to set me up with every man she knows."

"And she hasn't succeeded?"

"Believe me, it's not for lack of trying. Kyla thinks a woman needs a man to be complete."

He stared at her for a long moment before he spoke. "And what do you think?"

She took a sip of water. "I don't *need* a man . . ."

He raised his eyebrows.

"To be complete. I'm already there."

"I'll vouch for that."

She felt the heat rush to her cheeks and Brian smiled as if he could see her blush.

"But, I am surprised that you're not involved with anyone," he said.

"I could say the same thing about you. Why aren't you involved?"

"I've only been in California for a few weeks, remember?"

She smirked, "You could have left someone behind . . ."

"Jefferson said you owned an advertising agency, but you sound like a private investigator," he kidded.

"If I'm getting too personal . . ."

"You're not. I did leave someone behind, in Boston. I'm divorced."

Alexis arched an eyebrow. "Oh, I didn't know that."

"Does it make a difference?"

"Should it?"

"No."

"Then, it doesn't. Anyway, you're forty years old and I'd be suspicious if you didn't have some kind of past."

"How do you know I'm forty?"

"You grew up with Jefferson."

"I could be a year younger . . ."

"Or you could be chronologically challenged and be a year or two older," she teased.

He laughed again. "My mother used to call people like you a pistol."

"Is that a good thing?"

He took her hand. "You have no idea how good it is."

Dropping her eyes, she eased her hand away. "So . . . are glad to be back in California?"

He leaned his elbows on the table and nodded his head slightly. "Things are beginning to look up," he said.

She ignored his tone. "You like the clinic?"

"I love it. Jefferson has put together something wonderful here."

"Yeah, five years ago, no one was sure how this would turn out. A group of African-American doctors daring to do what few had done."

"I'm proud to be one of them."

"What is that now? Nine doctors?"

"Yup, all under one roof."

"Are you the only ophthalmologist?"

"Uh-huh. I'm a surgeon actually. I've been performing some of the newest techniques of laser surgery. Actually, it's called Laser Vision Correction and it's become a hot thing. Perfect vision without glasses or contacts."

"Were you in a group practice in Boston?"

"No. I was on staff at Boston General. That's one reason

I'm so excited about joining the clinic. Not only will I get to practice, but as a partner, I'm kind of an entrepreneur, like you. It's an exciting new adventure for me and if there is one thing people say about me, it's that I'm adventurous."

"But you're a long way from home . . ."

"I spent twenty years there, but I never considered Boston my home. It's true what they say. Home is where your heart is and my mother is still in San Diego."

The waiter/actor brought their food, smiled, and perfunctorily asked if they needed anything else, but turned away before they had a chance to answer.

Alexis smiled at Brian. "Would you mind? I'm going to bless the food."

"Yes, I would mind."

Her shoulders tightened, but before she could say anything, he reached for her hands.

"I'd mind, because *I* would like to say our first grace."

She bowed her head and her smile widened as she listened to his words. This man knew how to thank the Lord! When he finished, she picked up her fork and grinned. "Where did you learn to pray like that?"

He shrugged and he bit into his burger. "Been doing it all my life."

"Saying grace?"

"That and walking with the Lord."

She nodded her head slowly. "Me too."

"I know, Jefferson told me."

They laughed so loud that patrons from nearby tables frowned disapprovingly. Alexis cleared her throat and wiped her lips with the napkin. "Do you have a church home yet?"

"No, not yet. I've been spending all of my time getting settled, but next week I plan to attend church with you."

"Oh really?"

He laughed. "Don't think I'm finagling another date. Jefferson's already invited me."

"Well, that wouldn't be so bad."

"What?"

"If you were to finagle another date."

He bowed his head slightly and lifted his glass. "Well, Ms. Ward, to our next date."

She laughed and raised her glass too. "Cheers."

They chatted until the sun settled over the Pacific Ocean, bringing in the June evening chill. And as Brian drove her home and kissed her on the cheek at her door, she smiled, unable to remember when she'd had a better time.

The room glowed with the flickers from the cinnamon-scented candles and her moist skin glistened in the room's soft light. With half-opened eyes, Kyla felt a perspiration bead drip from her chin onto his face. Breathless, she wilted onto Jefferson's heaving chest, listening to his racing heart, his heavy breathing matching her own. The minutes rolled past before their pulses could be considered stable.

His fingers caressed her earlobe, moving against her flesh, arousing her desires once again. She took a deep breath, determined to hold back the feelings she already felt stirring inside. It had been a few hours and she was too exhausted to continue. What else could she focus on besides the sensation of his fingers dancing in the curve of her back? She started counting—one, two, three, four—his fingers moved to her shoulders, massaging her lightly. Five, six—he hugged her close, his breath tickled her ear—seven, eight. He buried his face in her hair—nine. She sighed as his lips followed his fingers. Where was she? One, two, three, four . . . She sat up and leaned against the back of the couch.

"Honey, we'd better go up to bed if we're going to make it down to San Diego in time for church with your mother."

"We can't, we're not finished."

"Jefferson, we have to get up early."

"You promised me that I could have anything I wanted for my birthday and I want you in every room of this house. So far, we've only done the kitchen and the family room. There's quite a few more we have to do."

"You've lost your mind," she teased. "There are nine rooms in this house. It would take us all night!"

"That's what I'm counting on."

She closed her eyes and leaned into him, running her hands over the tightness of his back. He kissed her head, her neck, then nibbled on her ear before his lips found hers.

"Didn't you just turn forty?"

"That's right, I just hit my prime."

"No, honey, you got that wrong. It's a woman who hits her prime when *she* turns forty."

"See, I'm just trying to help you out."

"But, *I'm* not forty yet."

"Come on, just one last time. Then, I promise, we'll go to bed."

"How can I resist a man who begs?"

He leaned over her, letting the sheet fall away and kissed her forehead. When the telephone rang, he moved his lips to hers.

Kyla pushed her hands gently against his chest. "Jefferson."

"The machine will get it."

"But, it might be your mom or Nicole," she said in a husky voice as she rubbed his cheek.

She picked up the cordless phone from the end table. "Hello."

"Kyla, this is Jasmine."

"Oh . . . hi Jasmine."

Jefferson shook his head. "She can't stay here! Not tonight!" He motioned for her to hang up and Kyla nodded.

"Kyla, is Jefferson there?"

Kyla frowned. "Yeah . . . he's a little . . . busy right now. Is there something you need?"

"I *need* to talk to Jefferson."

Kyla shrugged and put her hand over the receiver. "She wants to talk to you," she whispered.

"No," Jefferson said waving his hands.

"Honey, I left her a note today telling her if she needed us, she should just call . . ."

He shook his head. "I don't care. Tell her to call back . . . later. Much later," he said as his fingers glided up her leg.

"Jas, he's *busy*. Tell me what you need and I'll give him the message," Kyla said, shivering slightly now that his fingers had moved to her stomach.

"You're afraid to let the man *talk* to your best friend, Ky?"

"Well, if you want to just call back tomorrow . . ."

Jasmine sighed. "I wanted to know if he could do me a favor."

She waited a beat. "Okay?"

"My garage door is broken and I don't want to keep leaving my car outside."

"Okay, I'll let him know and ask him to call you back. I've got to go, Jasmine. Speak to you later." She hung up the phone and Jefferson clicked the button to turn off the ringer, then dropped the phone onto the floor.

"She's turned into a witch since Kenny left," Jefferson said.

"It's just that she's in a lot of pain." She wrapped her arms around his neck and pulled him close. "Promise me that nothing like that will ever happen to us."

"Never," he whispered, slipping his naked body over hers. As their lips touched and their tongues met, Kyla allowed herself to drift into the sacred land with the only lover she'd ever had and the only man she would ever love.

Jasmine hung up the phone. It sounded as if she had interrupted something. Well, too bad. She lifted the phone, punched in the Blake's number again, then hung up before it rang.

She picked up her phone book, flipped through the pages, picked a number, then dialed. "Hello, may I speak to Michael Newman?"

"Who is this?" a woman asked.

She didn't say the words she was tempted to say. "I'm one of his clients and I just received some news that I must discuss with him."

"Hold one moment, please."

Jasmine tapped her fingers against the table as she listened to the muffled voices, chuckling as she imagined the conversation on the other end.

"Hello."

"Hi, Michael, it's Jasmine."

"Oh . . . hello, Ms. Larson. I didn't know you had my home number." He cleared his throat. "Is there something I can help you with?"

"I'm sorry to call you at home, but I couldn't help it. I was thinking how much fun we had the other night and I wanted you so bad. I thought we could get together for round two. How quickly can you get here?"

"Well, I'm sorry to hear that Ms. Larson, but I think that can be handled in my office on Monday."

"I *know* you're not telling me no."

"That's exactly what I'm saying. I prefer to handle these things in my office."

"Michael, I don't like to be turned down."

"I understand. But, there's nothing I can do about that right now. This is a very bad time."

"Maybe I should have given my message to your wife?"

"I wouldn't recommend any moves like that, Ms. Larson."

Jasmine was surprised to hear the drone of the dial tone in her ear. "I cannot believe that Negro hung up on me!" She slammed down the phone. Picking it back up, she hesitated, then placed it back on the receiver. No need to make Michael any angrier. She wanted to keep him in her stable. At least he pretended to care about her when they made love.

She flipped through the pages of her address book, skimming past the names, then finally threw the book down. It was too late to call anyone anyway; they were all with their wives,

wives they spent the weekends with, but complained about during lunchtime trysts and evening rendezvous with her.

She stood at the window, staring into the silence of the night. Another night alone. She shook her head. How much more of this would she have to endure? Sighing, she clicked on the television, channel surfing until she settled on a Mary Tyler Moore rerun. Leaning back, she pulled the comforter over her and within minutes, found herself surrendering to a welcomed slumber. Tonight, there was no fear of hidden ghosts. Things were going to be different. She could feel it. When she closed her eyes, she dreamt to the tune of one of her favorite old songs: "A Change Is Gonna Come."

# Five

The gravel kicked up a cloud of gray dust as Jefferson screeched the Range Rover into the full parking lot, finally settling into a lone space in the back of the church.

"I told you!" Kyla said through clenched teeth.

"What? We're only about ten minutes late."

"I hate walking into church after the service has already begun. It's so . . . rude."

Jefferson chuckled lightly. "Rude? Do you think God cares what time we get here?"

"We should have been on time," Kyla said as he took her hand and they trotted across the lot. "Especially since we're visitors."

"We've been here a million times. No one considers us visitors anymore. Besides, this is *all* your fault. If you had let me go to bed last night . . ." he teased.

Kyla sighed exasperatedly as Jefferson opened the large wooden door and the melodic voices of the choir sailed towards them. Walking on the tips of her toes, Kyla tried to ease into the last pew when Jefferson grabbed her hand and pulled her towards the front of the church. Holding her head down,

51

she tried to smile, but couldn't ignore the clearing of the throats or the occasional "umph, umph, umph" she knew were directed towards them. The ten-second walk down the center aisle seemed to take much longer and finally they scurried into one of the front rows.

"Hey, Mom," Jefferson whispered as he kissed her cheek.

"What happened?" Constance Blake questioned softly as she leaned across Jefferson and patted her daughter-in-law's hand.

"It was Kyla, Mom. She wore me out last night," Jefferson whispered.

"Jefferson!" Kyla hissed as her mother-in-law smiled knowingly.

"I was exhausted."

"Jefferson!"

"She made me use muscles I'd forgotten I had."

"Jefferson!"

Finally turning to Kyla, he grinned. "Ssshhh!" He put his fingers over her lips. "The preacher's getting ready to preach. Quiet!"

Kyla playfully pushed his hand away, but intertwined her fingers in his when moments later he laid his hand on her lap. She nodded her head slightly as she tried to focus on Reverend Morrison's words, but her mind kept wandering. Between Nicole and church and the clinic and all the committees, there was never enough time for the two of them. But this weekend, they had played like newlyweds and she shivered as her skin tingled with just the thought of last night.

She tried unsuccessfully to hide a yawn, then forced herself to sit up straight. It had been almost two in the morning when they'd finally fallen asleep. But every second of weariness was worth it and she couldn't wait to get home tonight. She'd have to make Nicole go to bed early; they still had more rooms to conquer. She tried to stifle a giggle and jumped as Jefferson squeezed her hand.

"Baby, this is not the place," he scolded with a wide grin.

Blushing, Kyla scooted down against the cushions of the pew. They had been married *too* long.

As Reverend Morrison continued his message on focusing on the Lord, Kyla sighed with relief when he asked the congregation to turn to Ephesians 4:23. With an opened Bible in front of her, she'd have to concentrate now. But when the Reverend's voice boomed through the church, talking about deceitful lusts and how they all had to renew the spirit of their minds, Kyla's eyes opened wide. "Oh my God! He's talking about me!" she thought in horror. But the next moment, she sat back. She was only thinking about her husband and their wonderful life. And what better place to think about all of your blessings, than in church? Sneaking a quick glance at her husband's handsome, chiseled face, she smiled. She was blessed indeed.

Alexis waved to Pastor Ford, then scooted across the chairs as she made her way to the crowded aisle. She smiled and waited as the aisle cleared of the congregation and just as she was about to step from the church, she heard her name.

"Alexis, honey. Can I speak to you for a moment, please?" Miss Imogene called.

"Sure, Miss Imogene." Alexis smiled, though inside she cringed.

"How are you, dear?" She hugged Alexis. "Where are Kyla and Jefferson?"

"They went down to San Diego to pick up Nicole."

"Oh. Well, anyway, my dear, we've been waiting to get you in one of these Helps Ministries . . ."

"I know . . ."

"We could use some help in the bookstore or in the counseling room. I know you've worked a bit on Kyla's project."

"I have helped a little with The Compassion House," Alexis said weakly.

"Well, dear," Miss Imogene continued. "What do we have to do to get you more involved?"

"I'm sorry, Miss Imogene. I really want to participate in one of the ministries. It's just that I'm always so busy with work."

"Well, you have to get busy with God's work too, my dear."

Alexis hung her head. "I'll call you during the week to let you know what I've decided."

"That'll be good," Miss Imogene said, already turning her attention towards someone else. Alexis scurried down the aisle, keeping her head down so that no one else would stop her, and didn't take a breath until she got into her car. Banging her head against the headrest, she closed her eyes. Miss Imogene was right and this week she would do something about it.

But now, she had to find something to do today. Her eyes roamed to her car phone and she shook her head. Part of the dating rules—never call first. Desperation didn't look good on anyone.

She punched the button on her car radio that was programmed for 102.3. *Spread the Word* was one of her favorite radio programs and she bobbed her head to the familiar gospel tunes, grateful to have something to focus on. As she crossed Florence, making her way to Centinela, she slapped her hands on the steering wheel as the crossing train arms came down, halting traffic for an oncoming freight train.

"Ugh," she sighed. She leaned back and her car phone caught her eyes again. Before she could change her mind, she turned down the radio, dialing quickly and was surprised when a groggy voice answered.

"Oh no, sorry I woke you."

"Regina?" Brian said a bit sharply.

Alexis raised her eyebrows. "No, it's Alexis. I'm sorry. I thought you'd be up by now. You said that you had some work to do at your apartment this morning and I just thought . . ."

"That's okay. I should have been up. I mean, I *was* up . . . early. And, then . . . I . . . uh, went back to sleep."

"Well, I'll speak to you later."

"No, wait. I'm glad you called."

She smiled for the first time. "You are?"

"Yeah. I was gonna call you, but I didn't know what time you got out of church."

"I was just on my way home now and got caught at a train stop and thought this would be a good time to call you and . . ."

"You don't have to make excuses," his voice smiled. "I said I'm glad to hear from you."

She cleared her throat. "I wanted to thank you for yesterday. I had a great time."

"So did I."

The silent seconds that followed made her feel uncomfortable. "Well, that's why I called. I'll speak to you soon."

"Well, what are you going to do now?"

She shrugged as the traffic began moving. "Nothing, I'm on my way home. I might go into the office later."

"That doesn't sound like fun. Why don't we do something?"

"Okay," she said, hoping she didn't sound too anxious. "Any ideas?"

"You could come over here and help me unpack."

Her smile turned into a frown.

"Kidding! I was only kidding," Brian said. "Why don't we go out to brunch. You could show me around L.A. It's been many years since I've been here."

"I could do that . . ."

"Good. What time should I pick you up?"

"It'll take me another fifteen minutes to get home," she said as she turned onto LaBrea. "Give me an hour."

"I'll be there."

As she clicked the phone, she frowned slightly. She was about to have another date. Two in one weekend with the same person. It had been months since that had happened. "I'm gonna just settle back and enjoy this," she said aloud. And seconds later, she yelled, "But, who in the world is Regina?"

She turned the radio back on, blasting the song through her car and singing much louder than normal as she made her way north on LaBrea.

Jasmine clicked the remote, passing the same stations again. "One hundred channels and there's nothing on!" she sighed. She paused at Channel Nine and snickered as the television evangelist jumped across the stage like a bouncing ball. When he suddenly stopped and started asking for financial contributions, she laughed. "Yeah, right," she screamed at the screen. As she started flipping through the channels again, the telephone rang.

"What!" she exclaimed into the phone, sure it was Serena calling her back from yesterday.

"Is that any way to greet a friend?"

She paused for a moment. "Who is this?"

"You know who it is."

"Well, it certainly isn't a friend. Not the way you spoke to me last night."

"I was calling to apologize," Michael said softly. "I'm sorry. I couldn't talk. My wife was sitting right here watching my lips move."

"You still didn't have to be so nasty."

"You were the one who threatened me."

"Only after you made me feel bad."

"I didn't mean to make you feel bad, baby. But, that's why I'm calling. To say I'm sorry." He paused, waiting for her to say something. When she remained silent, he continued. "I can make it up to you."

She slumped down in the bed. "How?" she whined.

He chuckled. "What are you wearing?" His voice was soft.

She fingered the hem of her nightgown. "Nothing."

"Umm. My favorite outfit. Want some company?"

"What about your *wife*?"

"She's at church. I can be there in fifteen minutes."

"You're pretty sure of yourself, huh? Thinking that I'd be sitting here just waiting for your call."

"No. I just want to make up for last night."

She waited a beat. "I'll give you ten minutes to get here."

When she hung up the phone, she shimmied out of her nightgown and looked at herself in the mirror. After the call last night, she hadn't been sure whether she'd ever see Michael again. "I should've known!" she exclaimed to her reflection. "Who can stay away from this?" she said as she ran her hands along her wide hips. She turned sideways and admired her toned legs, but a second later, she ran into the bathroom. Today was going to be a good day.

# Six

"I hate when you do that."

"Do what?" Kyla panted through the speakerphone and slowed her pace on her stationary bike.

"I hate to hear you panting and sweating while I'm slaving here at work," Alexis laughed. "I could easily be talked into becoming a lady of leisure. Just one sign from anyone . . ."

Kyla grabbed a towel from the shelf and wiped her face. "I'd rather be in your shoes."

"Excuse me? I think your heart is pumping too fast. Did you just say you'd rather be slaving away over someone's desk?"

Kyla got off the bike and sat on the padded workbench against the mirrored wall. She took a sip from her water bottle. "You should try living this life."

"I'd like to, but unfortunately I don't have a husband who *lives* to take care of me."

"Now, don't get me wrong, I appreciate my husband. It's just that recently . . . I've felt like . . . I need something else. I think I want to pursue my career."

"Whoa! Are you talking about going back to investment banking?"

"No! That was too demanding, and with Nicole and Jefferson, there's no way. But, there are still a lot of things I can do."

"Yeah, but why? You're already so busy with the clinic and all of Nicole's stuff. When would you have time to do anything else?"

"That's what I'm talking about. Everything you just mentioned is for someone else."

"But what about The Compassion House? Do you know how many battered women will be taken care of because of that project? You should feel good about that."

"I do. The Compassion House is my heart. I've already met some of the women and their kids and I tell you, Alexis, I know it's going to change my life. But not even The Compassion House does it for me. I don't feel like I'm growing in all parts of my life and I think I could get part of me back if I went back to work."

"Girlfriend, I don't understand it, but if that's what you want to do, just do it."

Kyla sighed. "If it were that simple. But Jefferson won't even hear of it. When I try to talk to him, he tries to find another project to keep me busy. And if he *really* thinks it's bothering me, he'll buy me something—diamond earrings, a new car, anything. The bigger he thinks my concern is, the bigger the gift."

"Hey. Next time maybe you'll get a Rolls-Royce instead of a Lexus!" Alexis laughed.

"Alexis . . ."

"I'm sorry. It's just that this is hard for me to take seriously. Chile, you have a wonderful life," she drawled.

"I'm just tired of my life being only about Nicole or Jefferson. I feel like I'm living in my husband's shadow. I need more than that."

"Do you think you feel this way because you're so involved with the clinic?"

"That's part of it. I can't find myself away from Jefferson. Everyone says that I have it all, but when it comes right down to it what do *I* have?"

"Girlfriend, I am truly trying to understand where you're coming from as I sit here grinding away. Just give glory to God that you have a black man that is not in prison or gay or just sitting at home waiting for you to bring home all of the bucks."

Kyla laughed. "Don't be such a cynic. I keep telling you there is someone out there for you."

"Well for once, I might agree with you," Alexis paused. "I've been out with Brian."

"Get out of here! You actually *saw* Brian?" Kyla giggled. "Girlfriend, you've been holding out on me! I want all the details!"

"We've been out a few times . . ."

"You've been out with him more than once?"

"Why are you saying it like that?"

"Because you're the queen of the 'Get Rid of Them After the First Date' club."

"Those days just might be over." Alexis glanced at her clock. "Hey, I've got to go. I'll call you tonight."

"Oh no, you don't . . . you're not getting off that easy."

"Kyla. I have to go! Remember I'm still one of the working stiffs and since I own this place, I really *do* have to work."

"Okay . . . but let's meet later. I'm going to noon prayer and then I don't have to pick Nicole up until after five. So, can you get together for a late lunch?"

Looking down at her calendar, packed with meetings the entire day, Alexis frowned. There was no way she could afford the time, but she really did want to talk.

"Oh, come on!" Kyla's tone turned mischievous. "If you don't . . . I'll go to the clinic and just ask Brian about everything."

"No!" Alexis yelled, then lowered her voice when her secretary looked through the glass wall. "Okay, I surrender. Just promise me that you'll keep your nose out of my business."

"All you have to do is tell me what I want to know. So, what about meeting at Memphis at around three?"

"That's good, but I'm really casual today, so don't come marching in there making me look bad," Alexis kidded.

"Girl, please. There is no woman on earth that can do that to you! See you later."

"Wait, there is something else," Alexis paused. "I wanted to ask you something about Jasmine."

Kyla frowned. She hadn't seen or spoken to Jasmine since Saturday even though she had left a few messages about Jefferson wanting to look at her garage door. "What?"

"Have you noticed anything different about her recently?"

"Not really, except that she's still pretty upset about her divorce."

"No . . . beyond that." Alexis knew she'd have to tread carefully. "Kyla, just watch your back. I don't want Jasmine to . . . use you."

"Use me? She's my friend. She would never do that!"

"Kyla, I'm your friend too and I don't trust Jasmine. I think she's playing some kind of dangerous game with you and Jefferson."

"I don't know what you're talking about. She would never do anything to hurt me."

"Well, I don't know if you've heard, but there's talk about her and Patricia Newman's husband. You know her, she's in our Women's Prayer Group . . ."

"Alexis, I can't believe that you of all people are in the middle of this gossip. I've known Jasmine for over thirty years and she has never given me any reason not to trust her. I think all you're seeing is the difficult time she's having being alone."

"But there are other things . . . people are saying that Patricia's husband is not the only one . . ."

"Alexis, I think you're accusing the wrong person. I know the Newmans and Michael Newman is the cheat! He's tried to hit on me! I think it's just this little thing you and Jasmine have against each other. But nothing you can say is going to turn me against her. I have to stick by her while she's going through all of this."

Alexis sighed, knowing she'd have to find some other way to convince Kyla. Maybe face-to-face this afternoon would be better. "Look, just watch your back. I've gotta go. They're calling me for a meeting. I'll see you later."

Kyla clicked off the speakerphone and shook her head. She hated this childish rivalry that Alexis and Jasmine seemed to have going. It was obvious they would never become friends, but she didn't want to be in the middle of it anymore. The next time either one of them said anything, she would just stop her cold.

Looking up at the clock, she jumped from the bench.

Only an hour before noon prayer and she was never late. She kicked off her sneakers and headed into the shower.

Kyla had been kneeling, but now she rose and clasped her hands together, rocking in her seat, continuing to pray in the spirit. Today, the intercessors were praying for the health of the nation, focusing on the tribulations of the government and its leaders. Kyla closed her eyes and raised her hands to the Lord as the meeting came to an end. The group clapped their hands in a praise offering and Kyla smiled. Praying for others helped her to feel closer to God and helped her to realize all the blessings in her life.

As Miss Imogene closed out the meeting in a congregational prayer, Kyla whispered her thanks to the Lord. When they closed, she hugged the woman who'd been sitting next to her, then turned to Miss Imogene.

"Do you need me for anything today?" Kyla asked as she bent over to hug the older woman.

"No, honey. Nothing's on the schedule. But tomorrow, we'll be going through all of the donated clothes. Can I call you if we need an extra set of hands?"

"Of course."

"You are a dear." Miss Imogene patted her arm.

As Kyla stepped from the prayer room, she passed Pastor Ford's office and when she couldn't find Avery, the pastor's assistant, she tapped lightly on the pastor's door.

"Hi, Pastor. I didn't want to disturb you. Just wanted to pop in and say hello."

"Come on in," Pastor Ford said as she flipped her shoulder-length bob away from her face. With regal motions, she stepped around her desk and took both of Kyla's hands. "I'm just catching up on a few things."

"How was your trip?"

"Wonderful! You know any time I can get on the road and spread the Word, I'm ready. I'm just sorry I missed Jefferson's party. I heard you guys had a good time."

"It was great and Jefferson got your gift. He wanted me to thank you for the Daily Devotionals. You know we'll use it."

"I knew Jefferson would want a gift that he could share with you. It was for the both of you."

Kyla nodded. "Well, I know you're busy and I just wanted to pop in for a second."

They hugged again. "I'll see you on Sunday."

Hurrying through the hallway, Kyla bounced down the stairs to her car. She snuggled against the soft leather seats and inhaled the new-car scent. Turning on the ignition, she tapped her fingers against the steering wheel. There was still a little time before she had to meet Alexis and she smiled, knowing exactly what she'd do. She maneuvered the car away from the curb, still not used to the sleek lines of the sports model, so much smaller than the Mercedes they'd just traded in. Within minutes, she crossed Slauson Boulevard and pulled into the clinic's parking lot.

The African-American Complete Wellness Medical Center was housed in a new two-story futuristic-looking building. Here, for just a little more than a year, the clean white interior resembled a high-class health club more than a medical facility with nine medical specialists.

Kyla remembered when Jefferson first told her he had been asked to join a team of three other doctors to develop this clinic.

"This is a great idea, Kyla! Can you imagine a team of specialists providing medical services right in the middle of the Black community?" he had asked enthusiastically.

"It sounds good, honey. But, I just don't understand how this will work. Why do we have to invest *our* money?"

"Because it's a partnership where we will be completely in charge. We'll have to borrow some of the money, but none of us want to go too far into debt. That's why everyone agrees you should be involved. With your financial savvy, there is no way this won't work."

Kyla shook her head. "It's going to take a lot of time and money and medical expertise and . . ."

"It's going to take God, baby. We have God on our side."

Kyla had paused for a moment. "You're sure about this, aren't you?"

Jefferson had run his fingers lightly down her face. "Yeah, I'm sure. But the one thing we have to do is pray. Pray until we're both sure which way to go."

When Jefferson had pulled Kyla into his arms, she had closed her eyes and thanked God that their marriage was built on the Lord. They had spent the next few weeks praying and talking and praying some more, then finally decided to take on the venture.

Now, walking through the vestibule area, Kyla chatted briefly with Officer Daniels, one of the security guards who had been with them since the clinic opened. With the sky roof providing natural light, Kyla squinted slightly as she proceeded through the octagonal building to the receptionist's desk.

The new receptionist jumped up to greet her. "Hello, Mrs. Blake." LaKwanda always seemed to speak a decibel above the level of everyone around her.

"Hi, LaKwanda. How are you?"

"Just fine," she yelled.

"Are you enjoying your assignment here?" Kyla asked, referring to the high school Achiever's Program that LaKwanda had been hired through.

"A lot! I'm having so much fun, I can't wait to get back to school and tell everyone about this."

"Just let me know if I can help you with anything, okay?"

"Should I tell Dr. Blake that you're here?"

People in the waiting room turned towards them and Kyla purposely lowered her own voice hoping LaKwanda would follow her example. "That's okay. I'll just go straight up. I'm going to see Shannon first."

"All right," LaKwanda shouted and her shoulder-length braids swayed with every word she spoke.

Kyla proceeded up the stairs that gave her a total view of the 25,000-square-foot space, complete with offices, examination and conference rooms, a pharmacy, and a small cafeteria.

"Hi Kyla. I heard LaKwanda yelling," Shannon giggled. "I was just on my way down to rescue you."

Kyla shared in the laugh. "How are you, Shannon?"

"Just fine now that the proposal is finally finished. I still can't believe we're expanding the clinic again. But at least this time, we won't have to move."

"I know what you mean. Is Jefferson available?"

"He's just finishing up with a patient. Do you want to wait in his office?"

"No, I don't need to disturb him. Actually, I stopped by to see Dr. Lewis. Is he here?"

Shannon nodded. "Uh-huh. His office is right down the hall, that way," she said pointing.

"Okay, I'll see you later. Just tell Jefferson I'll see him tonight."

Kyla's heels tapped against the slick tiled floors as she strolled down the hall. She stopped outside Brian's opened door, standing boldly in the entranceway as he spoke into the phone. He looked up, smiled and motioned her in.

As Brian continued his conversation, Kyla walked through the office, glancing at the pictures and awards on the wall. At a picture of Brian with two little boys, she paused.

"Kyla. Good to see you. How are you?" Brian hung up the phone and came around the desk to hug her.

"Fine. And you?"

"Good. I'm finally getting settled in. I'll be doing my first surgery within the next few days."

"That's great. Jefferson didn't tell me. So, how does it feel to be back home?" She took a seat.

He perched himself on the desk in front of her. "I'm glad to be back where the sun *does* shine."

"I know that's right. I remember how cold it was in Virginia and it was nothing like what you had to suffer through in Boston."

"Yeah, but Boston was good to me."

She tugged at her ear and coughed. "Uh, I understand you met my friend Alexis."

She watched his smile widen. "Yeah."

When he didn't continue, she frowned. Was that all he was going to say? Several silent seconds passed before she added, "We've been friends since Hampton."

"I know."

"Well, I'm glad you two finally met."

"So am I. She's nice."

Kyla crinkled her eyes. "I heard you guys had a chance to really talk at Jefferson's party."

"Yeah. By the way, that party was great, Kyla. I told Jefferson that everyone is still talking about what a good time they had."

"Well, I'm glad . . ."

"There's my wife." Jefferson strutted into the office.

Irritated, Kyla twisted in her seat. "Oh, hi, darling. I was just chatting with Brian. I haven't had a chance to talk to him much since he moved back."

"Oh?" Jefferson raised his eyebrows in amusement. He was glad he had warned Brian that Kyla would be sure to come around, asking about Alexis. He wondered what had taken her so long.

Kyla stood. There was no way she'd get any information out of Brian now that Jefferson was playing policeman. Both men faced her, silent and steadfast with silly grins on their faces.

"Well . . . uh . . . I just wanted to stop by and say hello," she said.

"Hello . . ." Jefferson said, grinning.

Kyla rolled her eyes. "Well, Brian. We really have to get together soon. Maybe I should plan a welcome home party or something."

"I'd like that."

"Good. Then, I'll call you. Jefferson . . . I'll see *you* later."

With all the dignity she could muster, Kyla strode past them and heard their snickers as she darted down the stairs.

Let them laugh, she thought. If Brian's dates with Alexis were only casual, why was it all such a big secret? Anyway, she didn't need to get any information from them. She was on her way to get all the news she needed.

"Kyla! *Bon jour!*" Stephen Felix, the owner of Memphis waved his arms wildly as he greeted her.

"Hi, Stephen. What are you doing here? I heard you got a part in that new Spike Lee movie. Congratulations."

"Thank you, *mon cherie.*" He air-kissed both of her cheeks. "We just finished filming, so I came to check out my investment. You know how that is, dahling. But enough. I want to hear all about the big bash. Everyone is still talking about it. You made my restaurant famous, dahling."

Kyla chatted with the actor as she followed him to one of the tables. He pulled out a chair for her. "I know you're not eating alone today. Who's joining you?"

"I am!" Alexis flew to the table and slumped into the other chair. Dressed in old jeans, a white T-shirt and a navy blazer, Alexis still looked like she had just stepped out of a fashion magazine.

"Alexis, the most gorgeous woman on earth. When are you going to fulfill my fantasy and become the lady in my life?"

Alexis laughed. "When I forget about your six ex-wives."

He held his hand to his chest covering his paisley tie. "How you offend me! I've only been married five times, but I would adore you more than any of the others."

"Yeah, yeah, yeah."

"Well, I will just have to find a way to convince you. One day, you will be mine. Ladies, enjoy your lunch." With that, Stephen floated away in his usual style, his feet barely touching the ground.

Kyla and Alexis giggled. "Is he a mess or what?" Alexis chuckled. "I wonder if his mother still claims him."

"I'm sure she does, but he probably doesn't claim her! He thinks he's from the South of France and his mother would only remind him that he's from South Central. But I really think he wants to marry you," Kyla teased.

"Please. The man is thirty-something and has been married five times. That is almost chronologically impossible."

"Well, he's a piece of work, all right. But I don't want to talk about him. Tell me about Brian."

"Oh! What happened to, How is your day, Alexis? How is your business, Alexis? How are you feeling, Alexis?—none of that, huh?"

"Come on. Why are you teasing me like this?"

"Hi, Kyla, Alexis," the waitress said, interrupting them. "Are you guys just having your usual?"

"What about the Cobb salad?" Alexis asked, and Kyla agreed, though she really wanted the high-calorie peppered shrimp.

When the waitress walked away, Alexis leaned back and smiled. "Okay . . . Brian's really nice."

"Nice? What's up with that word? That's the same thing he said about you."

Alexis closed her eyes and frowned. "Oh, no, you didn't! Kyla, why can't you just stay out of my business?"

"Don't worry. I didn't mention your name. Well, maybe I mentioned it once. But he said you were nice."

Alexis leaned forward, elbows framing the table. "Is that all he said?"

"Yup. But that doesn't mean anything. I have a feeling

that Jefferson told him not to say anything to me. So come on, tell me more."

"Well . . . he's a Christian, did you know that?"

Kyla shook her head. "No, I didn't. Well you know what I think—there's nothing sexier than a Black man with his hands raised to the Lord."

Alexis laughed and nodded in agreement. "He'll be coming to church with us. Jefferson invited him."

"So, where have you guys been?"

"The first time, we went to Venice Beach . . ."

"Really? That's a funny place for a man with Brian's kind of money. I would have thought he would have been doing everything he could to try to make a good impression."

"And that's what I liked about him. He's not pretentious. He was more interested in us getting to know one another than anything else. We spent the entire afternoon just talking."

"Have you two talked about *everything*?"

Alexis frowned. "What do you mean?"

"Well, I don't want to get involved . . ."

"That'll be the day . . ."

"But, I do think you should know . . ."

"If you're talking about the fact that he's divorced, with two sons, that his ex-wife's name is Regina, she's a teacher, and they lived in a brownstone in Boston, where she and the boys still live . . ."

Kyla held up her hands. "Okay, okay."

"He's told me everything, though I did have to ask him about Regina when he called me by her name. But it was an innocent thing. So far, things are great. No secrets."

"Well, I just wanted to make sure you knew . . ."

"You don't have to look over my shoulder, Kyla."

"I'm not. So, when are you two going to get together again?"

"You have beat me and battered me and pounded me and blackmailed me into meeting you. And you still want more information?"

"All I asked is, when are you going out again?"

The waitress arrived with their salads and teas. As she walked away, Kyla and Alexis held hands, bowed their heads and gave thanks for the food they were about to eat.

"Ky, listen to me. I'm just going to chill and see where this goes. And I'm counting on you to let me and Brian do this without any pressure or interference."

Kyla's eyes opened wide. "Of course. I wouldn't *dream* of interfering."

Alexis rolled her eyes. "Anyway, change of subject. Are you going to talk to Jefferson about getting a job?"

Kyla sighed, wiping the corner of her mouth with her napkin. "I have to."

"You don't sound too confident."

"Because I know how he'll react. But I'm not going to back down this time. I've just got to do something else besides being the professional professional's wife."

"If you explain it to Jefferson that way, he'll understand."

They chatted through lunch and were still talking when the waitress came to clear the table.

"Now, promise that you'll tell me everything about your date tonight," Kyla started as they gathered their things to leave. "And, don't make any plans with Brian for the weekend. Remember we'll be in Santa Barbara for the Women's Fellowship with my mom."

"Oh, that's right!" Alexis bit her lip. "I do want to see your parents. Plus, we could get some shopping in . . ."

"You sound like you have something else to do."

"Brian's coming to church Sunday and I wanted to be there with him."

"I didn't know you meant *this* Sunday. I wonder if Jefferson remembers that I won't be there."

"Well, your mother's program is Saturday, right?"

"Uh-huh. I'll be staying until Sunday, but you could come back Saturday night or early Sunday morning and still make it to church with Brian."

Alexis nodded. "Then it's a plan."

Kyla glanced at her watch. "Oooh! I've got to get Nicole."

"And I've got to get back to the office to get some work done before I meet Brian." Alexis paused, frowning slightly, wondering if she should bring up Jasmine. She didn't want to make Kyla mad, but she had to warn her. "Kyla, I wanted to clear up what we talked about earlier."

"What?" she asked, digging in her purse for her credit card, unaware of her friend's look of concern.

"What I was trying to say . . ." Alexis began, "is that Jasmine . . ."

Kyla looked up and shook her head. "Don't say another word, Alex. I am really tired of this thing you and Jasmine have going. And really, I'm surprised at you! I expect this from Jasmine, but from you . . ."

"Kyla, I only brought it up again because you're not listening . . ."

"I've heard everything you've had to say. And you know what? This sounds just like some high school mess. I didn't participate in that then, so you know I won't be part of it now!"

Alexis had to force her mouth shut. She snatched her purse from the table and stared down at Kyla. Seconds slid by before Alexis spoke. "All right, Kyla. You don't have to listen, but I hope your ears are open to this one free piece of advice." She paused, as her eyes became slits. "That woman, that person that you call a *friend* . . . is . . . a . . . snake. And, I pray that one day you don't find her slithering around on her belly eating everything in *your* backyard."

Alexis turned on her heel, whipping her hair over her shoulder, and stomped out, leaving Kyla sitting with the check and credit card in hand and her mouth wide open in surprise.

# Seven

"A snake." Alexis' words reverberated in her mind. It wasn't that she was worried about their friendship; they'd had their fights before and had always been able to put disagreements behind them quickly. And Kyla knew this time would be no different.

Only this time, it *felt* different. Like Alexis was trying to deliver some covert message that she just didn't get. She tried to remember Alexis' exact words, but the only thing that stuck in her mind was the snake. An interesting choice of words.

Turning the corner, Kyla could see Nicole in the playground and she forcibly pushed thoughts of Alexis away. She slowed the car and honked the horn, getting both her daughter's and the school attendant's attention. The after-school monitor peeked through the fence and Kyla waved, ignoring the guilt she felt not walking to the playground the way the school's safety and security policies requested.

The monitor nodded and motioned to Nicole. With pigtails flying and backpacks bouncing, Nicole and Hannah came running to the car. After they climbed into the backseat, Kyla leaned over and closed the door behind them.

"Mother, you're late! Didn't you remember that Hannah was coming home with us today?"

Kyla smiled into the rearview mirror as she pulled the car away from the curb. "Hello, ladies. How are you today?"

"Fine, Mrs. Blake," Hannah whispered and Nicole sighed.

"You're never late, Mother. Where were you?"

"I didn't know I had to report my comings and goings to you, young lady. What's wrong with you?"

Nicole pouted. "I had to fight for Hannah *again*." The words were spoken as if she had performed her daily duty.

"Nicole, your father and I have talked to you about this."

"She was protecting me." Hannah's voice was so soft Kyla had to strain to hear. "Billy was picking on me and Nicole made him stop."

Kyla tried to hide her smile. "Well, what did Billy do, Hannah?"

Before Hannah could speak, Nicole answered, "He said that Hannah had a stupid name because it was the same whether you spelled it backwards or forwards. And, I told him that her name wasn't stupid because it's in the Bible. He didn't even know that! He didn't even know that Hannah was the mother of Samuel. And, I said he was the one with the stupid name because he was nothing but a bearded billy goat and if he didn't stop picking on Hannah I was going to punch him in the nose!"

Kyla sighed. Quoting the Bible in one breath and threatening the boy's life in the next. "Nicole, Billy was just being silly. Do you think you handled that in the right way?"

Nicole's eyebrows furrowed. "Maybe," she said, her voice suddenly soft.

"Really?"

A few beats passed. "Well, maybe not, Mommy. But I only said that to him because he made Hannah cry."

Kyla glanced again into the rear mirror and looked at the two girls: Hannah crouched down low, shoulders slumped, looking even now like she was going to cry. Nicole, staring back at her, defiant in her attitude. And Kyla softened. She had to admit that while she wasn't pleased with the way she'd done it, she was pleased that Nicole defended her friends. Just like Jasmine.

"It's good that you want to protect your friends, Nicole. But you have to handle it in the right way, especially as a Christian. Do you understand what I mean?"

"I think so," she paused. "A Christian should only kick someone's butt if nothing else has worked."

Kyla could not hide her smile. "Something like that. We'll talk about it later."

By the time Kyla turned onto their street, the girls were laughing and chatting about the upcoming summer vacation. And, when Kyla pulled into her driveway, the garage door was already up.

Nicole clapped her hands. "Daddy's home!"

Kyla grabbed her briefcase and when she looked up, Jefferson was standing at the door, casually dressed in an old sweat suit. "Hey, you." He kissed her cheek, taking her briefcase from her hand.

She wondered if he would say anything about what had happened earlier with Brian. Knowing her husband, he wouldn't. Unless she brought it up. She wouldn't.

"What are you doing home so early?" Kyla asked as she walked into the family room. Nicole and Hannah were sitting on the floor, already engrossed in the happenings on the Cartoon Network. "Hey, ladies. What comes first?"

Hannah looked up through her glasses, like she was going to cry, but Nicole barely glanced away from the television screen. "Oh, Mom. Can't we just look at one cartoon?"

"What did your mother say?" The deep voice resonated through the room and both girls jumped up.

Nicole picked up her bag and Hannah dutifully followed. "Come on, Hannah. I think we should go up to my room and do our homework," Nicole ordered as if she had suddenly come up with this idea.

"One day I'm going to learn how to do that," Kyla said. "I'm going to get our daughter to do what I ask the first time without having to give a second explanation."

"She knows she doesn't get a second chance with me. But with you . . ." Lying on the couch, he took Kyla's hand. "I'm pooped."

"I guess now that you're an old man, you're going to have to slow down a bit," Kyla laughed.

"Talk big now, but remember your fortieth is not too far away."

"But for the next few months, you and I will be part of different decades and I'm enjoying every day of it."

"I can see that," he grinned as he clicked on the television news. They sat silently watching the depressing information of the day.

"By the way, I ordered pizza," Jefferson said. "It should be here in a few minutes."

"Oh, you dear, dear man!" She kissed him on the forehead. "I'll go change."

As she moved to get up, he held her tightly. He kissed the

back of her neck, refusing to release his grasp. She giggled as his breath tickled her.

"You'd better let me go or you may have to finish what you started."

"Promises, promises." He loosed his grip and she ran up the steps, checking first on the girls, reviewing their assignments while they changed their clothes. Then, she shooed them away while she went to her room to change.

Dressed only in one of Jefferson's huge T-shirts, Kyla came downstairs while Nicole was setting the table. "What's up, Nicole? Don't your father and I deserve to eat with you?"

"No, Mother. This is for you. Hannah and I are going to eat in my room."

"What happened to asking first?" Jefferson asked.

Kyla's eyes darted between the two. "You know what? As long as you promise to eat all your food and not make a mess, you can eat upstairs."

Jefferson's eyebrow arched, but he remained silent. After the girls left with their plates, Kyla and Jefferson settled into the family room, trays set in front of them. Kyla bobbed her head to the jazz flowing softly through the speakers and chewed on a piece of pepperoni. Her eyes moved from point to point around the room, but she avoided Jefferson and his eyes, even though she could feel his piercing glance.

He finally broke the silence. "Okay, I can tell that something is wrong."

She looked up, but didn't say a word.

"Is it something with Nicole or the clinic?"

Kyla shook her head slightly. That was the problem. He couldn't imagine that there could be anything else in her life. "No, it's about me."

She could see the muscles in his face tighten. "What is it? Are you sick?"

"Have you ever thought about what I do all day?"

His eyes blinked rapidly. "What? I don't know what you mean."

"Have you ever thought about what a typical day is for me?"

He was silent for a long moment, then his eyes flickered understanding. "Oh. You want to talk about this work thing again. So what's wrong this time?"

"Nothing's wrong. That's what you always think. But that's not my truth." She pursed her lips, then proceeded. "I just wanted to let you know that once the summer is over and Nicole is back in school, I will be returning to work."

Without a word, Jefferson stood, taking his plate into the kitchen. Kyla remained in the family room for several minutes before following him. He was leaning against the refrigerator, sipping soda from the bottle. She walked past him, around the center island, placed her plate in the sink, then turned facing him.

"I know you're not happy about this, but this will in no way affect you or Nicole. You two will always come first in my life. This is something I have to do for me."

She paused, giving him a chance to respond, but he kept sipping on his drink, his eyes staring at the nothingness behind her. Taking a deep breath, she strained to keep her voice steady. "Look, I'm not going to let this turn into a fight. I just want to talk about it."

"What's there to talk about, Kyla?" his voice snapped at her like an overstretched rubberband. "You march in here and tell me you're going to find a job like I don't have any say in it. But what would I say anyway? You know how I feel."

"Yes I do, but what about how I feel?"

"Let me ask you something, Kyla. Why is it that Nicole and I aren't enough for you?"

"You are for the mother and wife part of me. But what about my other side? What about my other needs? You could never give up your career for me."

"That's a stupid thing to say. I have to take care of my family. That's what a man is supposed to do. Most black women would get down on their knees and shout hallelujah if they were able to stay home, raise their children and be a wife."

"Do you know how primitive that sounds? Why is it that all you want me to be is Dr. Blake's wife?"

"And why do you have a problem with *being* my wife?"

They held their stares before Kyla walked over and took his hand. When he tried to pull back, she tightened her grip, ignoring the churning in her stomach. Her pleading eyes bore into his and within moments she could feel the tension begin to ebb from his body, though his weak smile did little to cover the sadness that veiled his eyes. Right away, Kyla could feel herself weakening. She took the soda from his other hand and laid it on the counter, allowing her to take both of his hands into her own. He softened, putting his arms around her, burying his face in her hair.

"I love you."

"I know you do," she said leaning back, looking into his face. "And you know I love you and would never do anything to hurt us."

His eyes looked away. "If you want to go back to work, then I've failed."

She frowned. "Why are you turning this into something about you? This is about me."

He shook his head and pulled away, moving in slow motion to the dinette table and when he sat, he lowered his head into his hands. Kyla followed and stood behind him, massaging his shoulders, holding the silence that stayed for minutes.

Finally, he spoke. "You know, my father failed my mother . . ."

"Jefferson, that's crazy!"

"He did. When my dad died, he left us with nothing."

"It's not like he planned to die so young."

"That's my point. There was no preparation. So he left us with no insurance, no money in the bank. Dad's legacy was a mortgage and two small kids. Mama's life turned into a working merry-go-round. She worked two jobs during the week and another one on the weekend. There was never any time for anything else. After all the missed school plays and football games and band recitals, I vowed that my family's life would never be like that. I think that's the real reason I wanted to become a doctor so badly. With money, I knew that my children would never suffer, my wife would never suffer.

Her hands continued to move along his shoulders. She'd heard this many times. "And you've succeeded. I haven't suffered a day of our marriage. But don't you see? Our family doesn't fit into that box that was created by your father."

"But it's still not enough for you . . ."

"Jefferson, please understand that this is not about money."

His head barely nodded. "You know, when you led me to the Lord all of those years ago, everything I learned reaffirmed what I wanted to do, be the head of the household, be the protector of my family, but most important, be the provider. I learned how to be a real man for God. For the last eleven years, since you stopped working, I've done that. But if you return to work . . ."

"None of that will change."

"Kyla, I don't want to stop you from being you or from getting the satisfaction you need. But I don't want you to stop me from being me either. Why can't you get fulfillment taking care of Nicole and me? Look at everything you do for the clinic and everything you're involved in at church. What about the Compassion House? There are so many people that depend on you. Isn't that enough?"

Kyla shook her head, but before she could speak, Nicole came running down the stairs.

"Mommy, Mommy! We're finished and we were playing on the computer and watching TV and then Hannah said she wanted to call her mother."

"Okay," Kyla stood directing her attention to the girls, but her eyes followed Jefferson as he left the room.

The rest of the evening passed in a blur. They called Hannah's mother, cleaned up the kitchen and then Kyla allowed herself to be talked into watching a half hour of *Tom and Jerry*. But as the girls laughed at the antics on the television, Kyla's thoughts were upstairs with her husband. She was hoping for a chance to finish their talk.

"Mommy, can we go play in the game room?"

"There's nothing in there that you know how to play."

"I know how to play pool."

"Your father told you to stay away from the pool table

and anyway, it's time for you two to go to bed. We've got to get ready for the last day of school."

The girls cheered, continuing even as they dressed for bed. Once she was finally able to calm them down, she handed them both Bibles.

"Hannah, this is our devotion time where we study anything you want in the Bible."

"Do you do this at your house, Hannah?" Nicole questioned.

"No, my mother doesn't make me read the Bible except for when I go to church on Sunday."

"Well, you should read the Bible every day. That's what we have to do!"

"Hey, hey. What do you want to study tonight?" Kyla asked both girls.

"Let's show Hannah where her name is in the Bible so that next time someone makes fun of her, she won't feel so bad."

"That's a good idea. Hannah, have you ever read about the woman Hannah in the Bible?"

Hannah shook her head.

"Nicole, do you remember where that is?"

Nicole frowned in thought, then shook her head. "I can't remember. But, she was Samuel's mother, so is she in one of his books?"

"That's it." Kyla let the girls take turns reading about Hannah and her trials, her cry to the Lord and how the Lord answered her prayers. She watched the young Hannah cheer up as they read and talked about her namesake. They talked for an hour before she led the girls in prayer, allowing each of them to say what they wanted, then added her prayers to theirs.

As she tucked the girls in, Hannah reached up, grabbed her neck and smacked a kiss on her cheek. "Thank you, Mrs. Blake, for showing me my name in the Bible." Hannah grinned. "I thought Nicole was making it up in school today."

"See, I told you!"

"Hannah, just remember how special you are."

Kyla kissed Nicole, then turned off the lights with warnings of silence that she knew would go unheeded.

Leaving the girls, Kyla walked to Jefferson's office. She leaned her ear against the closed door, but decided not to disturb him. She would bring it up again, though. Maybe after she returned from Santa Barbara.

In their bedroom, she slumped into one of the chairs under the window. Tucking her feet under her, she skimmed through the pages of *Essence*, but couldn't keep her mind on any of the articles. Her mind wandered from Alexis to Jefferson, back to Alexis. At least she knew what she was up against with Jefferson, but with Alexis . . . all she could think about was the snake . . . and Jasmine. Just what did Alexis mean? Kyla picked up the telephone. It was time she had some answers.

Jasmine paced the living room floor, pausing only to look at the cars that drove by. It was after nine and he had not shown up. She paged Michael once again, but a half an hour later, he still had not responded.

She bit her lip, determined not to let the tears come again. After taking a deep breath, she turned out the lights and started up the stairs. The shrill ring of the phone startled her and she ran back down the stairs.

"Michael?"

"Jasmine?"

"Oh," Jasmine said disappointed. "What do you want?"

"I was calling to check on you," Kyla said.

"You don't have to do that. I'm fine," Jasmine said sharply.

"I left you a few messages . . ."

"And, I didn't call you back. So what?"

"What's wrong? You sound like you're mad."

"I'm not mad. I'm just sick of you sitting in judgment of me and throwing your life up in my face."

Kyla cringed as she pulled the phone away from her ear. She thought about hanging up, but she knew Jasmine's anger was a result of her loneliness. Stick with her, Kyla, she said to herself. She took a deep breath before she spoke, "Jasmine, I wasn't judging you . . ."

"What did you call me for? Is Jefferson going to help me with my garage?"

"Of course he is. If you need help, you know we're always here . . ."

"That's what you say."

"Look, Jasmine. This is going nowhere and I have another idea. Why don't we get out of L.A. together for a little while? I'm going to my parents' house for a special women's program with my mother's church this weekend and I'd like you to come with me. I know you'll have a good time and my parents would love to see you. It's going to be just us girls; Jefferson's not even going." Kyla blocked out the misgivings she had, since Alexis had already accepted her invitation.

Jasmine snickered. "Are you kidding? Two days with you *and* your mother? That's more self-righteousness than any person could bear."

"Jasmine!"

A long silence followed. "We need to talk, girl. I know it's late, but why don't you come over here? We can just sit and talk and you can stay over."

Jasmine hesitated. She didn't want to spend another night alone and it looked like she would not hear from Michael tonight, but she couldn't let Kyla know. "I don't want your high-and-mighty pity, Kyla," she said. "Just leave me alone!" She slammed the phone down, her lips quivering.

In her bedroom, she undressed and crawled into bed, determined not to let the ghosts haunt her tonight. She tried to focus on work—especially, the project coming up at the end of this week. They were introducing a new product and SONY management wanted to review her numbers. She had done all of the financial projections and was excited about making the presentation to the board.

But not even the work she enjoyed could keep her focused. Her mind was only filled with thoughts of Kenny. She wanted him so badly. She closed her eyes and allowed herself to dream. In her dreams, Kenny was a doctor with *his* own clinic, making all the money she ever wanted. Their marriage was a wonder, without the heated arguments and weeks of angry silence. Drifting deeper into sleep, her mind's images became clearer. In her dream, Kenny had never left. He was calling her name.

She opened her eyes at the sound of his voice and held out her arms, welcoming him back into their bed. When their lips met, he teased her, caressed her. Before she surrendered to him totally, she opened her eyes again, to take in his full being. And, the image of Kenneth Larson had transformed completely. As the new image devoured her, she sighed with pleasure. This was her perfect man. And, this man was Dr. Jefferson Blake.

Kyla hung up the telephone just as Jefferson came back into the bedroom. She forced the corners of her lips into a smile. "Truce?"

He smiled back. "Truce."

She watched him undress and leaned against his bare chest when he climbed into the bed. "I'm really worried about Jasmine," she said. She filled him in on the details of her conversation.

"Kyla, maybe you should just leave her alone for a while. Give her some time to figure this all out."

She shook her head. "We can't desert her now. We're all she's got. Serena and her dad try, but they're too far away."

"I'm not saying desert her. I'm just saying we don't really know how to help her. She probably needs someone to talk to . . . a professional. I can help her contact someone."

"No, it's not that bad. She was like this when her mom died. She wouldn't eat, she stopped going to classes and she wouldn't leave the house for anything. But Kenny was there to help her through all of that. In a way, I guess, Kenny has died to her because she's reacting the same way she did when her mom died. But this time, I'm the only one around to help."

Jefferson shrugged his shoulders. "Whatever," he said as he leaned over and picked up his Bible from the nightstand. "Do you mind if I read tonight?"

"Okay, then I'll pray."

They bowed their heads and held hands.

"Dear Heavenly Father," she began. "We come before you tonight giving you honor and praise. You are an awesome and mighty God and we give you glory, Lord, we bless you. As we prepare for our devotion tonight, Heavenly Father, open our eyes and ears to what You want us to learn. Help us to gain wisdom and knowledge from Your Word. And help us to always put You first. Guide our hearts and our lives and order our steps so that we may serve You. In Jesus Christ's name we pray, Amen."

Jefferson opened the Bible and began reading from I Peter 3. Then he turned to I Corinthians 7. As Jefferson read from the scriptures, referring to the wife's role to her husband, Kyla was pleased that she was married to a man of God, a man who would search the scriptures to find the answers for their life.

Kyla leaned into Jefferson and focused on making sure she opened her heart to the scriptures, wanting to get insight into what the Lord wanted her to hear. Jefferson was just the vessel; the words were the Lord's.

She closed her eyes, listening to the deep resonance of her husband's voice, feeling the scriptures, becoming a part of what Paul and Peter were saying. Kyla blocked out the troubles of the day, the anxiety of what she would do about a career, the problems with Jasmine, her argument with Alexis and her upcoming trip to Santa Barbara. She even blocked out thoughts of Nicole—for now. Everything was released from her mind so that she could lose herself in the words and presence of the Lord.

Brian parked his car in the circular driveway and tossed his keys to the doorman. "I'll be right back," he said. They entered the elevator and Brian pushed the button for the seventeenth floor.

"I don't live on seventeen. I live on the eleventh floor," Alexis said.

"I know." With a half grin, he bent toward her and when his lips covered hers, she let their tongues meet. He pulled her close, leaning into her body, and she ran her hands over the muscles of his back, drowning herself in the sensation.

The ping of the elevator startled them both.

"Brian," she started, her lips barely moving from his. "We have to get off."

"No, we don't. This is seventeen. We have a little more time." He pushed the button for eleven and they kissed until the doors opened again.

When they got to her front door, she whispered, "I really had a wonderful time tonight."

His tongue gently traced her lips before he reclaimed them and backed her into the carpeted wall. A moan escaped from deep inside of him, before he backed away. "It's time for me to go." His voice was soft and husky.

She bit her lip and nodded, not wanting to chance her own voice.

"I can't wait until you get back from Santa Barbara." He ran the tips of his fingers across her lips. "Until next time . . ." He got on the elevator and blew her a kiss as the doors closed.

Alexis stepped into her apartment and leaned against the closed door. His words played over and over. "I can't wait until next time . . . next time . . . next time . . ."

Her skin tingled. "Neither can I, Brian." And she knew that she was in big trouble.

# Eight

The alarm clock shrilled and Kyla pulled the pillow over her head.

"Kyla? Kyla, we have to get up," Alexis called from the other side of the king-size bed.

Kyla moaned her disapproval.

"Come on," Alexis shook her. "It's five o' clock."

"That is exactly why I'm not going anywhere," she cried from under the pillow.

"Your Dad said we have to be ready by five-thirty."

"Are you girls up?" Lynn Carrington peeked her head inside the darkened bedroom.

Kyla rolled over. "Come on in, Mom."

"Good morning." Lynn tiptoed into the room, still in her bathrobe but every strand of her short-cropped salt-and-pepper hair in place. "I wanted to let you know there's coffee and bagels. Your father is already up and rarin' to go." She turned on the small lamp sitting on the dresser.

"She's chickening out because it's still dark outside, Mrs. Carrington," Alexis said as she slid into her slippers. "I'm going to take a shower. Kyla, get up!"

Lynn Carrington chuckled and sat down in the rocking chair, pulling her robe tighter around her petite frame. "Well, honey. If you're going to go, you do have to get up."

Kyla flung her legs over the side of the bed, wiggling her toes in the brown carpet. "Jefferson had better appreciate what I'm doing," she said, "no soul should rise before the sun." She yawned. "Thanks again, Mom, for keeping Nicole." She had decided to return to Los Angeles early, rather than attend the second day of the retreat.

"We're thrilled to have her! We don't get to see her half enough since we left L.A."

Kyla removed her robe from the closet. "Well, you're not half as thrilled as she is. Her granddaddy is going to take her fishing every day and her grandmommy will spoil her rotten. And, this will give Jefferson and me a little time together. We could use it right now."

Lynn stilled the rocking chair. Her light brown eyes were filled with concern. "Is something wrong, honey?"

Kyla looked at her mother through the reflection in the mirror. "Oh, no. Just something we have to talk about." She forced a reassuring smile. "Not to worry. We're fine."

"Then, I'm really glad you're going back early. Communication is the most important thing in any relationship."

"Always the counselor aren't you, Mom? You never should have retired."

"Child, it's in my blood," Lynn said running her thin fingers through her hair. "But, I didn't learn this from being a guidance counselor. This is from *time served*." She chuckled. "Your father and I have been married *a mighty long time*."

"Oh good, Mrs. Carrington. You got her up. Come on,

Kyla," Alexis ordered as she shivered into the room wrapped only in a towel. Kyla sighed and went into the bathroom.

"Well, I'll get out of here so that you can get dressed, honey. Just come into the kitchen when you're ready." Lynn patted Alexis on the shoulder.

Alexis bent over and hugged her. This tiny woman had treated her like a daughter from the first day they'd met. "Thank you for such a great weekend. I don't know which was better—the King's Daughters Program or all the shopping I did."

Lynn threw back her head and laughed, her dimples deepening.

"I always love coming up here to your church. Just walking in, you know the Holy Spirit is there."

"Yes, Winston and I have been blessed. But you guys are too. You know how we love Pastor Ford. Now, you'd better get moving before Winston has a fit. You know how he is. Everything has to be right on time."

Alexis dressed, then threw her suitcase and bags on top of the bed. Waiting for Kyla, she sat in the rocking chair at the window enjoying the sound of the crashing waves. As the first light tried to peek through the early morning's darkness, she allowed her mind to wander to thoughts of Brian. Seeing his face in her mind's eye made her smile. She couldn't wait to see him again.

"Okay, I'm awake now." Kyla scooted into the room. She threw on her jeans and a T-shirt and tossed the rest of her clothes into her weekend bag.

"Why don't you go ahead and get something to eat. I want to say goodbye to Nicole."

"Okay." Alexis struggled with her bags. "Kiss her for me too."

Tiptoeing into the small room that her parents had added on and decorated in yellow just for their granddaughter, Kyla eased onto the canopy bed and stroked her daughter's hair. The early morning light cast a warm glow on Nicole's face and she stirred in her sleep. Kyla smiled, remembering how Nicole had begged to spend a few extra days in Santa Barbara and after all the pleading, she had finally agreed. Her daughter would have a wonderful time with her grandparents: here she could romp on the beach with her friends and bask in the center of her grandparents' love.

Nicole moaned and Kyla leaned over to kiss her, then wiped the lipstick imprint she'd left on Nicole's cheek. All of God's wonders and miracles were etched in this face that she loved so much. She kissed her again. "I love you, sweetheart," she whispered as she left the room.

"Good morning, Dad," Kyla said as she pecked him on his shaved ebony head. This weekend was the first time she'd ever seen him totally bald and she had teased him about his Michael Jordan look the entire time.

Winston Carrington's hearty laugh echoed through the large front room. "I wondered if you girls were really going to get up this early." He took off his glasses and folded the newspaper he'd been reading onto his lap. "Have a little something to eat and we'll be ready to go."

"I don't want anything. Too early for me."

"Well, not for me," Alexis said as she chewed on the last of her bagel. "I'm ready."

"Then let's get going, ladies. We still have to make sure that you can get on this flight," he said to Kyla.

"Oh, I'll be able to exchange my ticket. Who else will be leaving Santa Barbara at dawn on a Sunday?"

Winston chuckled, picked up a few of the bags and stooped low as he ducked his six-foot-six-inch frame under the door frame.

Lynn hugged Kyla and Alexis. "Kyla, make sure you call me when you get home. And don't worry about Nicole. She can stay as long as she likes."

"Don't tell her that! She may never come home. Come on, Dad."

"Now, you want to rush me?" he asked teasingly. "Y'all the ones doing all the kissing and hugging." He grabbed his wife around her waist, lifted her from the floor and swung her around.

"Put me down!" Lynn protested playfully as she slapped his hands. "You'd better stop acting the fool and get these girls to the airport!"

It was only a few miles to the town's small airport and just as she thought, Kyla exchanged her ticket without any problem, allowing Winston to leave them and return home for his early morning fishing date with his granddaughter. The boarding of their flight was announced after only a few minutes.

"Ladies, you can take any seat," the flight attendant smiled.

They struggled down the narrow aisle of the commuter plane, hands full of extra bags. Kyla chose two seats and handed her bags to Alexis, who managed to stuff several bags into the overhead bin.

"Girl, there's no room for these up there. I'll have to squeeze the rest under the seat."

"I think you overdid it this time, Alexis. And I always end up carrying your extra bags."

"Oh, stop complaining. Here, take these and stuff them under your seat."

Kyla sucked her teeth. "I'm surprised they let us on the plane with all of your stuff."

"Girl, just sit back and be happy that you're going home early to see your husband, all because of me!"

The jet's engines revved up and they settled back for the short flight to Los Angeles. Alexis thumbed through the airline magazine while Kyla leaned back, closing her eyes.

"You know, Brian's going to church with me this morning."

"That's right, I forgot."

"We were probably going to go out afterwards. Do you think you and Jefferson would like to join us?"

Kyla cracked open one eye. "Are you sure you really want us old married folks tagging along?"

"Actually, I'd appreciate it. I think I need to be chaperoned."

Kyla sat up. "Why?"

"I think I'm falling for this guy."

"Well, what did you expect? He's smart, fine and funny . . ."

"And I'm scared."

"That always happens at the beginning of any relationship. You're getting to know one another."

"That's the part I'm scared of. Getting to *know* one another." Alexis paused. "And . . . I mean 'know' in the biblical sense . . ."

"Oh . . . so, it's gotten to that point, huh?"

"I think so. I mean, the other night when we kissed . . . if we weren't in the hallway . . ."

"Really?" Kyla's eyes opened wide. "He kisses that well? Mmm, I want all the details."

"I don't know if it's his kisses or if it's because it's been sooo long. But honey, if he had kissed me any longer, my clothes would've just fallen off right there in that hallway!"

Kyla giggled. "That would've been a sight. Can you imagine what all of those hoity-toity neighbors of yours would have said?"

"Kyla, I'm serious!"

"I know, honey. I'm sorry. So, what are you going to do?"

"I don't know . . . I mean, I know that I'm not going to go to bed with him." She paused for a long moment. "Whew! That's the first time I've said it out loud and I mean it. I've been too good and I'm just too committed to the Lord to mess up this way now. But the thing is, I don't know how to bring it up with Brian."

"Well, he's a Christian. It should be something that's easy for you two to talk about."

"Spoken like someone who's been married for a trillion years. It's not easy no matter who you've got to talk to about it. And just because he's a Christian doesn't mean that he will agree. Lots of people say they're Christian, but you don't know what that really means."

"That's true . . ."

"And Christians are people too. We all believe a lot of different things."

"But there are some things that are pretty basic."

"Well, maybe to you and me, but I don't know what side of the fence he will be on. The man is a red-blooded African man. I can tell you *that* for a fact."

Kyla arched her eyebrow. "Really," she smirked. "And, how do you know *that*?"

"Never mind." Alexis sighed. "I just don't know how to

bring it up. I mean, over brunch should I just say, 'Brian, you really turn me on, but there's no way I'm going to go to bed with you'? Or do I wait and talk to him about it when we get to . . . that moment? And, suppose we get to what I think is that moment and I say, 'I'm not going to bed with you' and he says, 'I never asked.' Anything could happen." She flapped her hands in the air in frustration.

"Alexis, I think you're making too much of this. It'll come up naturally and knowing you, you'll handle it just fine."

"Probably . . . but let's say we even make it through all of that. Let's say that Brian and I do become an item. How are we going to practice this? How do you really remain celibate in today's times?"

"I know, girl! It would be a struggle for me." Kyla turned to face Alexis. "Look, I know you're serious about maintaining your relationship with God . . ."

"That is *so* important to me."

"Well, just remember to hold on to yourself. Don't let go of what you believe."

Alexis nodded.

"And, bring it up in the Singles' Fellowship," Kyla continued. "That's why you guys meet, right?"

"There are other reasons, but we do talk *a lot* about sex."

"Well, get their perspective. And take Brian with you!"

"That's a good thought. And along with that, I'll be doing a lot of exercising." Alexis sighed.

"Exercising?"

"Yeah, 'cause, girl, the only way I'll be able to keep my hands off of that man is by getting on my knees, then up again, then back on my knees and up again. Whew! That boy is *fine*!" she said, fanning herself.

Kyla laughed. She leaned back and closed her eyes once again.

Alexis looked out at the clouds and sighed in peace. Yes, she would pray . . . just like she always did. But even though she was concerned about Brian's views on fornication, she was grateful that she would be talking to a Christian man. The last man she'd gone out with told her that he believed the "supreme being was a seven-foot man who lived on Mars." She had barely been able to sit through that dinner, and after that disaster, she had made a commitment to herself—only a man of God would do. "Thank you, Lord," she whispered to the clouds. And, as she said that, she knew there was something else she had to do.

"Kyla, are you awake?"

"No."

"I have something I want to talk about."

"Please. I am tired of talking about your new man!"

"No, it's something else. I want you to know that I do try to hold my tongue, but sometimes I have a hard time. I try to walk as a Christian, but there are things that just get under my skin, especially when it comes to my friends." She took a deep breath. "I just want to apologize for getting you upset the other day. About Jasmine."

Kyla cocked her head and stared at her friend, waiting for the catch that she was sure was coming. But when Alexis just smiled back, Kyla said, "Apology accepted. Thank you."

"Now, don't get me wrong. I'm not sorry for what I *said*. I'm just sorry that it upset you. Because chile, that girl *is* a snake!" Alexis drawled.

Kyla laughed out loud. "You know, it's a good thing I love both you and Jasmine so much, because sometimes the two of you are a pain in my . . ."

"Kyla!" she giggled.

"What? All I was going to say is that you guys can be a pain in my . . . head. Sometimes the two of you give me a headache! What did you think I was going to say?" she asked innocently, and closed her eyes once again as the flight attendants prepared the cabin for the final approach to Los Angeles International Airport.

As soon as the cab started up the hill, Kyla set the flowers aside and began digging into her purse. She directed the driver and pulled out her wallet as he stopped in front of the house. Pulling the remote garage opener from her purse, she paid him, then got out of the cab as the driver placed her bags on the side of the curb. She closed the door gently; not that she thought there was any chance of Jefferson hearing her, it was much too early. But their bedroom did face the street and she wanted to surprise him the way he always surprised her.

The last time Jefferson had gone away, he had returned home a day early in the middle of the night—quietly, silently undressing and finally putting his long, warm naked body against hers. Kyla in her unconsciousness had embraced him, her husband fitting easily into her dream. She had been frightened when she opened her eyes and realized she wasn't dreaming—that she wasn't alone. But it took only moments to realize she was having the best kind of dream. Kyla shuddered as she remembered that time and smiled in anticipation of this homecoming.

Balancing her bags, she slung her purse over her shoulder and held the roses she'd purchased at the airport in front so they wouldn't get crushed. She smiled; she had great plans for them.

She pressed the garage-door opener and then stopped suddenly. Between their two cars was Jasmine's BMW. Frowning, she walked inside. "What is Jasmine's car doing here?" she thought to herself. She walked to the side of the BMW and looked inside. The car was empty except for the keys that sat on the driver seat. With the hand that held the flowers, she touched the hood of the car; it was cool.

Her frown deepened. "Jefferson must be checking her car for her and she left it here overnight." But even as she reasoned with herself, a fog washed over her as her stomach fluttered and her heart beat faster. A favorite scripture came to her mind: *For God hath not given us the spirit of fear; but of power, and of love, and of a sound mind . . .*

She stepped through the pantry into the kitchen. Her senses quickened—her ears perked, pupils dilated, even her nostrils seemed to flare. She looked around, a few dishes and glasses in the sink, but nothing unusual. She walked through the kitchen with slow steps into the dining room, finally stopping at the base of the winding stairs. She stood, listening. Silence. Then, a faint sound . . . running water. Kyla realized it was the shower in their bedroom.

She let out a deep sigh and smiled. Jefferson had probably just gotten up for church. Well, she had different plans; she and Alexis had already agreed to attend the second service. Running up the stairs, she imagined the look on Jefferson's face when he saw her.

At the top of the stairs, she could clearly hear the sound of water running, coming from their bathroom. Turning the corner, she dropped her bags in the hallway and was surprised to see the usually opened double doors to their bedroom securely closed. With one hand, she balanced the flowers and with the other she opened one of the doors.

The first thing to hit her was the smell, slightly musky, the aroma that lingers in a room after exercise . . . or lovemaking. Focusing on their bed, she saw Jasmine—leaning against the headboard, with the silk sheet around her. Her hair was tousled, curls falling carelessly onto her shoulder. And then, the sheet fell revealing her nakedness. Kyla's eyes blurred in confusion.

"Oh, Kyla . . ." Jasmine said matter-of-factly, as if she belonged in her best friend's bed.

The sound of Jasmine's voice made Kyla's head spin. She felt like she'd just awakened from a nightmare into a nightmare. Words swirled around in her head, but her dry mouth prohibited speech. With leaden legs, she reached deep inside herself, somehow finding the energy to move forward away from the bed, away from Jasmine and toward the sound of the running water. She had to find Jefferson. She had to let him know that Jasmine was in their house, in their bed. There had to be an explanation and he would have the answers.

She heard the hiss of the shower and could see the outline of his body, but the steam would not allow him to see her through the glass shower stall.

"Jefferson?" Her throat released a squeak.

"I'm almost finished, Jasmine. I said I would be out in a moment!"

A pained moan escaped from her constricted throat as she gasped for air. The next moment, a deep, animalistic howl came from the depths of her being.

Jefferson opened the shower door, peeked his head

through the cumulus clouds of steam that floated over his head and stepped out, completely exposing himself to Kyla.

"Oh my God! Kyla!" His words were barely a whisper.

"*Jefferson!*" She dropped the roses, unaware that she had been clutching them to her chest. Her hands covered her mouth trying to hold back the bile stirring inside. She whipped around before Jefferson could move toward her and ran. She didn't stop in her bedroom; she couldn't bear to look at Jasmine.

"Oh my God!" Jefferson repeated when he finally was able to move from his frozen state. "Kyla. Wait! Please!" He grabbed a towel from the heated rack and sprinted toward her, slipping over the flowers that were scattered across the marble floor. In the bedroom, Jasmine was standing near the door, wrapped only in a sheet.

"What happened?" Jefferson asked as he grabbed his robe, trembling with the emotion that rode through his body.

"I . . . don't . . . know," Jasmine's voice shook as she sat down on the bed. "I was in the other room and came in here to tell you something and . . . Kyla just came marching into the room before I could get to you."

"What did you say to her?" He was already moving into his closet.

"I didn't say anything. She just stomped past me and went into your bathroom. I wanted to stop her, to warn you . . . but I didn't know what to do."

"She wasn't supposed to be back! She was coming back tonight. My God! Where's Nicole?" he cried as he tied the bathrobe sash around his waist and ran out of the bedroom. He heard the door that led to the garage slam and he bolted down the stairs, into the garage in time to see Kyla backing her car out.

He chased the screeching car. "Kyla, wait. Please!" Standing in his driveway clad only in his bathrobe, he watched his wife speed down the street.

It took only a moment for him to move into action and he ran back into the house. "This can't be happening!" he screamed.

He took the stairs two at a time and stopped at the top in Nicole's room. There was no sign of his daughter and he shook his head. Was she with Kyla? He rushed back into his bedroom, shoving past Jasmine. "Get out of here!" he screamed as he went to his closet.

Jasmine froze. She knew that Jefferson would be upset at first. But she hadn't expected him to turn on her. Her words sounded tight. "Jefferson, don't blame me. This is *not* my fault. I didn't do this alone."

His eyes opened wide and he snapped at her in disbelief. "Jasmine, get out of my bed! Get out of my house!" His eyes glassed over and he looked right through her. "Jasmine . . . please . . . just . . . leave," he said lowering his voice and speaking the words deliberately as he tried to maintain some semblance of calm. He knew her words were true. He *was* to blame.

"You're right," he continued. "This wasn't your fault. But you have to leave. This was a mistake." Picking up his keys, he ran from the room.

When she heard the garage door close, Jasmine stood at the bay window. This window gave her the same view as the one in the guest bedroom—the one she had looked out of earlier when she heard the car drive up and saw Kyla getting out of the cab. Now, she watched Jefferson pull his Range Rover onto the street and speed away. She strolled back to the bed and lay back on the silk sheets.

She rolled her arms and legs across the sheets and marveled at their softness. She never had these kinds of things and for a moment allowed herself to wonder if her life would be different now.

This was working out even better than she had planned, though she would have preferred a few more rendezvous with Jefferson, just to solidify her hold. But she knew that wouldn't be a problem now. Kyla's unexpected arrival had changed everything. What a coup!

She pulled the comforter completely over her naked body and remembered how this wonderful morning had begun.

With the memory of last night still fresh, she had rolled over, reaching for Jefferson only to find the other side of the bed empty. She had sat up when he walked into the room.

His eyes had fixed on her for a moment and then he had turned away. "Please cover up. We need to talk." His voice had been taut.

"Jefferson, last night was so special for me . . ." She had reached for his hands.

He had pulled back. "Jasmine, get dressed. You can use the guest bathroom and then we have to talk."

"Okay . . . I just thought . . ." But before she could finish, he had walked out, ignoring her words.

She had sighed with disappointment. Kyla wasn't coming home until tonight and she had planned to spend the entire day in bed. They had made love only once last night before he had rolled away as if he were in some kind of mental agony, but she had intended to seduce him again this morning.

Now as she watched him walk away, her body raced with adrenaline. "Okay, think, Jasmine. Think. What to do next?" After a few moments, she had just shaken her head. She'd just have to wait until they talked, see where he was coming from. That would be okay, she had told herself. She had seized the opportunity last night and it had worked. Now, to take this further, she would need a plan. Married men were so easy the first time. Keeping them on the hook took special planning.

Picking up her slip, she had gone back into the guest bedroom. That was when she'd seen Kyla and had made sure that Kyla had seen her.

Well, she had gotten what she wanted and now she decided to leave before Jefferson returned. There was no need to irritate him. If she played this right, he would be back in her arms in no time. After the night they'd had, he would call her at his first sign of loneliness.

As she dressed, her gaze settled on the wedding picture of Kyla and Jefferson sitting on the bureau. She bit her lip and turned away quickly. She slipped into her shoes and then walked from the bedroom out of the house, not understanding the loneliness that seemed to suddenly engulf her. Just like when Kenny left.

She shook her head. "Why am I feeling like this?" She had won the ultimate prize, but the moment didn't feel victorious.

"Stop it!" she scolded herself. "I just have to focus on the fact that now I'll have everything *I've* wanted. If I do this right, I could be Mrs. Jefferson Blake." She got in her car and pulled into the street, shuddering with emotions that she couldn't quite understand.

# Nine

Kyla sped down the streets, smearing her tears across her face with the back of her hands. For the last hour, she'd been weaving through the city without a destination. Passing a freeway entrance ramp, she swerved, made an illegal U-turn and got on. She wasn't sure if she was going north or south. It really didn't matter.

Increasing her speed to seventy miles an hour, she set the cruise control. The freeway was Sunday-morning light. Most people had not even begun to stir, yet in the first few hours of this new day where the sun was already threatening to shine in its full glory, a lifetime had passed her by. Her tears built, pouring forth as the morning rewound, fast-forwarded, then rewound in her mind.

For a moment, Kyla felt the urge to see Nicole. She wanted to hold her child and she needed to be held—as a child. There was no doubt her parents would be there for her. But how was she going to tell them that the man they loved as a son, the father of their grandchild, had committed adultery . . . with her best friend!

"How could they do this to me?" It was still impossible

for her to believe. Both Jefferson and Jasmine loved her and would never do anything to hurt her. But they did. "How long had this been going on?" She searched her brain, trying to think back over the years, trying to remember every occasion when the three of them had been together. She tried to remember a look, a touch—and then it all became clear. This was why Jasmine stayed at their house so often. Her chest ached as she thought of them together while she was asleep in her bedroom.

She wondered if they had been together the entire time she'd been in Santa Barbara. Probably. That's why Jasmine's car was in the garage—she had moved in for the weekend. Why would the man she had given her heart to do this to her?

She began to tire and she knew she had to stop. Go somewhere, but where? To her parents? No, she wasn't ready to tell them yet. And Alexis was with Brian today. There was only one place left to go . . . but she would never go back to *that* house. Deciding to exit the freeway, she noticed a hotel at the base of the ramp. She turned into the parking lot and stopped her car in front of the bright pink building. She didn't even know what city she was in.

She sat staring out the car window, trying to find answers to the questions that haunted her. Her fingers rubbed the gold heart around her neck. What would happen to her now? What would happen to Nicole? Why would Jefferson give up everything they had? Did he really love Jasmine?

The trembling began at the soles of her feet and swelled to the top of her head. She wanted to go inside the hotel, to be alone, but her limbs were immobile. Seconds passed, minutes ticked by, it could have been an hour. But time didn't matter; she felt like it would never matter again. And as the sobs crawled up inside, she released them freely as her life crumbled to small pieces inside her heart.

Jefferson glanced once again at the clock on his dashboard, as he'd been doing every five minutes for the last two and a half hours. He didn't know what time had to do with anything, but somehow he felt more secure keeping track of it. That was all he seemed to be able to control right now.

The vision of his wife in their bedroom wouldn't leave his mind. How could he have been so stupid? This was never supposed to happen to him. Not just because he loved Kyla dearly and not just because when he had taken his marriage vows, he meant to keep them until the day he died. But because he was a Christian. "I'm a *Christian*," he said aloud, as if he needed to remind himself.

He shook his head in disbelief, not understanding at all what had happened. One minute Jasmine was there, the next they were in bed together. He didn't understand how he had fallen, how he could have yielded.

Once again, he glanced at the clock, but his hope had already begun to falter. He'd been driving the streets of Los Angeles, checking everywhere he thought Kyla could be. He had driven past the clinic, past their favorite restaurants, had talked to the doorman at Alexis' building. She was nowhere to be found. And what about Nicole? Was she with Kyla? Had she come home to find him in his shame? Maybe she was with Alexis, or still in Santa Barbara. And why had Kyla come home early? Why did this have to happen to him? The answerless questions flooded and overpowered him.

A thought rushed to his mind. Maybe Kyla had returned

home. Without anywhere else to go, maybe she'd taken Nicole back there. Feeling a ray of hope, he increased his speed, weaving carelessly through the streets, arriving home within ten minutes. As he turned the corner, he could see that the garage door was up, and he pressed down on the accelerator, sure that Kyla had returned.

But as he turned into the driveway, it was empty. Then he remembered. Jasmine had left the door open. Kyla had not been back at all. He sat inside his car, not having the energy to move into the garage. He couldn't go inside. It would only remind him of what he'd done and he couldn't handle that right now.

He pounded his fist against the steering wheel, then leaned his head down. What was he going to do? All the feelings he'd been fighting to keep at bay since this morning rushed forward. And, now with all hope gone, he finally broke down.

He cried gut-wrenching sobs, the way only a grown man could cry. His shoulders heaved, revealing the acute pain that tore at his center. He cried, wondering where was his precious Kyla. He cried, wondering what would happen to his life now. He cried for the poor example he had set as a man of God. He didn't think about passing neighbors; his emotions flowed, emitting the shame, pain, and anguish that had been stored inside from the moment he had touched Jasmine, even before Kyla had found him with her.

Unsure of how much time had passed, not caring anyway, he finally lifted his head. As he did, he heard a voice, though he wasn't sure where it came from. He looked through the windshield to the sky and the words came clearly. *My grace is*

*sufficient for thee: for my strength is made perfect in weakness.*
After a few minutes, Jefferson dried his tears.

He ran into the house, to their bedroom, then stopped when he saw the dull light on the answering machine—no messages. Hanging his head, he fell to his knees.

"Dear Lord," he prayed. "My first prayer is that you keep Kyla and Nicole. Please keep my loved ones safe, Heavenly Father. Keep them in Your hands. And Lord, I come to you on my knees, with a heavy heart. I am so ashamed, Father. I am so sorry for what I have done and I feel such guilt even asking for Your forgiveness. But, please forgive me Lord, for I have sinned. I have sinned against You and my wife. But I thank you, Father, for being a God of mercy and grace. And I thank You for Your blood, Jesus. Your blood that covers this sin for me. My humble prayer, Father, is that You help me find a way to make this up to Kyla. Help her to forgive me. Help Kyla to know that I love her with every fiber of my being." With his head still bowed, Jefferson continued to speak to the Lord, asking for help and direction. He remained on his knees until they ached and only then did he rise with hope.

He made a mental list of who he could call—people who Kyla might turn to. He knew he would have to choose his words carefully as he spoke; he could never reveal what had happened. Self-protection was not his goal—he didn't care what anyone thought of him. He was willing to shout his sin from the rooftop if he thought that would bring Kyla back. But, he had to be discreet for Kyla's sake. The revelation of his disgrace had to be in her hands.

He called his in-laws first and held his breath as Lynn chatted about the weekend she'd spent with Kyla and Alexis.

"But I'm sure Kyla has told you all about this already," Lynn said.

"Actually, she hasn't said too much. We haven't had much of an opportunity to talk . . . yet."

"Oh, too bad. I know how excited she was to surprise you. She really wanted the two of you to have some time alone. Did something come up?"

"Yes . . ."

"Anyway, Winston and I are thrilled to have Nicole with us for a few days. Did you call to speak to her?"

Jefferson almost collapsed from relief. But at the same time, he was saddened. With Nicole in Santa Barbara, Kyla was free to move around without having to return home.

"Hi, Daddy." Jefferson broke down at the sound of his daughter's voice. "I'm having a great time. I went fishing and I played with Misty and Kristy and Papa is taking us fishing tomorrow too. Can I stay here until Saturday, Daddy? Misty and Kristy are having their birthday party and I really want to go."

"We'll see, sweetheart. I just have to check with . . . your mother," he said softly.

"Can you ask her now? Can I talk to her about it?"

Jefferson clenched his fist. "She's not here right now. But, I'm sure she'll call you tonight."

"Where did she go?"

"Listen, Nicole, I promise I'll talk to her and we'll let you know, okay? I think it will be all right. I have to go now, honey. I love you and I'll call you tomorrow."

Next, he called Alexis, but there was no answer. He even called his mother, hoping that Kyla had found refuge in San Diego, but when his mother asked about Kyla and Nicole, he knew his wife was still missing.

He had been pacing the room and it wasn't until that moment that he noticed the bed—the sheets still disheveled, the comforter sprawled on the floor. With tears stinging his eyes, he tore the sheets off the bed and ran into the garage, dumping them into the garbage. He leaned against the cold wall and closed his eyes. There had to be something he was missing, something he had overlooked that would give him a clue about Kyla. Then, his eyes opened wide. Why hadn't he thought of that before? He knew exactly where she would turn in this situation. He jumped into his car and held his breath for the entire fifteen minutes it took him to get to the church. A few cars remained in the lot and his eyes quickly scanned the area for Kyla's car. But even though he didn't see the Lexus, he knew she was here. She had probably parked somewhere else, waiting for Pastor Ford to finish the second service. From the look of the almost-empty parking lot, second service had ended a while ago and Kyla was probably with the pastor right now.

He ran inside, almost knocking down Elder Roberts, who was locking up the front doors.

"Jefferson, man, where's the fire?"

"Sorry. I needed to see . . . Pastor Ford," he said, as his eyes searched the sanctuary. "Is she still here?"

"I think so. She's probably back in her office."

Jefferson could hear Pastor Ford's voice even before he entered her private alcove. When he stepped into her outer office, she was talking to Miss Imogene.

"It is time for both of us to go home," Jefferson heard Pastor Ford say.

Miss Imogene chuckled. "I've been trying to get you out of here for the last hour."

Jefferson coughed and the women looked up.

Pastor Ford took one look at him and frowned. "Jefferson." She paused, but kept her eyes on Jefferson. "Miss Imogene, I'll see you later."

Miss Imogene smiled as she passed Jefferson and the pastor motioned him into her office. She closed the door behind them.

"How are you?" The pastor's eyes narrowed with concern. "I missed you in church this morning."

"Pastor Ford, have you seen Kyla?" his voice shuddered as he spoke.

The pastor's frown deepened. "No," she said slowly. "What's wrong, Jefferson?"

He shook his head, unable to speak and fell into the chair in front of the desk. Wordlessly, Pastor Ford sat next to him and waited a few moments before she questioned him again.

Jefferson fought to hold back sobs. He was so sure that Kyla was going to be here, and now he wondered if he had any hope of finding her.

"Oh, Pastor . . . I don't know what to say . . ."

"Start at the beginning. Why don't you know where Kyla is?"

Jefferson swallowed and turned in the chair slightly so that he could face his pastor. But when Pastor Ford's soft brown eyes looked back at him, his face dropped. There was no way he could tell her.

"Jefferson, I want to help," she urged.

With his elbows resting on his knees, he held his face in his hands. "Kyla found me with another woman this morning," he said softly. He closed his eyes when he heard the pastor's sigh, but continued, "She came home early from Santa Barbara and I was with . . ."

Pastor Ford leaned forward and rubbed his back. "Okay, I think I've got that part," she said. "And, you don't know where Kyla is now." Her statement was a question.

He shook his head. He had used up all his words.

Pastor Ford stood and walked to the window, letting his confession sink in. "Have you prayed?" she asked.

He nodded. "That's the only thing I've done right today."

When she turned to face him, her eyes bore into his. "Are you in love with this other woman?"

He sat up straight. "Oh, God, no! Pastor, I love Kyla with all my heart. I have never cheated on her before and I don't even know why or how or . . ."

Pastor Ford held up her hands. "That's enough. That's what I thought, but I had to ask you so that I could know how to help." She walked to her desk and leaned against it. "Where else could Kyla be?"

"I don't know. I've called everyone we know. At least all the people that she would turn to. I was sure she would contact you."

"She may call me at home," Pastor Ford nodded slightly. "She's fine, Jefferson. I feel it."

Jefferson studied his pastor as she sat with her arms folded. "Aren't you going to ask me how I could have done it?" he asked, dropping his eyes.

She shook her head. "No, I don't need to know that. You know. The only thing that's important is that you've repented to the Lord. Now, Kyla can forgive you."

"Pastor, how will she be able to do that? I can't imagine that she'll be able to ever look at me again."

"It may take some time, but I know Kyla. She'll be hurt and in pain and angry. But, she's also filled with the Holy Spirit and that's where the forgiveness will come from. As long as you're truly remorseful."

"I am! I love Kyla with everything inside of me. And I just want to find her. I have to make things right." He paused. "Pastor, when she does come home, will you help us? I won't know what to do . . ."

Pastor Ford nodded. "I was going to suggest that. Let's just find Kyla first. I'll let you know if she calls me."

Jefferson forced a smile and stood. "Thank you, Pastor. I'll call you as soon as . . . I know something. I'm going to go back home. Maybe she's back or has called or . . ." his voice faded.

As he turned away, the pastor took his hand. "I think you're forgetting something. We have to pray."

"I've already prayed."

"Honey, you can't pray enough in this situation," she smiled.

Through his pain, he chuckled and held Pastor Ford's hand.

"Father," the pastor started. "We come before you now with praise and thanksgiving, for you are a God of grace and mercy. Thank you for your gift of salvation which includes the forgiveness of our sins, in the name of Jesus. We are grateful, Lord, and know that once we repent, you remember our sins no more. And as Jefferson and I bow before you now, Lord, I pray that you give Kyla and Jefferson the strength to face this trial in front of them. I pray, Father, that you will provide the direction and help that you promise in Your Word and we know Your Word is true. And, we thank you, Father, that somehow this will be turned around for your glory. Your name,

Father, will be exalted and we thank you and praise you for it. In Jesus Christ's name we pray, Amen."

Without saying anything, Jefferson hugged the pastor and left.

Alexis let the phone ring until the answering machine picked up, but decided not to leave another message.

"I guess they're not home," she said, turning to Brian. "I don't know what happened. Kyla said they'd meet us at the second service." She frowned. "Maybe they changed their minds and went to the first service."

"Maybe they just had an extended homecoming celebration," he said as he put his hands around her waist and pulled her close.

She bit her lip. "No, they wouldn't miss church if they could help it . . ."

"Hey, what's wrong? You don't think they could've changed their plans?"

"Maybe . . . I'm just surprised that Kyla didn't call."

"Well, maybe she couldn't pull away . . . if you know what I mean. Anyway, are you ready?"

"Sure . . ."

He frowned. "If you don't want to go out . . ."

"Oh, no." She looked up at him and smiled. "Don't mind me. I worry about my friends too much."

"That's one of the things I like about you." He kissed her forehead, then brought his lips down to hers, brushing against them. She closed her eyes, surrendering to the pleasure. After several long minutes, she stepped back, turning away from him. "Where did you say you wanted to go?"

"I hadn't decided, but now I'm wondering if maybe we should just stay here." His voice was husky and he moved towards her.

"No, I don't think so . . . I think we should go out."

He took her arm and his smile teased her. "Ms. Ward, are you afraid to be alone with me?"

"Of course not. Why would you say that?"

His eyes bore into her. "Prove it."

"Prove what? I just want to go out, that's all."

His smile continued to mock her. "Well, I've changed my mind," he said. "Let's stay here and . . . talk." He kissed her nose. "We can . . . get to know one another better. I think it's time, don't you?" He met her lips.

"Brian . . ."

His face nuzzled against her neck.

She bit her lip. "We *have* to talk."

He leaned back. "Okay."

Still standing in the circle of his arms, she stared at him and at that moment, she knew she was in love. She took a deep breath and perched herself on the couch's arm. "I don't know how to talk about this." She lowered her eyes. "I haven't had to in such a long time. Things just never seem to get this far . . ." When she looked up, he was sitting next to her, tapping his fingers against the back of the couch. Clasping her hands, she continued, "This is hard for me."

His smile widened. "Hard? I could say the same thing right about now. Okay, let me see if I can help you. You're trying to tell me that you like me, but you need to know if I'm sleeping with anyone and you need to know if I'm responsible—do I have protection." He kissed her hand. "The answers are no, no one, and yes, I'm very responsible," he said patting his pants pocket. "I'm ready for anything we want to do."

She chuckled nervously. "Well, that's all good to know. But what I'm trying to say is that we've talked about this a little, but I'm not sure how much you really understood. I'm a Christian . . ."

"So am I."

"Well, one of the things that is really important to me, as I'm sure it is with you, is walking with the Lord. Following all God's commandments . . ."

He frowned.

"And so . . . whew! I didn't know it was going to be this difficult. So . . . I'm just going to say this right out and let it go where it may . . . I don't know what you're going to think about this . . ."

"Honey, just come on and say it. Don't keep me in suspense. What is it? Are you HIV positive? Do you have herpes or something else?"

"No, no and no."

"Well, what is it? Don't tell me you're a virgin," he joked.

"Bingo!"

His smile vanished. "You're kidding, right?"

"I'm not kidding. I mean, I'm not exactly a virgin, but I have been since I made my commitment to the Lord."

"Oh . . ." The word dragged out long. "I thought you said you'd been a Christian for over twenty years."

She nodded.

"Wow! You must be climbing the walls!"

"Honestly, I have fallen a few times. Especially in the early years. But recently I have maintained this walk. It's a struggle, but I'm going to do all I can to keep this vow."

"Oh . . ."

"Brian, I wasn't really sure how to talk to you about this, because I'm not sure where you stand . . ." She wrung her hands.

"Well it's not like I've had to deal with anything like this in a while," he said. His eyes narrowed a bit as he tried to figure out if Alexis was serious.

"I didn't mean to spring this on you. I know you didn't ask or anything."

He grinned. "I was *definitely* asking . . ." he said, realizing that she *was* serious.

She laughed. "And my body definitely wants to say yes, but . . ."

He touched her shoulder. "You don't have to explain anymore." He stood and walked to the balcony, gazing out onto the traffic below on Wilshire Boulevard. This was a surprise, but he couldn't just jump all over her. "I'm disappointed. I admit it," he said at last, turning back to face her. "But I respect you and I respect the commitment you've made. And maybe this is good. I mean, if this relationship can move forward without sex, then that would be good, right?" His question sounded unsure.

She nodded. "And I want you to know that I understand how difficult this is going to be. Just looking at you right now let's me know it's not going to be easy for me."

"Well, at least I know I'm not turning you off."

Her eyes slowly roamed his body, from the top of his short haircut, to the soft lines around his brown eyes, past his mustached lip, down to his tight runner's body. "I'm not turned off at all," she said shaking her head slowly.

He shoved his hands into his pockets. "We'll just take this a day at a time."

With a smile framing her face, she walked to him, took his hands and kissed him lightly. "Thank you for understanding and making it easy for me."

"Easy, huh? Well, what should we do with our hormones?"

They both laughed.

"I can't say that this isn't different," Brian began. "But I'm willing . . . to give it a *try*."

"Okay . . ." As she stepped away she felt her eyes mist slightly, though she wasn't quite sure why. He had accepted all of this, hadn't he? He *was* willing to try. "Should we still order in or do you want to go out?"

"Let's stay in."

"Okay," she smiled weakly.

"I just want to know one thing. How far *can* I go?"

"Brian . . ."

"I mean is this okay?" He brushed his lips on her neck, sending her head reeling back. Then, his mouth moved to her earlobe. "What about this?"

Alexis closed her eyes and fell into the feeling.

"Is this acceptable?" His lips had moved to her closed eyelids and he planted soft kisses while his hands massaged her shoulders. "And, what about this?" His tongue searched her lips, then merged with hers. "I want to make sure I don't step over any lines," he murmured.

She opened her eyes. "I think they all work."

"That's good, because I want to make you happy."

Leaning back, her eyes pierced his. "Are you sure you're okay with this?"

He nodded slightly. "If you want the lady, you've got to go along with the lady's rules."

"Well, what about food? Still hungry?"

"Now more than I was before," he said with a smile.

"What do you want? Mexican, Italian, Chinese?"

"Let's try Chinese. I understand that MSG reduces the sex drive."

"Are you serious?"

"No, but I can always hope, because Lord knows, I'm going to need some help."

After the food was delivered, they sat back on the couch, eating Egg Foo Young and listening to Luther Vandross's smooth voice fill the room.

"This is kind of nice. Just you, me, Luther, and our hormones," Brian said as he reached out for her.

She jabbed him playfully with one of her chopsticks. "Let's stop talking about our hormones."

"What else is there?"

"Church. What did you think of the service this morning?"

He started nodding his head slowly. "Well, I've heard a lot about this woman and you guys were right. Pastor Ford is something else. I actually learned a few things this morning."

"That's how it always is with her. No matter where you are in your life, her words will reach you. She is truly anointed."

"Well, this gives me one more reason to be back in California. I do miss Boston, but it's more because of the boys than anything else."

"You don't talk about them much."

"I thought I talked about them all the time. I try not to bore my friends with all my kid talk."

"You could never bore me. Tell me about them."

"Brandon and Russell? There's not much to tell except that they're two great little boys and I live for the day that I can have them live with me."

She sat up. "Really?"

"Yeah, why are you surprised? I'm their father and would love to be in their lives full-time."

"I'm sure Regina would have something to say about that."

His nod was slow. "I'm sure. But, I think I'll be able to work it out."

His words sounded mysterious to Alexis and she frowned. The telephone rang.

"Hi, Jefferson. I was wondering what happened to you guys. We missed you in church."

"Uh, yeah . . . I know . . . listen, Alex, I was just calling to see if Kyla was with you."

Alexis frowned. "No. Didn't she come home this morning?"

"Oh yeah, but she . . . she left and I needed to talk to her."

"She's not answering her cellular?"

"Uh, no. I think she forgot to turn it on."

"Well, I haven't heard from her, but if I do, I'll tell her to call you. Jefferson, is everything all right?"

"Uh . . . sure. Fine. I'll speak to you later."

"What's wrong?" Brian asked as he dropped the food cartons onto the kitchen table.

"Jefferson was looking for Kyla and he didn't sound good."

"Did he say what was wrong?"

"No, he was evasive and now I'm worried."

"Oh, come on, honey. If something was wrong, you're the first person that Kyla would call."

"Maybe."

As they went to sit on the balcony, she listened to Brian's chatting and laughed along with him. But her mind moved away, settling into its own corner. Disheartening thoughts raged through her. Something was wrong, terribly wrong. She could feel it in her spirit. But she could not discern who the warning was for. When Brian took her hand, she faked a smile and said a prayer inside her head. "Lord, whatever it is, please keep us. Please keep all of your children safe."

# Ten

Kyla awakened suddenly, drawn from a fitful sleep. Confused, she looked around the darkened room. Then, the memories flooded her. She leaned over and clicked on the lamp that was bolted to the nightstand. The dull, low-watt bulb cast a brownish hue to the already dingy room.

Kyla swiveled and dropped her legs to the floor, facing the three-drawer dresser with its peeling veneer. This was a simple room, with only four pieces of cheap furniture and gray paint-chipped walls. She was surprised there was a television, telephone, and radio.

Standing, she looked through the murky window and for the first time noticed the small terrace adjoining the room. Sliding the door aside, she stepped onto the narrow concrete square and the cool night air softly kissed her face, making her realize how stuffy the room had been.

She glanced over the railing, taking in the full parking lot. Beyond the lot, the freeway was in full view. Traffic was Sunday-evening light. People were already home with their families. Tears stung her eyes and she fought to hold them back, but it was difficult. Sorrow seemed to engulf her, like she was mourning a death. In a way, she guessed she was. Stepping back into the room, she locked the door securely and still wondered where she was.

When she had stepped into the lobby this afternoon and walked up to the desk clerk, she hadn't asked any questions, even though the clerk had plenty of questions for her. She remembered how he had looked her up and down, suspicion blanketing his face.

"I'd like a room please."

He had raised one eyebrow. "A room?" The clerk had peered over the counter. "Do you have *any* luggage?"

"No."

He had scrutinized her credit card, turned it over then upside down, and checked the signature against her driver's license. Finally, begrudgingly, he handed her the keys to a single room. It wasn't until she had glanced at her reflection in the mirror that she understood the clerk's scrutiny.

Within minutes, she had collapsed on top of the tattered bedspread that covered the twin-sized bed. Exhaustion was a welcomed guest, preventing her from having to face all of the brand-new issues in her life. But unconsciousness did not grant complete immunity. She'd had a restless slumber, charged with dreams of Jasmine and Jefferson together.

Now as she stared out the window, her reflections moved forward. She had issues to resolve, decisions to make, things she had to face. The first thing she had to do was leave this hotel. But not just yet. Rubbing her arms, she returned to the bed. She had to do something. Maybe get something to eat. But the thought of food made her stomach somersault even more. She lay back, leaving the lights on, hoping they could keep away the ghosts. But even with the lights, she couldn't avoid it. As much as she couldn't bear to think about what she had found when she got home, she couldn't put it out of her mind. Jasmine and Jefferson. Jefferson and Jasmine.

Memories of her wedding day came to her mind. She pictured herself in her wedding dress, making the vows that she had written, words she still remembered. Vows they had promised each other. Vows they had promised God. On that day, Kyla knew adultery would never be an issue in their marriage. The man she loved lived to please God and that meant he would always honor his wife.

And throughout the years, when women had thrown themselves at the successful, handsome Dr. Jefferson Blake, she had not wavered. Temptation would always come; even Jesus had been tempted.

But, knowing the word of God and knowing her husband, Kyla knew from the bottom of her heart that Jefferson would *never* cheat on her. He loved her too much to bring her that kind of pain. He would never break his vows, not to her and not to God.

But he had. Her heart had been wrong. The security that she had built over the years had been a false one.

Then there was Jasmine. Her dear friend of more than thirty years. Her friend who would fight anyone who would try to hurt her. They had been through so much together, shared everything from homework to clothes . . . they knew each other's secrets.

Maybe this was all a misunderstanding. Maybe she had jumped to the wrong conclusion. Maybe Jasmine had only been spending the night like she had so many times before. She hadn't actually seen Jasmine and Jefferson in bed together.

And, she hadn't given Jefferson a chance to explain. Maybe he had a logical explanation.

Her laugh was bitter. There *was* a logical explanation . . . her husband was having an affair with her best friend. There were a lot of things to call it, but no matter how you explained it, it came down to the same simple thing.

She picked up the remote and flipped through the television channels, hoping to find something that would detach her from the roller coaster she couldn't seem to get off. With each channel, her emotions veered, from numbness to anguish and back again. She knew she had to do something before she tore herself into small, useless pieces.

Clicking off the television, she turned to the radio, finding her favorite Christian station. She lay back once again, trying to lose herself in the lull of the music, but was surprised when tears found their way back. She was not going to cry anymore, she couldn't allow herself to break down.

A shower. That's what she needed. She went into the bathroom and started taking off her clothes. She folded them, then leaned into the bathtub, turning on the water.

When she stood straight, she caught her reflection in the mirror and put her hand over her mouth in horror. Her eyelids were swollen and puffed, as if she'd been beaten. Her hair stood wildly over her head and her face was streaked with tears that had run through her makeup. But it was her eyes that exposed her pain. In their redness, she could see the end. She bit her lip and cringed; she looked like a battered woman.

Staring at herself under the harsh glare of the fluorescent lights, the tears that she'd been fighting so hard to control flowed. She stepped into the shower, hoping the water would soothe her.

But instead, for the first time since her ordeal began, she released the pent-up sorrow that had been building inside since she'd seen Jasmine in her bed. She cried from her center. The pain was not just emotional, it was physical. The ache was so sharp, so deep, she wanted to jump out of her skin to get away from it. She screamed from the depth of her core, putting a sound to the intense emotions that reared inside, fighting to find their place on the outside. Falling to her knees, the water poured over her aching body. She lifted her head, letting the salt of her tears mix with the tepid water surging from the showerhead.

How could love cause this kind of pain? It was unreal. She had never felt anything this extreme, this deep before. The enemy was vicious, holding her prisoner but she couldn't escape. There was nowhere to flee. The pain rose to her throat, choking her entire being until she was sure each breath would be her last. Curling up on the base of the cold porcelain tub, she coiled into a fetal position, bringing her knees to her chest, covering her heart. She had to protect her heart, knowing that if she didn't, it would burst from her.

As she lay there, the enemy traveled, bleeding from her pores, seeping out, covering her skin. All the love she felt for her husband, all the feelings that had unfolded throughout the years culminated now to form this.

The pain was so fierce, so furious, so profound that she knew she could no longer live with it . . . she wanted to die. She had to die. What did she have to live for anyway? This misery was too severe to endure. With this revelation, her tears began to subside. She wanted to die. She wanted to die. She wanted to die. The thought reverberated through her mind.

And as quickly as that wicked thought tried to control

her, another more powerful one countered. It jumped into her heart, crushing all thoughts of death. The thought came from one of her favorite praise songs and the words seemed to be hidden in the water drops that continued to pour upon her. She lay still on the base of the tub, listening as the words fell. Lifting her head, she cocked it to the side so that she could hear better.

The water streamed down the side of her face. Yes, she could hear the words in the soothing water. And as she listened, the words became clearer, still soft, but clearer. *Late in the midnight hour, when you feel all alone, God will turn it around for you* . . . She listened silently, letting the water minister to her. Then, she began to sing along, softly, slowly, off-key at first. *Late in the midnight hour, when you feel all alone, God will turn it around for you.* Lifting herself, she stood and raised her face to the ceiling, letting the water hit her directly in the face. She began to sing with the water, faster and louder . . . *Late in the midnight hour, when you feel all alone, God will turn it around for you.*

Her tears had been replaced by the words of the song. Turning off the shower, she stepped from the tub and stood in the middle of the bathroom raising her voice. She sang louder and louder, the words came faster and faster. She raised her hands in praise to the Lord. She cried out, knowing she was heard. God was right there, always there.

She knew what to do. She was a praiser! When all was bleak, when things were at their darkest, she knew how to enter into praise. And, she was a worshipper. When all was grim and she was discouraged, she knew how to worship.

She sang and sang, repeating that verse over and over . . .

*Late in the midnight hour, when you feel all alone, God will turn it around for you.*

She had found her peace; she had found her joy. It was in the Lord. She would take herself out of it and put it into God's Hands. The Word said she was the Lord's child. God would always take care of her.

Kyla had no idea how long she stood in that small hotel bathroom in the middle of nowhere, naked and dripping wet, praising her Lord. But time was not her concern. She was releasing herself. Losing control and herself in the presence of the Lord.

Finally, physically exhausted, mentally drained and full of hope, she wrapped a towel around her body, letting her thoroughly soaked hair drip onto her shoulders. Walking into the bedroom, she looked at herself in the mirror again, looked past her hair, past her face, into her eyes. And there, she saw life. The Lord had spoken.

She knew there were still many things she had to face; this journey was nowhere near the end. Nor was it going to be easy. She didn't know what she wanted; she didn't know what Jefferson wanted. But she knew what God wanted. He wanted her to stand, stand before her friends, stand before her enemies. And, she would proclaim that, following Psalm 118: she would not die, but live. She would trust in the Word of the Lord.

Sitting on the bed, she took a deep breath, then exhaled, releasing her fear so that she could now walk by faith. With faith, she knew she'd be able to face the day; she'd be able to stand up to it all. But first . . . she had to get some sleep.

She pulled back the thin stained blanket, threw the soaked towel on the floor and climbed in, pulling the sheets over her body. Her hair was still dripping wet, not a great idea for a black woman—perm or no perm. But, she would deal with that, and everything else, in the morning. Lifting up, she leaned over to turn off the light and her eyes focused on the clock radio. The large red digital numbers revealed the time clearly . . . *it was midnight.*

Jefferson glanced again at the huge round clock hanging above the mantel; it was exactly midnight. Sixteen hours had passed and now as a new day was birthing, he still did not have any idea where his wife was. He stood and walked through the house, turning on all the lights. He wanted their home to be shining like a Christmas tree when she returned.

Making his way back to the family room, he dropped onto the couch and sighed. Where could she be? He'd spent the entire day asking that question as he sat by the phone willing it to ring. But the phone had remained stubbornly silent. The waiting was his greatest pain. There was absolutely nothing he could do and it was killing him. Dr. Jefferson Blake was not a man used to waiting.

Now, as he held his head in his hands, his heart pleaded for his wife. All he wanted to do was see her, hold her, kiss her, and beg unashamedly for her forgiveness. He would do anything to get her back, but the fear that consumed him told him he might never have that chance.

The Bible on the end table caught his eye. They had Bibles throughout the house, almost as a reminder of the kind of life they wanted to live. Staring at the words on the leather cover, he read them aloud, "Holy Bible." Holy. Holy. Holy. He had tried to live his life as a righteous man, not perfect, just a man that loved the Lord. He was a husband, a father, a doctor, but the most important role in his life was that he was a man of God. All he had to do was look around his church on Sunday and see how important that was. There were not enough black men in the church and he believed he was called to be an example.

Jefferson's prayer had always been that when anyone looked at him, they would know he was a child of God. That God's light would shine through him. His life's walk was his witness. But what kind of testimony would he have to give now?

Already forgiven by God, he was grateful for the Blood of Jesus and God's abiding love, but would he ever be able to forgive himself? And what about Kyla, could she forgive him? Pastor Ford had said she would, but he had his doubts. He put down the Bible and stood, moving to the mirror that hung over the fireplace, but he couldn't raise his eyes. Not yet.

Where was she? Just the thought of her out there somewhere, alone and in pain was torture. He had to find her so that he could hold her, comfort her, assure her of his love.

He walked outside into the starless night. The early morning hours of Monday offered no hope as he was met only by a dark, still silence. Even the air didn't move; the neighborhood was at rest.

Thirty minutes passed and with a resigned sigh, he returned inside. It was time for him to face it—Kyla was not coming back. At least not tonight, he thought. He had to hold onto that thought—at least not tonight. Any other thoughts were too grievous to handle.

He wanted to call the police so that others would be looking for her, but he knew that no one would consider Kyla missing until twenty-four hours had passed. And what would he say anyway? That his wife had run away after she had found him in bed with her friend? He wondered how many times the police had heard that story.

He leaned back into the couch's pillows and closed his eyes. Exhaustion tried to claim him and he curled up on the couch knowing he would not get a good night's sleep, even though a full appointment book awaited him in the morning. But, it didn't matter. He would stay right here, by the door, so that he would hear Kyla as soon as she came in. And she would return; of that, he was sure. He had to be sure because if he allowed himself to think anything else, he knew he'd never survive.

Jasmine listened to the clock ticking the minutes into hours and in the darkness, she tossed with emotion. It was meant to happen. Her and Jefferson. And, she wasn't sorry. But why didn't it feel as good as she thought it would?

Finally, she sat up and turned on the light. It was just after midnight and she'd been trying to fall asleep for over two hours now. She should have been exhausted after she had spent the entire day getting her life in order—cooking, cleaning—all for Jefferson. Or was it just to keep busy?

She hugged her knees to her chest. She had hoped that Jefferson would have called her this afternoon, though she knew that was unlikely. He was probably still grieving. But Kyla would *never* return to him. Jasmine was sure of that. So, she would be here waiting for him as soon as he was ready.

Replaying the morning in her mind, she couldn't erase

Kyla's face from her mind. But why should she feel sorry for Kyla? Kyla had never done anything to help her.

Looking at the clock again, she picked up the phone. She needed to talk and her sister would just have to forgive her. The phone rang five times before a groggy Serena answered.

"This is Jasmine."

"Jasmine, what's wrong?"

"Nothing . . . I just had to talk to someone."

"Are you all right? Is everything okay?"

"Something happened today . . . I got involved with someone and I'm really happy about it," she said thinly.

"You don't sound happy. And why would you call me in the middle of the night to tell me this?"

"Well, because . . . it's Jefferson."

Silence hung in the air for several seconds. "Are you telling me that you got *involved* with Kyla's husband?" Serena whispered.

Jasmine swallowed hard. "Before you say anything, let me explain. He and Kyla broke up."

"Broke up?" Serena said, suddenly sounding wide awake. "Just last week you were telling me about a birthday party Kyla had given for him. Jasmine, this doesn't make sense."

"Well, why are you jumping all over me? They broke up and it was almost natural that Jefferson and I would get together. We've been friends for a long time."

"Yeah, and you've been friends with Kyla even longer. If she and Jefferson were having problems, you should've been the one trying to help her through—not stealing her husband."

"Stealing her husband?" Jasmine was indignant. "I didn't have to steal him."

"Okay, I'm sorry. I shouldn't have said that. But what I'm

trying to say is that even if they have broken up, do you think it's a good idea to get involved with your best friend's husband? What will this do to your friendship with Kyla?"

"I don't care about Kyla!" Jasmine snapped. "Why is it that everyone is always looking out for poor Kyla? You should be thinking about me, Serena."

"You *are* the one that I am thinking about. I don't want you to get hurt and this all seems so sudden. It just doesn't make sense."

"You know, I am so sorry I called you." Jasmine slammed down the phone. She should've known Serena would never support her. She was so much like Kyla.

This time when she clicked off the light, she was determined to fall asleep. It didn't matter what anyone said. She was going to have everything she wanted. And why shouldn't she? Kyla always got what *she* wanted.

Well, let people say what they had to say. She had her plans. And the first thing was to solidify her relationship with Jefferson and make sure he didn't try to go after Kyla.

A complete plan began to form in her mind. Tomorrow, she would make sure that Jefferson understood his future. She would go to him, apologize for what had happened, but convince him that they would be good together.

With it all clear in her mind now, she relaxed and inhaled the sweet smell of the blackberry potpourri that filled her bedroom. She wondered how long it would be before she had Jefferson in *this* bed.

Finally, she allowed herself to surrender. Tomorrow would be the most important day of her life. And with that thought, she fell asleep.

# Eleven

As the sun seeped through the French doors, Jefferson stirred. With great effort, he sat up and rubbed his eyes, then looked around, remembering. He jumped from the couch, tripping as he ran up to the bedroom. Empty.

He glanced at the steady glow of the light on the answering machine—no messages. Lifting the phone, he called information for the telephone numbers to area hospitals. The next minutes were spent checking hospital emergency rooms for anyone matching Kyla's description. Next, he called the police stations. Nothing. At least he knew she was safe, at least physically. He looked at the clock; it was just after six. Moving to the bathroom, he showered, then dressed. He made one last call and was surprised when he got the answering machine.

"Uh, Brian. This is Jefferson. I really need to talk to you, man. Uh, I don't know where you are so early in the morning, but I'm leaving for the clinic. Give me a call at the office if you get this anytime soon. Thanks, man."

Maybe Kyla had contacted Alexis and she was holding out on him. Brian would know. And, Brian would tell if he knew where Kyla was.

With slumped shoulders, he sank down onto the bed. How could he have been so stupid? His entire life was crumbling and for what? For a few minutes of lustful pleasure that he wanted more than anything to forget.

Shaking his head, he prepared for work and within an hour from when he'd awakened, he was sitting in his office, sipping watered-down coffee he had prepared in the Mr. Coffee machine that he had never learned how to use. Maybe he should have stayed at home—waiting. But when he looked down at his full calendar, he knew he couldn't do that. From ten o'clock on, every hour was filled. He looked up, peering beyond the window. He just had to see her today. She had to call or something. If she didn't, he didn't know what he would do.

He jumped when he heard the knock on his opened door.

"Hey, Jefferson. I was in the shower when you called and thought you needed something for the expansion proposal, so I decided to just come in. What's up?" Brian asked sitting down into one of the chairs.

"Uh, nothing. You really didn't have to come in, we could've done this over the phone."

"That's okay. I can get some paperwork done. What's up?" he asked again.

"Uh, I know you were at Alexis' yesterday. Did Kyla happen to call her?"

Brian frowned. "Not that I know of. But Alexis was worried when you guys didn't show up at church and then she was really concerned after she spoke with you. Is something wrong?"

Jefferson sighed and shook his head. "I don't know . . . are you sure Alexis hasn't spoken to Kyla at all?"

Brian nodded. "I'm pretty sure. What's going on with Kyla?"

Jefferson hesitated. "I don't know . . . I haven't seen her since yesterday morning when she got back from Santa Barbara."

"Are you serious? What's going on?" When Jefferson remained silent, Brian probed. "You've got to talk to me, man."

"I don't know . . . this might not be a good time. The office, other people may start coming in . . . we have to get to work . . ."

"Look, if Kyla's missing, there is no better time." Brian stood and closed the door. "There's no one else here, but as soon as people start arriving, they'll see your closed door." Brian stood over his desk. "So, talk to me."

Jefferson lowered his head. "Man, I've messed up. Big time."

"What?"

"I . . . whew, this is hard to say . . ."

When Brian sat down and crossed his legs, Jefferson continued. "I got involved with another woman . . ."

"What! You? I don't believe it!" Brian exclaimed leaning forward in his chair. "What happened? When? Who?"

"Whoa, wait a second . . ."

"I'm sorry, man. It's just that I can't even imagine you with someone besides Kyla. I never thought you'd leave her."

Jefferson sat up straight. "I am not leaving Kyla!" he almost shouted.

Brian held up his hands as if he were warding off an attack. "Okay . . ."

"First of all, it only happened once. I don't even like Jasmine . . ."

Brian's eyes widened. "You mean you've been kicking it with that woman Jasmine, Kyla's *friend*?"

"Like I said, it was only this one time."

"Man . . ."

"I can't even tell you what happened. One minute I was talking to her, and the next minute we were in bed." Jefferson pulled his hands to his face. "This is a mess."

"Yeah, I'll say. How did Kyla find out?"

"She walked in on us."

Brian bounced back in his chair. "Oh, God! You did this in your own house? What were you thinking?"

"I know . . ."

"Never do that in your house, Jefferson. You're a doctor, you have money. Take her to a hotel. In your house! Oh, man!"

Jefferson raised his eyebrows, but didn't respond.

Brian continued, "So, Kyla found you in bed with Jasmine."

"Well, not exactly. I mean, I was in the shower. I don't know where she found Jasmine."

"Wait!" Brian exclaimed, holding his hand high. He stood and leaned over the desk. "So, she didn't actually *see* you two together." His question sounded like a statement.

Jefferson shook his head.

Brian slapped his hands on his legs. "Well, then you're home free."

Now, it was Jefferson's turn to frown. "What?"

"You are home free. Just don't admit that anything happened."

"What?"

"Just tell Kyla that no matter what she saw, she's wrong."

"You want me to lie to my wife?"

"If that's what it takes to get you through this."

Jefferson narrowed his eyes. "Brian, there are a lot of reasons why, but I'm not going to lie to Kyla."

"Why not? This is only about sex."

"Well, I'm not going to lie. I love her too much to do that."

"And that's why she found you with Jasmine."

Jefferson winced.

"Look, man," Brian started. "I'm just trying to get you out of this. Believe me, the best way to handle these things is to just flat-out deny it."

Jefferson's chuckle was bitter. "You sound like you have some experience."

"Some. But that doesn't matter. I'm just trying to save you and Kyla."

"I understand that, but I can't go that way. I've already sinned against my wife. I'm not going to complicate this by covering it up with another sin."

"I understand what you *want* to do. What I'm talking about is what you *have* to do to save yourself."

"I don't care what you say, I'm not going that way."

Brian laughed. "Man, I'm talking about lying. You were in bed with another woman." He held out his hands as if he were weighing the options. "Tell me, which is worse?"

Jefferson's voice raised slightly. "I know what I did. And, I know how I'm going to handle it and it's not going to be by going backwards."

Brian shrugged. "Whatever, but I'm telling you, man . . ." He paused taking in Jefferson's unshaven face and reddened eyes. "So, you haven't heard from her at all?"

Jefferson shook his head. "I have no idea where she is."

"I'm sure she's okay . . ."

"That's my prayer."

"Jefferson . . . look, the best way for you to get out of this once you do find her . . ."

Jefferson held up his hands. "No more, Brian. I don't need any more advice like that."

Brian shrugged. "Well, let me call Alexis and see if she's heard anything."

"No, don't do that. I only called you to find out if Alexis had heard from Kyla. But if she hasn't, I don't want to tell Alexis about this. At least not yet. Oh man," Jefferson said shaking his head slowly. "I'm just praying that at some point today, Kyla will at least contact me."

"Well, if Alexis says anything, I'll let you know." Brian stood. "Jefferson, I know you'll find a way to work this out. It'll be all right." He reached around and patted his friend's shoulders.

"Thanks," Jefferson said. More than anything he wanted to believe his friend was right.

With trembling hands, Kyla opened the Bible and went straight to Isaiah 43. *When thou passest through the waters, I will be with thee; and through the rivers, they shall not overflow thee: when thou walkest through the fire, thou shalt not be burned; neither shall the flame kindle upon thee. For I am the Lord, thy God.* She closed her eyes, then placed the Bible back on the table.

Doubt had accompanied the light of day and now Kyla wasn't sure how she'd handle the future that loomed menacingly before her. Her eyes roamed to the mirror. She'd done well, she thought. With hair braided and wrinkles steamed from her clothes, now she looked more like a homeless person than a battered woman, something she ruefully considered an improvement.

Still staring at her reflection, she picked up the phone and dialed the number, her fingers moving quickly, before she changed her mind.

On the first ring, her daughter answered the telephone. "Hello, Carrington residence."

Tears stung her eyes, but Kyla was able to keep the shaking from her voice. "Hi, sweetie."

"Hi, Mommy! Where are you? You didn't call me back last night. Are you and Daddy coming up here? Are you going to go to Misty and Kristy's party? Can I stay?"

Kyla laughed through her tears. "Hold on. I can't answer so many questions. How are you?"

"I'm fine. I'm having a real good time. Papa and I went fishing again and then I played on the beach with Misty and Kristy. Can I stay up here so that I can go to their birthday party? It's Saturday and Daddy said he had to talk to you about it."

Kyla was sure her heart had stopped beating. "You spoke to your father? What did he say?"

Nicole was silent for a moment. "He said he had to ask you."

"Where was your father when he called?" Against her will, the questions flowed.

"He was home, Mommy. What's wrong?"

"Nothing, sweetie."

"Well, can I go to the party on Saturday? Can you and Daddy come up for the party too?"

"I don't know. Anyway, how're Mama and Papa?"

"They're fine. Mama went for a walk, but Papa is sitting right here. Do you want to talk to him?"

"No!" she said a little too quickly, knowing that as soon as her father heard her voice he would know something was wrong. Obviously, Jefferson had called but had kept his secret tryst just that—a secret—and for that she was grateful. She would break all of this to them when the time was right. "No, just tell Papa I'll call later, okay? I love you, sweetie. Kiss Papa for me."

"Okay, and kiss Daddy for me. Bye!"

It took a moment for her to replace the receiver. "Kiss Daddy for me." Kyla wondered whether her lips would ever touch Jefferson's again and a single tear rolled down her cheek.

Wiping it away, she shook her head. "Stop it, Kyla!" she scolded herself aloud. "You have to move on."

Not letting time pass, she dialed the second number and again, it was answered on the first ring. Just the sound of Alexis' voice made Kyla relax a bit.

"Hey, it's me."

"Kyla. Where have you been? Jefferson called me yesterday and I left a message for you this morning. I was really beginning to worry."

"I'm sorry."

"Kyla . . ." Alexis began slowly. "Kyla, what's wrong?"

She would have smiled if a lump had not formed in her throat. It was uncanny how she and Alexis could read each other.

145

When she remained silent, Alexis asked again. "Kyla, what is it?"

Kyla wanted to tell her friend, but only tears fell. This was unbearable—it hurt to think about it, but now it was impossible to say out loud.

"Kyla, please! Where are you?"

"I'm at a hotel," she sobbed. "I don't know where."

"Give me the telephone number," Alexis spoke slowly. "I'll call the hotel, find out where you are, then come and get you."

"No," she sniffed back her tears. "I'm going to be fine. It's just that this is so hard."

"Kyla, what happened?" Alexis asked, her own voice now trembling. "Did someone die?"

"Die," Kyla repeated. "That almost explains it."

"Oh, my gosh! Who?"

"Not who, Alexis. What . . ." Kyla paused, trying to build the nerve to continue. "When I got home yesterday . . . I found . . . Jefferson is having an affair!" The last words came out in a wail.

"Oh my goodness! I don't believe you! With *who*?" Alexis didn't try to hide her astonishment. This couldn't be true. Not Jefferson.

Kyla inhaled a deep breath. "With . . . Jasmine."

There was a moment's pause and Alexis knew from the pit in her own stomach that it was true.

"Kyla, I'm on my way!"

"No, Alex, you have to work. I'll just see you later."

"I don't care what you say. Either I'm coming to get you or you're going to get your butt to me as fast as you can!"

With lips that had been trembling only minutes before, a

half-smile came to her face. "Thanks, Alexis. Just give me some time and I'll meet you at your office."

"Come to my apartment. Are you sure you're going to be all right?"

"I'm okay, especially after talking to you. I'll see you in a little while."

"Okay, but if you're not here in an hour, I'm sending out the cavalry."

"Give me two hours. I drove for a long time."

"Kyla . . . you know I love you," Alexis said before she hung up the phone.

Leaning back against the soft leather of her chair, Alexis sighed and shook her head. Never did she believe Jasmine would go this far. But what was even more astonishing was that Jefferson had been such easy prey.

It just didn't make sense. Jefferson loved Kyla, but more importantly, he loved God. Not that these things didn't happen with Christians. In her years of walking with the Lord, Alexis had had her own trials and temptations, troubles and struggles. She was not surprised that Jefferson had been tempted, but she was surprised that he had stumbled. And, with *Jasmine.*

Alexis stood and hurriedly stuffed papers into her briefcase. Work would have to wait; she had a friend to rescue.

Jasmine couldn't concentrate and right now she needed to be focused. But there was nothing more important than what she was going to do this afternoon. She had to make her move on Jefferson before he and Kyla had any chance of getting back together. Kyla was surely up in Santa Barbara getting comfort from her mother and father. But that wouldn't last long. The Carringtons were probably at this very moment trying to convince Kyla to return to Jefferson. Jasmine knew she would have to have a quick plan of action if she had any hopes of achieving her goal.

She looked at her watch; only five minutes had passed since the last time she had checked. She sighed, then looked up as she heard the knock.

"Hey, Jasmine. I need you to do me a big favor." Rose, the Vice-President of Finance and her boss, leaned against the carpeted wall of her cubicle. "I'm not feeling well; so I'm gonna get out of here. Would you look over the sales projections and then send them upstairs for me?"

"Sure." Jasmine grinned at her luck. With her boss out of the way, she'd be able to leave early too.

"I really appreciate you covering me like this," Rose sneezed. "This is going to be a tough week with the presentation on Friday and I need to be in tip-top form."

"Don't worry about a thing."

"Thanks! By the way, I looked over your part of the presentation. You did a great job."

"Thank you."

Rose sneezed and brought a tissue to her face. "You know, you're next in line for the Senior Analyst position."

"That's what I'm hoping . . ."

"I'll be putting in a good word."

Jasmine smiled. "Well, you can get out of here. I'll take care of these numbers."

When Rose had left, Jasmine leaned back in her chair. She had planned to tell her boss that her grandfather/grandmother/godmother had died. All she had to do was remember which one of them she hadn't used before. But now that wouldn't be necessary. Leaning forward, she perused the sheets she'd been given, then pulled out her calculator. It would take her about an hour to complete this project. Good. That would still give her time to get home before noon.

She turned her attention to the numbers, ignoring the chatting associates and ringing phones that surrounded her. She was on a mission. When she finally looked up, it was eleven-thirty. Calculating the time in her head, she knew she'd be home within an hour. Then, with another two hours to cook, take a bath, do her hair, get dressed—it would be about three. Three o'clock. Maybe three would be her new lucky number.

Putting her hand over her mouth, she stifled her laugh, trying to hold down her excitement. She scribbled a note on top of the report she'd just finished, then dropped it in her "out" box. Taking a moment to straighten the papers on her desk, she grabbed her suit jacket, purse and briefcase and ran from her office. She didn't even look back when her secretary called after her.

"If I'm lucky, she'll just think I had some sort of family emergency," Jasmine thought. "Maybe she'll just think my grandfather/grandmother/godmother died," she giggled.

She ran into the parking lot and jumped into her car. Rose might be thinking about promotions and that was good. But she couldn't begin to think about that now. There was a big night with Jefferson to prepare for and she was going to be ready. Turning on the ignition, she pressed down hard on the accelerator and sped from the SONY parking lot.

To Alexis, it seemed like forever, but only two hours had passed before the doorman finally called up, announcing Kyla's arrival. Standing in front of her opened door she waited, and within minutes the elevator delivered her friend. At the sight of each other, they embraced and broke down in tears.

When Kyla stepped into Alexis' condo, she stopped crying. She always loved coming here; her friend's home was so different than her own. Alexis' mark of creativity was stamped throughout the high-tech, high-rise apartment.

Taking her by the hand, Alexis led Kyla to the black and white striped couch, hugged her again, then pulled back, quickly taking in her friend's appearance. The Kyla who was always perfectly put together, with every strand of hair in place and every outfit perfectly matched, looked like a waif. There were dark circles under her puffy eyelids and her wavy, unruly hair was braided.

"Well . . . here I am."

"Here you are . . ."

Kyla smiled. "I know you want to know what happened. All the details. You're just too polite to ask. Unlike me."

"You're right. I do want to know, but I'm worried about you. Are you hungry? When was the last time you had something to eat?"

"I don't remember."

"That means you need to eat."

"Alexis, just the thought of food makes me want to puke."

"Okay . . ."

"I just want to talk." Kyla turned away, unable to look at Alexis. "You know, I never thought this would happen to me. I just knew that Jefferson loved me."

"Jefferson *does* love you. No matter what happened. You have to believe that."

"I don't know what to believe anymore. Finding him in bed with Jasmine changes everything."

Alexis' eyes widened. "You actually found them in bed together?"

"Well, not together. Jasmine was in my bed. Jefferson was in the shower."

"In the shower. That makes sense."

"What?"

"Well, if it really happened, Jefferson was in the shower trying to wash her off of him."

"It was too late for that! And, what was worse was that he called me Jasmine. There are so many women in his life that he can't tell the difference in our voices."

Alexis reached for Kyla's hands. "Stop. With what you just said, I know what's missing. Girl, we need to pray."

"Alexis . . . I don't want to right now."

"And that's just why we have to. This is clearly spiritual warfare if you're talking about all of Jefferson's women. Here," she said reaching out again. "Give me your hands."

When Alexis bowed her head, Kyla followed, closed her eyes and listened to the words Alexis prayed. And when Alexis asked the Lord to lead them and help Kyla find peace in this situation, she opened her mouth and uttered in the spirit, praying that the Lord would answer them.

"Now," Alexis said as she dropped Kyla's hands. "Now we can talk. So, what did Jefferson say?"

"About what?"

"About what happened."

"Alexis, it's not like I stood there waiting for Jefferson to fill me in on all the details."

"Have you talked to Jefferson at all?"

"No."

"Well, you have to talk to him. Because there is one thing I know for sure. I don't know how she did it, but I know that your husband did not get into bed of his own free will with that . . . snake!"

Kyla turned and her eyes bore into Alexis. "You *did* call her a snake. Did you know about this all along?"

"No! No!" Alexis rushed to clear up that question. "I *never* thought anything was going on with the two of them. I still don't believe it now."

"You had to think *something*," Kyla said as she folded her arms in front of her.

"Now come on, Kyla. Think about it. You know me. If I thought anything, I would have not only told you, but I would've kicked Jasmine's *and* Jefferson's behinds myself! I just had a feeling, an intuition." She paused. "Whenever Jasmine was around you and Jefferson, she always made it a point to be *with* Jefferson."

"What do you mean?"

"It wasn't any one thing. Just a lot of stuff added together. I mean, think back to Jefferson's party. Remember when Jasmine wanted you to give her a ride home?"

Kyla nodded.

"That whole thing was kind of strange. It was so obvious that you and Jefferson wanted to be alone, but she seemed determined to break that up."

"Umm." Kyla thought back to the night of the party and

remembered when Jasmine had kissed Jefferson. She'd had a bad feeling then.

"And then, there were those times when she wanted to stay with you guys. That was strange too. But to tell you the truth, Kyla, I thought it was stranger that you let her stay. Sometimes you're a little too nice for your own good."

"That's not fair, Alexis. If you were in trouble, I would have let you stay with us."

"Yeah, and I would've stayed for a few days, but I wouldn't have kept running back to your house, like Jasmine did. There was just something weird about the whole thing. I don't think I would've let some woman stay at my house like that."

"You would've if you thought that woman was your friend." The friends sat in silence for a few moments. "Do you think they've been sleeping together all this time?" Kyla asked softly.

"No, Kyla. Definitely not."

"Well, obviously, there was something missing for him." She lowered her head in her hands. "I don't know what I'm going to do. I can't even think. My head is so loaded with visions of them together."

Alexis rubbed Kyla's back. "The first thing you have to do is talk to Jefferson."

"I can't . . ."

"Nothing can be worked out until you talk to him and find out what happened."

"So what do you propose, Alexis? That I walk into the clinic and ask Jefferson for a play-by-play account of what happened? I don't need to know. What I saw was more than enough. And, it wouldn't matter anyway. It's over between us. I'm never going back."

"Never going back? Kyla, what are you saying?"

She stood, moving to the balcony windows, and crossed her arms in front of her as her eyes teared. "I'm going to divorce Jefferson." Her voice was barely a whisper.

"Kyla, you haven't even *talked* to him. And this is not just about you. What about Nicole? You've got to think about your entire family."

"That's what I'm doing. Nicole is the most important person to me, but I can't live with Jefferson just because he's her father. Especially if he's in love with someone else."

"Jefferson doesn't love Jasmine! He loves you."

"I don't know how you can say that. There is no way he could have been in bed with her if he loved me."

"That would be true if we lived in some fantasy world. But that's not the way it is. There is no doubt in my mind that Jefferson loves you totally."

"Well, I choose not to accept the way he shows his love."

Alexis sighed. "You're probably really tired. Do you want to lie down for a while?"

"No, but, I have a big favor to ask you. I have to give Jefferson a few days to pack his things. Would you mind if I stayed with you until he moves out?"

Alexis kept her voice steady. "Of course. You can stay here as long as you need to. But are you really going to ask Jefferson to move out without knowing what happened?"

"My husband had sex with one of my best friends. What else is there to know?"

"Kyla, people have been able to work out marriages after adultery. This has happened to *thousands* of women."

154

"I don't care who it's happened to. It's never happened to *me!*" Kyla exclaimed, her voice rising an octave.

"Calm down. You know I'm only trying to help."

"Alexis, the way you can help me now is to let me stay here a few days. I'll give you money for food and everything."

"Oh, please. My business is doing well enough to feed us both for a few days," Alexis said, trying to make the conversation lighter. Narrowing her eyes, Alexis turned away so that Kyla wouldn't be able to see her face. "So, where do you think Jefferson is right now?"

"I don't know . . . I guess he's at the clinic."

"Then you know what you should do? Go home. This would be a perfect time for you to run over and get some fresh clothes."

Kyla looked at her watch. It was almost three. She could get in the house, get a few things before Jefferson ever came home.

"May I use your phone?" Kyla asked. With each number she dialed, Kyla's heart pounded harder. What if Jefferson were home? The phone rang six times before the answering machine picked up.

"That's a good idea, Alex," Kyla said as she picked up her purse from the table. "I'll be right back."

Alexis hugged her friend. "Everything is going to be all right."

"I know." Kyla took a deep breath. "I'm going to pull myself together, get control of this whole thing. Thank you, Alex. I am so grateful . . . I don't know what I would do or where I would go . . ."

"Girl, stop it. This is what *real* best friends are for. Now hurry back. I want to tell you what's been going on with me and Brian," Alexis said trying to get her friend to focus on something else. But when Kyla barely nodded, Alexis could feel her friend's pain.

Alexis closed the door and glanced at the brass clock on her wall. Three o'clock exactly. She picked up the phone, dialed the number and as soon as it was answered spoke quickly and boldly. "Shannon. This is Alexis Ward. Put me through to Dr. Blake. I don't care if he's performing surgery on the President of the United States. Tell him to get on the phone now!"

# Twelve

Jasmine edged her car against the curb, turned off the ignition and glanced at the clock. Three-fifteen. Perfect. She peered through the window, making sure she had a clear view of the Blakes' front door. Jefferson wasn't home yet; she had been calling all day. But that was a good sign—he wasn't sitting home pining away for Kyla.

She knew she had to see him tonight. There was no telling when Kyla would be back. Her mother was probably talking Kyla into returning at this very moment. But by the time Kyla finally did return, it would be over. She would have Jefferson totally in her possession by then.

She leaned back in her seat and allowed the tension to ebb from her body. All had gone well; from the meal to her outfit, she held all the keys that would lead her to Jefferson. She smoothed her hand over the red tank dress she'd chosen. Sleeveless, short, simple.

She flipped down the sun visor and reached to get her makeup kit from her purse. A smile filled her face. Perfect makeup, perfect hair, she was the perfect woman for Jefferson.

She arranged the casserole dish on the passenger seat,

wrapping the dish-warmer securely around it. Even if it cooled, she'd heat the chicken and rice once she got inside. Jefferson wouldn't mind. He would just be glad to have a woman who really knew how to take care of him.

This was the hard part now—just waiting. Not knowing what time he'd come home. But, she didn't care how long it took; she'd be here for him when he arrived.

Her head turned towards a loud screech—a little girl being chased by a boy. The street was filled with children enjoying these first days of summer. While the children annoyed her, she was grateful for the distraction. Jefferson wouldn't notice her car when he drove up and she'd be able to surprise him. They'd sit down together, eat, have a serious talk . . . by the end of the night, Jefferson would be hers, again. "Come home, Jefferson. Come home and see what's waiting for you," she murmured.

She looked down the block as a car approached. "No!" she exclaimed, as it got closer. "No! No!" she panted as she watched the cream-colored car slow to a crawl and finally turn into the Blakes' driveway. She watched as Kyla sat immobile, as if trying to decide what to do.

"What are you doing back so soon?" Jasmine hissed as she thought about the plans she had for the evening.

Minutes passed. Jasmine scooted down in her seat but kept her eyes glued to the Blakes' driveway. When Kyla didn't move, Jasmine slowly sat up. She calmed her breathing and tapped her fingers against the steering wheel. "Okay, Jasmine. Think. Think!" she said to herself, trying desperately to figure out how to revise her plan. Her fingers tapped more rapidly. She knew if Kyla got anywhere near Jefferson, she would wipe

Jasmine right from his mind. Poof! That simply, her chance at happiness would be gone forever!

As she sat there, a new plan formed in her mind. "Okay," she continued her conversation with herself. "I'll just walk over to her and tell her that Jefferson and I had a date. We're going out to dinner."

Jasmine bit her lip, then continued. "I'll tell her I'm sorry for what happened, but that this was all inevitable. I'll tell her that Jefferson and I are in love and that he was planning on getting a divorce anyway."

Her hands trembled as she opened her door and stepped out. She moved slowly towards the Lexus, then stopped suddenly as Kyla drove into the garage and closed the door behind her.

"Shoot!" Jasmine shouted. Now, she would have to walk up to the front door. But that might not work. If Kyla saw her standing outside, she would never open the door. Returning to her car, she banged back against the seat and closed her eyes, trying to calm the pounding in her chest. She had known that Kyla would come back home at some point, but what was she doing back so soon? Maybe she had only come to get some clothes. That had to be it! She was not here to stay. That's why she'd come when she knew Jefferson wouldn't be there, Jasmine reasoned.

Still, Jefferson might come home early, see Kyla, and who knew what would happen then. She glanced at the clock again. She couldn't be rash; whatever she decided to do, had to be well planned and something that would keep Kyla away from Jefferson permanently.

With a half-smile, she slowly nodded her head. She knew just what she would tell Kyla to make sure she never came back again. Yes, she would give Kyla just a few more minutes and if she wasn't out of the house by then, Jasmine would make sure that Kyla would regret this day for the rest of her life.

Kyla opened the door and stepped inside. She moved passed the stacks of food lined on the shelves in the pantry and into the kitchen, raised her hand to her mouth in an instant of agony.

In the family room, she noticed a blanket sprawled along the couch. All of the leather pillows were propped at one end. Her heart ached. She could tell Jefferson had slept here last night.

She lifted the blanket to her face and closed her eyes. Inhaling its scent, she could feel Jefferson against her, his arms wrapped around her, protecting her. She could feel the years of their marriage. Maybe she should just see him, just talk to him . . .

She shook her head and threw the blanket on the floor. She would not allow her emotions to override her good sense. She could never trust Jefferson again.

When she moved into the living room, she stopped. The stairs loomed before her. The stairs that had led to her discovery. She started up, grasping the brass handrail for balance. She tried to clear her thoughts, but her mind betrayed her with each tread. Each vivid image increased the hurt, the pain, the ache. She shook her head, rebuking the thoughts that invaded and willing her mind to focus on the task at hand.

"Maybe I should have asked Alexis to do this," she thought. "Or maybe I should have had her come with me."

At the top of the stairs, the bedroom was in front of her and she couldn't move. She noticed the bags she had dropped yesterday and picked them up, then walked across the hallway into Nicole's room. She pulled the outfits from the bag and began carefully hanging them in the closet. As she worked, she couldn't keep the questions from her mind. What would Nicole's life be like now?

Finishing, Kyla looked around the room and sighed. She went to one of the bookcases that lined the walls and picked up a book. As she fingered the pages, she eyed the yellow room. Minutes passed as she wondered about the future of her family.

"As God is my witness, Nicole, I will protect you through all of this." She wiped away the tears that had fallen onto the book.

With unsteady steps, she went to her bedroom and stood at the door. The bed was made, though not very well. Everything else was in perfect order. No sign at all of what had happened here; Jefferson's futile attempt to wipe it away. But no matter what he did, yesterday was now part of their history.

She remained still, her eyes glued to the bed. In that bed, their marriage and their entire lives had been changed.

She moved quickly to her closet, pulling underwear, clothes, shoes, and stuffed each piece into her weekend bag. It would only be a few days, she didn't need much. As she turned off the closet light, she glanced around the bedroom. Tears burned as her eyes roamed her favorite room. Almost every piece of furniture in the master suite had been specially designed to provide a retreat for her and Jefferson. So many wonderful times had been spent here. And, everything had ended here.

The ringing phone startled her and she stared at the machine. Had Jefferson somehow found out that she was here? With hesitant steps, she moved forward and turned up the volume of the answering machine. She heard the beep, then listened to the message.

"Hello, Kyla and Jefferson. This is Pastor. Kyla, please give me a call. It's important. Thanks, and have a blessed day, you two." It wasn't until the machine beeped indicating the end of the message, that she allowed herself to breathe.

At least it wasn't Jefferson. Noticing there were six other messages, Kyla rewound the machine and pressed the button for the first message to play.

"Jefferson, this is Jasmine. I've been trying to reach you. I want to get together tonight so that we can have the talk you wanted and . . ."

With a shaky hand, she turned off the machine in the middle of the message and held back a sob. All doubts were now gone. She and Jefferson were finished. She walked into the hallway and started down the steps. "How am I supposed to do this?" she cried. But even as the question left her lips, she already knew the answer. The Lord would get her through.

Jefferson sped up the hill. Never had he been as glad as he was at this very moment that he lived so close to the clinic. He knew Kyla would still be home; Alexis had timed her call perfectly, with just enough time to tell him exactly what she thought of him. Shannon had knocked on his office door, announcing that he had an emergency call and even though he was with a patient, he had excused himself and taken the call at

Shannon's desk, knowing that it had to be something pertaining to Kyla.

"Jefferson, this is Alexis."

And at that moment, Jefferson knew Kyla was safe. "How's Kyla? Where is she?"

"Oh, don't worry. I'm going to tell you. Not because of you. But for Kyla. Because no matter how much of a jerk you are, I think you two still belong together. But Jefferson, how could you?"

He had closed his eyes and leaned onto Shannon's desk. The headache that had started yesterday worsened with each syllable of contempt he heard in Alexis' voice.

"Alexis, please. I just want to see Kyla. Just tell me where she is."

"She's on her way home. Don't worry, she just left me. It'll take her ten minutes at least. So you have more than enough time to talk to me."

"Alex, whatever you're thinking, you're right. There is nothing you can say to me that I haven't said to myself. But I've got to go. I've got to see Kyla." He'd hung up the phone eager to finish with his patient.

Now, as he turned his car at the bottom of the street, he wondered if Kyla would ever be able to forgive him. Well, getting her forgiveness would become his job. He would tell her that no matter how many years it took, he would earn her love, her trust, her forgiveness.

The garage door opened and he sighed with relief. She was still here! As he pulled inside his stomach twisted with anxiety, but at least Kyla was home. He had barely turned off the Range Rover before he was out of the car and inside the house.

Jasmine couldn't believe it! She was just about to go inside and had to rush back to her car when Jefferson drove up. In his haste, he hadn't noticed her.

She slammed her fist against the steering wheel, then sat back so hard, the casserole dish in the seat wobbled. But, she was not about to give up.

Again, she got out of the car and almost ran to the front door. She tried to peek through the windows, but the curtains were drawn. As she raised her hand to knock, she stopped suddenly. Jefferson might get mad, she thought. She tried once again to peer through the window, then turned away. Back in her car, she sat straight up, her eyes posted on the house. She would wait, but not for long. She had every intention of winning this battle.

Kyla came down the stairs slowly, with the bag on her shoulder. It was as if her life were coming to an end.

She dropped her bag on top of the blanket and went to the fireplace. The pictures on the mantel stared back at her, and she picked up one of her and Jefferson. They'd been on a picnic that day, a year before Nicole was born. They were so happy. They were *always* happy. So, why had Jefferson turned to another woman? What was wrong with their marriage? Why hadn't he told her he was unhappy?

She picked up her bag, then moved through the kitchen into the pantry. There was no way she could stay a minute longer.

"Kyla!" Jefferson exclaimed. "Thank God you're all right."

Jefferson watched his wife back away from him and his

heart dropped. The fear that crossed her face matched the pain in his heart. "Kyla, please. I need to talk to you," he begged.

Her mouth opened wide, but words would not escape.

Jefferson stepped toward her, moving tentatively until he had backed Kyla against the center island in the kitchen. They stood close, their breathing taking on matching rhythms. Slowly, she lifted her head and locked her eyes on his face, searching for answers.

He lifted his arms. He knew that if he could touch her . . . if he could touch her they would be able to put this all behind them. He lowered his arms onto her shoulders.

"Get away from me! Don't you touch me! Don't you ever touch me!" Her vicious scream echoed throughout the room.

Jefferson jumped back. "No, Kyla, no. I love you! I have to tell you what happened."

"Love? How can you talk about love? You don't know what love is."

He lowered his head. He had planned the words he would speak if the Lord would only bring Kyla back to him, but now his words sounded so empty. "Kyla, I am *so* sorry. You will never know. There . . . there is really nothing I can say. Except that I love you with all my heart . . ."

The warmth of his voice seared through to her heart and her knees weakened. She moved away. "Do you think saying you're sorry is going to change anything?" she cried. She turned back facing him, ready for the fight. "How could you do this to me, Jefferson? How could you do this to us?"

"I . . . don't . . . know," he stammered. "I . . . Kyla . . ." He stopped. What could he say? "Kyla . . . you're right. Saying sorry doesn't change anything, but there is one thing that will never change and that is . . . *I love you.*"

"How can you even form your lying lips to say that to me? How can you say you love me when you were in bed with my best friend?"

"No . . . it's not what you think. That's not what happened."

Kyla searched his eyes. "Are you saying that you didn't have sex with her?"

Jefferson hesitated, hearing the hope in her voice and Brian's words came back to him. "Just tell her it didn't happen . . ."

He gazed into her eyes, then turned away. "No, that's not what I'm saying. All I'm saying is that there is no way I could ever explain to you what happened, because I don't even know . . . not really. But I do know that I love you and I will do anything . . . anything I have to do to make this up to you." Jefferson stepped towards his wife. "I know how much I hurt you, Kyla. It's all I can think about. I can't eat. I can't sleep. But I have prayed and prayed that somehow you'll be able to find it in your heart to forgive me."

"Forgive you for what? For having an affair? Or for being stupid enough to be caught with her in my bed?"

"There was no affair," Jefferson said wearily. "It was only that one time, Ky. Just Saturday . . ."

Kyla picked up her bag.

"No, please wait. It's true. We were not having an affair. It just happened this once. Jasmine came over. I kept trying to push her away . . . it just happened. It had nothing to do with my love for you . . ." Jefferson stopped, realizing how ridiculous it all sounded. When he saw the look on his wife's face, he continued in a whisper. "Kyla . . . I'm telling the truth."

"Let me tell you what the truth is, Jefferson. I come home

from a weekend with my parents. I find my husband in bed with my friend. *That's* the truth."

Jefferson's shoulders slumped. "Kyla, I will say this until you believe it. I am so sorry. I love you so much." His eyes pleaded for her understanding.

"I'm supposed to believe that you love me. Based on what?"

"Based on everything that we've had, Kyla. Based on all of the years. Don't base this on one night, one mistake."

"Everything we had and all of those years didn't keep your pants on and your butt out of our bed with my friend!"

Jefferson winced as her emotions pierced him. He had known she'd be hurt, but the depth of her pain and anger rocked him.

Silence hung between them before Jefferson slumped into the chair. When he looked up, tears filled his eyes and his voice was soft. "Kyla, all I can say is that I love you. Please just tell me, what do I have to do? What do I have to do to earn your forgiveness?"

She had to fight back her own tears. "Just like that? I'm supposed to forget all that happened? That might be easy for you. But what about me? It's not simple for me."

"It's not simple for me either. I hurt, because I hurt you. I would never do anything on purpose to cause you any kind of pain. I just want to make this up to you."

Kyla walked over to the chair where Jefferson sat and stood directly over him. With narrowed eyes, she stared down at him. He tried to meet her stare, but through her eyes, he could see her pain and had to look away. His entire body began to shake.

"Jefferson, you can *never* make this up to me. It's over between us. I want you out of this house and I want you out before the weekend."

"No! I . . . no!" He raised his voice as he stood. "I will not do that, Kyla. I will *not* move out. We have to find a way to work this out. What about us? What about our family? What about Nicole?"

"What about Nicole! Jefferson, what about the fact that Nicole was supposed to come home with me, and if she had *your daughter* would have found you in bed with her Auntie Jasmine. You weren't thinking about your family when you had Jasmine up in *my* bed."

Turning, she walked away from him, toward the door, but as she got to the pantry, she turned back. "If there is any bit of the man that I loved left in you, you won't make this difficult." She hurled her words across the room like sharpened spears. "Just leave, Jefferson. Get out. I want you out of my life!"

Kyla slammed the door, leaving a bewildered, shattered Jefferson buckled over in absolute, sheer pain.

As soon as the garage door opened, Jasmine sat up. It seemed like minutes passed before the Lexus pulled out. Jasmine peered through her windshield, making sure Kyla was alone.

She watched Kyla drive down the hill, then looked towards the open garage door. Jefferson was probably really upset right now and she could comfort him. But, there was something else she had to do. She had to make sure Kyla was returning to Santa Barbara.

Jasmine started the car and sped down the hill. At the bottom, Kyla's car was stopped at the light. She waited a half-block back, until the light changed before she pulled into the traffic behind Kyla. They drove for several blocks before Jasmine watched as Kyla drove past the freeway ramp.

"Oh no," Jasmine whispered. "Where are you going?" She continued to follow, her fingers tapping the steering wheel. When Kyla turned onto Wilshire, Jasmine had her answer. Kyla pulled up to the valet in Alexis' building and jumped from the car. Jasmine noticed the bag she had with her. At least that was a good sign.

She turned her car around. What was going on? Were they separating? How long would Kyla be gone? Now, being with Jefferson tonight took on greater importance.

She returned to the Blakes' house and turned into their driveway. The garage door was down. She smoothed her dress as she rang the front door. No answer. She rang the bell again. And again. And again. Still, no answer. She stood there for five minutes, ringing the bell before she finally slumped away.

Where was he? She wondered if she should wait, but knew in her heart that all the plans for tonight were over. She started her car and backed out of the driveway. The night may have been over, but Jasmine's plans were not. As long as Kyla and Jefferson were separated, she knew she had a chance. She would just have to make sure their separation was lasting.

# Thirteen

For the second time that day, Alexis stood in the hallway, waiting for the elevator. To her surprise, the doorman had just called up, announcing Kyla's arrival. After the call she'd made to Jefferson, she was sure he would have run into his house like a king staking claim to his kingdom, prepared to rescue his wife and save his marriage.

"Wow! What happened to you?" Alexis asked when she saw Kyla's face. "You look like you've just seen a ghost."

Kyla dropped her bag in the middle of the floor. "I did. I just saw two."

"Two what?"

"Two ghosts—Jefferson and Jasmine."

Alexis swallowed hard. "You just saw Jefferson and Jasmine . . . together?"

"Oh, no," Kyla said. "Not together. Jefferson came home early, but Jasmine was following me like she was in the middle of some *I Spy* movie. She tried to stay a few cars behind, but I saw her as soon as I turned onto Slauson. She followed me all the way to your front door."

"No way! This girl has really gone off the deep end. She

didn't try to say anything to you?" Alexis asked sitting next to Kyla.

"No, not that I would've stopped and talked to her. This whole afternoon was unreal. Just as I was ready to leave my house, Jefferson shows up!"

"Really?" Alexis pretended to be surprised.

"Yeah, he came home and came running in the house like I was supposed to be waiting for him. We had a huge fight, and when I left, that's when I saw Jasmine."

"I don't get that part. Maybe she wasn't really following you."

"I'm not being paranoid, if that's what you think. Like I said, I first noticed her when I crossed Slauson, but I didn't pay any attention until I was halfway up LaBrea and saw that it *really* was her."

"What do you think that was all about?"

"I don't know, but whatever her problem is, it's getting out of hand. First, she sleeps with my husband and now she's following me. She's scary."

"Kyla, she's crazy, but the witch is harmless."

"What she did with Jefferson wasn't harmless."

"Okay, but I still don't think there's anything for you to worry about. As funny as it may seem, I think she considers herself your friend and I don't think she wants to hurt you."

Kyla wrinkled her face and looked at Alexis sideways. "I can't think of anything that could have hurt me more."

Alexis' face softened. "I know, sweetie. I think she's acting out her hurt, not deliberately hurting you. So, did you and Jefferson get to talk at all?"

"Talk? I was screaming like a madwoman." Kyla rested

her elbows on her knees and held her head. "Alexis, I am so scared."

Alexis put her arms around her friend. "You're the one who's always quoting 2 Timothy 1:7. You know how the devil uses fear."

"I know God is with me and that this whole thing will somehow be turned around for His glory. But how can anything good come out of this?" She wanted to burst into tears again. The emotions were there, but now she felt hollow—like there was nothing left inside.

"Give it to God, girl. You're trying to handle this and you can't. Give it to God, and listen to what the Lord wants you to do. You taught me that."

"I'm trying. I keep praying and praising. But inside, everything is all mixed up. Then, when I saw Jefferson . . ."

"Wait!" Alexis said, then held up her hands as a thought came to her mind. "You still haven't had anything to eat, have you?"

Kyla shook her head.

"Look, if you're going to stay with me, you have to eat. I don't know how to take care of sick people." She went to her kitchen, banging the cabinets as she yelled out to Kyla. "So, I'm going to feed you."

Kyla sat in the living room, running her fingers along the stripes in the couch, and looked up when she heard Alexis return.

"The only thing is . . . I don't have any food," Alexis whined, her eyes drooped downward like a lost puppy.

For the first time in days, Kyla laughed, a hearty laugh from deep inside, replacing, for a moment, the fury that still festered there.

"Well, who needs food when you've got money?" Alexis pulled out her wallet and spread several bills between her fingers. "You know my philosophy: don't do anything you can pay someone else to do. Who should we pay to cook us some food?"

Wiping tears of laughter from her cheeks, Kyla said, "I told you, it doesn't matter. I'm not even hungry. This has erased my desire for food. I could start a new diet—the Infidelity Diet."

"That sounds like a winner!" Alexis squealed. "My agency will do all the advertising for you."

Kyla sat up. "Maybe some Chinese would be good. But first, can I take a shower and change my clothes? I'd hate to run you out of your own place with this serious body odor I've got going on."

Alexis was still chuckling. "Okay, go change and I'll order a lot of different things we can share. It'll be fun."

Within an hour, the two friends were sitting on the spacious balcony, enjoying the food and the serenity of the evening. The change in this neighborhood from day to night always amazed Kyla. Daytime hours were bustling with business, but by night, most people had returned to their suburban homes, transforming the area from business to upscale residential, creating a haven that still remained a wonderfully kept secret. Now, as she sat eleven floors up staring at the skyline of the city, tranquility blanketed her. The pressure of the last hours seemed to dissipate into the evening air.

"It is so beautiful out here."

"It is, isn't it? That's why I love living here," Alexis said, then added, "but nothing compares to the view you have from your home."

Kyla chuckled lightly. "Good job of bringing up the subject."

"I know you want to talk, and I'm going to listen," Alexis said as she kicked off her mules and leaned back in the lounger.

Kyla laid down her chopsticks. "I still can't believe this. I never thought adultery would be an issue in my marriage. I knew we would have problems, but . . . I never thought it would be another woman."

"Have you ever thought about how it happened?" Alexis asked.

"What do you mean?"

"Well, when you first told me, honestly, I didn't believe you. I kept saying to myself that the Jefferson Blake I knew would never do anything like this . . ."

"That's what I thought . . ."

"So, I was trying to think of all the ways Jasmine could have done it. I mean, Kyla, I know you're hurt right now, but when you can get past your anger and look at this objectively, you will see that this doesn't make any sense. Jefferson doesn't even like Jasmine. He told me that himself."

"When?"

"I don't remember, at some party or something. But my point is, while I don't know what happened, I can tell you that this was not your everyday, ordinary affair. What did Jefferson say when you saw him?"

Kyla sighed. "He didn't say much. He wasn't trying to defend himself. All he kept saying was that he was sorry and that he loved me."

Alexis smiled. "That's Jefferson. He's not making excuses or placing blame. He's just telling you the two most important things: that he's sorry and he loves you. You can't be mad at him for that."

A moment passed. "Saying sorry is not enough. I feel so bad right now I don't even have the words to describe what's going on inside of me. Sometimes I feel hurt, sometimes I feel pain. And then at other moments, I am so ashamed."

Alexis leaned forward, touching her friend's knee. "I know, sweetie. But with time, this will pass away and you'll be fine. You're hurt and I truly understand that, but Kyla, no one gets out of this life without some pain. It's just not possible. What separates us from others is how we deal with it. You're a strong Christian woman. That stands for something and you've got to act that way."

"I know what I'm supposed to do, but I just can't," Kyla said with tears stinging her eyes. "I can't just walk in there and forgive Jefferson. I can't even stand to look at him. It's too much for me to handle."

"No it's not! God told us that there would be many trials and tribulations and obstacles and adversaries. But our job is to stand and battle them all!"

"How am I supposed to do that?"

"Fight. You can't throw away a union that God blessed because Jefferson made a mistake. You've got to forgive."

"I don't have it in me. I already asked Jefferson to move out."

"And he agreed?"

"No, he said he won't leave."

"Good! At least one of you is willing to stand."

"It's easy for him, I didn't break his heart. I didn't toss him aside."

"Okay, I'll give you all of that. Even so, the two of you should *still* be together."

"How can you be so sure, Alex? How can you know that Jefferson is the one I should be with, especially after what has happened?"

"Oh come on, Ky. You've been married forever and this is the first time you've had any serious crisis in your relationship. You're just hurt now. But when you pray about this, you'll know that you're supposed to be with Jefferson. God blessed you and your marriage too much for you to think it was a mistake. 'Cause you know, girl, the Lord doesn't make mistakes."

Kyla stared over the balcony's edge and remained silent.

"I know you've got to feel *something*," Alexis continued. "You've got to know in your heart that you and Jefferson belong together, even with all of this."

"When I was at our house today, I had such mixed feelings. There were times when I felt that if Jefferson had been standing there, I could have killed him with my bare hands. But then, the very next moment, I wanted to take those same hands and put them around my husband. Hold him and have him hold me. I've never felt so confused in my life. I feel like I'm going crazy. I wish I could just disappear for a little while and come back when this is all over."

"Well that's not going to happen. You have to live through each and every step of this, no matter how painful. You and Jefferson have to resolve this together."

"I don't understand these opposing feelings I have. I can't forgive him, yet I still have feelings for him."

"It's the Holy Spirit, girl. God is speaking to your heart."

"I can't just forgive him."

"How can you say that? That's what your salvation is all about, Kyla. That's what Jesus is all about."

Kyla felt the tears starting to flow. "But this is not the same."

"You're right, it's not. What Jesus does for us is much greater."

"It hurts too much." Kyla put her head in her hands and started to cry again.

Alexis pulled her chair closer to Kyla's and took her hands. "There you go again. Talking about your hurt. Look, I know this is hard, but walking with the Lord is always hard. Kyla, I'm not saying that Jefferson doesn't have to answer for what he did. He has some explaining to do to you and to God. But you have to do what you know is right in the Lord's eyes. Our entire relationship with God is based on our forgiving so that He can forgive us."

"I know that . . ."

"So, you've got to *act* on what you know. You have to go to Jefferson and talk it out. God ordained your marriage, so you have to fight for it. You don't have any choice."

"But . . ." Kyla sniffed.

"You and Jefferson have to get together and pray. God will give you the answers and the direction. God will never let you down."

"I thought Jefferson would never let me down either."

"Kyla, we're talking about two different beings here. Maybe that's your problem. Jefferson is good, but he is not God. He's a man with flesh that leads him in the wrong direction every day, just like the rest of us. But, Jefferson already has God's forgiveness. And now, you have to give him yours."

"Do you think that's what this is all about, Alex? Do you

think I'm being tested for my ability to forgive?" Kyla's voice was soft.

"I don't know. Our faith is always being tested. But the Kyla I've grown to love has it inside of her to come through all of this. The Kyla I know has God."

Kyla reached over and hugged her friend. She held onto Alexis tightly, fighting back the tears that continued to beat against her eyelids.

"Hey, what time is it?" Alexis asked pulling back. "It's almost seven-thirty. We're going to be late for Bible study. Let's go. We can clean up this mess when we get back."

"You go. I'm going to stay here."

Alexis put her hands on her hips. "What? Kyla Blake miss a Monday night Bible study? What will Pastor say?"

"Absolutely nothing, because she knows I'm always there."

"And that's why you have to go tonight. Especially tonight, Kyla."

Kyla was silent and when she finally spoke her voice quivered. "I can't go, not tonight."

"Why not?"

"Because . . . Jefferson might be there."

"Oh . . ." Alexis sighed. "Kyla, you can't stop going to church just because you might see Jefferson. What about The Compassion House? Are you going to let that go too since Jefferson is on the board?"

"I don't know. Pastor called while I was home today and left a message that she wanted to talk to me. I'm sure it's about The Compassion House and I'm going to ask her to let someone else take over for a while . . ."

"Oh, brother . . ."

"Alexis, you just don't understand."

"I guess I don't." Alexis looked at her friend, at a loss for what to say next.

"If you're going to make it to Bible study, you should get going."

Alexis squinted at her watch. She hated missing it, but maybe there was something the Lord wanted her to do here. "Well, maybe neither one of us has to miss Bible study," she said, finally.

Kyla frowned.

"Let's just have our own study here tonight. We can read, talk a little, pray a lot . . ."

"I hate to have you miss it . . ."

"That's okay. But you've got to promise me one thing."

"What's that?"

"That I get to lead the study. We'll study the scriptures I come up with."

"Alexis . . ."

"Those are the terms," Alexis said, holding up her hands indicating that was the way it was going to be. "You start cleaning up out here and I'll get my Bible. Be right back."

A few minutes later, they were sitting at the dining room table with an opened Bible and notepads.

"Okay," Alexis started. "We're going to start with Matthew 6:14–15. Would you mind reading it out loud?"

Kyla turned to the scripture, then rolled her eyes. "Alexis . . ."

"Remember the terms. I'm missing Bible study tonight so that we can do this together. And, I'm leading. So . . ."

Kyla sighed. *"For if ye forgive men their trespasses, your heavenly Father will also forgive you: But if ye forgive not men their trespasses, neither will your Father forgive your trespasses."*

Alexis smiled. "That's enough! Bible study is over. Now, let's pray."

"Hey, honey. You must've been expecting me. I didn't even hear the phone ring," Brian chuckled.

"I caught it on the first ring." Alexis sat up in her bed. "I didn't want it to wake Kyla."

"She's there with you?" Alexis could hear his surprise.

"Yeah . . ." Alexis said, not sure how much she wanted to tell Brian.

"Thank God!" When she didn't respond, Brian continued, "It's okay, Alexis. Jefferson told me everything."

"Everything?"

"Yeah, don't sound so surprised. We've been friends for a long time."

"No, it's not that," Alexis said turning up the light in her room. "I didn't think he would say anything to anyone."

"Why not? He's hurting, you know."

"Kyla has a lot more to hurt about."

"Jefferson is really upset that he brought this kind of pain on her."

"Well, I think Kyla has a right to be in pain."

Brian laughed. "Listen to us trying to say who's suffering the most. What we should be doing is everything in our power to get them back together."

Alexis' grin was wide. "I knew there was a reason I liked you."

"I knew there was a reason you liked me too. Does Jefferson know that Kyla's with you? He's been going out of his mind trying to find her."

"I think so. I tried to get them together this afternoon, but that was a disaster. Kyla is so hurt, she won't listen to anything." Alexis sighed. "I don't know how Jefferson could have done this."

"Don't start judging him."

"I'm trying not to. Whenever I find myself going there, I remember how Jesus dissed the Pharisees because they were so judgmental. So, I am not casting stones, but I still don't understand."

"Well, Jefferson doesn't know what hit him. Apparently, Jasmine went after him."

"Did he tell you what happened?"

"Alexis . . ."

"Okay, I don't want to know the details."

Brian gave a light chuckle. "Don't worry. They'll make it through this. They love each other."

"And they both know the Lord."

"Which is the most important ingredient for any successful relationship," Brian said.

"Amen."

"That's why our relationship is going to work."

Alexis was glad that he hadn't said that to her in person where he would've been able to watch her blush and see her knees go weak.

When she remained silent, Brian continued, "So, what do you think we can do?"

"I'm going to keep working on Kyla. You make sure Jefferson doesn't give up."

"Don't worry about that. Jefferson will never give up. And there's another thing we can do," Brian said.

"What?"

"Pray."

Alexis sank into her pillows and smiled as she listened to Brian's plan. He told her that he had already prayed for the Blakes, but that the two of them should develop a prayer of agreement. He asked her to turn to Matthew 16:19, which she did, even though she already knew the scripture. *Verily I say unto you, whatsoever ye shall bind on earth shall be bound in heaven; and whatsoever ye shall loose on earth shall be loosed in heaven. Again I say unto you, That if two of you shall agree on earth as touching any thing that they shall ask, it shall be done for them of my Father which is in heaven.*

Then they prayed, asking for the Lord's direction as they stepped in to help their friends and binding satan's power so that the union that God had ordained would last. They prayed that Kyla and Jefferson would open their ears and hearts to hear the words the Lord wanted them to hear.

When Alexis hung up the phone, she turned off the light and snuggled under the comforter. "The most important ingredient for any successful relationship is for both people to know the Lord," Brian had said. "That's why our relationship is going to work."

She turned onto her back and stared at the ceiling. She was consumed with thoughts of Brian more and more. There hadn't been anyone like this in her life and though she feared admitting it aloud, she knew where this relationship was going.

But that was fine with her. He had all the right ingredients: he was intelligent, funny, had his own career, and was not at all threatened by her success. But, most importantly, he was a Christian. A walking, practicing Christian. Not someone who just talked about it. He was a man who lived it.

"Just like Jefferson," she sighed aloud. But she wasn't going to let what had happened to Jefferson taint her belief in Brian.

She turned over, pulled the pillow over her head, and drifted into a peaceful sleep.

# Fourteen

Jefferson bolted up in the bed. He was surrounded by darkness, except for the streetlight that cast a bronze hue throughout the room. Glancing at the clock, he saw it was midnight. Again. For the second night in a row, he was awake to greet a new day. As he leaned over to turn on the light, his Bible caught his eye and he picked it up, hugging it close to his chest.

"God, I hope you're right," he said, his eyes raised towards the ceiling.

The headache that had attacked him this afternoon had not retreated, even with sleep. It seemed to serve as a reminder of this storm in his life. As if he could forget!

His eyes wandered to his wedding picture on the dresser. He'd been so happy with Kyla and he shook his head now, wondering if they'd ever capture that happiness again. The way things had gone this afternoon, he wasn't sure about anything.

It had taken him awhile to get himself together once Kyla had left. At first, he had run behind her, hoping somehow she would still be there. But the garage and the street were empty. Returning to the house, he had come up to their bedroom.

184

This room that he'd had such difficulty facing now seemed to call him. He had laid on the bed, closed his eyes and let silent tears fall. Before yesterday, he couldn't remember the last time he'd cried, and now, he couldn't seem to stop. Men weren't supposed to cry, he'd been taught. So with all the tears he'd shed over the last two days, he wondered if that meant he didn't think of himself as a man. But it wasn't tears that made him doubt his manhood.

Exhaustion from the two emotion-packed days finally took him prisoner and he had collapsed into a restless slumber. He kept waking, intermittently, to the voices of Kyla and Nicole; but it was just wishful dreams.

Now, he reached over to Kyla's side of the bed and rubbed his hands along the comforter, imagining his wife's body lying next to him. He held that image, knowing that she would come back to him. She just had to.

How had it all come to this? Jefferson knew about all the statistics that said that most married men would commit adultery at some point in their relationships. And, in the past, he had had his temptations, though he knew with all certainty that he would *never* succumb. He knew from the moment that Kyla had captured his heart with her innocence, there would never be another woman for him. He thought back to their first date . . .

"This was really nice," Kyla had said as Jefferson walked her to her dorm room after they returned from dinner. "I had a good time."

Smiling down at her, he had leaned against the doorpost, moving in for the kiss. She kissed him back, a soft gentle one, and when he tried to probe his tongue further, she had stopped.

"I think we should just end this now," she had said.

"Really," he had said, his voice husky. "I was thinking I could come in."

Kyla shook her head. "I don't think so."

"Why? I thought you said that your roommate was away for the weekend."

"She is."

"Well," he had said returning his hands to her waist. "I figured we'd have some private time."

Keeping her smile, she shook her head again. "There is something I think you should know."

"Don't talk," he said kissing her on the neck. "Talking is not what I want to do."

"That's what I have to tell you. I don't do this."

He leaned back and looked in her eyes, waiting for her to finish the joke. When she didn't, he asked, "Huh?"

"I'm a virgin."

Immediately, Jefferson's hands had dropped to his side. "Uh . . . well . . ."

Kyla laughed. "That's exactly what everyone says when I tell them."

"Well, uh, I guess . . . I should say . . ."

"Good night?" Kyla had said, still smiling.

"Yeah, good night."

Jefferson had returned to the Kappa House flabbergasted. It was unbelievable. The sixties revolution had overflowed into the seventies and he didn't think there were any virgins left at Hampton Institute, or in all of Virginia, for that matter. That night, he made up his mind—he would never see her again. There were just too many available women on campus. He didn't need to deal with all the issues of a virgin.

So, with his decision made, no one was more surprised than he when he called her a few days later to go out again. And on this date, he decided to find out what her game was.

"So, uh . . . you're a virgin?"

She had laughed. "Yup."

"You say that like it's normal or something."

"It is to me. It's part of my commitment to God. I'm a Christian."

"Well . . . uh, I know some Christian girls who aren't virgins."

She hunched her shoulders. "I can't talk for anyone else, I can only talk about me. I made a vow when I was thirteen years old through a program at my church. I vowed then that I would remain celibate until marriage. I don't think I really knew what that meant back then, but as I've gotten older, it has become really important to me."

"But it's been a long time since you were thirteen. I mean, things and times have changed. How did you make it through three years here without being . . . challenged?"

"Oh, don't think it hasn't been a challenge," Kyla chuckled in her soft manner. "It hasn't been easy, but it has become simpler."

Although Jefferson had been unable to explain it to himself at the time, they continued to see each other, between the time he spent with other women, until he was no longer able to deny his feelings for Kyla. And even when he began to see Kyla exclusively, she could not be persuaded to sway from what she believed.

"I'm sorry, Jefferson," she had said to him on many occasions. "But marriage is the only way I can be released from this vow."

At first, Jefferson believed this was a woman's elaborate ploy to lure him into a permanent commitment. But even when he tentatively proposed to her, hoping that she would consent to sleep with him, her views did not falter. She told him they should put off marriage until he finished medical school.

"Your hormones must be wrapped in an iron box. I can't deal with this," Jefferson had tried to explain to her. "All of this fondling and caressing and stroking isn't enough. It's killing me. I'm frustrated. I was pretty active before I met you, if you know what I mean. And, I do love you, but . . ."

"Jefferson, as much as I love you, I love God more. I don't want to lose you, but I just can't compromise. I can't break the promises I made to the Lord. Trust me, you wouldn't want me to do that either."

Jefferson had been baffled . . . and in love. No matter what, he couldn't move on. It was at this point that he felt he had to find out more about the spiritual center of the woman he loved. She had often invited him to church, but he had refused, maintaining his belief that church was made for weddings and funerals.

But Kyla had continued to invite him, never pushing, until he had finally agreed to go. When he attended the Sunday services, he could *feel* what she had in her life and at the same time, he really noticed the void in his.

The pastor spoke with such passion and conviction that Jefferson had been instantly moved. The message was different from the ones he'd heard before; it wasn't the normal fire-and-brimstone and to-hell-you-will-go sermon. This pastor spoke of hope, saying that faith and hope went together. He spoke of life, not death. Everlasting life!

Suddenly, it hit him. When the minister gave the invitation to people who wanted to know the Lord, Jefferson took Kyla's hand and shakily walked to the altar. Though he didn't know what to expect, Jefferson wanted to know the same God that gave Kyla her strength. He wanted to know the God that gave Kyla her peace and joy.

Jefferson had been saved that day, accepting Jesus Christ as his Lord and Savior, and he had walked with the Lord ever since. When he and Kyla had been married almost three years later, he had been celibate the entire time. And while none of it had been easy, Jefferson remembered that their wedding night was the most beautiful, sensual, sexual experience he'd ever had in his life.

Now, as he lay on the bed stroking the comforter, he wondered what his life would be like from now on. For more than sixteen years, he had kept his marriage vows. Kyla was still the only woman he wanted. The only woman he could imagine his life with.

He sat up and went to the window. Everything seemed so out of control, like someone else was guiding the ship of his life. He had only been trying to help his wife's best friend. But something else had taken over. He remembered Jasmine had called him on Saturday . . .

> *"Jefferson, I really need some help with my garage."*
> *"I told you before, Jasmine, I don't know how to fix those things."*
> *"Well, what am I going to do?"*
> *When Jefferson heard her tears, he reluctantly agreed.*
> *"Thank you so much, Jefferson. I can't tell you how much I appreciate this. Why don't you stop by at about eight tonight?"*

"That's too late, Jasmine. It'll almost be dark then. Why can't I come by this afternoon?"

"Uh . . . I have to go out . . . tonight will really be better for me. And it won't matter if it's dark. You'll be working inside anyway."

Jefferson acquiesced, and on his way home from the video store that evening, he stopped by Jasmine's house. He rang the doorbell several times and was about to turn away, when she finally came to the door.

"Oh . . . Jefferson," Jasmine exclaimed. "I really didn't expect you so soon." She leaned against the post like she was posing for a magazine layout.

Jefferson swallowed hard. His eyes quickly roamed her body, taking in the slinky lingerie that hugged her. "Ah . . . Jasmine. I just came by to look at your garage. Look, I'll come by tomorrow after I pick Kyla up from the airport."

He turned and started walking to his car. "No, Jefferson, please." She followed him into the street, seemingly unconcerned that she was dressed like a hooker. "I didn't expect you so soon or I would've been dressed. I was just trying this on when you came. Please stay. I really need to have my garage fixed."

"I said I'll do it tomorrow."

"Listen, I'm really embarrassed to have to tell you this, but the door has to be fixed now. I'm three payments behind on my car note and they've already threatened to come and take my car. I just need a little time to get my finances together . . ." Jasmine hoped Jefferson wouldn't remember that she'd only had the car for two months.

Shaking his head slightly, Jefferson stuffed his hands in his pockets and shifted his feet. "I don't know . . ."

"Please . . ."

Warning bells blazed in his head, but he talked himself out of it. "Don't be ridiculous," his voice inside said. "This is Jasmine, Kyla's friend. Nothing's going to happen."

Finally, he moved toward her and Jasmine smiled. He followed her into the house and stood awkwardly at the door.

Jasmine walked to the couch, swaying her hips, feeling the hem of the short, satin slip tickle her thighs right below her buttocks. She sat down on the couch, crossed her legs and the slip rode up her legs exposing even more.

"Jefferson," her laugh came from her throat. "Why are you standing over there? Come over here and sit down. We can talk . . ." she said, licking her lips.

He didn't meet her eyes. "Jasmine, the only reason I came over here was to fix the garage. Do you want me to take a look at it or not?"

Her smile grew wider. She could hear the huskiness in his voice. "Whatever you say." She stood and went to the garage, leaving him standing right where he was.

Turning back, she wanted to laugh out loud. He was pathetic. Just like all the other men. Just two minutes of looking at her in this little piece of a slip and they were like puppies. "Are you coming?" The question sang from her lips.

Jefferson followed, still ignoring the signals that hadn't left his brain. "I'm only helping a friend," he kept saying to himself. "I'm only going to help her and then I'm going home."

Taking the ladder she had set against the wall, he put it under the remote for the opener and glanced at Jasmine as she leaned against the laundry machine. He wondered what Kyla would think of Jasmine now. He'd been trying to tell her that Jasmine was in trouble. And as Jasmine paraded around the garage in her nightgown, he knew he'd been right.

He tested the ladder's legs for sturdiness and his gaze met Jasmine's once again. Looking away, he tried to ignore the stirring inside. "Jasmine, why don't you go and put something on while I do this, okay?"

She strutted to where he was standing and moved close, her breath falling on his chest. "What's wrong, Dr. Jefferson?" Her voice was seductive. "What's wrong with what I'm wearing?"

Jefferson crossed his arms. "Look, Jasmine. I think you're playing some kind of sick game and I'm not going to play with you. So get dressed while I work on this, okay?" He tried to make his voice stern, hiding the arousal he felt.

She grinned. "Okay, Dr. Jefferson. Like I said before, whatever you say." She stood still for a moment, her eyes bearing into his before she tossed her hair and strolled away.

Once inside, she ran up the stairs and had to constrain the squeal that rose inside of her. This was going great! She changed into a bra and panties and went to the mirror, turning from side to side. She still looked mighty good for a woman of almost forty. With strong, sturdy legs and toned arms, the only thing she would've changed about her pear-shaped figure were her breasts. She had considered implants—but she couldn't think about any of that now. Her body was fine; it always got her what she wanted and tonight would not be any different. Putting the sheer, floor-length sheath over her, she allowed herself a final glance in the mirror.

Tying the robe around her waist, she slipped into the feathered slippers. He had asked her to change and that was *just what she'd done. She ran back down to the garage and took a deep breath as she stepped inside. "I'm back."*

He was holding the ladder, his back to her, and when he turned around, the ladder fell from his hands. Jasmine couldn't help her giggle. *He's so pitiful,* she thought. *It's amazing what a woman can do with her body to make a man forget how to carry a ladder.*

"There's . . . there's . . . nothing . . ." he stuttered as he struggled to get the ladder upright. "There's nothing I can do. You need a new opener altogether. Just go to any hardware store and they'll install it for you."

She strutted to him. "But I want you to put it in for me," she pouted.

Jefferson shook his head. "I'm sorry. I'm not good with this kind of stuff." He stepped from her quickly, feeling like he was a pawn in a chess game. *He made one move; she made two.*

"Well," Jasmine started as she sashayed across the garage, blocking his exit, "I really appreciate all that you've done for me, so far . . ." She put her arms around his neck and kissed him, nudging her tongue inside his mouth. It was seconds before he yanked her arms away.

"Jasmine. I'm sorry I couldn't help you." Moving around her, he went into the house and left through the front door.

She panicked. *What had gone wrong? He was responding to her; she could feel him when they kissed.* She followed him outside, prepared to give her best performance. "I'm so sorry, Jefferson. I don't know what got into me." Forcing the tears to her eyes, she held her hand across her chest. "It's just that I feel so alone . . . please, please forgive me."

"I'm sorry you're having problems, but I'm not the

one to help you fix them." He got into his car and backed from the driveway, never looking at her again.

It wasn't until a car drove by and honked that Jasmine realized she was still standing outside half-naked. Running back into the house, she charged up the stairs into her bedroom. "Maybe I was a little too pushy," she said as real tears punched against her eyelids. "He's too conservative for this. I've got to find another way."

She put on a pair of jeans and a cutoff T-shirt, then brushed her hair, letting the soft curls frame her face. She put on a pair of pumps, grabbed her purse and keys and, just as she was about to leave, glanced at the lingerie that she'd thrown across the bed. Without hesitation, she picked up the slip and stuffed it into her purse. As she ran down the stairs and got into her car, the idea formed and swam in her head.

She drove the five blocks up the hill to the Blakes' house and parked in the driveway. Taking a deep breath, she rang the bell and within seconds, he answered.

"Jasmine . . ."

"Wait, before you say anything, Jefferson, I just came over here to apologize."

"You don't have to apologize. I understand. Now, good night." He started closing the door.

"Wait, please don't do this, Jefferson. I feel so bad."

"I said it was okay."

"Well, may I come in?"

"Not a good idea."

She forced a smile. "That's okay. But I will stand out here as long as it takes to explain this to you and beg for your forgiveness. So, if you don't mind what the neighbors will say . . ."

Jefferson tapped his fingers against the door. Why was

*he even thinking about putting himself in this position? Yet Jasmine was Kyla's friend and he was an adult. This was his home and he would never do anything he didn't want to do.*

*He opened the door, just barely, letting Jasmine in. She stood in the hallway entrance and waited as Jefferson remained by the opened door.*

*"Do you mind if we go in and talk a little?" she asked as she motioned with her head toward the family room. "I could really use a friend."*

*Through narrowed eyes, he looked her up and down. She looked so innocent, standing there in jeans and a T-shirt. And, he could tell that she really meant what she said; she just wanted to talk. She was still going through a tough time because of Kenny. He knew that had been hard on her. She needed to talk. Maybe he could convince her to see a therapist.*

*He closed the door, motioned for her to go into the family room, and followed. They sat on the couch, Jasmine purposely sitting as far to one end as she could, as far away from him as possible. He knew then that he had been right to let her in. She just needed a friend and Kyla wasn't there for her now.*

*She lowered her head. "Jefferson, I am so sorry. I really can't explain what got into me." She paused. "It's just that you and Kyla have been such good friends to me . . . so, naturally, I would just turn to you."*

*She looked up, through her eyelashes. "I haven't been with anyone since Kenny . . . I just looked at you and . . . I lost it. You're such a strong, wonderful man. And, no matter what, you've always been there for me. All I can say is that Kyla is very lucky to have you. And if I ever have the opportunity to be involved with someone again, I just pray that he will be just like you. I just hope that you will be able to find it in your Christian heart to forgive me . . . please."*

*His shoulders relaxed and she smiled slightly.*

*"So, will you?" She opened her eyes wide.*

*He smiled. Maybe Kyla was right. Jasmine was just lonely and distraught since Kenny deserted her.*

*"Will you?" she repeated.*

*"Will I what?"*

*"Forgive me? I couldn't handle it if you were still mad at me."*

*"Apology accepted."*

*"So . . . still friends?" Jasmine extended her hand, though she still maintained her distance.*

*Jefferson took her hand. "Friends."*

*A few moments passed before Jasmine spoke again. "Were you going to watch these?" she asked, pointing to the videos lined on the table.*

*"Yeah."*

*She turned the titles over in her hand. "I've been dying to see . . . Woodbridge House."*

*"Yeah, I can't wait to see that one either. Kyla hates action movies, so I plan on having a night of all action!"*

*She lowered her head again. "Jefferson, I know I messed up before . . . but, would you mind if I stayed and watched one of these with you? I just don't think I could go home alone right now . . ."*

*Jefferson was silent as a war raged inside of him.*

*"I promise, all I want to do is watch videos. Just like a couple of old friends," Jasmine said.*

*"Sure, you can stay. Wanna watch Woodbridge House?"*

*"Sure!"*

*"Okay, you pop the video in and fast-forward past all*

*those movie trailers. I'll get the popcorn. Do you want
something to drink?" he asked as he went into the kitchen.*

*"You're going to pop some popcorn?"*

*He laughed. "No, I brought this from Trader Joe's.
What do you want to drink?"*

*"Anything will be fine," Jasmine yelled.*

*"Well, here it is." He put the bowl and glasses on the
table. "Are you ready?"*

*She nodded and smiled. "You have no idea just how
ready I am."*

*He smiled back. "Okay, let's get this show on the
road!" he exclaimed, leaning back with the remote in his
hands.*

Jefferson stood up from the chair and went to the nightstand, picking up his Bible before returning to the window. He
wondered how many more hours of sleep would escape him.
From the window, he could see the street below, calm with the
peace only the middle of the night could bring. It was so different from the turmoil that filled his life.

For the last few days, he had wanted to place the blame
somewhere, but now as he looked back, he saw what he'd always known; the fault fell at his feet.

Scooting the chair closer to the window, Jefferson peered
out into the blackened L.A. sky. He felt such peace in his
heart; but in his head, confusion reigned. Sitting back, he
closed his eyes and remembered the rest of the evening . . .

*They had watched the movie together, but Jefferson
couldn't concentrate. Out of the corner of his eye, he had
watched Jasmine as she snacked on popcorn, her eyes never
leaving the television screen. And as she brought the pop-*

corn to her lips, each time, Jefferson was reminded of the kiss. He watched as her tongue licked away the salt that lingered and he shifted, trying to find distraction in the movie.

The two-hour movie stretched much longer and when it finally ended, he yawned. "I can't believe this, but I'm really tired. I'm going to have to take a rain check on the rest of these."

"You're not going to watch them? I was looking forward to The Sky Below."

"Well, I don't have to return them until tomorrow if you want to take it with you."

"Okay . . ." She hesitated. "Jefferson, I have a big favor to ask." She paused again. "Would you mind . . . if I stayed here tonight . . . please?"

Seeing the frown on his face, she added quickly, "Please don't think I'm going to try anything. Believe me, I've learned my lesson. The only reason I'm even asking you this is that my house . . . it's so scary sometimes. That's what I think today was all about with you. I hate being there alone."

"Jasmine, I'm sorry, but you can't stay. Kyla's not here . . ."

"Jefferson, I thought you forgave me. And . . . I don't know if Kyla has told you, but recently . . ." she bit her lip, "I've been getting calls . . ."

"What kind of calls?"

She sniffed. "I don't know . . . threatening calls. From a man saying that he knows that I live alone. And I get scared, especially on the weekends. That's why Kyla let's me stay over with you guys so much."

"Have you called the police?"

"Uh-huh, but they said there's nothing they can do until he tries something . . . like breaking in or attacking *me . . ." Jefferson winced. "I'm having an alarm installed when I get the money."*

*Jefferson's eyes blinked rapidly. He was married; how could he let her stay while Kyla was away? What would people think? But, on the other hand, how could he turn her away? She was Kyla's friend and she always stayed over. And if someone was threatening her . . .*

*"I wouldn't ask if I weren't scared."*

*Seconds of silence hung in the air. "It's no problem." He said the words matter-of-factly, just the opposite of what he was feeling. "You know where everything is. Just stay in the guestroom. I probably won't be as good a host as Kyla."*

*"That's okay, I don't want to be a bother."*

*He nodded.*

*"Jefferson, thank you so much. I can't tell you how much this means to me."*

*"Well, I'm going to go upstairs now. Good night." Jefferson bounded up the stairs with prayers for morning to come quickly. He undressed and got into bed, hoping he would fall asleep right away. But he tossed for endless minutes, and when sleep eluded him, he decided to read. The current bestseller and his Bible both sat on his nightstand. He reached for the Bible, but then picked up the novel. After an hour, but only ten pages, he still wasn't ready for sleep. He should have been exhausted since he had risen early and worked in the yard most of the day.*

*He put the book down as he heard Jasmine come up the stairs and finally close the door to the guest bedroom. He sighed and turned his attention back to the courtroom battles of his favorite author, but he couldn't stop thinking about the kiss.*

*He got out of bed and went into their bathroom, turning on the cold water at full blast. As he glanced in the mir-*

ror, dark eyes bore back at him, freezing the moment, making him ask, who is this man? Finally leaning over, he rinsed his face with the frigid water, hoping that these alien feelings would follow the water down the drain.

He returned to his bedroom and just as he was about to get into bed, he heard a sound. Jefferson stopped. Jasmine had come up a while ago, so he knew it wasn't her. She was probably asleep by now. Just like he should have been.

He stood still and wondered if Jasmine had locked all the doors. He'd been so eager to get upstairs that he didn't check the house the way he normally did. He would have to go downstairs. He went to the closet to get his robe, but decided he didn't need it. The house was warm and Jasmine was already asleep. He was just going downstairs . . . just downstairs. To check on the house. Nothing else.

As he put his hand on the knob of his bedroom door, he heard the floor panels in the hallway squeak. Someone was outside his bedroom door and he opened the door quickly.

She was standing there, dressed in the red slip, waiting for him, like a vision in a dream. Without a word, she took his hand and leaned into him. She kissed him gently, letting him feel her, then followed him as the gentle kiss built with his desire. She moaned. He led her back to his bed, laying her down like a delicate flower and kissed her with surprising zeal. His fingers slid underneath her slip and he caressed her. He didn't allow himself to think about what was happening. And he never heard Kyla's voice nor the voice of God inside of him.

Opening his eyes, he massaged his head. He was so ashamed. He had betrayed his wife and gone against everything that he believed as a man of God. As hard as it was for him to explain, he had fallen and it was his fault.

But, he couldn't let his marriage go. Not for this single mistake. He wanted his wife; he wanted his family. And he was going to do whatever he had to do to keep it all together.

Looking down at the Bible in his lap, he knew this book held all his answers. Only God could bring him out of this misery. Jefferson closed his eyes and prayed.

"Heavenly Father, I don't know what to say. I feel such shame and guilt. But I know that You have forgiven me and I thank You for Your grace and mercy. With Your grace, I have peace and I thank you for that, Lord. Jesus, I thank you for the blood. Your blood that covers me now and that covered me before I was born. Now, Father, my prayer is that You lead me. Show me what You want me to see. Speak the words that you want me to hear. I am yours, Lord . . ."

He opened his eyes and turned the pages of the Bible.

First, the Lord led him to Isaiah 43:25, *I even I, am he who blots out your transgressions, for my own sake and remembers your sins no more.* Then to I John 1:9, *If we confess our sins, he is faithful and just and will forgive us our sins and purify us from all unrighteousness.* Then to the Book of Psalms 103:12, *As far as the east is from the west, so far has he removed our transgressions from us.*

As tears rolled down his face, the Lord continued his healing. He read and read, quoting scriptures out loud, savoring them in his heart. He hungered for the Word with an ardor he'd never before experienced. And the Lord fed his spirit, satisfying him, making him full.

The pages of the Bible seemed to turn themselves and he continued reading, unable, unwilling to stop. The hours passed and, finally exhausted, he turned to Hebrews 8:12, *For I will be merciful to their unrighteousness and their sins and their iniquities will I remember no more . . .*

Jefferson remained still as the words he read sank into his heart. Finally, he walked to his bed and, still fully clothed, climbed under the covers. The peace that he'd felt in his heart now consumed his entire being. He knew that he would have his family back; not because of himself, but because of God's grace. He didn't know how it was going to happen, but he knew that was God's business.

He closed his eyes, knowing that the torment that still grieved him would gradually be lifted. God's forgiveness was instant, but now he had to forgive himself. He began to drift into sleep, but before he fell into complete unconsciousness, God had one more message for him. The words of a Psalm that he wasn't even familiar with came to his mind . . . *weeping may endure for a night, but joy cometh in the morning.* Then, he slept.

# *Fifteen*

Before the alarm clock shrilled, alerting her to the six o'clock hour, Jasmine slapped the off button. Stretching across the bed, she rubbed her hands along her legs, aching from lack of sleep. She turned over and looked at the phone.

She still hadn't spoken to him, even though she'd called him until the late hours of the night, but he had not answered and now Jasmine felt her time was running out. As long as Kyla was in L.A., there was always the chance that the Blakes could reconcile.

The numbers on the clock flipped to 6:10. Still too early to call, but desperation was beginning to override courtesy and she picked up the receiver, dialing the number without hesitation. When she heard Jefferson's voice on the answering machine, she slammed the phone down. "Where is he?" she muttered, in exasperation.

The ringing phone startled her. "Hello," she exclaimed, barely able to keep the excitement from her voice.

"Good morning."

Jasmine slumped back against the headboard. "Serena . . ."

"I was just calling to see how you were doing. I didn't wake you, did I?"

"No."

"So . . . how are things?"

"If you were calling to find out how *things* are with me and Jefferson, they're just fine."

"I hope you know what you're doing."

"Serena, if you've called to lecture me, just save your quarter."

"It just seems that this happened rather suddenly. Are you sure it's all over between Jefferson and Kyla?"

Jasmine sighed. "Yes . . ."

"That's hard to believe."

Jasmine held her tongue.

"I'll keep praying for you . . ." Serena said.

"Do that . . ."

"And call me. And call Dad. He misses you and knows that something is wrong."

"I'll think about it . . ."

"And, Jasmine. I love you."

"Yeah," she sighed again.

It was almost six-thirty when she hung up and went to stand at the window. Joggers and walkers filled the street, making use of the early-morning hours before the workday began. She sighed. It was time for her to get ready for work. But there was no way she could. Jefferson had to be able to get in touch with her and she didn't think he had her work number. She could just leave it on the answering machine or at his office, but this was too important. She only had a few days to solidify their relationship, so she couldn't leave any of this to chance. She'd have to wait for his call.

Jasmine dialed a number quickly, then pinched her nose and spoke. "Rose, this is Jasmine. I think I caught the cold you had yesterday. I was up all night and just came back from the pharmacy. I'm going to take something now that'll hopefully knock me out, but I'll check in with you this afternoon. Sorry about this." She coughed before she hung up.

Now all that was left was to come up with a plan for her and Jefferson. It was time to move into aggressive mode. She dialed the Blakes' number once again and waited for the answering machine.

"Jefferson, it's me," she said sweetly. "I'm still trying to get in touch with you. Please call me, I think we need to talk. I've taken the day off so that we can get together. Call me."

She dialed the number to the clinic and left the same message with the service. Then sinking back into the bed, she sighed. Not at home, not at work—where was he? And then it hit her. With *Kyla.* They were probably together at Alexis'. She flipped through the phone book hoping she still had the number. She did, but knew she couldn't just call. Alexis wouldn't let her anywhere near Kyla.

Standing, she paced the floor. "Maybe I should just give this all up!" she exclaimed aloud. "If Jefferson and Kyla are together . . ." But as soon as the words were out of her mouth, her resolve returned. "No! It's already done and it's *my* turn to be happy." She'd wait for an hour or two, she decided. If she didn't hear from Jefferson by then, she'd do whatever she had to do to keep the two of them apart.

The coffee was already cold, but that didn't bother Jefferson. Today, he was drinking out of habit. Even though he'd only had a few hours of sleep, he felt surprisingly energized. The Lord had a way of doing that.

He tapped the keyboard of his computer, checking the records of patients he would see later and stopped as he heard the steps on the stairs. He turned around.

"Hey, Brian. What are you doing here so early?"

"It's not so early, it's almost eight. How long have you been here?"

"I don't know . . . a few hours."

Brian sat down. "I take it Kyla's not back?"

"No, but I saw her yesterday."

"Yeah, Alexis told me. You know that's where Kyla's staying, right? I found out last night, but it was too late to call you."

Jefferson nodded. "I didn't know for sure, but I figured as much. Alexis was the one who made sure I got to see Kyla yesterday."

"But it didn't go well?"

"Not at all . . ."

"Then I take it you didn't take my advice."

Jefferson frowned. "No, I didn't. I told you before, I wasn't going to do that and frankly, I'm surprised at you."

Brian shrugged. "Hey, if you love the lady . . ."

"That's exactly why I won't lie to her. It's bad enough what I did; I'm not going to complicate it further."

"So what *are* you going to do?"

Jefferson shook his head. "I don't know yet. But I'm going to fight. Kyla means too much to me to give up. I'm going to do whatever I have to do."

"Whatever, huh? That covers a lot of territory."

"Well, I'm willing to do anything. Except lie."

Brian's smile vanished and he became still, but within a few seconds he smiled again. "Sorry if you don't like my methods, but I was just trying to help a friend who was in bed with a woman that wasn't his wife."

"Good morning, Dr. Blake, Dr. Lewis."

Jefferson coughed and Brian lowered his head. "Good morning, Shannon."

"Dr. Blake," Shannon walked in and handed a folder to Jefferson, "Dr. Blunt and Dr. Cameron are waiting for you in the downstairs conference room."

"Thanks, Shannon," Jefferson said standing. "Could you please close the door on your way out?"

When Shannon left, Brian spoke. "Hey, man, I'm sorry. I shouldn't have said that. I didn't know anyone else was here and . . ."

Jefferson held up his hands. "Forget it," he sighed. "Look, I'll see you later, okay?" he said as he left the office.

Brian shook his head and wondered if Jefferson and Kyla would ever get back together with the way Jefferson was handling things.

"Man, you should have listened to me," he said to himself as he walked down the hall to his office. "You really should have just listened to me!"

"Okay, sweetie. I'll speak to you either later tonight or tomorrow. I love you."

Alexis walked into the kitchen just as Kyla hung up the telephone. "How is Nicole?" she asked as she got a mug from the cabinet and poured coffee from the coffeemaker.

"She's the bright spot in my life," Kyla sighed. "She's having a good time with her friends and not even thinking about coming home."

"Good thing," Alexis said as she sat down at the dinette table, "with the way things are between you and Jefferson. I mean, you haven't even talked to him . . ."

Kyla held up her hands. "Please, don't start that again."

"Well, it's good that Nicole has someplace *stable* to be."

"Well, I'll be *stable* in a few days. As soon as Jefferson moves out."

"I thought you said he wasn't going to do that."

"He will, once he sees that he doesn't have a choice. I'm not sure about many things with my husband, but I'm sure that he doesn't want his estranged wife and child to be homeless."

Alexis sighed. "Didn't you get anything out of our Bible study last night?"

Kyla folded her arms. "Forgiveness doesn't mean that I have to live with the man who betrayed me."

Alexis stood, taking her cup to the sink. "I can't believe you're saying it's all over without even talking to Jefferson."

Kyla rolled her eyes.

"Well . . . I'm going into the office. Are you going to be all right here?"

Kyla nodded. "Yeah, I don't have to meet with Pastor Ford until this afternoon, so this morning I plan to try to get a little of myself back. I'm going to meditate and pray and I think I'm going to fast today, too."

"That's a good idea. When you pray, just pray hard and call me if you need anything." Alexis picked up her briefcase and jacket.

Kyla closed the door behind her friend and smiled. She'd meant what she'd told Alexis. She was fine and would be, no matter what she decided to do. Because the Lord was with her. He said that in one of her favorite scriptures, Hebrews 13:5, *I will never leave thee nor forsake thee.*

Picking up the Bible from the table, she looked around, trying to decide where she would read. She headed for the balcony, set on enjoying the morning sun, when the phone rang.

Kyla laughed. She knew it was Alexis, calling from her car, just to check on her or give her some more advice.

"Hello."

Silence. But Kyla could hear breathing.

"Hello," she repeated.

Suddenly, the dial tone hummed in her ear.

She shrugged, but the moment she replaced the receiver, it rang again. She let it ring a few times before she picked it up again.

"Hello?"

This time the line clicked dead immediately.

Less than fifteen seconds later, the phone rang again and Kyla started to shake. She knew, she just knew, it was Jasmine.

Jefferson rushed back to his office and took off his lab jacket, replacing it with his sports coat. "Okay, Shannon. I'm on my way to UCLA. I'll be there the rest of the afternoon, but I'll be back this evening, probably after you've gone."

"Okay," she said as she followed him into his office. "There's just one thing I need to tell you, though."

"What?" Jefferson was distracted, focusing on the papers on his desk.

"Well, it's kinda weird, but you've had a few phone calls this morning. Jasmine Larson has been calling . . ."

At the mention of her name, Jefferson's head popped up. "Jasmine Larson?"

"Yeah." Shannon started looking at the message slips she held in her hand. "She's called six times in the last two hours."

Jefferson could hear the dubiety in her voice and he lowered his eyes. "Uh . . . if she calls back, please ask her not to call me here. Tell her I'll be gone for the rest of the day and she can reach me at home tonight. But, do not, under any circumstances, give her my pager or tell her where I am." Jefferson knew his simple instructions would be followed without question. If he didn't want to speak to Jasmine, she'd never make it past Shannon.

"Okay," Shannon agreed. "Is there anything else?"

"No, no. I just need to make a quick call."

When she closed the door, Jefferson rolled through his Rolodex and dialed the number. He was put through right away. "Good morning, Pastor. How are you? I'm fine, considering everything. The reason I'm calling is that this battle has moved to another level and I pray that you can help me."

# Sixteen

"Dr. Blake's office," Shannon answered the phone with a sigh.

"May I speak to Dr. Blake, please?"

"I'm sorry, Mrs. Larson, but as I told you before, Dr. Blake is out and is not expected back for the rest of the afternoon."

Shannon could hear Jasmine's sigh. "Well, is there a number where he can be reached? This is urgent!"

"I understand, but Dr. Blake is somewhere where he cannot be disturbed. I will make sure he gets *all* your messages."

"What about his pager? Give me that number."

Shannon tried to keep her voice even. "During office hours, this is the best place to leave messages for Dr. Blake. I promise . . ."

"Is he meeting with his wife?" Jasmine interrupted.

Shannon paused. "Mrs. Larson, I have given you all the information I can and . . ." Before she finished, Jasmine slammed the phone in her ear.

Shannon hung her phone up with a heavy sigh. It was only noon and she wondered how many more times Jasmine would call today. She'd had to handle unruly clients and boisterous patients before. But this was different. Despite Dr. Blake's obvious desire to stay away from her, Jasmine Larson was determined to get what she wanted. Shannon couldn't wait for Dr. Blake to call and tell her what he wanted her to do with this woman.

Kyla was flipping through the pages of the *Christian Today* magazine, though she wasn't focused on any of the articles. Her hands shook slightly with the thought of what she was about to do.

"Okay, Kyla. Pastor will see you now." Kyla forced a smile at Avery, the pastor's assistant, and tossed the magazine onto the table before she stepped into the office.

"Hi, hon. Sorry you had to wait, I was on a long-distance call." Pastor Ford came from around her desk to hug Kyla.

"It's no problem." Kyla's voice was soft. "Pastor Ford, I got your message. I assumed it was about The Compassion House."

The pastor leaned forward on her desk and smiled. "I have some great news. I've been contacted by several organizations that want to fund the project for us. Kyla, this is getting bigger than we ever thought. I think it's going to end up being a full-time job for you. Are you ready for this?"

"I don't know . . ."

"This is so exciting." Pastor Ford tapped her manicured fingertips atop her desk. "Isn't it good how the Lord has built this little idea into something so big for this community? What's the date of the opening again?"

"Pastor, there's something I have to tell you." With downcast eyes, Kyla continued, "I need to take a leave of absence and have someone else lead The Compassion House for a little while." Kyla raised her eyes and looked directly at her pastor. "It's not that I want to leave the project altogether—it's just that right now, I need a little time to myself . . ."

"May I ask why?"

She glanced away. "It's personal."

"I think it's spiritual. You're in the middle of a spiritual battle, Kyla Blake, and you've laid down all of your weapons! I saw Jefferson. He told me everything."

Kyla's eyes blazed. "He *told* you? He didn't have any right to do that."

"He had every right. The two of you should have come to me when this first happened."

Kyla stood and walked to the window. "Well, I'm sure he didn't tell you the whole story. Just the part he wanted you to hear."

"That's probably true. Let me see . . . he told me that you found him in bed with another woman and he wanted to know if I had any time to speak with the two of you together about healing."

Kyla blinked but remained silent.

"Oh, and he did add one other thing. He said that every part of him loved you and he was willing to do anything to heal your pain and rebuild your trust." When Kyla remained quiet, the pastor continued, "So, did he tell me everything?"

Kyla nodded.

"When would you like to make an appointment for the two of you to come in?"

"I don't know; I haven't decided what I'm going to do."

The pastor raised her eyebrows. "What you're going to do?"

"Jefferson and I are . . . separated, I guess. I'm staying with Alexis until Jefferson has a chance to put his things together and move out."

The pastor nodded her head slowly. "I have to say, I'm a bit surprised. I thought you were strong in the Lord."

Kyla met her glance. "I am!"

"I thought being strong in the Lord meant that your heart was fixed."

"That's what it means . . ." Her voice was slightly softer.

"I thought being strong in the Lord meant that you would stand through whatever was thrown your way." Pastor Ford paused. "Kyla, let me ask you something. Do you think you've been set aside by God not to have trials in your life?"

Kyla remained silent.

"You may not be saying it, but you're acting that way." She paused again, before adding, "Jesus has given you the power to deal with what you're going through."

"Pastor Ford, it's the Lord who has gotten me this far. It's just that my heart has ached every second since I found Jefferson with . . ."

The pastor came around the desk and took Kyla's hand. Her voice was gentle. "I understand, Kyla. I'm not even married to Jefferson and *I* feel bad. I feel bad for you and for him. I feel bad for me as his spiritual leader. But I know this can be turned around."

"I don't know how," Kyla's voice trembled.

"Kyla, other women have gone through this and have come out on the other side kicking butt. Sisters have come through adultery with stronger marriages, better self-images, greater love. This is your chance to look the devil in his face, call him a liar, and show him that you know how to stand."

"I'm trying to stand," she said weakly.

"It's more than just trying. It's *doing* what you know is right. Jefferson called me this afternoon and told me you won't even talk to him."

"That's because I don't know what to say . . ."

Pastor Ford smiled. "Then all we have to do is figure that out." She reached across her desk and handed Kyla her Bible. "The Word of God is very clear on this, Kyla. This is about forgiveness."

"That's what Alexis says, but how can I just excuse and forget what Jefferson did?" Kyla asked, barely able to hold back her tears.

Pastor Ford held up one hand. "Oh, no. I did not say anything about excusing Jefferson. He has a lot of work to do to earn your forgiveness and your trust. What I'm talking about is releasing him from *your* judgment. Because judgment is not your job. That belongs to God."

"I'm not trying to judge Jefferson. I just don't want to be one of the weak women who let men walk all over them."

"First of all, Jefferson is not like that. And secondly, it takes a person who is strong to forgive, Kyla. Forgiveness has nothing to do with weakness because by forgiving you're walking in Christ's example. Turn to Psalm 32:1."

Kyla read the verse silently. *Blessed is he whose transgression is forgiven, whose sin is covered.*

"God says that those of us who receive God's forgiveness are blessed. God bestows blessings on sinners. And that is each one of us, Kyla. The blessing in this life is that we have salvation *and* the forgiveness of our sins."

"I know that God forgives us, and I'm grateful for that. But how am *I* supposed to do that?"

"Kyla, forgiveness in this situation is a two-person process. Both you and Jefferson are going to have to work on this. But remember, it's a process that will take time and will be continuous. And there won't be an ending point; you'll be working on this for the rest of your life because forgiving doesn't mean that you'll forget. But Kyla, forgiveness is a direct order from the Lord. Turn to Luke 17:3." Pastor Ford began quoting the scripture from memory. "*If thy brother trespass against thee, rebuke him; and if he repent, forgive him.* Kyla, Jefferson has repented. He asked for the Lord's forgiveness first. He came to me and I prayed with him. Now, he's asking for your forgiveness."

Kyla wiped a tear from her cheek, smearing her makeup in the process.

"Kyla," the pastor continued, "I can give you scripture after scripture where the Lord tells us to forgive, just as He has forgiven us. This is the basis of our relationship with God."

"This is just so hard . . ." Kyla sniffed.

"Oh, I know it is, honey. But the Lord never said this walk was going to be easy."

"I can't erase the picture from my mind of walking into *my* bedroom and seeing another woman there. My brain is filled with visions of Jefferson and Jasmine together."

"I think that's why the Lord made forgiveness such an important part of the Christian doctrine. God knew the hold these kinds of sins would have over us. But forgiveness breaks the hold and sets you free."

With tears in her eyes, Kyla nodded.

"This is a crisis, Kyla. It's spiritual warfare and you have to do all that the situation demands. You have to pray, call on the name of Jesus, listen to the Lord's voice, and then move forward. You *have* to forgive. And you know how you can do it? Remember that God is with you, inside of you, filling you with the strength you need."

Kyla nodded again and Pastor Ford stood. "I think it's time for us to pray, but before we do that, what was it that you came in here to tell me?"

And through her tears, Kyla laughed.

Still in her bathrobe, Jasmine paced through the living room. This had not been a good day. No matter what she did, no matter who she called, Jefferson was nowhere to be found. There had to be something she could do to find him.

She sat down on the couch and brought her knees to her chest. As she rocked back and forth, thoughts of the past days floated through her mind. It wasn't like she wanted to break up Kyla and Jefferson. But what kind of marriage could they have had if it was so easy to get Jefferson into bed? Obviously, Jefferson was attracted to her. Enough to risk his marriage.

Everyone would blame her, but this wasn't her fault. Jefferson could have easily turned her away, but he didn't. And she hadn't really planned on Kyla finding out, but when she returned home early, it was inevitable.

Now, Jasmine felt she was close to having a real relationship in her life. Kyla had always been the lucky one. Now it was her turn. She had to do whatever it would take to get to the finish line. Finally, she went into the kitchen and removed the casserole dish from the refrigerator. "I've got to keep working my plan," she said.

Leaving the bowl on the counter, she ran up to her room and changed into the same dress she'd worn yesterday. "Okay, Jefferson," she said as she sauntered down the stairs. "We are going to have our night." Looking in the mirror, she smoothed her dress and ran her fingers through her curls. Pleased, she got the dish, picked up her purse and locked the door behind her. He had to come home sometime, and tonight she'd be there waiting right at the front door.

# Seventeen

"Argh!"

"What's wrong?" Kyla asked, looking up from Alexis' bedroom floor where she had the newspaper sprawled in front of her.

"Oh, nothing. I almost dropped this nail polish." Alexis carefully placed the bottle on the nightstand.

"That would have been nice. Red polish all over your white carpet."

"This is *not* red. It's Wanderlust."

Kyla rolled her eyes. "Whatever it's called, it would have looked like red on your carpet. That's why I suggested you put a different color carpet in here."

"I love my black-and-white apartment."

"It's so hard to keep clean."

"So what? I don't have to do it."

Kyla laughed. "And speaking of someone who refuses to lift a finger, how come you're doing your own nails?"

"Cause I haven't had the chance to get over to Nancy's."

Getting on her knees, Kyla leaned against Alexis' bed. "I hope it's not because of me."

"It's not you. Dr. Lewis is the one who's really keeping me busy."

Kyla smiled. "How're things with the two of you?"

"Great!" Alexis grinned. "I think this is moving towards the stage where you can call it a relationship. We've got as far as needing to have 'the talk.'"

Kyla scooted up onto the bed and folded her legs under her. "How did it come up? Was he trying to . . . you know?"

Alexis laughed. "You are all up in my business."

"Well, you're up in mine. So tell me . . ."

"Well." Alexis started waving her hands in the air to dry her nails. "We were here waiting for you guys. And we started kissing and before it got too far, I stopped him."

"Just like that?"

"Yeah, girl. I had to put on the brakes. One more minute and I would've been all over him."

Kyla laughed. "What did you say?"

"I told him that I wasn't a virgin, but I had been celibate and planned to stay that way until I got married."

"And what did *he* say?"

Alexis shrugged. "I don't really remember. It was all I could do to just concentrate on my words. But he did agree, though I don't think he was too happy."

"So, he hasn't been practicing celibacy?"

"We didn't go into that much detail, but I don't think so. It's interesting; when a man says he's a Christian, it can mean something totally different than when a woman says it."

"That's not fair, Alexis. You don't know what *anyone* means when they say they're a Christian."

"I know, but you know how these guys are. They will stand on every part of God's Word *except* for the part about fornication. Remember Donovan? He actually told me that God wasn't talking about *us* when it came to fornication. I asked him where in the Bible did God specifically exclude us? So I didn't expect much from Brian when it came to this sex discussion. But, surprisingly, it went well."

"Have you guys been out since then?"

"No, it happened Sunday and . . ."

"I've been here ever since. I hope I'm not getting in the way."

"You're not. I speak to Brian every day and he's coming by in the morning to take me to breakfast. I guess he wants to stay away from those hot and heavy nighttime dates for a while. But that's cool. So, speaking about our men . . ."

Kyla brought her legs up to her chest. "Leave it alone, Alex. This is the first time in days I've had a chance to relax."

"I was just going to ask about your talk with Pastor today."

"I already told you, I'm going to stay as the project leader with The Compassion House. She's even talking about it becoming a full-time position."

"You know that's not what I'm talking about."

The phone rang.

"Good," Kyla said. "I've been saved by the bell. It's probably your man calling."

"Hello . . . oh, hi, *Jefferson*. She's right here," Alexis said with wide eyes focused on Kyla. "No, it's *your* man calling," Alexis said, putting her hand over the receiver.

"No!" Kyla said, crossing her arms in front of her. "I don't want to talk to him."

"Kyla, take the telephone."

"I said no, Alexis."

They stood, holding their stares and finally Alexis brought the phone back to her ear. "I'm sorry, Jefferson, but my friend is acting like she lost the left side of her brain." Kyla watched as Alexis nodded her head. "Uh-huh, uh-huh," Alexis kept repeating. "Okay, Jefferson. I'll give her the message. Good night."

Alexis hung up the phone, her eyes bearing into Kyla. "You know you're being ridiculous."

"How come you keep jumping on me? It was Jefferson who cheated."

"And you know what, Kyla, I'm sorry about that. I really am. But when he stands before God on judgment day, his sin won't be any worse than any you've committed. So, you need to find a way to move on."

Kyla rolled her eyes and stomped out of the room. She paced in her bedroom, angry with Alexis, but angrier with herself because she knew Alexis was speaking the truth.

The knock on the door made her jump, and she turned as Alexis peeked into the room. "I just came in to tell you good night." She closed the door before Kyla could say anything, but not more than a second passed before Alexis opened the door again. "One other thing. Jefferson said to tell you that he loves you. He loves you with all of his heart and all of his mind. Not that that would mean anything to you!" And this time when she closed the door, Alexis missed the smile that had slowly edged onto Kyla's face.

Jefferson was holding his head in his hands when Brian knocked on the door.

"I wasn't sure if you were still here."

Jefferson didn't raise his head. "There's no place else for me to go." His voice was weary.

"Nothing's changed?" Brian asked as he leaned against the door.

"I can't even get Kyla to talk to me." Jefferson raised his eyes. "I don't know what I'm going to do. I want to try to work this thing out, but she won't let me."

"You know she won't be like this forever."

"I hope not."

"Just give her time. It's only been a few days. And she's hearing it from every end. I know Alexis is working on her."

"Yeah, Alex may be mad at me, but she's on my side, thank God."

"And you can't expect Kyla to just come running back to you. This is a lot for her to deal with."

"I understand that, but we have to work through this together."

"She's probably thinking that your mind wasn't on being together when you were with Jasmine."

"Thanks, Brian. I feel *so* much better now that I've had the chance to talk to you."

"Hey, I'm only trying to get you to see it from her side so you'll be better equipped to handle this thing."

"I'm afraid that the longer this goes on, the more she'll get used to being without me and that is driving me crazy! I don't want to live my life without Kyla and Nicole."

"But what if she tells you she needs some space? Are you prepared to give it to her and move out?"

"I'm not going to move out! I'll never do that. I'll sleep in another room if I have to; I'll do anything *except* move out."

"Okay, remember I'm on your side. This will all work

out." Brian patted Jefferson on his shoulder. "What are you doing tonight?"

Jefferson shrugged. "I'm finished here; I guess I'll just go home."

"Let's grab something to eat."

"No, thanks. I'm not in the mood to go anywhere."

"We can have something delivered to my place. It'll give us a chance to hang out."

"I'm not very good company . . ." Jefferson said, shaking his head.

"Well, I am. All you're going to do is go home to that big house and sit around feeling sorry for yourself. Come with me, we'll have pizza, and I'm sure there's a game on tonight. I can take some of your money."

"Oh yeah?" Jefferson smirked. "Still a Red Sox fan, huh?"

"You know it, and if we're lucky, they'll be playing one of your pitiful California teams. Whadda ya say? We haven't had a chance to really hang out since I got back."

Jefferson was thoughtful. "I guess I could. I already know that Kyla isn't coming home tonight . . ."

"You don't have to sound so excited," Brian grinned. "I know I'm a poor substitute, but at least I'm something."

"Maybe I should go home and change."

"What do you need to change for? Just take off that tie and roll up your sleeves. I've gotta warn you though, I haven't finished unpacking. There are boxes everywhere!"

Jefferson chuckled. "Thanks, man. I appreciate having something to do tonight."

"No problem. I just got Direct TV and with all of those

channels, we'll be able to find a game or two. Let me just grab my stuff." Brian trotted out of the office.

Jefferson gathered his jacket and bag. Even if it was just for a few hours, he was grateful for the distraction. But he knew Kyla would not be far from his main thoughts. And that's just the way he wanted it.

"Jefferson said to tell you that he loves you with all of his heart and all of his mind." Alexis' words played back in her ears. Kyla turned over and clicked on the light. Those same words were part of the marriage vows he'd written and he'd said them to her often through the years.

"At least he didn't forget," Kyla said to herself. She got out of bed and walked to the window. The city lights had dimmed long ago and a nocturnal peace had fallen atop Los Angeles. Hugging her arms against the coolness of the room, she returned to the bed. "With all of his heart and all of his mind."

It was just after eleven. He was probably just getting into bed, watching the news, then reading his Bible. Before she could change her mind, she picked up the phone. She frowned when the answering machine came on and she hung up, dialing the number again. Surely, he was in the bathroom or something.

For the next fifteen minutes, she called continuously, never leaving a message, but finally accepting that he was not home.

Her decision came within seconds and taking a breath, she dialed another number. She closed her eyes, her pounding heart the only sound in the room. As the phone began to ring, the pit in her stomach warned her to hang up. What was she going to say anyway? But she had already dialed and she had to go all the way. She had to know.

"Wait! Keep ringing!" Jasmine yelled to the phone as she put her key in the door. It was probably Jefferson.

"Hello," she said breathlessly.

Jasmine heard breathing on the other end.

"Hello," she repeated.

"Jasmine . . ." the voice was a whisper.

In a split second, a thousand thoughts ran through her mind and an idea came to her. "Oh, Kyla, hello." Jasmine made sure her voice was calm. Then she yelled over her shoulder into an empty room, "Jefferson, Kyla's on the phone." Jasmine heard Kyla's moan and then the dial tone droned in her ear.

Jasmine hung up the phone and collapsed onto her couch. She kicked off her shoes and sighed. The hours that she had sat in front of Jefferson's house had made her return home discouraged. But Kyla had just turned that around.

If Jefferson wasn't with Kyla, then they hadn't worked anything out. But, she had a feeling that she had to move her plan into overdrive. She had to get Jefferson back in bed. Just one more time and then, he would be hers.

# Eighteen

Jasmine jumped. Her hands groped the table and picked up the phone. "Hello," her voice was groggy with lack of sleep.

"Jasmine, you sound awful."

Sitting up, she peered around the room through tired eyes. "What time is it?"

"It's after eight. Still not feeling well, huh?"

Jasmine shook her head. "Uh, no. I didn't have much sleep, Rose."

"Well, I guess you won't be in today . . ."

"I'm really tired . . ."

"It's that awful flu. Well, stay home and rest. I guess I'll have to handle the presentation from here."

"I'm sorry . . ."

"Don't be. You probably caught the flu from me. Call me later if you're feeling better."

Swiveling her stockinged legs onto the floor, she held her head. She didn't know what time she'd fallen asleep. She stumbled into the kitchen, dumped a spoonful of instant coffee and water into a cup, then put the drink in the microwave. The hot cup felt good against her hands. At least I don't have to think about work, she thought. She went back into the living room and the mirror above the mantel caught her eye. Her eyes were puffy and the makeup she hadn't taken the time to remove was streaked across her face. She looked sick. She had to stop sleeping on the couch.

Jefferson would be at the clinic by now, she thought as she sipped her coffee. But today, phone calls wouldn't do. She left her cup on the living room table and went upstairs to get dressed.

"Wow! You were up early," Alexis said as she joined Kyla in the dining room. "I heard you out here before I even got up."

"I'm sorry, did I wake you?" Kyla looked up from her Bible.

"Oh no. I was up; I'm just surprised that you were."

"I've been up all night it seems. I'm going to see Jefferson this morning."

Alexis grinned. "Finally! Kyla, this is all going to work out. I know it doesn't seem that way right now . . ."

Kyla held up her hand stopping Alexis. "I'm going to see Jefferson . . . so that we can begin talking about getting a divorce."

"What? How did you move from not talking to him to getting a divorce?"

"I called Jefferson last night . . . and he wasn't home. Then I called Jasmine and found out he was there."

"I don't believe it. What did he say?"

"He didn't say anything. I hung up before he could get to the phone."

Alexis frowned. "And he didn't try to call you back?"

Kyla shook her head. "No."

"That doesn't make sense. He knows you're staying here. Something's not right."

"All I know is that he was with her last night."

"Kyla, don't jump to conclusions. You've tried and convicted this man before he's had a chance to present his case."

"He doesn't need a trial. The evidence is obvious."

Before Alexis could respond, the intercom rang and the concierge announced that Brian was on his way up.

"I'll just go into the bedroom and leave you guys alone."

"No, don't do that. We're going out to breakfast. Why don't you join us?"

"No, I don't think so."

Before Alexis had a chance to protest, the doorbell rang.

"Good morning," Alexis smiled as she opened the door.

"Hey, honey." Brian kissed her. "Hey, Kyla."

Kyla forced a smile. "How are you, Brian?"

"I'm doing good. I just left your husband."

"You did?" Alexis asked, her eyes darting between Kyla and Brian.

"Yeah, he fell asleep on my couch last night. We stayed up pretty late talking. You know," he said turning to Kyla, "he's pretty shaken up by all of this."

Kyla sank down in the chair. "He was with *you* last night?"

"Yeah," Brian frowned. "Why?"

"Kyla thought Jefferson was with Jasmine," Alexis explained.

"No way. He doesn't even want to be in the same state with that woman. I can vouch for where he was. He didn't plan on staying, but, like I said, it got late and he slept on the couch."

Alexis turned to Kyla. "I hope this sends you a message. Jasmine is willing to do anything."

Kyla didn't respond, but breathed deeply. She felt surprisingly relieved as thoughts swirled in her head. Jefferson hadn't been with Jasmine and he was feeling as bad about all of this as she was.

"Brian, let me go get my things. I'll be ready in a moment."

When Alexis left the room, Brian sat down at the table with Kyla. "So, how are you really doing?"

"I guess a little better now that I know where Jefferson was last night. But I'm still confused. I have so many mixed feelings."

"That's understandable. But Jefferson is sick about all of this too. He loves you and wants a chance to prove it. I've known him for a long time and I've never seen him like this."

"Well, some might say the same thing about me."

Brian laid his hand on top of hers. "I know you're in pain, Kyla. But don't you even want to try to work this out?"

Kyla felt her eyes begin to water. "I'm afraid."

"Of what?"

"Of being hurt like this again. I wouldn't survive if Jefferson ever . . ."

Brian leaned back in his chair and exhaled. "You need to tell Jefferson that. Tell him how you feel and then listen to him."

"Is everything all right out here?" Alexis walked into the room tentatively.

"Yeah, we're fine. You ready?"

"Uh-huh. Kyla, are you sure you won't join us? We'd really love the company."

"I think you two can get along without me. I'll be fine. I have some things I have to . . . work out."

Kyla closed the door behind them as they left and went to the balcony. The tears that fell today were ones of relief. Without any more thought, Kyla went inside and picked up the phone.

"Hi Shannon. This is Kyla. How are you?"

"Fine, Kyla. I haven't spoken to you in a few days."

"I've been . . . away. Is Jefferson available?"

"Yes, I think he's just finishing with a patient."

"I can call back . . ."

"No. He said to put you through immediately if you called. Hold on a second, please."

Kyla sat and tapped her fingers atop the endtable as her heart pounded harder with each passing second.

"Kyla."

She stood at the sound of his voice. "Hello, Jefferson."

"I'm so glad you called . . ."

"I just wanted to know," she started as she shifted her feet. "Can we get together today?"

"Of course. I just have to see if there is anyone here who can cover me."

"Oh, no. I don't mean right now. I don't want you to cancel anything . . ."

"I don't mind."

"I would prefer if we got together this evening. After you've finished."

"Okay . . ." Jefferson said, still wondering if he should clear his calendar. "It looks like I'll be finished by six . . ."

"Then I'll meet you sometime after that. Let's just meet . . . I'll meet you at home."

There was an uncomfortable pause. "Kyla, I can't wait to see you."

She waited a beat. "I'll see you later, Jefferson."

"Okay, and Kyla? I love you."

She hung up the phone.

Jasmine looked in the mirror. She was ready to go. Yesterday she had played it safe, but there was no way she was going to sit around today.

As soon as she opened the car door, the smell hit her. She'd forgotten about the two-day-old casserole that sat in her car overnight. She sucked her teeth. It would take days for the foul odor to evaporate from her car. Taking the dish inside, she returned with air freshener and sprayed it liberally throughout. She forced a smile. There was no way she was going to let anything put her in a bad mood this morning.

Within minutes, she pulled into the parking lot of the clinic. She'd been inside only once before, during the grand opening, and she smiled now as she parked next to Jefferson's Range Rover. Quickly, she got out of her car, walked past the security guard, and went into the building. Not knowing where Jefferson's office was, she stopped at the receptionist's desk.

"I'm here to see Dr. Jefferson Blake."

"Is he expecting you?" The young girl's braids swayed and Jasmine wondered why she was yelling.

"Yes, he is. I just need to know where his office is."

"I have to call his assistant."

"Why can't you just tell me where his office is?" Jasmine snapped.

The young girl's eyes got wide. "I'm sorry. I have to do it this way." Her voice seemed to get louder.

"Is there a problem here?" The security guard came over to the receptionist.

Jasmine's eyes wandered up and down the gray-suited guard. She smiled, and moved forward to stand closer to the man. "Uh, no. There's no problem, officer . . ." she squinted to look at his name tag, "there's no problem, Officer Daniels. I just need to know where Dr. Blake's office is."

The girl looked at the guard. "I was just telling her that I have to call Shannon first. I'm just following the rules."

"Go ahead and dial," the guard said.

As the girl spoke into the phone, Jasmine smiled at the guard, but he looked away and Jasmine was sure that it was the gray at his temples that stopped him from reacting to her. She tapped her foot as she tried to make out what the girl was saying, and she finally hung up the phone. "Shannon will be right down. You can have a seat if you want."

The guard motioned to Jasmine. Turning, she swayed her hips as she moved slowly towards the seat. When she looked back, he had already turned away, not taking any notice of her. Jasmine sucked her teeth.

Another young woman in a chocolate brown suit came down from the second floor and walked straight to Jasmine. "Hello, I'm Shannon Gray, Dr. Blake's assistant. May I help you?"

Oh, no, Jasmine thought. This is the woman I've been fighting with on the phone. "Yes, I need to see Dr. Blake, please." Jasmine tried to keep her voice calm.

"I'm sorry. Dr. Blake's calendar is completely full today. Is there someone else who can help you Ms. . . ."

Jasmine knew she was asking for her name. "I only need to speak to Dr. Blake for a few minutes. I'm sure if you told him I was here, he'd find a way to squeeze me in."

"All right." Shannon frowned. "I'll tell him. And you are . . ."

Jasmine inhaled. "Mrs. Jasmine Larson," she said holding up her chin.

Jasmine watched as Shannon's eyes narrowed. "Yes, Mrs. Larson. I'll let Dr. Blake know."

Jasmine's eyes followed Shannon up the stairs. From the reception area, Jasmine had a complete view of the octagonal-shaped building and she kept her eyes on Shannon as she walked around the railing, finally stopping outside one of the offices. As Shannon knocked and went inside, Jasmine smiled. She wouldn't have to go through all this the next time.

She picked up a magazine and flipped through the pages, her eyes constantly darting up. She stood as Shannon came into view and proceeded down the stairs.

"I'm sorry, Mrs. Larson. Dr. Blake said he won't be able to meet with you."

Jasmine blinked rapidly. "This is important. I have to speak to him."

"He asked that you call him at home."

"I'll just sit here and wait," Jasmine said as she returned to the seat and picked up the magazine she'd been reading.

Shannon sighed. "I'm sorry, but he's with a patient and has a full schedule for the rest of the day."

"Is everything all right?" The guard came over again.

"I've just been explaining that Dr. Blake cannot see Mrs. Larson today . . ."

"And, I *said* I would wait," Jasmine said, raising her voice slightly.

"I'm going to have to ask you to leave the building."

Jasmine raised her head slowly and glared at the security guard. "What?"

"You can call Dr. Blake for an appointment, but if you don't mind . . ." Officer Daniel's voice seemed to get deeper.

Jasmine stood, grabbed her purse, and under her breath, cursed them as she stomped from the clinic.

"Are you okay, Shannon?" Officer Daniels asked.

"Sure. I'm fine." With purposeful steps, she went back to her office. She'd been trying to figure out how to take care of this since the phone calls started yesterday. She tried to speak to Jefferson, but he had brushed it aside. He didn't want to talk to her about it. And Shannon understood. Especially if she was right about what was happening. But now, it was clear to her that Jasmine wasn't going to disappear, and if Jefferson didn't know what to do, she did.

Alexis was beaming. "Kyla, I'm so glad. Things will be fine after you talk to Jefferson."

"I don't know, Alexis, and I don't want you to get your hopes up. I'm just going to talk to him."

"Well, that's a start. I have a feeling that Jefferson will do the rest. What time are you meeting?"

"Sometime between seven and eight at our house. I wanted to let you know where I'll be . . ."

"Hopefully, you'll be there all night and tomorrow and the next day and the next day. Call me tonight."

"I will. But I hope you and Brian will get out, now that you won't have to baby-sit me."

"That's a thought," Alexis laughed. "Maybe I'll cook dinner for him or order in as we sit anxiously and wait to hear from you."

"Whatever. Have fun."

Alexis was still smiling as she hung up the phone. Finally! She had to let Brian know. As she reached for the phone, it rang.

"Ward speaking."

"Alexis? This is Shannon Gray, Dr. Blake's assistant."

"Yes, Shannon." Alexis immediately sat up in her chair. She knew Shannon well from the years she'd worked for Jefferson. And though she'd spoken to her often, she was sure this was the first time Shannon had ever called her.

"I feel a little strange calling you. And I probably shouldn't . . ." Shannon hesitated. She knew she was doing the right thing. Alexis would know what to do. "I just wanted to let you know that Dr. Blake is having a problem . . ."

Alexis frowned. "What kind of problem?"

"Well, Jasmine Larson keeps calling him, even though he's made it clear that he won't speak to her while he's at the office. But, the thing is, she showed up at the clinic this morning. I had to have security escort her out."

"Did she speak to Jefferson?"

"No, he wouldn't see her. But, Alexis, I think this has gotten a little embarrassing for Dr. Blake. The only reason I'm calling you is because I'm afraid of what she'll do next. Like follow him to the hospital or follow him home, I don't know what . . ."

Follow him home. Oh no, Alexis thought. If she followed Jefferson home today and he was meeting Kyla . . .

"Shannon, do you have Jasmine's number?"

Shannon exhaled. "Yes. I hope you know that I don't believe in getting involved in Dr. Blake's personal business, but when I tried to speak with him about Mrs. Larson, he just brushed it aside, saying it wasn't very serious. But, I think this *is* very serious now."

"You did the right thing. Thanks for calling me."

Alexis stared at the telephone number. Maybe I should call Jefferson myself, she thought. But then she shook the thought away. He had enough to deal with. She'd handle this. It was time for Jasmine to meet one of Kyla's real friends. Alexis put on her jacket, grabbed her purse and rushed out the door.

The windows shook as Jasmine slammed the door. She threw her purse on the couch and screamed. What was she going to do now? There was no use calling Jefferson. Shannon would never put her through. At least she had left that note on his car. He'd call her once he read it, but that might not be until tonight.

The doorbell rang and she frowned. No one knew she was home, except Rose and . . . Jefferson. She ran to the door.

"Hello, Jasmine. May I come in?" Alexis asked as she walked past Jasmine.

"What do you want?" Jasmine stood at the opened door.

"May I sit down?" Before the words were out of her

mouth, Alexis had already sat down on the couch. "We have to talk."

Jasmine slammed the door. "I don't know what you want, but I have nothing to say to you. I would prefer it if you would just leave my home."

Alexis' eyes surveyed the room, then she smiled as she stared at Jasmine. "We can either have a nice *friendly* chat or this can be nasty. It's your choice." Her smile disappeared.

Jasmine swallowed hard, but she was not about to let Alexis intimidate her. "What do you want?"

"I have just one question for you. What is your basic malfunction?"

"What are you talking about?" Jasmine knew what Alexis wanted, but she had no intentions of discussing anything with her.

Alexis' voice seemed to drop an octave. "Jasmine, I was trying to do this nicely, but it's not possible. So, let me say what I came to say. *Leave Kyla and Jefferson alone.*"

"Who do you think you are?" Jasmine yelled. "Coming into *my* house and telling me what to do with *my* friends! Well, I have news for you. I was friends with Kyla way before you even came into the picture. You have no right to come in here and try to tell me what to do!"

Alexis stood, towering over Jasmine. "Oh, I have every right. Because I know what a real friend is. You know what, Jasmine?" Alexis started as she folded her arms in front of her. "I always knew you were scum. I did. But even I never believed you would slither this low. You're right, you have known Kyla a lot longer, which makes it even more amazing that you did what you did. How *did* you trick Jefferson into going to bed with you?"

"Trick him! Is that what you think?" Jasmine laughed. "Jefferson could have easily said no, but he wanted me."

"Ha! Maybe the way a dog wants a bone—to chew on for a second, then throw away. Let me give you this news flash. Jefferson doesn't want you. He doesn't even like you. He loves Kyla. So, be smart—stay away from them," Alexis said menacingly.

"You think you can walk into my house and *threaten* me? Are you out of your mind? You have some nerve. Dressed in your expensive clothes like you're somebody . . ."

"Expensive clothes don't make you somebody, Jasmine. You've proven that."

"Well, I'm not scared of you, Alexis. I don't care who you are or how many businesses you own. You can't stop what's happening with me and Jefferson. We'll be together tonight and there is nothing you can do about it."

Alexis shook her head slowly. "I never thought I'd live to see the day when I'd feel sorry for you. You have lost what little mind you did have. So, because you don't have much sense left, I'm going to break this down. Stay . . . away . . . from . . . Jefferson. Walk away now, while you can still walk."

"And if I don't? What are you going to do?" Jasmine screamed.

Alexis removed her purse from her shoulder and placed it on the table. She began to take off her jacket.

Jasmine's eyes widened. This woman couldn't be serious.

Alexis folded her jacket and placed it on the couch. "If you don't stay away from Jefferson, I'm going to . . . Kick. Your. Behind."

Her voice may have been steady, but Jasmine could tell by the way her eyes blazed that Alexis was serious.

Jasmine paused, letting Alexis' words settle. She looked her up and down and measured her chances. She wasn't about to get beaten in her own home. "And you call yourself a Christian."

Alexis inhaled a deep breath and took moments to release it. As Jasmine hoped, Alexis paused. "You're right. I am a Christian. And that gives me even more reason to protect my friends."

Jasmine's heart was still pounding. Maybe her strategy didn't work, but then she exhaled as Alexis picked up her jacket.

"Jasmine, next time, I won't let you off so easy. Stay out of my way and stay away from Jefferson and Kyla. They're working things out. And as soon as you realize you were a mistake, then you can move on and spin your poisonous web elsewhere!"

"I told you, Alexis. I'm not afraid of you!"

Alexis raised her eyebrows. "Then you're stupider than I thought. You *should* be afraid."

After Alexis stomped out, with shaky legs, Jasmine ran to the door and locked it. Her fisted hands beat against the sides of her legs. *Everyone* was trying to keep her away from Jefferson, but it was not going to work. After several minutes, she allowed her breathing to become steady. They were all only making her more determined. And with everything in her, she was determined to win.

# Nineteen

It was almost seven when Kyla arrived. Taking a deep breath, she pulled into the garage next to the Range Rover. As soon as she turned off the ignition, the door to the house opened and she gasped as she caught a glimpse of him. He was wearing her favorite outfit—a tight, black, short-sleeved turtleneck and fitted black jeans. His muscles seemed to be popping everywhere. With a smile but hesitant eyes, he held the door open wide for her.

"Hey, you," Jefferson smiled.

Like a moth drawn to a flame, she longed to run into his arms and forget all that had happened. Instead she stuffed her hands into the pockets of her denim duster and stepped past Jefferson, conscious of the charge that shot through her when her arm brushed against his chest.

He followed her into the kitchen, where she turned to face him, not sure of where to go next. He kept a safe distance, but his eyes bore into hers, screaming his emotions.

"Do you want something to eat? Or drink?"

She shook her head. "No." She paused. "I feel like . . . a visitor."

241

He reached for her, but pulled back when she stiffened. "Kyla, I want you here; I want you home. I want you to come back . . ."

"Let's go in there," she said, pointing to the family room.

Even when she sat, she didn't remove her hands from her pockets and the shaking had reached her shoulders.

"Are you cold?"

"No," she frowned.

Silent seconds dragged as long as minutes and hung between them.

"Kyla . . ."

"Jefferson . . ." They spoke simultaneously, then shared a nervous laugh.

"I love you, Kyla."

Her eyes dropped, then she lifted her face, staring back at him. Her face hardened against his stare. It was a moment before she spoke. "I hate you." The words were so soft and the silence that followed so long, that Kyla wondered if she had really said the words or just imagined them. But, as she watched mist cover his eyes, she knew he'd heard her. "I *hate* you," she repeated more emphatically.

Jefferson swallowed hard and nodded.

Shaking her head slightly, she continued, "Jefferson, how could you do this to me?"

"I . . ."

"How could you do this to us? Why didn't you tell me that you weren't happy . . ."

"That's not true. I was . . . I *am* happy with you."

"Then how could you do it?"

He hung his head. "I don't know. I made a terrible mistake . . . I can't even explain it."

"Those kind of mistakes were not supposed to happen to us, Jefferson."

"I know. I don't understand it myself."

"You don't understand it?" she asked as she stood. "Well, let me see if you can understand *this*." Facing the pictures on the mantel, she inhaled, willing herself to speak without tears. "The mistake *you* made ripped the guts out of me! I feel like I've been in surgery, but the doctors forgot to use anesthesia and then they forgot to close me up. I feel like I've been torn apart, split open, and left raw."

Jefferson brought shaky hands to his face, holding them under his chin as if he were praying. He nodded and waited for her to continue.

Walking back to the couch, she sat on the edge and faced him. "You were in my blood, Jefferson, deep inside my bones. Every fiber of who I am loved you like a crazy woman, and now," she paused and her hands fingered the gold heart around her neck. "Now, every space where there was love is now flooded with pain. There is no place on my body that doesn't hurt, and I'm afraid this pain will never go away."

Instinctively, he reached for her hands and this time, she didn't pull back. "Kyla, it will go away. I promise you. I will take it away. I will do anything I have to do."

Her head shook slightly. "You gave it to me, but you can't take it away. I have to do that and I don't know if I can."

"But Kyla, you didn't do anything . . . I'll do it . . ."

"Yes I did. I lived in a make-believe world, blind to everything. I trusted you, I trusted Jasmine. I opened my home and my heart to that woman and . . ." She stopped.

"Kyla, the only person to blame is me. I will put us back

243

together. Counseling, working with Pastor Ford, whatever it takes. I want to help you heal, help us heal."

"You want me to heal?" She looked him directly in the eye. "Heal from what, Jefferson?"

His eyes narrowed. "From all the pain I caused you. From everything . . ."

"Does that include AIDS?" Her voice was barely a whisper. "Are you going to make sure I don't get AIDS from you?"

He blinked rapidly. "What?"

"Did you use a condom, Jefferson?" Tears were beginning to fill her eyes once again.

"Of course not. I don't use condoms . . ." And then it hit him. He was a doctor and he had never considered the possibility of disease. "No, it wasn't planned," he said. "I didn't want to . . . she came over here and seduced me . . ." His eyes couldn't meet Kyla's glance. "No, I didn't."

"Then, this could just be the beginning."

"I'll get tested . . ." He was surprised at how thin his voice sounded.

"And, what about Jasmine? Suppose she becomes . . . pregnant."

He was silent for a moment before he spoke, "She's not pregnant."

Kyla's head reared back. "She's not? How do you know? Are you shooting blanks now?" Even she winced at her angry words.

"I will take care of everything. I'll get us back to where we were."

"You can't do that. Nothing will be the same again."

"All I know is that I love you and I'm holding on to the

belief that you love me. And God is here with us, still in control. The Lord will help us make things right."

"I don't know . . ."

"Tell me, Kyla. Tell me that you don't love me. Tell me that everything from the last sixteen years has been wiped away."

She sat still, silent.

He lowered his eyes. "Please give me a chance to work through this."

"I don't know if I can," she whispered, her voice quavering.

Slowly, he moved towards her and knelt, his hands resting gently in her lap. "We love each other and what we have is so much stronger than what I've done."

She closed her eyes. "I just want . . ."

"What? What do you want?"

She looked up, and against her will, her hands touched his face, her fingers traced the lines around his eyes. "I want to love you again . . ."

He breathed. "That's what I want . . ."

"But I can't."

"Yes . . . yes you can. We can make it. Our love was strong; it *is* strong. And I believe in us. That's what you have to believe too."

"Our love wasn't strong enough to keep you away from another woman."

He swallowed. "That was because of me, Kyla. Because of my shortcomings as a man. It was not about you or our love. You've got to give me another chance."

She shook her head. "I can't open myself up like this again . . ."

A tear eased down his cheek. "Kyla, there will *never* be another time like this. I can promise you that . . ."

"You made that promise before."

He grimaced. "I did. And with what has happened, with all the pain I've caused you, I know that I could never do anything like this again. I am begging you. I am begging for your forgiveness."

Kyla remained still.

"Can you try to forgive me? Just try?" His eyes pierced her with that question. "Try to remember the life we had before this, Kyla. Remember the love you know I had for you. It is still there. Try to remember . . ."

Her eyes softened and he knew she was remembering.

"Can you try to forgive me?" he repeated. "I know it's going to take a lot of work. I know it may take months, even years. All I'm asking is that you give me a chance. I will spend every day of my life being the man that you thought I was. Being the man that you loved. All I want is a chance . . ."

"Just a chance . . ." she whispered.

"That's all I'm asking."

She brought her hands to her face to hold back the tears that wanted to burst forth.

"Just a chance . . . to show you that I love you with all that is in me," Jefferson continued.

She moved her head up and down.

He didn't want to wish or hope, but couldn't help saying his next words. "You'll come back? You'll stay?"

Again, she nodded.

In slow motion, he stood, and with tentative movements, leaned forward, reaching for her hands. When she didn't resist, he pulled her to her feet and hugged her close. They held each other tightly, trying to find the familiar space. Taking the tips of his fingers, he brushed her face and moved his lips to hers. She pulled away, shaking her head.

He put his fingers against her lips. "It's all right, Kyla."

Turning away, her watery eyes roamed the room, trying to find a safe space.

He moved away, fighting his urge to hold her and giving her the space she needed. Forcing a smile, he said, "It's still early. Why don't we go out and get something to eat?"

She shook her head. "I'm not hungry."

"Neither am I, not really."

As she stood there, looking like a lost child, his heart reached out to her. And he wanted to do the same, but he continued to hold back. He didn't want to chase her away.

"Tomorrow, I'm going to call Pastor and try to get us in to see her right away. And I'll take care of those . . . other things you mentioned."

She couldn't look at him. She nodded.

It felt awkward, the stranger's kind of silence that surrounded them. "We can watch television or something. Whatever you want to do."

"Actually, I'm kind of tired. I think I'm going to call Alexis, then turn in. If that's all right with you."

"That's fine. I'll come up with you . . ."

Her words came quickly. "I'm not going to sleep up there . . ." Her eyes looked up towards their bedroom. "I'll sleep in the guest bedroom."

"Okay."

The stranger's silence returned.

"I'll go in now."

"Kyla, before you go . . . maybe we can pray together."

Her smile seemed weary. "Of course."

She returned to the couch and took his hands. They bowed their heads and Jefferson prayed. "Dear Heavenly Father, we come to you with praise and thanksgiving . . ."

Kyla tried to focus on Jefferson's prayer, but her mind was filled with a million thoughts. She squeezed her eyes tighter, trying to block out everything she was feeling. Was she doing the right thing? Maybe they needed more time apart?

"And," Jefferson paused from what he'd been saying and opened his eyes, looking directly at Kyla. "Help Kyla to know that I love her with all my heart."

At the mention of her name, Kyla opened her eyes. They stared at each other for a moment before Jefferson continued, "In Jesus Christ's name we pray, Amen."

Kyla dropped Jefferson's hand and stood. "Good night," she said. He moved towards her, then stopped when she held up her hands. "No, Jefferson. I'll see you in the morning. We can talk more then."

He watched her walk into the bedroom, and though his heart ached, he forced a smile. At least she was home. One step at a time.

"I can't believe you have me doing this," Brian complained as he turned off Slauson and started up the hill towards the Colony Homes.

"You were the one who said we had to do anything to get them back together."

"They *are* together. And we're about to interrupt them,"

"We're not going to interrupt them if we don't have to. I

just want to make sure that Jasmine doesn't show up like she said she would. No! Don't pull into their driveway!"

Brian swerved and kept driving straight. "Where am I supposed to go?"

"Down the street. I don't want anyone to see us."

Brian sighed deeply and turned the car around.

"Work with me a little, honey," Alexis said, as she rubbed her hand along his leg. "We won't be long." He parked a few houses down and Alexis peered through the windows. "They're home. The lights are on." Her eyes searched the street. "And there's no sign of Jasmine's car."

"I can't believe things have come to this. You're turning me into a voyeur."

"Don't get your hopes up; we're not going to be peeking into anybody's windows. We'll wait a while and if Jasmine doesn't show up, we'll leave, okay?"

"We're wasting time. She's not crazy enough to show up here."

"She's not, huh?" Alexis asked pointing her finger. "Guess who's coming to visit."

They watched a car approach slowly, then turn into the Blakes' driveway.

"I am not going to let her do this!" Alexis was bolting down the street before she completed her words. When Jasmine stepped from her car, Alexis was waiting. "Hello, Jasmine," she said.

"What are you doing here?" Jasmine's voice did not hide her surprise.

"I thought you understood English."

Jasmine slammed her car door. "Alexis, this is none of your business."

"I told you to stay away from Jefferson."

"Who are you?" Jasmine was indignant. "His body-guard?"

"No, I'm in charge of pest control. Jasmine, this is ridiculous. Why don't you go home and haunt your own house?"

"I don't care what you say or what you think. This is between me and Jefferson. No one else. And besides that, he *wants* me. You're making me out to be the villain and it's Jefferson who took *me* to bed. Now, excuse me, he's waiting for me now."

"Jasmine, you're crazy and you're a liar. Jefferson doesn't want to see you. He's with Kyla right now."

Jasmine took a step towards Alexis. "I don't believe you." Her voice was tight.

"She's telling you the truth."

The voice came from behind her and Jasmine spun around, squinting in the dark. She smiled. "Hi, Brian. I don't know if you remember me. We've met a few times, I'm Jasmine."

"I know who you are."

Her smile widened. "Are you going to see Jefferson? So am I," she said as she glared at Alexis.

"I'm not going to see Jefferson and neither are you." Brian walked up the driveway and stood next to Alexis. "I'm just here to back up the woman I love. Alexis told you, he's in there with Kyla, and I don't think they want to be interrupted."

Jasmine started shaking her head slowly. "I can't believe this. Do you two really think you can stop me from going in there?" When Alexis and Brian remained still, Jasmine tossed her hair over her shoulder. "All right, I'll go, but don't think anything has changed," she said directing her words to Alexis. "You can't follow me around for the rest of your life."

"I will if I have to," Alexis said sweetly.

They watched as she screeched out of the driveway and disappeared down the street.

"Do you think she'll come back?" Brian asked.

"She will, but not tonight," Alexis said smiling at Brian. "She'll be afraid that my hero will be sitting out here waiting for her."

"She's not going to give up, is she? What was Jefferson thinking?"

"I think it was just lust and a temporary loss of sanity." Taking his hand, she led him back to the car. "But at least he won't have to deal with her tonight."

"Only because you were here, Ms. Ward." Brian leaned against the car and with his hands around her waist, pulled her to him. "You never stop surprising me."

"Well, you pull some surprises yourself, Dr. Lewis. You said that I was the woman you loved."

He smiled. "Did I say that? I didn't realize it."

"That's even better. It came from your subconscious."

He pulled her closer, squeezing her breasts against his chest. "Are you a psychiatrist now?"

"No, I just know these things. Some people might say that we haven't known each other long enough to be mentioning the 'L' word. And, men are never the first ones to say it."

"I didn't know that." His eyes teased her.

"Did you mean it?"

"Yes."

"Then I'm going to help you out."

"How?"

"Take back what you said."

"But I mean what I said."

"Work with me, Brian."

"Okay . . . I take it back."

She took a deep breath. "Dr. Lewis, I think I'm falling in love with you." She paused, letting the words sink in for both of them.

His eyes held a serious gaze and then he smiled. "I feel exactly the same way."

In the darkness of Oak Avenue, they kissed passionately, their hands exploring each other, touching nerve endings that ignited fiery explosions inside both of them.

"Alexis," Brian said her name breathlessly. "I want you."

"Yes," she moaned.

He pulled back slightly and his glazed eyes searched hers. "Are you saying . . ."

She smiled. "Let's go home, Brian. It's time for us to go home."

Jasmine stomped into her house, threw her purse on the couch and sighed. Maybe she should have pushed past Alexis, but she was just too tired to second-guess herself now. Exhaustion blanketed her. It had been days since she'd had a good night's sleep. About as long as it'd been since she'd seen Jefferson.

She held her head in her hands and closed her eyes tightly. Were Kyla and Jefferson really back together? If what Alexis had said was true, then it was over for her.

Her eyes popped open. Kyla hadn't come back. She knew Kyla as well as anyone and she knew Kyla wouldn't forgive Jefferson that quickly. She was too self-righteous and all caught up in that Christian thing. Jefferson had sinned and that went against everything Kyla stood for. She was sure Kyla and Jefferson couldn't have reconciled.

At least that was her prayer. Jasmine chuckled wearily as she thought about praying, something she hadn't done since she was a child. But, maybe it was time to pray and put God to the test. She couldn't lose the only chance she had at happiness. Without Jefferson, she didn't know where her life would be. "Just one more time, Jefferson," she said aloud.

Standing at the window, she plotted a plan, something that would work whether Kyla was back home or not.

They'd driven the twelve miles in silence. Brian pulled into the circular driveway.

Alexis closed her eyes and breathed deeply. "Brian . . ."

"You don't really want to do this, do you?"

Looking at him, she shook her head and wondered how did he know? Could he hear her pounding heart against her chest? Or was it the voice screaming inside her head that gave her away?

"Then, why did you say you did?" he asked, unable to hide his annoyance.

"I didn't really say anything. Brian, I'm sorry. I'm not teasing you. I just got caught up back there . . ."

"We both got a little caught up and I thought you were ready . . . for this."

She turned her body to face him and took his hand. "I am ready, that's not the question. I want you as much as you want me. But it's my commitment to God—I just can't break that.

No matter how much my flesh wants to go that way. I've made a commitment to be celibate."

"I thought we were making a commitment, too. To each other." He paused. "I love you, Alexis."

She felt as if her breath was being taken away. She had to make him understand. "I love you too, Brian. But that doesn't mean I should back away from the things I have to do for the Lord."

Brian's face tightened. He had never waited longer than a week for any woman and he didn't want to accept this. "So, what am I supposed to do?" he snapped in anger. She pulled her hand away from his. "I am sorry. I don't know what else to say."

Staring out the window, Brian shook his head. A minute passed before he spoke. "I don't know what to do about this, Alexis. I'm getting frustrated . . . something is going to have to change soon."

Alexis was quiet for a moment. "Are you giving me an ultimatum?" she asked as she clasped her hands together trying to stop the shaking.

"I don't know what I'm saying. But I don't feel like talking about this anymore."

Alexis took her keys from her purse and jingled them in her hands. She looked at Brian, sitting stoically in his seat. She wanted him so much and didn't want to lose him. "I'll speak to you tomorrow?"

He nodded.

She stood on the curb and watched the BMW skid from the driveway. And, her heart stopped. They had professed their love for one another, and now she wondered if she would ever see him again. She bit her lip as she fought to hold back tears.

How could she have put herself in this position? She had gone too far, placing herself continuously in situations with Brian where neither one of them could win.

As the elevator rose to the eleventh floor, she closed her eyes. She knew she had made the right decision. She couldn't look back; she was committed to her walk with God. She had to hold on to her convictions. When the elevator doors opened, she made a vow to herself. If she got a second chance with Brian, she would work hard not to take her flesh to places where her spirit did not want to go.

# Twenty

Brian had been driving the streets of Los Angeles for over an hour when he made his decision. He had come too far with Alexis. He was going to church, praying over meals, talking about God in the middle of normal conversations. Over the past few weeks, he had even started reading his Bible. He'd done all of this to impress Alexis and he wasn't about to lose her now.

Maybe I should just move on, Brian thought. Los Angeles was overflowing with willing women. But, he had found the woman he wanted to be with. Alexis had all the things he was looking for in a mate: she was attractive, smart, funny, and had her own money, so he knew she wasn't into him for his. And even though he wasn't into God the way she was, he did like that she was a Christian. She would make a great mother for his boys. With her as his wife, no judge would deny him custody.

Turning back to Wilshire, he hoped that she was still awake. Though that didn't matter—this was too important and had to be cleared up tonight.

"Hello, again, Dr. Lewis," the doorman said. "I didn't expect to see you again this evening."

Brian tossed him the keys.

"Will you be here for just a few minutes or should I park your car in the garage?"

Brian hesitated. "Park the car."

It only took a moment for the concierge to call up to Alexis' apartment. "You can go right up, Dr. Lewis. Have a good evening."

That would have to change. He didn't want to have to get permission every time he came to see her. He'd convince her to give him a key. That shouldn't be too hard.

He took deep breaths as he rode up in the elevator, still unsure of what he was going to say. When he got to the eleventh floor, she was already waiting at her door.

"I hope I didn't wake you."

"No, I couldn't sleep," Alexis said as he stepped inside. "I read my Bible for a while, and now I was watching a *Columbo* rerun . . ." She folded her arms in front of her.

Reading her Bible, he thought. I guess I won't be staying tonight.

"Why did you come back?" she asked soberly, breaking the silence.

He stared at her for a moment, as she stood steadfast, with her back against the door. Her hair was tousled like she'd been asleep. And as his eyes skimmed down her body, he could tell that she had on very little underneath her bathrobe. He was sorry he wouldn't be staying. He brought his eyes back to hers. "I wanted to apologize," he said sincerely. He moved to the couch and she followed him, but sat at the other end. "I don't want us to argue about this."

"Neither do I," she said quickly. "I'm just sorry I put us in that situation."

"You didn't do it by yourself." He took her hand and raised it to his lips. "I do love you."

She smiled. "I love you, too . . ." she paused and her smile faded. "But . . ."

He raised his eyebrows. "I don't like the sound of that, but . . ."

She entwined her fingers in his. "You have to know that nothing's changed. Brian, I am sorry if you're not able to understand or handle this . . ."

He raised his hands. "Stop. You don't have to explain. I know where you stand and I'm going to support you in this. If I want the woman . . ."

"Are you sure you're going to be able to live with this? Because, I don't want us to go any further if this is not what you want."

"I want you. I have to admit that I want you in every way. And, when two adults are in a relationship, usually that means physically too."

"That's what the world thinks."

"Uh . . . yeah, the world. But, I understand. I mean, I agree with you. We have to stand on the Word of God."

"That's what I have to do."

"Well, we'll just take this relationship slowly. I mean, we did move to a new level tonight."

She smiled hesitantly. "We did, but I hope . . ."

He held his finger to her lips. "You don't have to say anything else."

She nodded.

"I've gotta go. I do have a job I have to go to in the morning," he chuckled.

He put his arm around her shoulder as they walked to the front door.

"Thank you for coming over. When you drove off, I didn't know . . ."

He kissed her, a gentle kiss, and then backed away. "I'll see you tomorrow," he whispered, and closed the door behind him. He smiled as he rang for the elevator. At least things were back on an even keel. He would play the game her way—at least for a little while. He would give her a little time, make sure she trusted him.

As he sped down LaCienega heading home to Baldwin Hills, he thought about his plans. He had fallen for this woman hard, he knew he was in love. But he was used to having his way. Very soon, Alexis Ward was going to be his in every way.

# Twenty-one

"Kyla, Kyla, it's me. Jasmine. Guess who's here with me?"

Jefferson suddenly appeared at Jasmine's side. "Hello, Kyla," he said softly as he put his arms around Jasmine's waist. "I'm so sorry to tell you this, but I'm leaving you. Jasmine is the woman I love. She's the one I want to spend my life with." She watched as they turned away from her, slowly proceeding up the stairs, the stairs that led to her bedroom. She tried to move, but her legs had become lead weights bolted to the ground, preventing her from saving her husband.

"Sorry, Kyla. Good night, Kyla. Sorry, Kyla. Good night, Kyla."

They were mocking her, saying the words over and over again. Her hands covered her ears. "No, no, no!" she screamed and sprang up in the bed.

Terrified, she clicked on the light, her eyes quickly surveying the room. Only the sound of her heavy breathing interrupted the stillness. Pulling the sweat-damp sheet to her chest, she frowned. She *had* heard them, she was sure of it.

She picked up her watch. Just one-thirty.  Hours had

passed, but a sound sleep refused to come. Their voices haunted her; their images filled her dreams. She knew she wouldn't be able to close her eyes again.

Dressed in her underwear, she jumped from the bed, shivering against the cool air. Twisting into her jeans, she dressed quickly, stopping only to put on her watch and tie her hair back. With shoes and purse in hand, she twisted the bedroom's doorknob, moving noiselessly into the hallway. The entire downstairs was engulfed in darkness and she groped through the family room and kitchen, into the garage. Closing the door, she stooped to slip on her shoes and, as she stood, her eye caught a glimpse of a white paper sticking from the windshield of Jefferson's car. The paper looked like it had slipped down into the hood and gone unnoticed. Curiosity pulled her to the car.

Her hands shook as she read the note. *Dearest Jefferson, I wanted you to know that I had a wonderful time the other night. You are an incredible lover and I can't wait until we get together again. I only hope that I gave you half the pleasure that you gave to me. I will be waiting for your call. Love, Jasmine.*

She fell back against the wall and read the note again. This was real. The intimacy she had shared with her husband was gone forever. Jasmine knew Jefferson as she did. She'd seen him naked, knew how his body felt, knew how he felt inside of her, knew what his tongue, what his caresses, felt like. Had he done the same things with Jasmine that he did with her?

Choking a sob, she stuffed the note in her bag and got into her car. It wasn't until she was on the freeway that she picked up her cell phone. It rang a few times, but finally a groggy Alexis answered.

"Alexis, this is Kyla. I need you to do me a big favor."

"Kyla? What time is it?"

"It's late, I'm sorry. But I just need you to do something for me."

"Okay . . . where are you? How did things go with Jefferson?"

"I'm on my way to my parents and I want you to call my mother . . ."

"You're driving to Santa Barbara *now*? Is Jefferson with you?"

"Yes, I'm going to Santa Barbara and no, Jefferson is not with me. I can't talk about it right now, but Alexis, would you please call my mother?" When Alexis hesitated, Kyla continued. "I really need your help. I want you to call my mother and tell her I'm on my way. And tell her what happened . . ."

"Don't you think you should do that?"

"I will, but I just can't . . . I don't know how to bring it up. I think it would sound better coming from you."

"I don't know . . ."

"Please, Alex. Then she'll be waiting for me, and I really need her right now," Kyla sobbed.

"Ky, maybe you should come over here and drive up in the morning. You don't sound good . . ."

"I'm fine, really. I need to get up there. I need to see my mother, I need to hold Nicole."

"Okay . . ." Alexis was alert now. "I'll call her. But call me when you get there or else I'll worry all night."

"I will."

"Kyla, I know it doesn't seem this way right now, but you'll make it through."

"I'll call you when I get to my mom's."

Steering with one hand, she reached into her bag and pulled out the note. *You're a wonderful lover.* Jasmine was talking about *her* husband. The man *she* loved. The man who loved only her.

As she headed north on the near-empty freeway, she sobbed with the knowledge that, no matter how hard they all tried, things would never be the same again.

He picked up the phone on the first ring.

"Hello."

"Jefferson, this is Alexis."

"Alexis, didn't Kyla call you?"

"Yeah, she did. How did you know?"

"She said she was going to call you and let you know that she was staying here. I'm sorry . . ."

"Jefferson, I don't think we're talking about the same thing. Kyla *just* called me. She's on her way to Santa Barbara."

He sat up in the bed and turned on the light. "What are you talking about? She's downstairs asleep in the guest room."

Alexis sighed. "Not anymore. Something must've happened."

"Nothing happened," he said, swiveling his feet onto the floor. "She said she would stay but wanted to sleep in another room." He slammed his fist against the bed. "I knew I should've slept downstairs! I should've slept on the couch! What happened? What did she say?"

"She didn't say anything. She just said she had to see her mother and she sounded upset. Do you think she talked to Jasmine?"

"Jasmine? No, she hasn't been here and this is the first time the phone rang all night."

"I don't know . . . I don't have a good feeling about this . . ."

"Alexis, I don't have a clue as to what could have happened."

"You have to go after her."

He glanced at the clock. "I can't . . . my patients tomorrow."

"No, not tonight. She needs some time with her parents. But go after her tomorrow. She loves you, Jefferson. That's why she's hurting so much."

"I know. Oh God, how could I have done this?"

"It is too late in the night for you to ask me *that* question. You don't want to hear my answer. So, are you going to go tomorrow?"

"Yeah, of course. I just have to figure out some things. I'll call you. And let me know if she calls you back. Alex, thank you. I don't know how Kyla and I would have gotten this far without you."

"Just bring her back, Jefferson, and make her happy!"

As soon as he hung up the phone, he ran downstairs to check the room. The sheets were ruffled and the blanket had been thrown on the floor. Besides that, there was no sign that she had even been in their house. He lay down, folding himself under the covers, taking in her slight scent that still lingered in the sheets.

"Oh, Kyla." He wrapped his arms around the pillow and curled his legs. What was he going to do? Was this nightmare ever going to end?

Her car wheels crunched under the gravel driveway and before Kyla could put the car in park, her mother opened the door. She ran to her mother's arms.

"I've been sitting here at the window waiting for you."

"Mom, I'm so sorry."

Lynn Carrington leaned back and wiped her daughter's face. "What do you have to be sorry about?"

"Everything. You're up in the middle of the night . . ."

"Now, hush. And come on inside."

Her mother was her crutch and Kyla leaned against her until they were inside. Winston was standing at the door and closed it behind them. Without a word, he hugged his daughter, holding her as sobs escaped from her throat. Tears filled his own eyes as he held her close until her sobbing subsided.

When he finally pulled back, he looked at her and smiled. "I want you to know this, honey, you are going to be fine. You hear me?" Winston asked.

She nodded and blew her nose into the tissue her mother had given her.

"You are a strong, beautiful woman. But the most important thing is that you are a child of God and this ain't nothing but the devil."

"I know . . ."

"Now, I'm gonna leave you with your mother, but you know," he said gripping her shoulders, "when you need me, I'm right here."

She smiled through her tears. "I don't want to keep you guys up. We can talk in the morning."

"I'm gonna go on to bed now. You're going to stay with your mom and I'll be sleeping in your room."

"No, I don't want you to do that."

"Now, you just come on, Kyla. Let your dad go ahead and take care of his business and we'll take care of ours."

She hugged her father. "Thank you," she said kissing him on his cheek.

"You guys go on to bed now. I'll see you in the morning."

With arms locked, Lynn and Kyla walked down the hall and stopped in front of Nicole's bedroom. "I want to just look in on her."

Lynn smiled. "Of course. Take your time. Just come in when you're ready."

She tiptoed in and found Nicole on the bottom of the bed, covers kicked off. Kyla released a soft laugh. Picking her up, she turned Nicole around, replaced the cover, and kissed her softly before she left the room.

"Did she wake up?" Lynn asked when Kyla came into the room.

"Are you kidding? That child will sleep through anything."

Lynn chuckled as she adjusted the covers on the queen-size bed. "She's come by it honestly; you were the same way. Why don't you get out of those clothes and get in bed?"

"I didn't bring anything . . ."

"Here, take this. It's just a T-shirt, not one of those fancy things you young people wear."

Kyla's smile was bittersweet. She tossed off her clothes, threw on the T-shirt, and climbed into the bed, resting her head in Lynn's lap.

"I remember when I was little, the best times were when you let me stay up late and we would talk for hours about anything I wanted to."

"Yup," Lynn said stroking her hair. "Those were some of my best times too."

"It seems like such a long time ago." They were silent for a few moments. "Oh Mom, I don't know what happened. How did everything go so wrong?"

"I don't know, honey. But these things happen, unfortunately."

"It never happened to you and Dad."

Lynn hesitated before speaking again. "Why don't you just get some rest now. We'll talk about this in the morning."

It wasn't long before Lynn felt the soft rhythm of sleep from her daughter, but she continued to run her fingers through her thick hair and she prayed that somehow Kyla would find her way through this. She knew her daughter would make it as long as she stood strong in the Lord.

# Tweny-two

Before morning revealed the new day's light, Jasmine had awakened with her dream still fresh in her mind—Jefferson had told Kyla that he was leaving her. Now, as the early morning sun shone, Jasmine glanced at herself in the mirror and smiled at that memory. She turned, checking out her dress from every angle, holding in her stomach a bit as the knit held her body tightly. Good thing she hadn't had much of an appetite these past few days. But, after this morning, that would all change. Taking a final glimpse, she grabbed her keys and purse and confidently stepped to her car.

Jefferson's skin still glistened from the shower's steam. He was wrapped only in a towel as he spoke into the telephone.

"Brian, I don't know how to thank you."

"Just bring Kyla back and end this."

"That's my prayer, man."

"Well, God answers prayers. Kyla loves you. All you have to do is remind her. I'm just sorry I can't cover you this weekend . . ."

"That's okay, Brian. Hopefully, I will only need today."

Dropping his towel onto the bed, he jumped into his clothes and tossed the rest of his things into his bag. In a few hours, he'd be reunited with Kyla and Nicole and he couldn't wait another moment. He moved quickly and was in the garage when the doorbell rang. He pushed the garage door open, peeked into the driveway, and felt his heart drop when he saw Jasmine's car. A moment later, she appeared.

"Jefferson," her voice echoed across the concrete. "I didn't think we were ever going to get together again."

His eyes quickly glanced over the purple dress that clung to her body.

"I've had quite a time trying to reach you," she continued. "I'm sorry it's taken so long. I know you wanted to talk to me."

"I don't know why you thought that."

She chuckled flirtatiously. "You said you wanted to talk to me—the other day, after . . . well, you know."

"Oh, you didn't need to come over here for that, Jasmine. What I wanted to talk about then was how we were going to handle this mistake with Kyla. But now . . ."

She frowned. "Mistake? Kyla? What happened between us wasn't a mistake." Her heels tapped against the concrete as she moved closer to him. She rubbed his arm. "What happened was pure desire and it's been coming for a long time. You wanted me, I know that Jefferson. And that's fine, because I feel the same way about you. I haven't been able to stop thinking about us since this happened."

Pulling away from her, he opened the door to the Range Rover and threw his bag inside. "Jasmine, please don't make this any worse."

"That's not what I want to do, believe me. But there is

electricity between us that you can't deny. The passion was real. The way you held me and kissed me. The way you made love to me . . ."

Jefferson shook his head as Jasmine continued talking. Here he was, surrounded by his garden tools, Nicole's bicycle and toys, Kyla's Rollerblades—this garage was filled with signs that a normal family lived in this home. Yet, he was standing here, listening to this woman talking about the night they made love. It was surreal.

"I don't want to go over this," Jefferson said. "What happened was wrong and now we have to move on. I'm on my way to Santa Barbara now to fix things with Kyla, and I'm going to bring my family back home. I'm sorry," he said shaking his head.

Jasmine stood with her mouth open, stunned by his words. "And what about me, Jefferson? Do you think you can take me to bed like a toy and when you've had your little fun, then throw me aside?"

"Jasmine, you don't know how sorry I am for what I've done to you. But, after saying I'm sorry, I don't know what else to say. I love Kyla."

"Just like that, it's over?"

"There was nothing between us, Jasmine. Just bad judgment on my part." He glanced at his watch. "I've got to get on the road."

She turned from him and, with slumped shoulders, walked away. As he backed out of the garage, he stopped next to her car. "I'm sorry, Jasmine."

Through bleary eyes, she looked at him. "Sometimes sorry is not enough, Jefferson. Sometimes there's a higher price to pay."

He opened his mouth, but then silently shook his head. There was nothing he could do to get her to understand. When Jefferson drove down the street, he never looked back to see Jasmine sitting in her car, her body shuddering with sobs that surprised even her.

"Mommy!" Nicole jumped on the bed and hugged Kyla before she had a chance to sit up.

"Hi, sweetie," Kyla murmured through sleepy eyes. "I missed you."

"I missed you and Daddy too. Did you come up for the birthday party? Is Daddy coming too? When did you get here?"

Kyla wiped her eyes. "You sure are full of questions. What are you doing up so early anyway?"

"Papa's taking me fishing. Do you wanna come with us?"

"Now Nicole, I told you your mother got here late last night. Give her a chance to rest, okay? Anyway, your grandfather is waiting for you," Lynn exclaimed as she entered the room balancing two mugs of coffee. She turned on the low-light nightstand lamp.

Nicole kissed her mother again and bounced off the bed. "I'll see you later, Mommy. Bye, Mama."

Kyla pushed herself up, drawing the blanket over her. "Oh, Mom. Just seeing her makes my heart ache. I'm so grateful that she was up here with you and Dad."

Lynn sat in the rocking chair and pulled her bathrobe tighter. Holding her mug to her lips, she took a sip. "Me too."

"What if she had been with me when . . ." She paused, as

she leaned back against the headboard and looked directly at her mother. "How much did Alexis tell you?"

Lynn sighed. "Jasmine and Jefferson. You found them together." Lynn placed her mug on the carpeted floor. "I don't want to know any other details. Honey, why didn't you call us when this happened?"

"I couldn't face anyone. I was so hurt and embarrassed."

Lynn stopped rocking and cocked her head. "Kyla, you know there is nothing you can't talk to your dad and me about. We love you and will support you, no matter what is going on. And why were you embarrassed? You didn't do anything."

Kyla let her eyes linger on the window. The first beams of light were beginning to shine through the sheer curtains and Kyla strained to peer out at the ocean. "I can't explain it," Kyla began, keeping her eyes on the window. "But, I felt like my womanhood was put in question and being attacked. What kind of wife was I? Obviously not good enough for Jefferson, so he turned to someone else." Kyla picked up her coffee and watched Lynn shake her head.

"I know it might not make sense to you," Kyla continued, "but I felt like I failed him in some way."

"You know that's not true."

"That's what Jefferson said."

"So you *have* talked to him?"

Kyla nodded. "Jefferson and I got together a couple of times. The first time, I was so angry, I just told him I wanted a divorce. Then, we got together last night, and I agreed to at least stay in the house."

"So if you guys were working things out, why did you leave?"

"Mom, I couldn't even sleep. I heard voices and I had

dreams . . . Oh Mom, I don't know what to do." Lynn moved to the edge of the bed and held her daughter. "I never thought Jefferson would do anything like this to me."

Lynn shook her head. "When Alex called us, I didn't know what to say. Your father and I haven't even talked about it; I think we're still in shock."

"I'm past that stage. After I got over finding them together, I was loaded with anger. But even most of my anger is gone. All I do now is hurt," Kyla sighed. "I wish the anger would just come back. That was a lot less painful."

"You're just going through all the stages of healing. All of these emotions will help you work through this."

"I don't feel like I'm healing. I feel like I'm going crazy. Last night, I ran from my own house. I couldn't even stop to tell Jefferson I was leaving."

"He's going to be worried. Maybe you should call him."

She shook her head. "Every time I hear his voice, Mom, the ache in my heart sinks deeper. And it's just settled there, like it's never going to go away."

"That's normal, honey. The deeper you loved, the deeper the pain."

"I loved him totally," Kyla said as she leaned down, resting her head in her mother's lap like she had done last night. Lynn held her, stroking her in the kind of silence only a mother and daughter could share. Kyla closed her eyes and savored the comfort she felt. If she could stay like this in her mother's arms, she'd never have to face the pain again.

Finally, Lynn asked, "Do you love Jefferson?"

It took her less than a second to answer. "With all my heart," she said through tears. "But I don't want to love him."

"I know he loves you."

Kyla sat up, her eyes searching her mother's face. "How can you say that after what he did?"

"What he did was terribly wrong. But I know that man loves you. I've known that from the moment I met him."

"That was before. How do you know that he loves me now?"

Lynn waved her hand. "I'm not thinking about this single incident. I'm basing this on the sixteen years that you have together."

Kyla shook her head. "I wish I could be as sure as you are."

"How sure I am doesn't matter. But one thing I know is that you can't sit around trying to wish this away. As painful as it is, it's done. Now you've got to move past all of this."

"What do you think I should do?"

"No, child," Lynn said, shaking her finger at Kyla. "You're grown. You and Jefferson are going to have to figure this out."

"But I know you have an opinion."

"I do . . . I think you need to reach down deep inside of you and pull out what's there. This is the time for guts and God."

"God is the reason I've made it this far."

"That's who you lean on, honey. Hebrews 13:5 tells you that. The Lord will never leave you."

"God's been with me, Mom. I know that. But that hasn't shielded me from all the hurt."

"God never said He would do that. The Lord only promised to give you the tools to stand against all of this. The Word of God says: *Rejoicing in hope; patient in tribulation; continuing instant in prayer.* You have to rejoice in the hope of your future with Jefferson and be patient as you try to work this out together, having the faith that it will happen. And, you have to stay on your knees."

"It sounds easy."

"But know it's not. The Lord just wants you to have faith. Because faith will give you hope, faith will give you strength, faith will give you the weapons to fight. And who knows what this is all about?" Lynn continued, "I've known from the moment you came from my womb that the Lord has a mighty work for you to do, Kyla. And sometimes, when God is preparing you for something, you have to be broken so that you can totally depend on Him. You might think that you're being persecuted right now, but remember that when you are, the glory of God is upon you. As long as you use this to magnify the Lord."

"Mom, I know all of that in my head, but it's my heart that hurts. And my heart keeps telling me that I have to be afraid, because this could happen again."

Lynn took Kyla by her shoulders. "Girl, I don't even want to hear you talk that way. That ain't nothing but the devil using the same tactics and, in this situation, he's using fear. But you have to stand against that, Kyla. How many women of God do you think have had to stand against something like this?"

"Well, you never had to," Kyla pouted.

Lynn raised her eyebrows, holding her daughter's stare and, after several seconds, Kyla's mouth dropped in disbelief.

"Dad?" she whispered.

Lynn nodded slowly. "When we were first married. I didn't even have all the years under my belt that you've had to know that Winston loved me."

Kyla held her hands to her mouth. "Oh, my God. I never knew . . ."

"There was no reason for you to know. We worked it out."

"But when? Who? What happened?" Kyla asked, shocked at her mother's nonchalance.

Lynn shook her head as she stood and went to the bureau. She picked up her wedding picture and it was several moments before she spoke. "None of that is important," Lynn said, her words still slightly charged with pain even though it had happened thirty years before. "I only told you now because I want you to know that you *can* survive."

"But you and Dad have a wonderful marriage."

"We had to work it out."

"How did you do that?"

Lynn was thoughtful for a moment. "But, God," she said. Kyla's eyebrows furrowed in puzzlement.

"That's how I did it. Whenever questions or doubts came into my head, my answer was always, 'But, God . . .' So, when I said, 'Lord how am I going to make it?' I answered, 'But, God . . .' When I began to wonder about all of the details of his affair, I would say to myself, 'But, God . . .' If your father called and said he was going to be late and the fear tried to ease its way back into my soul, I would get down on my knees and pray, and then sing. And all the time I knew, 'But, God.'"

"I'm so sorry . . ."

"Why are you sorry? I'm not."

Kyla was surprised. "You're not? How can you say that?"

"Even though I still think about it occasionally and still feel some pain, his affair became a new beginning for us. It brought us closer to the Lord and to each other. Your father has spent every day since then trying to make it up to me."

"That's exactly what Jefferson said he would do. Spend the rest of his life being the man I thought he was."

"That's a strong statement for a man to make."

Kyla nodded.

"Sometimes I think about what my life would've been like if I had left your father. And I know it wouldn't have been as good as it's been with him."

Kyla stood and went to the window. Daylight had completely arrived and she watched the soft waves break onto the beach. She pulled at the gold heart around her neck. "I want to be sure, too. But I'm not."

"Honey, if Jefferson made a habit of this, that would be a different thing. But that's not the case. I don't know how he got himself into this, but I do know that your husband is a man of God and the Lord has already forgiven him. Jefferson wants your life to be together. And I think you do too."

Kyla nodded.

"Then get your pride out of the way. You know what Proverbs says."

"*Pride goeth before destruction, and a haughty spirit before a fall,*" Kyla quoted the scripture. "Is that what you think is holding me back, pride?"

"I don't know. But I do know what's inside of you—the peace of God."

Kyla wiped away the tears that were falling onto her bathrobe.

Lynn walked to the nightstand and picked up her Bible, and handed it to Kyla. "Here, take this. I think it's time for you to have one of those deep conversations with the Lord. I'm going to leave you alone."

"Why don't you stay and we can do this together?"

With a smile, Lynn shook her head. "Not this time. This is between you and God." Lynn leaned down and kissed her daughter's head.

Alone, Kyla stared at the book in her hand. Then, after a few moments, she skimmed through the pages of the New Testament, finally stopping at Luke 6. She read through the entire chapter, then paused, reading verses 36 and 37 several times. *Be ye therefore merciful, as your Father is also merciful. Judge not, and ye shall not be judged: condemn not, and ye shall not be condemned: forgive, and ye shall be forgiven.*

She closed the book and got down on her knees. She needed to pray.

Jasmine thought she had recovered quickly, but when she closed the front door behind her and glanced at the clock, she realized she'd been sitting in her car for well over an hour after Jefferson had driven off.

"It's over," she whispered to herself as she'd done a hundred times in the car. "There is no way I can get Jefferson now." She blew her nose again into the crumpled tissue that she'd had in her purse and sat for a few more minutes, going over everything in her mind. The worst part was that she had lost her best friend—and for what? Jefferson didn't even want her.

How could I have been so wrong? she thought. Jasmine was sure that once Jefferson had gone to bed with her, he'd want her again. But he was blinded by his commitment to

Kyla. She shook her head. In the past, it had been so easy to get a married man. But Jefferson was different. And she didn't know what to do.

"Why didn't he want me?" she asked aloud.

Jasmine needed to be with someone who would hold her and tell her what she needed to hear. It took her only a few seconds to dial a number. "May I speak with Michael Newman, please? This is Jasmine Larson."

Within a few moments, she was put through to his office. "Jasmine, how are you?" he asked.

"Just fine," she responded, trying to put enthusiasm in her voice, though she could feel tears stinging her eyes. "I haven't heard from you in a few days and I wanted to know if we could get together tonight. It would be a great way to bring in the weekend."

"Hold on a second, Jasmine." She could hear movement in the background and assumed he was closing his office door. "Okay, I can talk now. Jasmine, I've been meaning to call you."

"Well, you won't have to now. We can meet somewhere this evening or you can come over here and I can make sure this is a night you won't forget." She was surprised at how seductive her voice sounded, even with a tear streaming down her face.

"That's what I wanted to talk to you about. Uh . . . we won't be able to see each other anymore . . . my wife . . . someone called her and told her . . . I denied it and that's why I wanted to talk to you. I wanted to make sure that if you see Patricia, you don't tell her *anything* about us."

Jasmine was silent.

"Jasmine? Are you still there? Did you hear what I said?"

"You said you don't want me to tell your wife."

"Of course not. You and I . . . we were just kicking it. But

I don't want to lose my wife. I mean, there are the kids and my business . . . if I'm going to make partner, I have to be stable. I have to keep my family together. You understand, Jasmine, don't you?"

"I understand . . ." Her voice was like stone.

"Maybe when things are a bit less heated and a little time has passed, you and I . . . we can get together again . . . you know how I feel about you, baby, don't you?"

"I know how you feel about me . . ."

"I'm sorry, Jasmine. Just hearing your voice makes me want to run over there. But we've got to do the right thing. I'll try to call you, maybe in a few months. But in the meantime, it would be best if you didn't call me. Here or at home."

Jasmine had no idea how long she held the phone to her ear. She wasn't aware until the mechanical voice came on. "If you would like to make a call, please hang up and try again . . ."

Michael had said what Jefferson said—"I'm sorry." These men had used her for their own pleasure and now they were running back to their wives.

Her tears started to flow again. If she hadn't been focusing on Jefferson, Michael would still be there for her. And, if Kyla hadn't come back from Santa Barbara so early, she would have had a better chance with Jefferson. But everyone was going back to their families, tossing her aside like trash.

A few hours passed as she sat in the silence with her thoughts. Finally, she wiped the lingering tears and lay back on the couch. She was exhausted, but she had to get some rest. So that she could take care of business. Because, no matter who they were, no one was going to get away with treating her like this. Like she had told Jefferson—there was always a price to pay.

# Twenty-three

It was almost noon when Kyla rose from her knees and went into the living room. Lynn was sitting in front of the bay window, dressed in jeans and a white oxford shirt, reading her Bible. Kyla held back for a moment. The sunlight flooded through the glass, casting a glow on Lynn's caramel skin. Her short haircut made her look much younger than her sixty-five years, though Kyla could see the soft creases that had begun to form around her mother's eyes and cheeks. Peace hung like a halo over her and Kyla smiled. This woman was her example.

"Hi, Mom."

Her mother looked up with a smile. "You're up?"

"I didn't go back to sleep," Kyla said as she knelt in front of the window. "I read a little and spent the rest of the time praying. Praying and listening."

The doorbell rang, just as Lynn was about to speak. "Now I know your father didn't forget his key." Lynn got up and fussed all the way to the door. "I told you to take your key, Winston. I told you . . ." She stopped as she opened the door.

"Oh, Jefferson."

Kyla jumped up.

"Hello, Mom," he said as he leaned over and kissed Lynn, though his eyes were set on Kyla.

"Good to see you, son." Then Lynn turned to her daughter. "Kyla, look who's here."

"Hey, you," he smiled through uncertain eyes. Jefferson stuffed his hands in his pockets. "I was a bit worried. I didn't know what happened."

The three stood awkwardly at the entrance before Jefferson spoke again. "Can we talk?"

"Of course you can," Lynn said. "I'm going to leave you guys alone."

"I don't want to run you off," Jefferson responded.

"Oh, no. I need to get down to the church. There's something I have to add to the Sunday bulletin."

"Mom, you can stay. I wanted to go for a walk anyway." Turning to Jefferson, she said, "Just give me a few minutes to change. Mom, I'm going to borrow one of your tops, okay?"

Lynn waved her hands. "Take anything you need, honey."

When Kyla left the room, Lynn motioned for Jefferson to take a seat. "Who's taking care of the clinic?"

"Fortunately, it runs without me, but a couple of the other doctors are covering my patients." He paused. "Uh, Mom, I wanted to . . ."

Lynn held up her hands. "Jefferson, this is between you and Kyla."

He lowered his head. "I wanted to say that I am so sorry and you can be sure nothing like this will ever happen again. I will spend the rest of my life making this up to Kyla."

He held his breath as Lynn's eyes pierced him. A lifetime of seconds seemed to tick past before she smiled. "I believe you, Jefferson."

He exhaled. "I wish I could get Kyla to believe me."

"I'm not the one whose heart you broke. Kyla has a lot to deal with and it's hard because she loves you so much. I do want to say one thing though." Lynn paused. "If you ever . . ."

Jefferson nodded before she could finish. "I promise you . . ."

"You don't have to say anything else. Just make my daughter happy."

"Okay, I'm ready." Kyla came from the bedroom and her eyes moved back and forth between the two.

Jefferson stood.

"There really is no need for you to go anywhere. I'm going to the church and it should be a little while before your Dad and Nicole return. Why don't you just stay here?" Lynn gathered her Bible and papers from the table. "I'll see you in a little while."

The two of them stood staring at the door as Lynn closed it behind her. Kyla finally broke the silence. "This really feels strange."

Jefferson's shoulders relaxed. "I don't want it to be this way."

"Why don't we sit down?" Kyla motioned to the couch, but then sat in the chair across from him.

"So, Nicole's out with your Dad?"

Kyla nodded. "Fishing again. That's why she loves to come up here."

"Hanging out with her grandfather is her favorite thing to do," he chuckled and looked directly at Kyla. "I'm glad you're still talking to me. I wasn't sure what to expect. When Alexis called me in the middle of the night . . ."

"I knew I couldn't trust her," Kyla chuckled.

"She called because she's our friend."

Kyla nodded. "Jefferson, I have something that belongs to you." She stood and pulled out the paper she'd been carrying from her jeans, handing it to Jefferson.

He frowned, then took the paper, swallowing hard as he read Jasmine's words. "Where . . ."

"I found it on the windshield of your car. I guess it was meant for you and I shouldn't have taken it, but . . ."

He tore the note into small pieces. "Kyla, I am so sorry."

"That was tough to read. It somehow made it all real. Even more real than when I walked in on the two of you."

"If there was any way that I could take back . . ."

"But you can't."

He nodded. "Kyla, all the way up here, I was trying to think of the perfect thing to say. The right words that would turn this all around for us." He paused. "But honestly, I couldn't think of anything, because there is no excuse. The most important thing I can say to you now is the truth. And that is, I love you so much."

She held his stare for several seconds. "For the first time, I think I believe that, Jefferson."

His eyes opened wider. "Are you saying . . ."

"I'm not saying anything except that I believe you love me. But that doesn't erase anything. I can't get it out of my head—you making love to Jasmine."

"We didn't make love. We had sex; it was only physical."

She raised her eyebrows. "I guess with that revelation I'm supposed to feel better."

He sighed. "Of course not. I just want you to understand that it was nothing like what we have together."

Kyla nodded. "I'm trying to understand that." She stood

and walked to the window. "During these past days, I've wondered what was wrong with me. I wondered if you had gotten bored. I wondered if I wasn't satisfying you. I wondered if it were because I wasn't experienced."

Jefferson rushed to her. "Kyla, it was none of that, it wasn't you at all."

"I even thought it may have been because I was a virgin when we married. I know Jasmine has been with a lot of men . . ."

Jefferson lowered his head and closed his eyes. "Kyla, please."

With her index finger, she raised Jefferson's chin and stared into his eyes. She could feel his breath on her face. "Did you enjoy it, Jefferson? Did you enjoy making love to her? Was it better than being with me?" The questions quivered from her.

"Kyla . . . I . . . no . . ."

She held up her hands and turned from him. "I'm sorry. I don't know why I asked you that. I just wish I didn't hurt so much."

"And I wish that I had never hurt you," Jefferson said as he turned her, making her face him. "Kyla, I want us to get back to where we were. I want . . ." He stopped, choking on his words.

She reached out and stroked his face. "Jefferson . . ." This time, when he lowered his lips to hers, she didn't resist, and allowed herself to take in the softness of him. He wrapped his arms around her and pulled her close, trying to fill himself with her.

The sound of the key at the door broke them apart.

"Daddy, Daddy!" Nicole ran in and jumped on her father. "I saw your car outside. When did you get here?"

"Hey, sweetie. How are you? Boy, did I miss you." Jefferson knelt down, hugging Nicole, and for the first time in days, embraced the feeling that he would have his family back together.

"Are you coming to Misty and Kristy's birthday party tomorrow?" Her arms were still wrapped around her father's neck.

"Uh, no. I forgot all about it. I'm sorry, honey, but I have to get back to L.A."

"When are you leaving?" Kyla and Nicole asked at the same time.

Jefferson stood, facing Kyla. "Tonight. I'm on call this weekend. I only came up to see you and hope that I could get you to come back with me."

"Hey, Jefferson," Winston walked into the house, eyeing his daughter and son-in-law.

"Dad, here let me help you with all of that," Jefferson said as he grabbed the fishing gear. "How are you?"

"Uh, just fine," he answered, looking at Kyla. He relaxed when she smiled back at him. "Is everything all right?"

"It's fine, Dad." Kyla hugged him tightly. "Jefferson and I were just . . . talking."

"Daddy, why can't you stay?" Nicole whined.

"Honey, you don't know how much I wish I could. But I've got to go to work in the morning and I know you understand that."

Nicole nodded. "Well, maybe you can play at the beach with me. Do you want to go down to the beach now? Please?"

Jefferson looked between Kyla and Nicole. "I don't know, honey. I really need to talk to your mother."

Kyla nodded her approval. "Go with her. She hasn't seen her daddy in over a week." Kyla smiled, tugging at her daughter's pigtails.

Jefferson's eyes questioned her. "Are you sure? I really wanted us . . ."

"We'll finish later," she nodded reassuringly.

"Well, young lady, what are we going to do?"

Nicole clapped her hands. "First, let's go get Misty and Kristy and then we can all go down to the beach. I have to put on my bathing suit. Are you going to get in the water too, Daddy?"

"No, I'll leave that all to you."

"Okay." She ran off to her bedroom.

"I tell you, that girl never runs out of energy," Winston chuckled as he sat on the couch and sighed. "I can't keep up with her."

"We really appreciate you keeping her up here," Jefferson said.

Winston dismissed Jefferson's comment with a wave of his hand. "Nonsense! It's a delight to have her."

"I'm ready! Let's go, Daddy!"

Jefferson gently ran his fingers across Kyla's face. "I'll be back."

Winston put his arm around his daughter as they watched Jefferson and Nicole walk hand-in-hand through the sand to the beachfront house next door. "I was surprised to see Jefferson here."

"Alexis called him and told him where I was." They were

silent as Jefferson and Nicole disappeared around the corner. "Daddy, this has been one of the worst times of my life."

"I know, honey. But the thing I know most is that you'll make it through."

"I'm beginning to think I might. I prayed for a few hours this morning."

"That'll always do it. As long as you're not doing all the talking and you're spending a fair amount of time listening."

Kyla chuckled. "Remember when you told me that prayer was not a monologue, but a dialogue? I was absolutely shocked."

"You remember that? You couldn't have been more than five or six."

"I think I was seven and for a long time after that I was afraid to pray. I thought I'd hear this booming voice come out of the sky and that scared me to death."

"I remember we had to say your prayers with you for a while after that."

Kyla nodded. "But once I understood, it changed my life. I learned to listen and hear the Lord. And to know God's voice. With the time I spent this morning, I know what I have to do."

Winston nodded and pulled Kyla back into his arms. "You know your mother and I are behind you."

"I thank God for you and Mom every day."

"Then the Lord hears the same things. Because every day in our prayers, we thank God for blessing us with you."

The two stood, watching the waves of the surf crash onto the shore. And, for the first time in days, Kyla felt the peace of the Lord.

# Twenty-four

The chair's legs squeaked against the hardwood floor as Jefferson pushed his chair away from the table. "Mom, I can't tell you how good that was. Thank you so much for dinner."

"This was nothing. If I'd known you were coming, I would have fixed you something really good. I'm sure neither one of you have eaten well these past few days."

Jefferson and Kyla looked at each other and smiled. "No. I haven't eaten much. But I hope that is going to change," Jefferson said.

"Daddy, I wish you didn't have to go. I really want you to stay for the party," Nicole said as she chewed on the last of her fried chicken.

"Honey, I wish I could, but the party is for kids anyway. You won't miss me," he said as he tickled her neck.

Nicole giggled. "I will miss you! But Mommy's going to be here, right? You're staying aren't you, Mommy?"

The moment froze. Kyla's fork clanked as it dropped to her plate. Finally, she nodded slowly. "Yes, honey. I'm going to stay."

Jefferson's shoulders dropped and Winston and Lynn exchanged glances.

"Well, I think I'm going to have to get on the road . . ." he started, then his voice seemed to disappear.

Winston cleared his throat. "Uh . . . Jefferson, before you go, can we go for a walk? I'd like to talk to you."

Kyla glanced between her parents. "Daddy . . ."

Lynn placed her hand on her daughter's shoulder. "Kyla, it'll be fine. While the men are out talking, you can help me clean up this mess."

"Can I help too, Mama?" Nicole piped in, unaware of the tension that had filled the room.

"Of course, why don't you start taking some of these dishes in?" As Nicole took the bread plate, Lynn carried the bowl of rice into the kitchen.

Kyla was alone at the table and she eyed her father and Jefferson as they moved to the front door. Her father put on his cap and bomber jacket and Jefferson held the door opened until they stepped outside. Kyla sighed.

"Let your father handle his business," Lynn said as she returned to continue clearing the table. "They'll be all right."

"I didn't know Daddy was going to say anything," Kyla whispered as she watched Nicole rinsing the plates before she put them in the dishwasher.

"He's your father, honey. And you're his baby girl."

"But I don't want him interfering in this. I have to handle it."

"He knows that, Kyla. But maybe he can give Jefferson some . . . insight."

Kyla nodded as she handed her plate to Lynn. When her mother went back into the kitchen, Kyla went to the bay window. The light at their front door was the only illumination on the beach and Kyla couldn't see very far. She couldn't tell which way they'd gone. She sighed. She didn't like not knowing what her father would say, but she had no choice now. She would just have to wait and see.

The waves seemed to crash louder in the dark and, as they walked along the shore, Jefferson pulled his jacket tighter around his neck.

"Are you cold, son?"

"No, I'm fine," Jefferson said and then hesitated. "I want you know that I am so sorry . . ."

Winston held up his hands. "I know you are." Stopping, he turned to face his son-in-law. "Jefferson, I love you as if you were my natural son and, though I am very disappointed, I want you to know that nothing has changed with the way Lynn and I feel about you."

Jefferson hung his head. "I appreciate that, sir."

They continued walking along the concrete strip that separated the beach-front homes from the sand. "I realize that this is none of my business. But, I love Kyla more than my own life and I hate to see her hurting like this."

Jefferson swallowed. "I . . . I feel the same way. I don't know how . . ."

"There's nothing you have to explain to me. I wanted to give you a chance to talk if you felt like you had to."

"I just want to know what I can do to make this up to her. I just want to find a way . . ."

"It's going to be a long process . . ."

"I know."

"In fact, it will never end. Every day, for the rest of your life you're going to have to find a way to assure her of your love."

"I *want* to do that. I will do anything."

"You say that now, but you are going to have to do it every day and it's going to be tough. And sometimes you're going to think that it's not making a difference, but I can tell you that it is . . ."

Jefferson frowned and glanced sideways at his father-in-law, but he remained silent.

Winston continued as if he was in a trance. "Sometimes it's going to seem like you're going backwards. Everything will be okay, then, boom! Out of nowhere, she'll begin to question you again. You'll be tired of answering her questions, you'll be tired of her insecurities. But that's just women, Jefferson. A woman needs to feel safe and you've shattered her cocoon of safety. Now, you're the only one who can build it back. She can't do it. You have to do it for her no matter how long, how much counseling, how much time it takes. It's up to you . . . that is, if you're really committed to your marriage."

"I am, Dad."

Winston nodded his head. "Then, I think you two will be fine. Just remember to keep God as your center. Lean on the Lord to show you the way. That's the only way you're going to make it."

"Yes, sir. I love Kyla. I don't think you could even begin to understand . . ."

Winston paused, then said sadly, "I understand."

They walked for several minutes in silence.

"Thank you, Dad."

Winston stopped again and stared into Jefferson's eyes. "I hope you understand *everything* I'm saying, son."

With a faint smile, Jefferson nodded. "I do."

Winston patted Jefferson's shoulder. "Let's go back. I know you have to get on the road.

While Nicole and her mother finished up in the kitchen, Kyla sat in the living room and finally breathed when she heard the key in the door. She searched their faces for some sign, but they only smiled.

"That was fast," Lynn said as she came to the door and took her husband's jacket. "Jefferson, do you want some coffee or something before you leave?"

"No, thank you. I really have to get going. I have to be up early in the morning . . ." He turned to Kyla, trying to plead with her in silence.

"Well, son, we'll see you soon. Drive safely." Winston hugged Jefferson.

"Yes," Lynn said adding her hug. "Traveling mercies and next time you talk to your mother, please tell her hello for us."

"Well, sweetie," Jefferson started as he knelt down.

"Bye, Daddy." Nicole hugged her father.

"Enjoy the party. I'll see you in a few days, okay? I love you."

"I love you too, Daddy."

Lynn took Nicole's hand. "Come on, honey. Let's go watch some TV with your grandfather."

They stood alone, silently for several moments before Kyla spoke, "I am glad you came up here today."

"So am I, but . . ."

She took his hand. "Please. Just a little more time."

He lowered his head. "I understand."

Kyla could tell from his voice that he didn't, but she knew he was willing to give her the space that she needed. "You'd better get going."

He nodded and zipped his jacket. "I'll call you when I get home."

"I'll be looking forward to it."

He ran his hand against her face. "I don't want to leave . . ."

"But you have to," she said softly. "And it's okay, because I'll be home . . . soon."

He hugged her and breathed deeply when she leaned into him. She stood outside watching until the Range Rover was no longer in sight. Closing the door, she leaned against it for several minutes, enjoying the warmth she felt. One thing that was promised in the Word of God was hope. Faith built your hope. And for the first time in days, Kyla felt the hope that had been promised by the Lord.

Jefferson yawned and shifted in his seat. It had been a long ride, but he was smiling. While he had hoped that Kyla would return with him, he knew now that they would be together. He felt even more confident that he'd be able to handle it. After the talk he'd had with his father-in-law, he understood that one could recover from such a devastating mistake. *And now, Lord, what wait I for? My hope is in thee.* He loved Psalms 39:7.

The Lord had filled him with hope. Kyla had said that in just a few days she'd be home. And she had hugged him. Hugged him like she loved him. Now, as he exited from the freeway, he held onto the memory of that. "Thank you, Lord."

He turned his car onto LaBrea and pulled down the visor to block the headlight glare from the oncoming cars. As the music from his church choir flowed through the car, he began to relax. He was close to home, in so many ways. There would still be a fight in front of them, but finally he was being given a chance to appear in the battle.

# Twenty-five

The sheer, light blue curtains swayed slightly in the breeze from the open window. Jasmine was lying casually on her bed and she glanced at the clock. It was still a bit too early to call. She'd wait another five minutes. She checked her phone book, though she knew she still had the Carringtons' telephone number. Her parents had been good friends with them until her mother died and her father left for Florida.

She rolled over on her stomach and sighed. Maybe she shouldn't make this call. She didn't even know if Kyla was still there. Maybe she should just let the whole thing go. Nothing had turned out the way she planned and who knew what would happen after she talked to Kyla.

Well, she would drop the whole thing—right after she talked to Kyla. She couldn't let them get away with the way they had treated her. Jefferson, Alexis, Michael—all of them had treated her like riffraff and it was time for them to pay. Jefferson would suffer the most. How would he explain it to Kyla after she told her that their affair had been going on for some time? It would be a long time before he ever used her or any other woman. And after Kyla, it would be Patricia Newman's turn. Then, she would go on with her life.

She looked at the clock again. It was time.

Kyla's fork clicked against her plate, still filled with scrambled eggs as she dropped it. She sighed.

Glancing over the newspaper, Lynn frowned at her daughter. "You know what's wrong with you, don't you?"

Meeting her mother's glance, Kyla shook her head.

"You miss your husband."

"I waited up for him last night, but he never called. I guess he just thought it was too late."

Lynn dropped the newspaper onto her lap. "You're not doubting him, are you?"

"No, not really," Kyla said, knowing she sounded uncertain. She didn't want to tell her mother that she had stayed up half the night wondering where Jefferson was. It was only when she prayed that she had finally fallen asleep.

"Why don't you call him?"

"I did a little while ago. But, I guess he already left for the hospital and I don't want to bother him while he's on call."

"He's probably just trying to give you space."

Kyla simply nodded.

"Do you know what I think?" Lynn asked. "I don't know what in the world you're doing here. You should be in L.A. with Jefferson."

"It really doesn't matter," Kyla said, as she swirled the eggs on her plate. "He's going to be working all weekend anyway."

"But he still has to come home. And the sooner you two

start putting your life back together, the better. You've already decided to give your marriage a try, so . . ."

"How do you know that?"

"Because I didn't raise no fool . . ."

Kyla laughed.

"And because of the way you two were with each other last night. At dinner, it was like he was seeing you for the first time. That man loves you to death."

"I do want to go back. But there are still some things that . . . I have to work out."

"Like getting back in bed with him?"

Her eyes opened wide. "Mom!"

"What? You don't think I know about these things?"

"Of course, but no one wants to think of their parents . . . in that way."

"Well, it doesn't matter what you think, I know the reason you didn't go back with Jefferson last night was because you're afraid of the intimacy, right?"

She hesitated, then pushed herself back from the table. "I wonder if he's going to be comparing me to Jasmine. Or if I'll be thinking of the two of them together." She folded her arms across her chest. "Will Jefferson find me as desirable as he once did?"

"Why don't you ask him?"

Kyla raised her eyebrows. "You want me to just come right out and ask him?"

"Yes."

"I can't do that. It's too embarrassing. I can't even believe I told you."

"Embarrassing or not, it's something you're going to have to face."

Kyla sighed deeply. "I don't think I should move back in with Jefferson until we've started counseling and gotten past some of this. It will just make things easier when we get back to . . . that point again."

"You think you should wait to renew the intimacy between the two of you?"

"You sound like you don't agree."

"I don't. Being intimate is going to be one of the things that will help rebuild your marriage and help you and Jefferson get connected again. You can't put aside such an important part of your relationship."

The hardwood floor creaked under her feet as Kyla went to sit on the couch. "How can I get close to him while I'm still feeling so hurt?"

Lynn followed her into the living room. "Well, if you're really committed to making your marriage work, you're going to have to get past these feelings." Lynn sat next to Kyla and took her hand. "You have a decision to make—do you want to feel safe or do you want to be with Jefferson?"

Kyla paused. That's what she had been asking herself all night. "Shouldn't I be able to have both?"

"You will, but not right away. There's so much healing that you have to do. Just because you forgive Jefferson doesn't mean you'll forget. Years from now, you will still remember the exact details of what happened. But soon, it won't bring you down as much. You'll be able to relegate this time to a little corner in your mind. And one morning, you'll wake up feeling very safe and very happy."

Kyla nodded. "I want that so much."

"But the healing starts somewhere. You need to get in that car, Kyla, and go get your man. Get him in every way."

Kyla smiled. She did want to see Jefferson. She wanted to hold him and have him hold her. She wanted her life back. "But what about Nicole? She'll be so disappointed when she gets back from breakfast and I'm not here."

"Child, your daughter loves you, but this is a big birthday weekend for Misty and Kristy. By the time they get back, they'll be getting ready for the party and I think Nicole will barely notice that you're not here."

That's what she wanted her mother to say. She remained thoughtful for a moment. "I think I'll do it," she said, standing and moving quickly. "I'll just go before I can change my mind."

Lynn smiled. "Are you going to call Jefferson and let him know you're coming?"

"No, I think I'll just surprise him . . ." She paused.

Lynn held up her hands. "Don't even go there."

As Kyla turned towards the bedroom, the telephone rang. "Do you want me to get that, Mom?"

"No, you go get ready. It's probably your father calling to tell me that he's going to have brunch with some of the fellows after choir rehearsal or something like that." Lynn was still chuckling as she picked up the phone. "Hello."

"Mrs. Carrington?"

Her shoulders stiffened at the voice.

"Mrs. Carrington, this is Jasmine."

A million thoughts stormed her, but she remained silent.

"Mrs. Carrington, can you hear me?"

"What can I do for you, Jasmine?"

The frozen tone penetrated through the telephone wires and Jasmine swallowed. Lynn had been like a second mother to her and, even with all that had happened, she realized now that she had hoped for a warmer response. "Mrs. Carrington . . . I . . . I know you know what's happened and I just wanted to say that I am so sorry."

"I'm not the one you should be telling this to."

Jasmine exhaled. At least she would get to speak to Kyla and go through with her plan. "That's why I called. I understand that Kyla is staying with you and I wanted to speak with her."

"You think Kyla is here?"

She paused and then frowned. "Yes . . . Jefferson told me . . ."

"Jefferson? So, you're still trying to ruin my daughter's marriage?"

"Uh . . . no. I . . . just called Jefferson to . . . speak to Kyla."

"Uh-huh . . ."

"Mrs. Carrington, may I speak to her?"

"No."

It was a moment before it registered. "No?"

"That's what I said. Jasmine Cox Larson, I am so surprised at you. You think I'm going to just put you on the telephone with Kyla so you can continue this game of destruction . . ."

"I told you, I want to tell her I'm sorry."

"That's what you say, but why don't I believe you?"

Jasmine pursed her lips. "I don't know. But this is not really between us, is it?" Jasmine dropped the softness in her voice.

"Don't pull that tone with me, young lady. I spanked your behind many times when you girls were young and I'm not against doing that now. Do you hear me?"

Forgetting that she was on the phone, Jasmine nodded.

"Now, before you talk to Kyla, you have to talk to me."

Again, Jasmine nodded.

"You know, your mother, God bless her, must be crying in heaven. I tried to warn her. I used to say, 'Now, Doris, you've got to get that girl in line.' You were out of control when you were just a tiny tot. But your parents just thought that you were a little rambunctious. That's what they used to say. But I knew it. I knew that one day we would all be paying. And, as sorry as I am about it, my word has become truth."

"Mrs. Carrington . . ."

"Jasmine, I just want to know, why? Was it worth it to you? Was it worth it destroying everything around you?"

"I didn't do it by myself, Mrs. Carrington."

"That's true and Jefferson will have to answer for his sin. But the thing about my son-in-law is that he is willing. He is willing to pay because he knows he was wrong. But you, I'm not so sure. I am not sure that you are willing to atone for what's happened."

"That's why I want to talk to Kyla."

"What did you really call for, Jasmine? What is it that you really want to say?"

"I want to apologize."

"Umph . . ." Lynn paused for a moment. "Well you know what, I'll pass that message on for you. And in the meantime, stay away from Kyla and Jefferson."

"So you're not going to let me talk to her?"

"No, I'm not. But, like I said, I will pass the message on."

Jasmine's voice tightened. "You're acting like we're children. You can't keep me away from Kyla."

"No, I can't. But I'm not worried. When you two do meet

up again, I think you're going to have a mighty tough fight on your hands. In fact, if I were you, I'd want to prolong that meeting for a while . . ."

"I'm not afraid . . ."

"See, that's your problem. You don't fear anything, Jasmine. You think you can do everything by yourself. Well, I hope you never look back and regret all you've done because, by the time you do, you will find that there is no one who will care."

"That's not true . . ."

"With the way your life is going, by the time you finish with everyone and everything, you'll be all alone. Look at the way things are now. You've already turned away your family, your husband, and now the one person that loved you like a sister. And, I don't imagine that you have a lot of friends busting down your door. I hope you will sit back and ask yourself what is happening. Because if you can answer that question honestly, then maybe you can save yourself."

"I don't need to save myself from anything. I'm fine. I don't need anyone . . ."

"That's where you're wrong. It's clear that you do need something . . . you need the Lord. Go back to God, Jasmine. The Bible says that the Lord is married to the backslider. God will welcome you with opened arms and overflowing love, and, right now, the Lord is all you have. But the good news is, God is all you need."

"Mrs. Carrington, I don't need you to preach to me."

"And I don't want to preach to you . . . all I want to do is tell you the truth."

Lynn had to pull the receiver away from her ear when Jasmine slammed the phone down, disconnecting them. She shook her head. She would pray for that girl. After all, Doris had been a good friend and, as angry as she was at Jasmine, she still felt responsible for her in some way.

"Mom?"

Looking up, Lynn smiled. "You're ready, honey?"

"Uh-huh. Are you okay? "I heard you on the phone. You sounded like you were a bit upset."

"Oh, no. I was just trying to lead someone to the Lord."

Kyla grinned. "That's my mom, always the witness."

"That's what we have to do, honey. Save souls. So, this is it."

Kyla wrung her hands. "Are you sure . . ."

"Get rid of that spirit of doubt and put your trust where it belongs."

With shaky arms, Kyla hugged her mother. "Mom, you have no idea how much . . ."

"Yes, I do. Now, get. And call me when you get home."

"I will," she yelled as she traipsed out the front door.

Closing the door gently behind her daughter, Lynn smiled. They would be all right. She was sure of it now. And not because of how she and Winston had raised Kyla, though God knows they had tried to do right by their only child. But Kyla would be fine because the Lord was the center of her life. And the greatest blessing was that she had married a man who believed the same thing.

Lynn tapped her hands along her legs, making a mental note of all the things she had to do. Now that Kyla was taken care of, there was a party she had to focus on. Nicole would be back any minute and there was much work to do.

Holding her hand to her chest, Jasmine felt her heart pounding. The mirror reflected her fear-filled eyes. "I don't care what she said, she's not my mother! She doesn't know what she's talking about! She doesn't know me!"

But even as the words screamed from her lips, her stomach twisted. She had called Kyla to get back at Jefferson, but Lynn had turned it all around. She ran her hands along her arms, trying to warm herself against the chill that had suddenly filled the room.

The telephone book on the nightstand caught her eye and she picked it up, flipping through the pages. Lynn had told Jasmine that she was alone. And as she looked through the names in her book, Jasmine knew she was right. Who could she call if she were really in trouble? Who could she call if she were sick and needed help? Who could she call now? Loneliness swept over her, filling her with a sadness deeper than she had ever felt.

As tears trickled down her cheeks, she returned to the phone, dialing quickly.

"Serena, this is Jasmine. I need two big favors."

"And how are you too, dear sister?"

"I'm sorry. It's just that this is so important," she sniffed.

"Jasmine, are you all right?"

"Would you mind a visitor for a few days? I have to get away."

"Really? You want to come to Florida? Great. Dad would love to see you. And, me too, of course. When do you want to come?"

"I'm coming tonight."

"Tonight?"

"Yes. And another thing. Is your Bible handy?" Jasmine's voice trembled.

Jasmine listened to the moment of silence before her sister answered. "Yes?"

"Good, because I need you to send a big old prayer up to God for me."

It was after eleven and Kyla looked around the family room. Sighing, she lit the final candle and went into the kitchen. Any minute, he would come walking through the door. Brian had called to tell her that Jefferson had left the hospital and, as each minute ticked by, the pounding in her chest grew more intense.

The creaking of the opening garage door made her jump. Taking a deep breath, she walked towards the door, then quickly turned around. The family room was better. When his car door slammed, she clasped her hands behind her back and said a quick prayer.

"Kyla!" He sounded frantic as he yelled through the pantry, then appeared in the kitchen.

"Hey, you." Her voice was soft.

He stepped towards her; his dark skin glowed through the flickering candlelight. "You're home?"

She nodded and watched an unsure smile fill his face.

"Home for good?" The hopeful words were a whisper.

She smiled. "Yes . . . at least, I think so. I hope so . . ."

"Kyla," he said as he stepped toward her.

She held up her hands and he stopped. "Wait. Before you say anything, there's something I have to say."

Standing steadfast, he stuffed his hands in his pockets as his eyes searched her face for answers.

Taking a step towards him, she spoke. "Jefferson, there are a lot of things I'm confused about right now, but I do know three things. One," she started as she moved slightly closer, "you hurt me. More than I can ever say . . ."

When he opened his mouth to speak, she shook her head to stop him.

"No, it's okay." She took another step forward. "I am hurt, but I know we can get through this because the second thing I know is that I love you and . . ." She moved closer. "I know you love me."

He nodded as tears began to fill his eyes. "I do . . ."

She held up her hands, stopping him again. "And the third thing is . . . God is all up in this place. The Lord is here, just like He promised. I wish God would take this burden away from us, but I know that won't happen. But, God will see us through. And knowing that," she said, now standing so close she could feel his heart beat, "I know we can make it."

He reached for her hands and pulled them to his face, kissing her palms. "I promise you . . ."

"Please," she said shaking her head. "No promises. At least not right now. Let's just say that we're going to work on this."

He brought his lips to hers and the tears that trickled down her face mixed with his. She took him in, loving him, holding him, needing him and finally knowing for sure that somehow they would find their way.

# Twenty-six

Every few seconds, a drop of water dripped from the faucet and Jasmine wondered how her sister could take it. She heard the key in the door, but remained at the small round table. Slow footsteps echoed through the house, then seemed to quicken as they approached the kitchen.

"Oh, good morning! Did you sleep well?" Serena asked.

Jasmine's eyes roved over her younger sister, clad in a pink and yellow flowered dress and she shuddered. "Yeah, but I'm still a bit tired. Those red-eyes are killers."

"Tell me about it! I've taken enough of them. Do you want me to fix you something to eat?"

Jasmine shook her head. "No, I had some tea and toast. Where are the kids?"

"With Dad. I made them promise not to say a word about you. He'll bring them home in a little while. Dad will be thrilled to see you. He's been so worried and so have I."

"I've told you many times that you don't have to worry about me."

"With what's been going on with you over the past few months, how could we not worry?" Serena asked as she leaned against the kitchen sink filled with the morning's dishes. "First, you break up with Kenny and hide it from us . . ."

"I told you." Jasmine picked up the cooled tea and took a sip.

"Only after I called your house and Kenny told me that he was moving out *that day*. And then, there's all of this stuff with Jefferson . . . what else could I do but worry?"

"Well, now there's one less thing to worry about. It's over between me and Jefferson."

"That's what you said last night, but what happened?" Jasmine asked as she sat at the table and laid her elbows on the plastic tablecloth.

Jasmine sighed and looked away from her sister's eyes. "Nothing. It was just a little mistake."

"A little mistake? That's not the way you sounded on the phone."

"Well, that's the way it was. We got involved for a minute and now it's over."

"Jasmine, how did you allow yourself to get involved with Jefferson Blake, of all people?"

"I guess I was lonely and he was there . . . things just got out of hand."

"I can't believe . . ."

"Serena, the last thing I want to hear right now is one of your lectures. And, I know what you're going to say anyway— Kyla's my best friend, she's like a sister to me, Jefferson's been like a brother . . . I know the whole deal." Jasmine rolled her eyes. She didn't want to hear from her sister the same words that had been playing in her own mind over and over again.

"I wish you had remembered the whole deal before all of this . . ."

"Serena!"

Her sister held up her hands, then she wiped her sweaty palms on her dress. "Okay, it's just that I don't understand. And, it's such a shame because Jefferson will probably pay big-time for this. I'm sure he and Kyla will be getting a divorce now."

"I don't think so," Jasmine said shaking her head.

"You think she'll forgive him?" Serena was surprised.

"Probably. She's like you . . . she's a Christian. Aren't you guys a forgiving bunch?"

"Still. That's a lot to swallow." Serena sighed. "I just can't believe Jefferson did this. He's such a man of God . . ."

"Key word . . . *man*. And that's my specialty."

Serena smiled. "You should specialize in God, Jasmine."

"No, thank you. I'll just leave all that God stuff to you . . . and Kyla."

"How can you say that after we were raised to know the Lord?"

"No, we weren't. We were *forced* into going to church."

"It's the same thing. Children are not equipped to make the right choices."

"I'm an adult now and I've made my choice."

"Living without God is not a good choice."

"But it's my choice."

Serena shrugged her shoulders. "Anyway," she started, as she hoisted herself from the table, "Dad will be here about four and then we have to go back to church for a youth program. You should come with us. Aunt Em and Uncle Ben will be there. And probably Lucas, Joe-Joe, Willard, and their wives. Everyone will be glad to see you."

"Sounds like roll call for the *Beverly Hillbillies*," Jasmine said, rolling her eyes.

Serena looked at her sister out of the corner of her eye. "I know you think you're too good for us little-city folk, since you're still out in L.A."

"How do you do it, Serena? How do you stay here?"

"I love it here. I love being around Daddy and his family. This is where he grew up."

"Yeah, but he got out when he was sixteen."

"And returned as soon as he could. He knew what was best. Sometimes I wish we had been raised here. Maybe then, you wouldn't have had all of these . . . issues in your life."

"Like you don't have any issues," Jasmine smirked. "Well, I'm grateful that we grew up in L.A. I couldn't imagine becoming countrified like you."

Serena rolled her eyes. "I'm going to throw some stuff together for dinner. Wanna help?" she asked as she pulled lamb chops from the refrigerator.

Jasmine looked her sister up and down. Polyester flowered dresses, church programs that lasted all day, lectures about family—Jasmine sighed. She needed to get on a plane bound for L.A. "What do you want me to do?"

"Here. Take these potatoes and peel them."

"Peel potatoes?" Jasmine twisted her face as if she had a bad taste in her mouth.

Tying an apron around her waist, Serena raised her eyebrows. "What?"

"I don't peel potatoes."

Serena plopped the potato peeler into her sister's hand. "You're not in Hollywood now. You're home, honey. Get to peeling."

Jasmine sucked her teeth as she picked up the first potato. Serena wiped her hands on the front of her apron and smiled. "Welcome home, sis," she said as she planted a kiss on her sister's cheek.

Kyla's knees shook and she took another deep breath, trying to calm her shaking. Reaching over, Jefferson patted her hand and she forced herself to smile. She needed something to focus on and her eyes roamed the pastor's office, finally settling on the oak bookcase overflowing with Bibles. More than fifteen hours had passed. She knew, because she had counted every one in her head. Keeping track somehow made her feel better. Every passing hour was their victory. They were still together; she had not run away.

Though leaving would have been impossible, with the way Jefferson had planted himself at her side. Even after they had talked until the early hours of the morning and she had finally told him that she would sleep downstairs, he had not left her. Her eyes smiled as she remembered their conversation last night.

"Thank you for understanding, Jefferson," she had said as she stood, preparing to go into the downstairs bedroom. "I'm . . . just not ready."

"I'm disappointed, but I understand," he had said. Then, he let the ends of his lips curve into a smile. "But this time, you're not going to get away."

When she had frowned, he had gone to the laundry room, returning with a blanket. He threw it across the couch with a flourish.

She had shaken her head. "No, I don't want you to sleep down here. It's too uncomfortable."

"I'll be fine. Believe me, it'll be better than waking up and finding that you've gone again."

"I promise, I won't leave."

"Just call this my insurance policy."

She had hesitated. "Well then, maybe I should try . . . maybe I can go . . . upstairs."

"No, honey," he had said gently. "Not until you're ready. I'll be fine here, really. I'll probably have the best night's sleep I've had in days. Just knowing that you're close by . . ."

It had been that way for the last fifteen hours.

"Hey, you two," Pastor Ford said as she swept into her office. "Sorry I took so long. You know how it is after the service. Everyone wants to say hello."

"Pastor Ford, I can't believe you wanted to talk to us today. After two services, we know you're ready to go home and enjoy the rest of your day."

Jefferson nodded and added, "We're grateful for you, Pastor, but we could start counseling tomorrow or the next day."

With a wide smile, the pastor shook her head and her shoulder-length bob swayed. "Don't worry about me. You just don't know how great it was to see the two of you walk into the sanctuary this morning. I almost danced at the altar. Anyway, I just wanted to talk to you a little and set up a counseling schedule." She paused. "I am so pleased."

"So are we," Jefferson said.

"Now," the pastor started as she leaned back in her chair. "You know, there are probably people who would say that with God in your life, you don't need a counselor or a pastor to get all in your business . . ."

"We *want* to do this with you . . ." Jefferson interrupted.

"I know you do. I just want to make sure you understand my purpose." Leaning forward on her desk, she continued, "I see my role as the person who's going to help you ask and answer the tough questions. In the beginning of this healing process, the two of you will be tiptoeing around each other like you're in a minefield. You'll be afraid to say things because you don't want to hurt the other's feelings. Or there may be things that you're just too afraid to bring up. But, in order for you to get through this grief, everything must be said, the tough questions must be asked. And, that's where I can help you. Any questions?"

As they shook their heads, Jefferson squeezed Kyla's hand.

"One thing, though, and I'm sure you're both already very aware of this . . . it's going to be painful. At times, very painful. Jefferson, you have to be prepared to answer anything that Kyla needs to know. And Kyla, you're going to hear some tough things. But I promise, there will be life and love and understanding and trust . . . on the other side." She paused, looking at both of them. "If I had to put my confidence in people pulling through an ordeal like this, you two would get my vote."

Again, they nodded, but this time, Kyla pulled her hand away from Jefferson, resting it softly in her lap.

"Before we leave, there is something that I want to know. What are your expectations?"

Complete silence was her answer.

"Jefferson?"

He cleared his throat. "Well, my prayer is that Kyla and I will talk and get past this so that we can go on with the rest of our lives. I want to understand all that I can do to help her forgive me and trust me again."

The pastor nodded. "Kyla?"

Bowing her head, it took a few moments for her to speak. "I just want my heart to stop aching." Her words were soft and slow.

When Kyla looked up, she was sure she saw tears in the pastor's eyes. "Go on."

"I just want this," she said pointing to her chest, "to start beating regularly."

When Jefferson reached for her, Kyla moved to the other side of her chair and the pastor held up her hand, nodding, reassuring Jefferson.

"That's fine." The pastor's voice had taken on a soothing cadence. "Like I said, today was to make contact and get on the same wavelength. I didn't want this to be a long session, but now that you've brought it up, Kyla . . ." she hesitated before saying, "it's important for you to understand that this pain is not just yours. It belongs to all of us, including me as your spiritual leader. So we all have to find a way to work through this."

With tears threatening, Kyla nodded.

"So tell us about it. Tell Jefferson about your pain."

With the slightest movement, Kyla shook her head. "I don't know if I can," she squeaked. "I don't know if I can do it without breaking down . . ."

"That's okay. There are going to be plenty of times when we're all going to break down. It's normal, Kyla. You're fine."

The silence filled the space again for a few moments. "No matter what I say, Jefferson will never know how I feel."

"Do you think it's important for him to know?"

She nodded.

Pastor Ford resisted her desire to get up and hold Kyla. As much as she wanted to do that, she couldn't—this was the first step. The healing would start with Kyla's words. "Well, he can't guess," the pastor said. "You have to tell him."

When Kyla shook her head, the pastor turned to Jefferson. "Jefferson, do you want to know?"

He opened his mouth, but his words were stuck inside. Swallowing hard, he nodded.

"Tell her. Tell Kyla that you want to know."

His eyes pleaded with her. "Kyla, I want to know," he said soberly.

It was probably only seconds, though it seemed like minutes were passing. She wished she was anywhere but in this office at this moment. Kyla looked up and stared through Jefferson. "Do you really want to know, Jefferson?" Her question sounded sarcastic.

"Yes?" Fear had turned his statement into a question.

She took a deep breath. "I thought I was special to you. I thought that what we had was special. But my pain comes from knowing that I was disposable. You were willing to throw away all of it, including me . . ."

"No, Kyla. That's not true."

Pastor Ford shook her head. "Jefferson, what Kyla is telling us is what she's feeling. You can't tell her that it's not true."

"That's not what I mean . . ."

"I think the best thing we can do right now is listen. No

matter how hard it is, let Kyla get it out. There'll be time to respond."

Jefferson nodded.

Kyla breathed again before she spoke. "I don't know who I am anymore. My whole life has been a lie. You're not the man I thought you were. We don't have the marriage I thought we had . . . everything is turned upside-down. I feel like . . . there's not enough air on this earth for me to breathe because I realize I mean nothing to you."

Jefferson couldn't hold back. "That's not true!"

"I couldn't mean anything to you, if you could be so intimate with someone else and you never considered how I would feel."

"I didn't think you'd be hurt . . . I didn't think you would find out . . ."

She stood and paced in front of the desk, seemingly ignoring his words. "I feel like the earth has just stopped spinning and, because of that . . . sometimes I feel like . . . I want to die."

"Please . . ."

Her pacing stopped suddenly and she stood over him with piercing eyes. "But the worst times are when I wish that you were dead. Because losing you that way . . . would be so much easier than having to live through the humiliation of this."

A screaming silence followed, broken moments later by the violent sobs that rose within Kyla, jerking her body with every breath. Jefferson jumped from his chair, pulling Kyla into his arms, letting her tears fall onto his chest.

Pastor Ford remained still, letting them hold each other as she held back her own tears. After several minutes, she exhaled deeply. "Well, I think we've started. What about meeting again on Tuesday?"

Still holding Kyla tightly, Jefferson nodded.

"Kyla, can you sit down for just one more moment?"

Nodding, she leaned down into the chair and Jefferson knelt next to her, still holding her hands.

"We're going to close on something that is going to be so important to you in the days to come. I'll read the scripture, but tonight or tomorrow you should meditate on this. It's Ephesians 4:26. And it says, *Be ye angry and sin not: let not the sun go down upon your wrath: Neither give place to the devil.*" The pastor looked up. "If there is any piece of advice I can give you, it's to commit this scripture to your spirit. Do not give the devil a foothold in this situation. He's going to use this, abuse this, do whatever he has to do to get you off your course. But that's just his job. Your job is to stand. And you can only stand by doing the Word."

The pastor came around to the other side of the desk and smiled warmly. "So, for someone who didn't want to take too much time, I think we accomplished a lot, wouldn't you agree?" She hugged Kyla for a long moment. Then, pulling back, her eyes bore into Kyla's. "You . . . just . . . stand."

Still holding Kyla's hand, she reached for Jefferson and bowed her head. "Now, let's pray."

The Florida sun was still hanging proudly as Jasmine waved to the 1989 Honda backing out of the driveway. Closing the door behind her, she sighed. It had been quite a homecoming. Her father, much grayer now, had held her hand the entire time, like he had been able to read her mind and knew that she would disappear if he let go. She had felt like she was suffocating in the small rooms, overflowing with family. Relief flooded her now as she finally had some peace.

"Ouch!" she yelled as a piece of torn plastic from the couch's slipcover scraped against her leg. Moving to the other end, she sat and stared out the window, her gaze moving along the block at the other small cottages that aligned this street. She shook her head. It was a different state, but this looked just like the neighborhood where she'd grown up. It was like Serena had never left home.

Sighing again, she sauntered into the kitchen and sat down at the table, running her fingers along the stiff plastic tablecloth. With the frayed flowered curtains, paint-chipped cabinets, faded yellow paint, and rusted appliances lining the counters, this room was exactly like the one where she had eaten her childhood meals.

She had worked so hard to escape this kind of life. And, she had succeeded. She belonged to the group of rising affluent African Americans. That's why she lived in the Colony Homes. That's why she only wore designer clothes and drove a luxury car. That's why she was willing to stretch every dollar she had. It all helped her to get as far away from this kind of room as possible. And Jefferson would have been just another key to her success.

Jefferson. She couldn't stop thinking about him, especially after what Lynn Carrington had said. Maybe she was alone, but she wouldn't have been had things worked out between her and Jefferson. But what would happen now? Would Lynn's predictions become her reality? With her elbows resting on the table, Jasmine folded her hands and looked up at the ceiling. "God, I don't even know how to do this really, not anymore. I don't remember how to pray, but I hope just talking will do it. I didn't mean to hurt anyone. I really didn't. I just don't want to face every day by myself. I don't want to be alone. So, now that these last weeks are behind me, please help me. I need all the help I can get from You. Please, help me to find that special someone in my life. Please help me get my life together."

She pulled her hands down and stood, then remembered and looked back up to the ceiling. "Amen." Running to the bedroom she was sharing with her nieces, she picked up the keys to the rental car. With her purse on her shoulder, she got into the car and put on her sunglasses, trying to recall the exact route. She'd forgotten to even ask if they attended the same church.

Maneuvering through the streets of Pensacola, she had to admit, there was something about this little town where her dad was born that she really did love. The houses were smaller than she was used to, but there was a feeling of community that she never felt in Los Angeles. "Maybe I should move here," she said aloud, then laughed hysterically. "No way! This place is too country for me!"

With the passing miles, the streets became more familiar and she coasted along, the images of the past weeks traveling with her. She hadn't meant to cause any *real* harm to Kyla and Jefferson. Everyone was making such a big deal out of all of this when it was really nothing. People had affairs all the time. Jefferson had probably already told Kyla that it was only that one time. It looked like God had handled everything for them.

She chuckled. All afternoon God had been coming into her thoughts. She wasn't even sure she believed God existed.

How could an unseen spirit control everything? And, if there was a God, why didn't anyone have any real proof?

But, on the other hand, as she looked around now at the hills and the birds and the clouds in the sky, maybe this was all the evidence that was needed to prove God's existence. Something had to create all of this. Jasmine laughed. "Why am I spending all of this time thinking about God?"

Minutes later, she pulled up in front of the church, relieved that Serena's car was in the parking lot. They would all be so surprised—and glad to see her. Well, this was the least she could do. While she was in Florida, she'd do her best to make them feel good. Let them know that there was no reason to worry about her. She was fine and always would be. There was no one walking the earth who was better at surviving than Jasmine Cox Larson.

Her sandals crunched the gravel as she moved toward the front, and her eyes focused on the message on the marquee: Are You Searching For Him? She stopped for a moment, feeling like it was a personal message. Maybe, maybe not. She had been searching for something. What she really wanted was a man in her life.

She continued towards the large double doors and as she moved forward, out of nowhere, words came to her mind. "*O give thanks unto the Lord; for he is good: for his mercy endureth for ever.*" She wasn't sure if that was from the Bible or not. She hadn't quoted anything from the Bible since she was a child and had no idea why these words were coming to her right now. Maybe a repressed memory from a long-forgotten Sunday school lesson. Maybe. She smiled as she walked through the doors and searched the crowded seats for her father and sister.

Seeing the top of her father's head, she crept down the aisle and slipped into the pew.

Her father didn't even look surprised as she squeezed his hand. "Welcome home, honey," he whispered.

Smiling, she clasped her hand tightly in his. She did feel like she was home.

# Twenty-seven

Jasmine looked at the apple-shaped clock that hung above the kitchen sink. It was already four in the morning and she had not had one hour of sleep. The pitch blackness of the night was threatening to fade and she knew dawn would be arriving soon. She poured milk from the pot sitting on the gas stove and began sipping, hoping this would bring slumber. But minutes later when she finished, she still felt as awake as she had several hours before.

She'd been feeling unsettled all evening. Ever since she went to church. *Are you searching for Him?* The words from the marquee were set in her mind. And then, there was the children's program. Just as she entered the church, the children's choir began singing their first song—*I will lift up my eyes to the hills from which cometh my help, my help cometh from the Lord, the Lord which made heaven and earth. He said he will not suffer thy foot, thy foot to be moved, the Lord that keepth thee, He will not slumber nor sleep* . . . The words of the beautiful song shocked her. Hadn't she just prayed for help? Could it be that God wanted to help her? She had prayed, but she never expected God to hear. It wasn't like she deserved God's love or attention.

"What are you doing up?"

Jasmine jumped at the sound of her sister's voice. "I couldn't sleep. I hope I didn't wake you." She tightened her silk robe around her waist.

"Is it jet lag?" Serena yawned, as her feet scuffed along the linoleum floor. She sat down at the table with her sister. Pink foam rollers crowned her head.

"Maybe . . . I have a question for you. How do you know God exists?"

Though the question surprised her, Serena answered casually, "Well, in the beginning, my belief was total blind faith. Our Sunday School teachers told us God was real and I just believed. And as a child, I loved the scripture, in fact, it was the first one I learned—*Blessed are they that have not seen, and yet have believed.* But, as I've gotten older, it's become easier to believe because I just look around. Look at my life."

Jasmine looked at her sister incredulously. "How can you say God exists by *your* life? Look at you—your husband died, leaving you with two young children. You're stuck in this little town . . ."

"That's what *you* see. When I look at my life, I see a God who brought me through my husband's death and gave me enough money from the insurance so that I now own my home. I have two beautiful children who help me carry on the memory of Robert. And, God has blessed me with a position with Xerox that I couldn't have imagined. Every need I have is met and most of my desires. I have a peace and joy in my life that I don't even understand. So, this can't be anything but God."

The ticking of the old clock was the only sound in the

kitchen and Jasmine nodded slowly. "So, how did you get all of this? How did you get God in your life?"

Serena smiled and reached across the table to touch her sister's hand. "I just asked," she said softly.

"I don't think I could ask God for anything. I've done too many things . . ."

"Honey, Jesus came for sinners. He wants you just the way you are. God wants to be in your life."

"I keep hearing Mrs. Carrington's voice in my mind," Jasmine started. Her eyes were glazed as if she were remembering the conversation. "She said I would be alone, but the truth is, I feel like I'm already there. There's no one in my life that really cares about me." Jasmine waved her hands as Serena started to protest. "I know there's you and Dad, but there's no one else. I feel like I'm going backwards and I have to try another way. And," she continued as her voice began to quiver, "I'm scared. I don't know what's going to happen if things keep going this way. I don't want to be alone."

Serena got up and knelt next to her sister. "With the Lord, you'll never be alone." She took Jasmine's hands into hers. "Let me help you find God again."

Jasmine began to tremble. "Serena, you don't know the things I've done . . ."

"It doesn't matter."

"Jefferson wasn't the only one. There have been so many others—married men . . ."

Serena kept shaking her head. "It doesn't matter. God wants you in exactly the place you're in." Serena went into the living room, returning with her Bible. "Jasmine, are you ready for a change in your life?"

Jasmine nodded, though she wasn't sure she could do

this. How could she go to God when her life was such a mess? Didn't she have to straighten out a few things first? And what would this mean anyway? Did she now have to go to church every Sunday? Was she supposed to give up sex? Was she supposed to give up parties—though Kyla and Jefferson were always going to parties? What would God expect from her now? She held her head, shaking it slightly. This was so confusing.

"I know you probably have a lot of questions," Serena said, as if reading her sister's mind. "But, there's only one place to start. Everything will fall into place as you get to know the Lord. All you have to do is ask Jesus to come into your heart."

"I don't know how to do that," Jasmine cried.

"I can show you." Serena opened her Bible. "Let's start with John 3:16. That explains why we have the gift of salvation. *For God so loved the world that he gave his only begotten Son, that whosoever believeth in him should not perish, but have everlasting life.*" Serena looked up at Jasmine. "God loves us. That's why we have the gift of His grace and mercy. And it's a gift, Jasmine. There is nothing you can do to buy it because we have all sinned. Look at Romans 3:23. *For all have sinned, and fall short of the glory of God.* Every being on earth has sinned, so, Jasmine, you don't have to worry about what you've done. All sins are equal in God's sight."

Jasmine simply nodded.

"*But the wages of sin is death; but the gift of God is eternal life through Jesus Christ.* We were all going to suffer eternal separation from God, but the Lord gave us a way out—a way to have everlasting life." Serena turned to Colossians 1:14. "*In whom we have redemption through his blood, even the forgiveness of sins.* Christ died on the cross so that no matter what we did—even sleeping with our friend's husband," Serena paused and smiled as Jasmine rolled her eyes. "No matter what we've done in the past or what we will do in the future . . . Jesus has already paid the price."

"I remember most of this stuff from Sunday school, but I never understood *how* to get God in your life."

Serena turned to Romans 10:9 and read aloud, "*That if thou shalt confess with thy mouth the Lord Jesus, and shalt believe in his heart that God hath raised him from the dead, thou shalt be saved. For with the heart man believeth unto righteousness: and with the mouth confession is made unto salvation.*" Serena closed the Bible.

Jasmine frowned. "All you do is say that Jesus is Lord and you're saved?"

"Say it and believe it in your heart. Believe in your heart that God raised Jesus from the dead. And then, we pray and you're saved."

"We pray and it's over."

"We pray and it's the beginning," Serena smiled. "Are you ready?"

Jasmine took a deep breath and nodded, though she still felt a bit unsure.

Serena knelt in front of her sister once again and took her hands. "This is what's called the Sinner's Prayer. Once you pray these words, you never have to do it again. Jesus will always be in your heart."

Jasmine barely moved.

"Repeat after me," Serena said. "Dear God, I come to you recognizing that I am a sinner in need of a Savior. I believe that Jesus is the Son of God. I believe that he died on the cross and God raised Him from the dead. I believe He lives. Jesus, come into my heart, be my Lord and Savior. Jesus, I receive you now.

I thank you that you shed your blood for the remission of my sins. Through this, my confession of faith, I am now a child of the Almighty God in Jesus, name. Amen."

Jasmine looked up and searched her sister's eyes. "Is that all I have to do?"

Serena nodded as tears ran down her cheeks. They hugged, holding each other for several minutes. And, as the morning light seemed to suddenly peek through the small kitchen window, Jasmine sighed, feeling like a burden had been lifted.

# Twenty-eight

Since Avery was not at her desk, Kyla gave a quick knock on the pastor's door, then stuck her head inside. "Pastor Ford, I'm sorry to disturb you . . ." she said.

"Kyla, come on in. Is it that time already?" She glanced at the mahogany clock on her desk.

"No, I'm a bit early. I was hoping that I could speak to you for a few minutes . . . before Jefferson got here. I hope you're not too busy."

Pastor Ford shuffled the papers on her desk. "I can go back to this." She stood from behind her desk and motioned for Kyla to have a seat on the couch. "Let's sit over here. I've been waiting for you to come to me."

Kyla frowned. "Come to you for what?"

She leaned back. "You've been in counseling for a month now and though it's going well, there are still some things that you're going through."

Kyla slowly shook her head. "Pastor, sometimes I'm afraid to have you look at me. I feel like you know everything that's going on inside."

Pastor Ford grinned. "I don't know everything. Just the

things God wants to reveal." Pastor Ford paused and peered at Kyla. "You can get started whenever you're ready."

Kyla bit her lip. Just how far do I want to go with this, she thought. "I do feel that counseling is going well," she said deliberately. "I know Jefferson is doing everything he can to rebuild my trust, but . . . there's something wrong with me." She stopped to look at the pastor's reaction. When Pastor Ford remained still, Kyla continued, "It's in my mind. I have all of these images of Jefferson and Jasmine together. It's driving me . . ."

"Kyla, this is all normal," the pastor said gently as she leaned forward.

"I thought you would say that, but how can it be? The thoughts come to me all the time—while we're watching TV or when we're in the car or even when we're . . ." She lowered her eyes.

"Even when you're in bed with Jefferson," Pastor Ford finished her sentence.

Kyla nodded. She hadn't expected to talk about their sexual relationship. She had hoped that if she could get rid of the thoughts, everything else would return to normal.

"Kyla, let me know if you think I'm getting too personal—but have you and Jefferson been intimate?"

She sighed deeply. "Yes, but I don't feel the same. I don't feel normal."

"Kyla, normal is going to be different from now on. You and Jefferson have different issues in your life. You're at a new place. Now, I'm not saying things can't be good. In fact, I think things are going to be much better. This is going to make your relationship mature and grow like nothing else can. You can't compare your life two months ago to where you are now."

"I understand that, Pastor Ford. But, when I'm . . . intimate with Jefferson, I feel like Jasmine is there."

Pastor Ford reached for Kyla's hand. "First of all, you're doing fine. You're only a month into your healing and you have made progress."

"I thought I'd be further along by now."

"Kyla, forgiveness is a process that takes a lot of time. It's not going to happen all at once. Just moment by moment, inch by inch, you two are going to fight your way back to each other."

Kyla leaned forward, holding her face in her hands. "I'm afraid that if I can't get back to the way we were—if I can't . . . respond, Jefferson will turn to someone else."

The pastor waved her hands. "Kyla, that is the devil trying to get in the middle of your healing. But, when the devil comes after you like this, point to the Cross. Remind the devil, rebuke him in the name of Jesus and he'll flee from you." Pastor Ford squeezed Kyla's hand, then stood, taking a sip from the water glass on her desk. "Have you talked to Jefferson about this?"

"No, the rest of our life is going well, I don't want this to be a stumbling block."

"It will only become one if you don't talk about it. We can discuss this in counseling, but why don't you try talking to Jefferson first? Jefferson is patient and accepting and the most important thing is that he is willing. I believe not only will Jefferson understand, but he will help you through this."

Kyla sat silently still for a moment. "Pastor, I want to love Jefferson completely."

A short knock on the door surprised them and Jefferson stepped inside.

"Did I hear my name?" Jefferson smiled and he hugged

Kyla. "Hello, Pastor. You guys didn't get started without me, did you?"

Pastor Ford smiled. "There is no way we would do that! Why don't you guys have a seat and we will get started."

Jasmine pulled the card she had purchased over a month ago out of the Bible. The blank white page loomed threateningly in front of her. Taking a deep breath, she finally pushed her pen along the paper.

> *Dear Kyla and Jefferson:*
>
> *There is so much I want to say, but I think it's best if I keep this short and simple. So here goes . . . I'm sorry. That's it. No other explanations are needed because I believe my reasons for what I did don't matter. And I'm ready to move on with my life. I am glad to know that you are both moving on too. My dad talked to your parents and told me that. I did want you to know that I will be away for a little while, spending some time with my dad, Serena and the kids. I don't know how long I'll stay in Pensacola—it's such a hick town, but we'll see how things go. So much of my family is here and it feels good to be around family right now. I'll be renting my house so that if I come back to Los Angeles, I'll have a place to stay and won't have to ask if I can stay with you guys. That's a joke, in case you didn't get it. Anyway, maybe one day we'll be able to find our way past all of this. Maybe, maybe not. I guess we'll have to wait and see. Well, that's it. I don't have anything else to say, so I think it's best to end this right here. Give Nicole a kiss for me . . . All the best, Jasmine.*

Not taking any time to look over the note, she folded the paper, stuffed it into an envelope and tossed it on top of the pile with the other mail Serena had stacked on the table. Standing, Jasmine smoothed her pantsuit and picked up her keys. She had promised Serena that she would meet her at Bible study. "Bible study," Jasmine chuckled softly. Her life really was changing . . . slowly and for the better.

# Twenty-nine

Alexis threw her keys on the table. "Whew!"

"Tired?"

"Very. We've all been through quite a bit these past months."

Brian pulled her back against him and hugged her around the waist. "But look at how far it's all come. It was great having dinner with Kyla and Jefferson tonight. It looks like all of their problems are over."

"Don't think anything is over."

"Well, they've made it through the first month . . ."

Alexis chuckled as she leaned into the couch. "Thirty days and counting. But even though they have a fight in front of them, they'll be fine. They have God and Pastor Ford. I believe God wants them together."

He pulled her towards him and she nestled in his arms. "I've got to say this. I'm glad it happened to Jefferson and not me. I wouldn't have been able to deal with it."

"Well, just stay away from Jasmine," she said, slapping his leg playfully. "In fact, just stay away from all women, period!"

He laughed. "With the woman I have in my arms, why would I want to look at anyone else?"

Alexis wrinkled her brow. "You know, that's a good question."

"Modest, aren't we?"

"I'm not talking about me. I still haven't been able to figure out how this happened to Kyla and Jefferson. There is no doubt in my mind that Jefferson loves Kyla and loves the life he has. So why did he do this?"

Brian shrugged. "I don't know . . . lust, curiosity, boredom . . ."

"Is that what happens to men? A few hours of pleasure is worth the risk of losing everything?" Alexis tried to keep her voice light, but she was puzzled. None of it made sense to her.

"Don't be sexist," Brian protested. "Both men and women fall, but everyone falls for different reasons."

"It's just not worth it. Jefferson could have lost everything—his wife, his family, his home, his reputation. It's too much to give up for a few moments of physical release."

"You make it sound so romantic."

"I may not have been there, but I can tell you there was no romance involved. All Jasmine was to Jefferson was a place for him to dump . . ."

"Whoa," he interrupted her, shaking his head. "You're tough."

"I should be. This just seems like another example of a man not being able to control himself, and it doesn't make sense to me."

"Well, even the Bible says that we will all be tempted. Look at Jesus, He was tempted for forty days . . ."

"But He stood."

"He was Jesus Christ. Give Jefferson a break. He's not God."

"I'm not saying that. I'm asking, how can a man who knew better, a man who is so strong in the Lord, how could he fall?"

"Do you know how many scriptures in the Bible speak about temptation?"

Alexis shook her head.

"There are so many," Brian started. "Jesus said in Matthew, *Watch and pray, that ye enter not into temptation: the spirit is indeed willing but the flesh is weak.* Jesus said 'watch and pray,' like temptation is always going to be lurking in our lives. Jesus knew. And then, Peter says, *The Lord knoweth how to deliver the godly out of temptations* . . . Listen to those words. Even the godly will be tempted. There are so many other scriptures about this. From the days of Adam, God knew our flesh would be weak."

"But Galatians 5:16 says *Walk in the Spirit, and ye shall not fulfill the lust of the flesh.* And anyway, how do you know so much about these scriptures? What's up with that?" Alexis gave him a sidelong glance, half-serious, half-teasing.

Brian laughed. "Does it bother you that I know so much about what the Bible says about temptation?"

"I just want to know *why* you know so much."

His smile disappeared. "You know, when this happened to Jefferson, I couldn't understand it either. I mean, I've always held him up as the example to follow. And knowing how much he loved the Lord, I felt like you—it just didn't make sense. So, I went into my Concordance and looked up scriptures. I wanted to have some way that I could understand. I figured if I could understand, maybe I could help."

Alexis was silent for a moment. "You're a good man, Dr. Lewis," she said finally.

Tipping her face with his fingers, he brought his lips to hers. When they broke their embrace, she leaned back in his arms.

Sitting in the dimness of the room's light, Alexis couldn't remember a time in her life when she'd felt such peace. She was with the man she loved and her best friend was building her life back. Minutes passed before Brian spoke again. "Maybe I could stay with you tonight," he said softly.

"Brian!" After what she had just been thinking, her disappointment was clear.

"No, not what you think. It's just that we've been through so much in the past weeks and I feel like we can exhale now. All I want to do is hold you and let you know that I love you."

"I know you love me."

"We don't have to have sex."

She looked up in his eyes. "There was one scripture you forgot to mention. It's the one that says, *and lead us not into temptation . . .*"

Brian chuckled. "Is that your way of saying that if I were to stay, you wouldn't be able to keep your hands off me?"

"That's exactly what I'm saying and we agreed that we wouldn't put ourselves in that position. In fact, with all of this talk, I think it's time for you to leave."

"Are you throwing me out?"

"You got it."

He laughed again. "Well, it's nice to know that I affect you in that way," he said standing. "You know, we can't go on like this for much longer. My heart and my . . . well, let's just leave it at my heart. But I can't take this. We're going to have to do something about this soon." He leaned over and kissed her. "And, I have a few ideas."

"What ideas are you talking about?"

"Maybe I'll share them with you later. Ciao."

And as she watched him walk out the door, goose bumps began to rise on her arms.

"Good night, Mommy."

"Night, sweetie."

Kyla turned off the lights and went back downstairs into the family room, sinking onto the couch next to Jefferson. He smiled and pulled her close as he flipped through the channels, finally settling on the late-night news.

"I had a good time tonight. It's been a long time since we've entertained here at home."

He kissed the top of her head. "Yeah, it was fun. Brian and Alexis have been good friends to us."

"I thought Brian was going to pass out when you told him that we were going to speak at the Marriage Fellowship next month."

Jefferson rubbed his hand along her arm. "He doesn't understand what Pastor says about testimonies and how they can help others. I'm excited about doing it, are you?"

Kyla nodded. "It's a bit scary, but I think it will be good. I'm going to invite some of the women from the Compassion House. Even though they're all single, they've been married, and some of what we say may help."

He squeezed her tightly. "I am so proud of you," he said, as she kissed the top of his head. "We're going to miss you at the clinic, but I'm glad Pastor made you the Executive Director of the Compassion House. I think you're going to make a big difference down there."

"I hope so. I think the Compassion House is going to make a difference for a lot of people."

Leaning from his arms, she reached over to the endtable and picked up the stack of mail. Sorting through the envelopes, she stopped as one caught her eye.

"Jefferson . . ."

"Umm?" He didn't turn away from the screen.

"There's something here . . . I think you should see . . ."

"What is it, honey?" Tossing the envelope onto his lap, she watched as his eyes scanned it, then looked up at her. "It's from Jasmine."

"Go ahead and open it," Kyla said standing, crossing her arms in front of her.

"We don't . . . have to open it . . . Kyla," Jefferson stuttered.

"No, go ahead. I think you should."

"It's addressed to both of us. Maybe . . . we should read it . . . together."

Her eyes bore into his. "No," she said strongly. "You read it."

Turning away, Kyla suddenly felt hot as she wrung her hands and paced behind the couch. Jefferson unfolded the paper and nervously scanned the letter. Then, he stood and handed the note to Kyla.

"It's fine. Read it," he said softly.

It took her only a moment.

Jefferson clicked the remote, turning the television screen to black. "This just doesn't seem to end. Kyla, I am so sorry for all of this . . ."

"I know that. I really do now." She bit her lip. "It's just that sometimes I wonder . . . do you think about her?"

Jefferson held his arms out. "Come here." He paused as he took her hands and pulled her back down onto the couch. "Kyla, I love you. I don't think about Jasmine at all. The only time she comes to my mind is when I'm thinking about the damage I did to you."

She was silent for a few moments, then nodded. "I talked to Pastor Ford a little about my concerns." Her voice was soft. "I can't stop thinking about you and her."

"There is nothing for you to think about."

"Sometimes, when we're together, I wonder if you prefer her to me . . ."

Jefferson hugged Kyla tightly. "I don't know how to get you to believe me or how I can make you feel safe again." He lifted her face so that he could look directly into her eyes. "Nothing like this will ever happen again. I only want you and I will make sure that every day of your life, you know that."

She nodded as tears filled her eyes. "I want to believe you."

"You have to believe me and I will do whatever I have to do. Even if that means that we should wait before we . . . make love again . . ."

"Oh, no, I'm not saying that," she said holding his hand. "I just want to know that when we're together, it's me that you want. It's me that you're thinking about."

He gently pressed his lips against hers. "You are the only woman in the world I want." His lips nuzzled against her neck and she leaned into him. "Let me show you." His voice was husky. "Let me prove it to you." His tongue found hers again. Finally pulling back, his eyes searched hers. "I want to make love to *my wife*." Taking her hand, he lifted her from the couch. "I want to show you just how much I love you."

She followed as Jefferson led the way, and with slow steps they climbed the stairs to their bedroom.

Alexis turned on the lamp in the living room. The incessant knocking continued and she tightened her terry cloth robe. Who could it be? And why hadn't the concierge called up? She slowly approached the door as each knock became louder.

"Who is it!" She peeked through the peephole. "What the . . ." She opened the door. "Brian, what are you doing here?"

Brian stepped inside, dressed in a tuxedo with a red bowtie and matching cummerbund. With his hands behind his back, he leaned over and kissed her.

"What are you doing here?" she asked again, her voice showing confusion. "And, why are you dressed like this?" Her eyes roamed up and down his body. It was Armani. Even in the middle of the night she knew that. And it fit him, showing his body's perfection.

He grinned and looked down at his clothes. "I had to dress up for one of the most important moments of my life."

She finally closed the door that she had held open. "It's three o'clock in the morning. Where are you going dressed like that?"

"I know it's late, sweetheart. But that's all part of the surprise. I wanted this to be something we would always remember."

Alexis ran her fingers through her hair. "What are you talking about?"

His smile widened as he took her hand into his and pulled her toward the couch.

"Brian, what's going on?" She was impatient.

His smile disappeared. "Alexis, I know that we haven't known each other for very long, but I know that I love you . . ."

"I love you too, Brian, but it's late . . ."

He edged his body from the couch and bent down on one knee. Alexis frowned in confusion, then opened her eyes wide. She raised both hands, covering her mouth.

"Alexis, there is a part of me that had been empty until I met you. You filled that hole in my heart. And, I love you for it." Brian's voice was soft as he pulled the velvet box from inside his jacket. "I want to spend the rest of my life loving you. I want to protect you and take care of you. Alexis, will you make me the happiest and most blessed man in the universe and agree to become my wife?"

He tipped opened the box and Alexis gasped. Even in the dim living room light, the diamond flashed like lightning and colors shimmered and bounced against her dark, slender hand as he placed the ring on her finger.

She had no idea how long she sat there staring at the ring, but when Brian's thumb rubbed away a tear from her cheek, she finally lifted her eyes to meet his.

"You haven't said anything and I'm getting a little nervous. Will you marry me?"

"I don't know what to say," her voice cracked.

"Say yes."

"Yes, yes!" she said as she hugged him.

Brian gently pulled her down onto the floor with him and

held her on his lap. And before he lowered his lips to hers, he said, "Alexis, I promise to love you completely, openly, and honestly for the rest of my life."

She was weak with emotion and closed her eyes, promising that she would remember every second of this moment for the rest of her life.

# *Thirty*

They could hear the pastor's muffled voice through the door to the side room and Kyla peeked into the sanctuary. Alexis and Brian were sitting in the front row and even from where Kyla was standing she could see Alexis' sparkling diamond. She was thrilled for Alexis and Brian and smiled as she thought of them getting a head start and attending their first Marriage Fellowship. Her only regret was that her parents had decided not to attend. She knew it was her mother's choice. Instead, they had taken Nicole to San Diego for the weekend.

"It's almost time," Jefferson's voice came from behind her. "It's time for us to pray." Holding hands, they bowed their heads. "Heavenly Father," Jefferson started. "We come before you with praise and thanksgiving for this special day. As we speak of the testimony you've given us, let the words of our mouths and the meditation of our hearts be what you want, Lord. Let our words flow from you so that each person receives the message that you want delivered. Today is a day to exalt, honor, and bless your Holy Name and we thank you. We thank you, Lord, that you did as you promised in 2 Samuel—

you lightened our darkness. We give you all the glory, we give you all the praise. In Jesus Christ's name we pray, Amen."

Kyla held on to Jefferson tightly as thoughts of the past months flowed through her mind. It was more than a cliché, when people said that the Lord had brought them a mighty long way. Kyla now truly understood those words.

"Are you ready, my love?" Jefferson asked, pulling back slightly.

"I'm ready to do anything with you."

He smiled. "I love you."

Holding hands, they walked into the sanctuary and toward the altar, ready to deliver God's message. Ready to do all things in the name of Jesus.

"Well, as most of you know, this is a special Marriage Fellowship today," Pastor Ford said. "We're talking about a subject that is familiar, but not usually exposed this up close and personal. As many of you know, or may have been told, or may have heard through whispers in the hallways, Kyla and Jefferson Blake are here today to share a very personal experience and I am so proud of them. When people speak about personal experiences in their lives, they are exposing themselves to ridicule, critiques, other's opinions of what you should have done or what you should have said—all of that. This is a difficult step to take and many would say it's not worth it. But what the Blakes know is that when the Lord gives you a testimony, it is to be shared for the edification of others. So, as I said before, I am proud of what this man and woman of God are about to do."

The pastor looked over at Jefferson and Kyla and smiled.

"Now, I am pleased to say that I was able to play a role in this process. When the Blakes came to me, they were broken, they were in a state of confusion, they had *both* suffered. But they both loved the Lord, and that's why I knew they would pull through.

"During our sessions over the last six months, we have experienced the complete spectrum of emotions. We all cried, we all screamed. Once, Kyla even threw my coffee mug against the wall and broke it."

There was an audible sigh from the audience and the pastor laughed. "But never fear. She went out the next day and brought me a new one." Everyone laughed and the pastor continued. "But I am telling you that in spite of it all, under the mercy and grace of God, the Blakes have survived. Now, I know you are all eager to get on with the program. So, I want to bring up, Kyla and Jefferson Blake."

They stood to the standing ovation of the congregation, and Jefferson placed his hand on Kyla's elbow, leading her to the podium. He kissed her on the cheek, then returned to his seat allowing Kyla to speak first, as they had agreed. It wasn't until he had sat down that he realized his hands were shaking, not from fear, but exhilaration.

When the crowd settled down, Kyla took a deep breath and spoke. "Good afternoon, church. Praise the Lord."

Jefferson's eyes never left his wife. This was a new Kyla Blake emerging. The one who was always behind the scenes, planning and preparing was gone. He looked into the audience. Every eye was on his wife, riveted by this beautiful woman who was giving her testimony unashamedly. He cringed as she opened up fully, revealing the pain of the aftermath of her discovery. This was the most difficult part for him to hear, and he still asked himself how he could have caused the woman he would lay down his life for this kind of agony. It was still a marvel to him that they had made it through. And, he had no doubt it was all God's doing.

Listening to Kyla continue to share, he shook his head at the beauty of the Lord. *Bless the Lord, O my soul: and all that is within me, bless his holy name.* The Lord had not only forgiven him, but had given him another chance. The Lord had brought him through his shame, giving him a chance to stand proudly—showing him how a man of God could stand, even after falling.

Jefferson moved to the edge of his chair. The crowd applauded and Kyla turned to her husband. He stood and walked to the podium, kissed Kyla and escorted her back to her seat. Then he returned to center stage, his eyes searching out into the silent, still crowd, waiting to hear from him; hear the words from the cheating husband.

"Thank you for your kind welcome. I stand before you today, a saved man. I am a man who loves the Lord. And because of God's tremendous grace and mercy, I am a man who is loved *by* the Lord. I am a man who is grateful for the blood of Jesus." He paused. "If you have your Bibles, please turn with me to John 16:33."

He waited until he heard the sound of turning pages subside. Then he read the scripture out loud. *"These things I have spoken unto you, that in me ye might have peace. In the world ye shall have tribulation: but be of good cheer, I have overcome the world."*

He paused for a moment, then spoke. "It is with this promise from the Lord that my wife and I have been able to move past our tribulation. Move beyond our trial. Because we know that even with all of this world's sorrows and pains, with all of the distress and afflictions, our Lord conquers *all* of these things and is able to make us whole again."

This time, he paused because of the applause from the crowd. Sounds of praise rose throughout the congregation. When he spoke again, his words flowed smoothly, from his heart. As he looked into the eyes of the people, he knew he was having an impact. He was doing the right thing. For Kyla. For himself. For the Lord.

When Jefferson completed his presentation, he thanked the congregation for their attention and everyone in the sanctuary stood, showing their appreciation with resounding applause. Kyla and Pastor Ford joined Jefferson in front of the altar. After several minutes of a standing ovation, the pastor motioned for the congregation to return to their seats.

"I'm only going to keep you for one more moment," Pastor Ford said. "I want to end with a scripture that I think we should all meditate on. You can turn to it, if you wish. The book of James 1:2. *My brethren, count it all joy when ye fall into divers temptations; Knowing this, that the trying of your faith worketh patience. But let patience have her perfect work, that ye may be perfect and entire, wanting nothing.*" She paused. "You know I don't normally do this, but I want everyone in this room to understand this scripture. I'm going to read the same scripture from the Living Bible. *Dear brothers, is your life full of difficulties and temptations? Then be happy, for when the way is rough, your patience has a chance to grow. So, let it grow and don't try to squirm out of your problems. For when your patience is finally in full bloom, then you will be ready for anything, strong in character, full and complete.*" She closed her book and looked around the sanctuary. "I think the only thing left to say now is . . . Amen."

It had taken over two hours to get everyone out of the church. People continued to approach Kyla and Jefferson asking questions, offering congratulations or just hugging them for support. Now, Kyla, Jefferson, Alexis, and Brian stood in the pastor's office talking excitingly about what had transpired.

"Pastor Ford, thank you for everything," Kyla said as she picked up her jacket, finally ready to leave. Jefferson nodded his agreement.

"I have to thank you guys. What you did today was special and you've helped countless people. But there is one more thing I want to do. Alexis and Brian," the pastor said turning to them, "would you mind if I spoke with Kyla and Jefferson alone?"

"Of course, Pastor Ford," Alexis said and then hugged Kyla. "We'll see you guys later." Kyla and Jefferson said their goodbyes to Brian and then turned to Pastor Ford with questioning glances.

The pastor picked up her Bible from her desk. "Follow me!" she commanded.

Holding hands, Kyla and Jefferson followed her into the sanctuary. She turned on the light above the altar, leaving the rest of the large room darkened. Standing at the podium, she motioned for them and they stepped directly in front of her.

"You know, when we began this counseling a few months ago, I knew the Lord was going to work this. But as I watched the two of you today, I knew this was a miracle. And there is a message in this miracle. The Lord is showing that through Him, at any time, we can have a new beginning."

Kyla and Jefferson nodded.

"And it occurred to me that we should bless the new beginning of this union. You're starting over. There is nothing wrong with your history, but the doors of your future are wide open and we have to rejoice. Can you both turn facing me, please?"

In the semidarkness glow of the room, they followed her instructions.

"Now, give me your rings."

"Our rings?" They questioned together.

"Yes, your wedding rings."

Kyla realized what the pastor was about to do and new tears formed in her eyes.

"Now, holding hands and facing each other, I want you to rededicate yourselves to each other and your marriage." When they looked at her blankly, she continued, "Just speak from your hearts. The Lord will lead you. Jefferson, you first."

Jefferson swallowed hard before he spoke. "Kyla, when we were married almost seventeen years ago, I didn't know what I had done to deserve you. And I thanked God every day of each year for letting me love you, protect you, and cherish you. Now, as we stand here because of my transgression, I can only thank the Lord again. But the words 'thank you' are too small to communicate the depth of my gratefulness to the Lord and to you. I thank God for His love and mercy." He paused, overcome with emotion. "I thank you, Kyla, for finding it in your heart to forgive me and for loving me when I wasn't even sure I loved myself. I promise once again in front of God and Pastor to love you, honor you, protect you, cherish you, forsaking every woman on earth. There is only you. As I stand before the Lord and make these promises, I thank God for the woman chosen for me. I thank God for making me whole with you. And I promise that I will love you, Kyla, as Christ commanded. I will love you as Christ loved the church . . ." Jefferson paused again as his voice quivered. He looked at the pastor and hunched his shoulders.

"Is that everything you want to say?" The pastor asked, her own eyes moist with emotion.

He nodded. "Oh, there is one more thing. Did I say I love you?"

They laughed and Kyla with the back of her hands wiped her tears that had fallen.

"I guess it's my turn." She took a deep breath. "I am so grateful to the Lord for bringing you into my life. Because, with all the good times, and even with what we went through, I love you with all that is in me. And I know that's the way it's supposed to be. You are my husband. The head of our house. The father of my child. The man the Lord wants me to honor. And I do. I thank you for your patience and for standing by me as we climbed back to where the Lord wanted us to be. I promise to love you, honor you, cherish you and I too, will forsake all others. There is only you. My prayer is that the Lord will continue to shine His mercy upon us and use us for His purpose, so that others may come to know Him. I promise you that the best of our life is in front of us. I love you."

Pastor Ford had to clear the lump in her throat before she spoke. "Let's bow our heads." And as the pastor prayed, it was all Kyla could do to not fall down on the altar and give thanks to the Lord. The pastor prayed over their wedding rings, and then they took turns placing the rings back on their fingers, just as they had done all those years before.

The ride home had been completely silent and now Kyla's eyes followed Jefferson as he came around the front of the Range Rover to open the door for her. She slowly slipped from the vehicle, sliding into his arms and without a word, he brought his lips to hers. The kiss began gently, but their urgency built, and he pulled her backward into the house. Jefferson used his hands to find their way, while their tongues continued to search and communicate. In the dark kitchen, Jefferson pushed Kyla against the center island. The hardness of the counter pushed into her back, but all she could feel was Jefferson leaning into her as they fought to become one. Her breaths came in small shudders as she shivered against his touch. Her mind was racing, but she couldn't capture any of her thoughts. She only wanted to fill her head with her husband.

Minutes later, Jefferson pulled back slightly and with a swift, smooth movement, lifted Kyla into his arms. She put her arms around his neck, pulling him as close as she could. He moved gingerly through the darkened house and carried her up the stairs, just as he had carried her into the hotel the night they were married. He gently laid her on the bed and covered her body with his.

Her heart pounded through her chest, but then she realized it was his heart she felt. She let her hands roam over the hardness of his back and arms. She wanted to feel every part of him.

Finally he sat up, giving himself enough room to remove

her jacket. He returned to her, kissing her, tantalizing her with the tips of his fingers. Every part of her body was on fire. He massaged her shoulders through the silkiness of her top and she moaned from deep inside as his fingers found their way underneath, touching her bare skin.

With experienced fingers, he unbuttoned her blouse, then, removed her skirt. His eyes and fingers drifted over her body. "You are so beautiful."

Standing, he removed his clothes, in what Kyla was sure was just moments, and then he joined her. She sighed as his tongue traced her curves, making her body tremble. She lifted her head, her tongue begging to find his again and she took him in.

With her eyes closed, she let her hands and mouth communicate everything she wanted to say. She needed to let him know how much she loved him. And, she wanted to let him know that she forgave him.

She drifted, giving herself away totally. She was unconscious with love and she let herself discover her husband in the way she'd known him before. She let him take her completely—her entire body and mind. Just like the first time.